About the author

Ian McFadyen was born in Liverpool and has enjoyed a successful career in marketing. He lives in Hertfordshire with his wife and has three grown-up children.

Blood on his Hands is the eighth in the series featuring DI Carmichael, all published by The Book Guild.

By the same author:

Little White Lies, Book Guild Publishing, 2008. (Paperback edition 2012)

Little White Lies (large print edition), Magna Large Print Books, 2010.

Lillia's Diary, Book Guild Publishing, 2009. (Paperback edition 2012)

Lillia's Diary (large print edition), Magna Large Print Books, 2014.

Frozen to Death, Book Guild Publishing, 2010

Frozen to Death (large print edition), Magna Large Print Books, 2014.

Frozen to Death, (Italian edition), Bibi Books, 2018

Deadly Secrets, Book Guild Publishing, 2012

Deadly Secrets (large print edition), Magna Large Print Books, 2014.

Deadly Secrets (Italian edition), Miraviglia Editore, 2014

Killing Time, Book Guild Publishing, 2015

Death in Winter, Book Guild Publishing, 2016

The Steampunk Murder, Book Guild Publishing, 2018

BLOOD
on his
HANDS

Ian McFadyen

The Book Guild Ltd

First published in Great Britain in 2019 by
The Book Guild Ltd
9 Priory Business Park
Wistow Road, Kibworth
Leicestershire, LE8 0RX
Freephone: 0800 999 2982
www.bookguild.co.uk
Email: info@bookguild.co.uk
Twitter: @bookguild

Typeset in Baskerville

Printed and bound by CPI Group (UK) Ltd, Croydon, CR0 4YY

ISBN 978 1912881 949

British Library Cataloguing in Publication Data.
A catalogue record for this book is available from the British Library.

To Lauren McFadyen

xxx

Chapter 1

Tuesday 30ᵗʰ June

Barney Green emerged from the chancel and, with his customary broad grin, strode quickly into the chapel where Mrs Carter and Mrs Gillespie were busy carefully positioning the long stems of bright-coloured summer flowers into the massive arrangements that would adorn the church come Sunday.

"Beautiful as always, ladies," he remarked with genuine warmth in his voice and an appreciative gentle nod of his head.

Lindsay Carter and Kerry Gillespie needed no more than those few simple words as a reward for the many hours they would spend each week making Moulton Bank C of E church look so welcoming and smell so delightful.

Like love-struck teenagers, the two middle-aged women gazed back in the young vicar's direction, with broad smiles and doe eyes.

"I'll see you both later," he continued, as he strode down the aisle towards the large south door.

Barney Green was always cheerful. It was one of the characteristics that made him so popular with the burgeoning congregation since he'd taken over from Reverend Pugh, the long-standing and altogether dowdier cleric who'd retired a few years before.

Whatever was happening around him, and whatever crisis he was called upon to resolve, Barney Green could be relied upon to tackle each situation with boundless energy and a persona heaped with warmth and constructive optimism.

Barney was a deeply religious man, but unlike the more traditional, sombre vicar he'd replaced, his interests and passions extended well beyond the confines of the Bible; and his thoughts were, more often than not, centred on more secular pursuits.

As he merrily made his way down the aisle, it was the lyrics to a new song he was learning to play that were uppermost in his mind.

That, however, was until he caught sight of the man with the haunted, gaunt look on his face, standing at the entrance, his arms stretched out in front of him, the palms of his hands facing upwards and covered in blood.

Chapter 2

It had been an uneventful week so far at Kirkwood police station with nothing having arisen that required either Inspector Carmichael or any of his team to leave the building in the past couple of days. So, when the call came through from Barney Green, the vicar at his local parish church, Carmichael was relieved to at last have something to occupy his mind.

He listened intently as the vicar explained the conversation he'd just had and the frightening admission that had been forthcoming from the ashen-faced man who sat trembling in the church vestry.

"Stay with him, keep him there," remarked Carmichael, "I'm leaving now. I'll be with you in half an hour."

Upon hearing the tone in Carmichael's voice, his three officers stopped what they were doing and looked over in their boss's direction.

"I need one of you to come with me," Carmichael shouted as he headed over towards the door.

"I'll come," replied DC Rachel Dalton, who had picked up her jacket and was on her feet before either DS Watson or DS Cooper had a chance to react, leaving her two colleagues open-mouthed and uncharacteristically lost for words.

* * *

"Is everything all right, vicar?" Lindsay Carter enquired as Barney Green walked back towards the vestry where he'd left the man while he'd called Carmichael.

"Is that man OK?" added Kerry Gillespie before the vicar had an opportunity to reply.

Barney Green put on a forced smile, but his pallid face and worried-looking eyes revealed his true emotions.

"Why don't you ladies stop for today?" he remarked. "You've been hard at it for hours. Why don't you come back tomorrow to finish off?"

Neither Lindsay Carter nor Kerry Gillespie had any great desire to leave, but they both nodded politely, realising that they were unlikely to get anything out of Barney Green regarding the mysterious man he'd ushered into the vestry fifteen minutes earlier; and he clearly wanted them out of the way.

"We'll see you in the morning then, in that case," remarked Lindsay Carter, although she doubted the vicar heard her, as he'd already left them standing alone and was now just a few metres away from the vestry door.

The two women waited, motionless, for a few seconds, until the vicar had disappeared back into the vestry.

"I wonder what that's all about," whispered Kerry Gillespie before starting to tidy up the flowers.

Lindsay Carter shrugged her shoulders. "Search me," she replied as she picked up the broom and started to sweep up the trimmed stems that had fallen on the floor. "But whatever it is, it's got Reverend Green concerned. I've never seen him look so serious."

Barney Green had no idea what he was going to say, or how he was going to keep the man in the church for the thirty or so minutes it would take for Carmichael to arrive, but he figured he'd think of something.

What he didn't expect when he entered the room was for it to be empty and for his visitor to have vanished.

Chapter 3

"So, what's happening?" enquired Rachel as she and her boss sped out of the police station car park.

"We're heading over to the C of E church in Moulton Bank," Carmichael replied. "That was Barney Green on the call at the station. He reckons a man has just come into the church with blood on his hands, claiming to have committed a murder."

Rachel's eyes widened. "Really," she remarked. "Is he serious?"

Carmichael shrugged his shoulders. "Well Barney Green is serious about it," he replied, "but only time will tell whether his visitor is telling the truth or not. So, the sooner we get there the better."

* * *

Barney Green rushed out of the vestry, his cheeks now completely colourless. "Did you see that man leave when I was on the phone?" he shouted down the aisle towards the two ladies who were fastidiously gathering together the cut flowers and sweeping up the floor.

"No," replied Lindsay Carter, "nobody's come out."

"Blast," remarked the vicar, "he must have gone out the back door and into the graveyard."

5

Turning smartly on his heels, Barney sprinted back into the vestry, then out through the small back door.

It had been over fifteen years since there had been a burial at the church, the plots having all long since been taken, but for over a hundred and fifty years prior to that the dearly departed Protestant congregation of Moulton Bank had, one by one, been laid to rest in the hallowed grounds of the church, set halfway up Ambient Hill looking down on the small Lancashire village.

Although Mr Pendlebury, the church sexton, did a sterling job keeping the graves neat and tidy, there were many large trees and bushes dotted around which severely hindered Barney Green's view of the entire graveyard.

Thinking quickly, he decided there were two options the fleeing man could have taken: either he'd have gone down the path to the north of the church, or he'd have headed around the side of the church to the main entrance which led to the road. Barney Green opted for the latter.

Panting and fraught, Barney arrived at the front gate on Ambient Hill about thirty seconds later.

Straining his neck, at first looking up the hill and then looking down, he could see no one. Even the road was empty of cars, which was very unusual.

"Bugger and damn," he cursed, just as his two middle-aged admirers arrived at his side, having tidied up their workstation and quietly departed the church.

"Has he vanished?" enquired Lindsay Carter, her question stating the obvious.

"Do you want us to help you look for him?" added Kerry Gillespie, her tone suggesting she was desperate for the vicar to say yes.

Barney Green thought for a few moments.

"If you could both please go into the graveyard and see if he's there, that would be very helpful," he replied. "But stay together, don't on any account split up. I'm going to run down to check out the car park."

Even though the vicar's insistence that they didn't split up had caused the two women to exchange a quick look of shared trepidation, they were delighted to be asked by their favourite cleric to assist him and they shot off back down the path.

Barney Green took a deep breath before sprinting the twenty yards down the hill which led to the church car park entrance. Being young and in good physical condition, this took him no time at all.

"Bugger," he muttered under his breath when he arrived to find only his own car and the old red Skoda that Kerry and Lindsay had driven up in. "He's either gone up the hill or he's in the church graveyard."

With Kerry and Lindsay already looking in the graveyard, Barney decided there was nothing for it; he'd have to now go up the hill to look for the mystery visitor.

He checked his pockets for his car keys, before remembering that he'd left them in his jacket which was hanging on a peg in the vestry.

"Bugger," he remarked for a third time, before he set off, running as fast as he could, up Ambient Hill.

Chapter 4

It took Carmichael and Rachel Dalton just over thirty-five minutes to arrive at the church car park and a further couple of minutes to walk the short distance from Carmichael's black BMW to the church entrance.

The large oak door was open and even before the two officers had managed to cross the threshold, they realised something was not right. The pained expressions on the faces of the vicar and his two helpers, sitting silently on separate but adjoining pews near the church entrance, told their story.

"I'm sorry, Steve," Barney Green remarked uncomfortably, "he's gone."

"Why didn't you keep him here like I asked you?" remarked Carmichael irritably.

Barney Green shrugged his shoulders. "Sorry," he replied. "After I finished talking to you, I went back to the vestry and he'd gone. I was only away for five minutes."

"So, have you checked the grounds and the road?" Rachel enquired.

"Churchyard, car park, up the road and down the road," interjected Lindsay Carter. "But he's just vanished."

Barney Green looked up from his seated position and nodded disconsolately.

"Mrs Carter's right," he remarked. "It's amazing. He appeared from nowhere and disappeared in the same way."

"Like a ghost," added Kerry Gillespie, her statement uttered in a way that suggested she half believed what she was suggesting.

"I suspect there's a more earthly explanation," pronounced Carmichael with the slightest hint of a smile on his face, "but let's take things step by step."

Then, turning his head sideways to face Rachel Dalton, he added, "I suggest you two ladies stay here with DC Dalton and provide her with an account of what you saw and a description of the man, while Reverend Green and I go through to the vestry, so I can see how our mystery man made his escape."

The two middle-aged women exchanged a quick look before nodding in agreement.

* * *

Carmichael followed Barney Green into the vestry, tucked away at the back of the building. Given the size of the church, Carmichael was surprised just how small it was. He took a few seconds to take a good look around.

"So, this is where you left him when you called me," Carmichael remarked.

Barney Green nodded. "Yes," he replied, "we spoke for a few minutes in the church near where we were just sitting, then I brought him in here. He was sitting in that chair when I left to call you."

As he spoke, Barney Green gestured to the well-worn but comfortable-looking brown armchair positioned below the impressive stained-glass window, which looked out across the open fields to the east of the church.

"And that's the door you think he fled through?" Carmichael remarked, pointing to the large pine door at the far end of the room.

Barney Green nodded again. "He must have gone through there," he replied. "Other than the door into the church, it's the only way out of here; and as neither Mrs Carter, Mrs Gillespie nor I saw him come back into the church, he must have left via that door."

"Which wasn't locked?" Carmichael remarked.

Barney Green shook his head. "No," he replied, "it's only ever locked in the evening."

Carmichael took the few short steps to the window and looked out across the fields.

"Before we go outside, can you tell me exactly what this man said to you?" Carmichael asked.

Barney Green folded his arms across his chest.

"Well," he replied, "I realised that all wasn't well as soon as I saw him at the back of the church. He had such a haunted, troubled look on his face. I asked him if he was all right, at which point he just said, 'You need to help me, I've just killed someone.' It was then I saw his hands, which were stretched out palms upwards. They were stained with blood."

Carmichael turned back to face the vicar.

"Was the blood dry or did it look fresh?" Carmichael enquired.

"It had dried," Barney Green replied, "but his hands were covered in it."

"What about his clothes?" Carmichael probed gently. "Did you see blood on them?"

Barney Green looked a little puzzled, then shook his head. "I don't recall seeing any blood on his clothes," he replied rather vaguely.

Carmichael smiled and nodded reassuringly. "Did he say anything else, while you were in the church?" he asked.

"I asked him what his name was," continued Barney Green, "but he didn't reply, he looked in shock. I then asked him who he'd killed, and he just said, 'I've slit his throat'."

"He definitely said his throat?" interrupted Carmichael.

Barney Green nodded. "Yes, definitely."

"So, what did you do then?" Carmichael enquired.

"I suggested that we both came in here," replied Barney Green. "I sat him down there in that chair and I told him I'd get us both a cup of tea."

"That's when you left him and came out to call me?" Carmichael remarked.

"That's right," replied the vicar. "From first seeing him in the church to leaving him sitting here couldn't have been more than ten minutes in total. So, other than him claiming to have killed a man by slitting his throat, I didn't get anything else out of him."

"Do you think he was being honest with you?" Carmichael enquired. "Could it have been some sort of sick prank he was playing?"

Barney Green shook his head. "Of course, I can't be certain," he conceded, "but I believed him."

"Can you describe what the man looked like?" Carmichael asked.

Barney Green nodded. "He was about the same height as me, medium build, he had dark brown hair, greying slightly at the sides, and was wearing a navy or black jacket and I think dark trousers and black shoes, although I'm not totally certain about the trousers and shoes."

"And how tall are you?" Carmichael enquired.

"Oh, five foot eleven inches," replied Barney Green.

"What sort of age would you say he was?" continued Carmichael.

Barney Green thought for a few seconds.

"Maybe in his early to mid-forties," he replied without any great conviction. "I'm not good with ages."

"Not to worry," Carmichael replied reassuringly. "I'm sure Mrs Carter and Mrs Gillespie will provide DS Dalton with a good description of your visitor; and a good stab at his age, too. I've no idea why, but women seem to have a knack of remembering far more than most men when it comes to those sorts of details."

Barney Green nodded. "They didn't get close to him like I did, but I sincerely hope they're more help to you with his description than me," he replied.

Carmichael smiled. "I assume you told the ladies about your conversation with the man?" he remarked.

Barney Green nodded. "I didn't at first," he replied, "but they could see I was concerned so reluctantly I felt I had to."

Carmichael nodded. "I understand," he replied sympathetically, before taking a few steps towards the door. "Now let's have a good look outside."

Chapter 5

The door from the vestry opened out onto a small flagged area with a high retaining wall to the farmer's field beyond. As Carmichael emerged from the dimly lit room into the open air, the extreme contrast that greeted his senses was intense.

It was a beautiful summer's day, one of a dozen or so days they'd enjoyed, unbroken by rain; and apart from a few fluffy white clouds and the faintest trace of a vapour trail from a plane long since departed from view, the spectacular, tranquil, azure-blue sky above seemed ceaseless.

Carmichael walked slowly towards the three stone steps leading up to the graveyard.

"Presumably our man would have come up here," he remarked as he reached the top.

"Yes," replied Barney Green, who'd followed Carmichael out of the church and up the path. "He'd have then either gone on into the churchyard or turned left and followed the path around, back to the front of the church."

As he spoke, Barney Green stretched out his left arm to point to the pathway.

"Earlier, one of the ladies mentioned that between you you'd checked the churchyard, the car park, up the road and down the road," recalled Carmichael.

"When I came out here before, I guessed that he'd most likely have made his way around to the front," replied Barney

Green. "I ran around that way. I met Mrs Carter and Mrs Gillespie there and they came back around here to look for him while I ran first down to the car park, then up the road to the top of the hill."

Carmichael nodded. "I see," he remarked, "but you saw nothing."

Barney Green shook his head. "Nothing," he confirmed, "he'd vanished."

As he finished his sentence, DC Dalton joined them. She'd finished talking with the two ladies and had followed Carmichael and Reverend Green into the churchyard through the vestry door.

As he saw Rachel Dalton, Carmichael placed his hand on Barney Green's arm.

"Why don't you go back inside and make yourself a cup of tea," he suggested with a comforting smile. "DC Dalton and I will have another look around here and I'll come and see you in a few minutes' time."

Barney Green looked over at DC Dalton, who gave him a warm reassuring smile.

"Of course," he replied, before walking briskly away down the steps and disappearing through the vestry door.

Chapter 6

With the door from the vestry closed, Carmichael looked across and fixed his piercing blue eyes on Rachel Dalton.

"What did they have to say?" he enquired.

"Not that much really," Rachel replied. "They were able to give me a good description of the man, but they didn't speak with him and they maintain they didn't overhear anything that was said between the man and Reverend Green."

Carmichael sniggered. "I told Barney they'd have a better memory than him," he remarked. "What description did they give you?"

Rachael took out her pocket book to refer to her notes.

"Respectable-looking man with dark hair, aged about forty-five," relayed Rachel. "Height, approx. six foot, smartly dressed, with an expensive-looking navy blazer with gold or brass buttons, white open-necked shirt, dark grey trousers, again expensive-looking, and brand-new brown Derby shoes."

Carmichael nodded. "I'm impressed," he remarked. "Anything else?"

Rachel looked down again at her notebook. "They said he wore no rings and they can't recall him having any other jewellery. But he did have, in their words, a very expensive-looking watch."

Carmichael smiled. "Any other striking features?" he asked.

"No," Rachel replied. "They say they only saw him for a matter of moments when the vicar ushered him up towards the vestry. They did say he looked very troubled."

Carmichael nodded again.

"OK," he said, "let's see whether he's left anything to help us find out where he went."

Upon finishing his sentence, Carmichael started to walk slowly along the narrow path, his eager protégée a couple of short steps behind him.

* * *

Back at Kirkwood police station, Watson yawned and stretched his arms skyward before rising out of his seat and ambling over to the window.

"I wonder how Carmichael and Rachel are getting on," he remarked.

Cooper looked up from his computer screen.

"Without knowing what the call he received was about it's hard to say," replied Cooper, before his attention returned to his computer screen.

Watson puffed out his cheeks and rested his elbow on the narrow window ledge.

"Do you notice how every time there's a juicy case, he always goes himself," he remarked. "Normally with Rachel, too. Me and you get all the boring stuff."

Cooper didn't bother to look up from his screen.

"I think you're imagining things, Marc," he replied. "I think you'll find the load's quite fairly distributed. In fact, when there's CCTV footage to scroll through or reams and reams of old documents to pore over, it's normally poor Rachel that gets lumbered with that."

Watson, still looking out the window, shook his head.

"Nah," he remarked, "I reckon Carmichael has a soft

spot for young Rachel. He was like that with Lucy Clark; remember when he first arrived? He took her to the US on his first-ever case here, leaving us more experienced officers behind, and she was just a rookie WDC."

"But she's a sergeant like us now," replied Cooper, "and I hear she's not far from becoming an inspector. Anyway, I always liked Lucy, she was a good officer. Maybe Carmichael saw that too. Maybe that's why she got to go to the US rather than us."

Watson took a few seconds to consider his colleague's opinion. He also wondered whether, like him, Cooper had received an invite to Lucy's wedding a week on Saturday. He decided not to say anything in case he hadn't.

"No," he said loudly. "He just likes to have a pretty face around him."

Cooper sighed and looked up from the computer.

"To be brutally honest with you, Marc," he added, "if I'd a choice of partnering either you, Lucy, or Rachel, you'd come a distant third. Especially when you're in one of these arsy moods."

Watson turned back from the window.

"Do you fancy a coffee?" he enquired.

* * *

"Some of these graves are well over a hundred years old," Carmichael remarked as he made his way past the weather-worn headstones dating back to the years around the time the church was built.

"Yes," replied Rachel, "my…"

Before she had a chance to finish her sentence, Carmichael had stopped suddenly at the foot of the largest and most imposing tombstone, which had been erected encased in a sturdy stone base and stood over eight feet tall.

"And this is the finest of them all," he remarked. "This chap must have been important."

"He was," announced Rachel. "It's the man whose money paid for the church to be built and who built the old village school just down the way."

"You seem to be well up on the local history," remarked Carmichael, his tone indicating surprise, but also an air of approval that his officer was so knowledgeable. Carmichael read the epitaph.

"Here lies Matthew Dalton, aged 67," Carmichael read aloud, "businessman, benefactor and friend to all in this parish. Husband to Ruth, father of Henry, Alfred, Emma, Louise and Rachel. Though his achievements were many he remained grounded as a Moulton Bank man and will ever remain so."

Carmichael paused for a few seconds, before turning back to face his young colleague. "A relative, I take it?" he said.

Rachel smiled and nodded. "I can never remember exactly," she replied rather vaguely, "but he's either my fourth or fifth great-grandfather. My father would be able to tell you; but yes, by all accounts, he was quite a big cheese around here in the mid-nineteenth century."

Carmichael nodded approvingly. "That's something to be proud of," he remarked with sincerity in his voice. "However, it's not going to help us find out how our mystery would-be killer made his escape."

Rachel's initial reaction was a faint smile; however, within a few short seconds her expression changed to one of curiosity as her eyes focused on the ramshackle fence that divided the churchyard from the farmer's field beyond.

"But maybe that might," she announced, pointing at a fragment of grey fabric trapped in the wire at the top of the fence.

Chapter 7

Within an hour of them finding the fragment of fabric, Watson, Cooper and four uniformed officers had joined Carmichael and Rachel Dalton at the church. As soon as they'd arrived, all six had been despatched by Carmichael into the cow field which stretched eastwards up Ambient Hill where the mystery man had, in all probability, taken flight, presumably now with a gaping hole in his grey trousers.

Carmichael had made a call to his old friend Norfolk George, the editor of the local newspaper, and had conscripted the help of a local artist, regularly used by the police, who was inside the church with Barney Green, Lindsay Carter and Kerry Gillespie attempting to create as good a likeness as they could of the man with blood on his hands.

"How are you doing?" Carmichael enquired.

"I think his nose was a little more pronounced than that," remarked Lindsay Carter.

"And his chin was squarer," added Kerry Gillespie.

"I think we're almost there," replied Rachel, although if she was being totally honest, she wasn't sure.

"Once you've finished, get a copy over to Norfolk George at the *Observer*," instructed Carmichael. "If he can have it by three o'clock this afternoon, he's promised it will be on the front page of this week's paper, which is out on Thursday."

"Right you are, sir," replied Rachel. "I'll make sure that happens."

"Also, get the sketch distributed to all the police stations within a hundred-mile radius of us," he continued. "See if our man is known to any of them. You can take my car."

As he finished talking, he handed Rachel the keys to his BMW.

"I will, sir," replied Rachel as she took the keys from his hand.

Carmichael started to walk away. "I'm going to join Watson and Cooper," he remarked. "I want to see if they've found anything."

Carmichael marched swiftly towards the vestry and the rear exit. However, before he'd disappeared from vision he turned back to face the group in the front pew of the church, hunched over the artist's sketch pad.

"When you get to the station," he shouted back at Rachel, "also see if they've had any reported incidents recently that may tie in with our man's confession to Reverend Green."

Rachel nodded vigorously, so her boss could see she'd got the message.

* * *

Natalie Carmichael, Carmichael's youngest child, had never bunked off school before. Of the three Carmichael children, she was the one who appeared to enjoy school the most. As far as her parents were concerned, everything was fine. At her parents' evenings it was always one long procession of beaming teachers, praising Natalie to the heavens. Her marks were all first rate, her behaviour was excellent, and she loved nothing more than to join in with anything and everything the school could throw at her, be it sports or academically related.

It was therefore completely out of character for her to have chosen to spend the whole of Monday, and most of the three hours that had already elapsed since she'd left home that Tuesday morning, sitting alone under a bridge on the bank of the Leeds-to-Liverpool canal, immersed in her thoughts and oblivious to the fact that her father was no more than half a mile away scouring the fields around the C of E church looking for a potential murderer.

* * *

"So, have you found anything yet?" Carmichael enquired as he reached where Watson and Cooper were standing.

Cooper shook his head. "Nothing," he replied.

"Unless he was planning to clamber over this drystone wall," added Watson, "my guess is he must have gone over that stile down there."

Watson pointed at the rickety-looking wooden structure ten metres from where they were standing.

"And where does that lead to?" Carmichael enquired.

"The pathway splits on the other side," replied one of the uniformed officers, who was standing close to them. "If you go up to the right it takes you to the car park at the back of the Amblers' Rest Café at the top of Ambient Hill."

"And if you take the other route?" enquired Carmichael.

"That takes you down the side of the hill towards Low Moor," continued the officer. "You eventually come out at the top of Stoney Lane."

"And how far roughly is 'eventually'?" Carmichael enquired.

"A good couple of miles, sir," replied the officer.

Carmichael considered their options for a few moments.

"Which one of you drove over here?" he asked his two sergeants.

21

"I did, sir," replied Cooper.

"Then in that case," continued Carmichael, "I suggest that you and I take a drive to Stoney Lane where the path emerges."

Cooper nodded.

"And what about the rest of us?" Watson enquired.

"Well, I'd like those three to carry on searching around here," Carmichael announced, pointing at the three uniformed officers who were some way off still searching for any signs of the missing man.

"Then I'd like them to go up to the café and ask if they've seen anything of interest in the last couple of hours. I'll leave you to organise and brief them, Marc."

"And what about us?" Watson enquired, meaning him and the uniformed officer who was still with them.

"I want you two to head off down the footpath," Carmichael replied with a wry smile. "If you move sharply you might even get to the other end at Stoney Lane before us."

As soon as he'd finished speaking, Carmichael gestured to Cooper with a faint movement of his head, turned away and started walking briskly towards the church. He didn't bother to wait to see the dejected expression on Watson's face, but he knew it would be there.

Chapter 8

"What do you make of all this?" Cooper enquired as he and Carmichael trundled down the winding country roads towards Stoney Lane.

"I'm not sure what to think," replied Carmichael candidly. "Barney Green is fairly sure the man he saw was telling him the truth, but it's all very bizarre."

"Maybe it's some sort of practical joke?" Cooper suggested.

Carmichael shrugged his shoulders.

"If it is," he replied, "it's a sick practical joke, that's for sure."

* * *

Natalie Carmichael looked at her watch. It was only 12:45pm, which meant that she still had another three hours before she would be able to return home.

She checked her mobile phone to see if there had been any text messages sent to her or if there'd been any new messages posted on Facebook or Twitter.

Other than another Facebook message from Sophie, her best friend, saying how jealous she was that Natalie was having a few days off in bed, and how she wished she had a bad cold, too, there was nothing.

Natalie took out the remnant of the chocolate bar she'd been nibbling all morning and put the last chunk in her mouth.

Bunking off school was incredibly boring, she concluded with a deep sigh; but then she remembered it was now lunch break at school, one of the times during the day that she'd come to dread the most.

* * *

Within fifteen minutes of leaving Watson and the rest of the police officers, Cooper's beaten-up old Volvo arrived outside an isolated, pretty cottage situated next to a smart, new-looking stile and a signpost pointing east, which read: "Ambient Hill 2.5 miles".

"Park a little way down the road," instructed Carmichael. "There may be tyre tracks near the footpath, which we might want to check out."

Cooper thought this highly unlikely, as there had been no rain in the area for at least two weeks; however, he did as he was ordered and brought the car to a halt some twenty metres down the lane, where the narrow road was wide enough for cars to pass by.

"It's a bit deserted around here," Carmichael remarked as the two officers made their way towards the footpath.

Cooper nodded. "It's not my cup of tea," he replied, "but for anyone wanting to live off the beaten track I expect it's just the ticket."

Carmichael was the first to arrive at the stile. "Doesn't look like we'll be getting any tyre tracks from here," he remarked, looking down at the parched earth at the side of the road.

Cooper shrugged his shoulders. "No," he responded. "But if our mystery man did come this way, maybe the old dear in the back garden saw him."

As he spoke, Cooper nodded his head in the direction of a

tiny old woman with a large straw hat, tending her sweet peas, seemingly oblivious to the presence of the two police officers.

Carmichael negotiated the stile and walked the twenty paces so that he was almost level with the lady.

"I wonder if you can help me?" he enquired in a loud voice.

The startled old lady took a step backwards and peered cautiously at the two tall men standing over the fence.

"You made me jump," she replied, putting her right hand against her chest.

"I'm sorry," said Carmichael, his voice still loud, but as friendly as he could make it.

"There's no need to shout," replied the old woman. "My legs may be a little shaky nowadays, but my senses are all in perfect working order."

"Sorry," remarked Carmichael, with his best welcoming smile. "We're police officers," he continued. "We were wondering if you saw anybody coming down the path in the last few hours?"

The old lady considered the question.

"Why do you ask?" she replied.

"We're trying to find a man who we think may have come down here," continued Carmichael. "Have you seen anybody?"

The old lady shook her head. "Sorry, my dear," she replied. "I've been here since just after breakfast and nobody has come past, as far as I saw. And I'm sure I'd have noticed."

Carmichael smiled once more. "Thanks anyway," he remarked before starting to walk away down the path.

"What has this man done?" shouted the old woman before Carmichael and Cooper had gone no more than five paces.

Carmichael turned back to face the old lady. "It's nothing to worry about," he assured her. "We just want to ask him a few questions."

The old lady smiled back and nodded. "Well if I see someone strange, I'll let you know," she shouted. "Who should I ask for at the police station?"

Carmichael walked back to the old lady and handed her a card.

"My name's Inspector Carmichael," he said in a quiet, comforting tone of voice. "You can get me on this number at Kirkwood police station."

The old lady took the card from Carmichael and studied it carefully.

"I can tell from your voice that you're not from around here," she remarked. "Somewhere in the south, I'd guess."

Carmichael smiled. "North London originally," he replied, "but I've been here a few years."

The old lady looked up into his deep-blue eyes. "They reckon it takes two generations to become accepted around here," she remarked.

Carmichael smiled. "I'll have a long wait then, in that case, won't I?" he replied with a wry grin. "Anyway, I won't keep you from your fine-looking sweet peas, Mrs... "

"Heaton," interjected the old woman. "Mavis Heaton. And they are fine, aren't they? They shouldn't be flowering yet by rights, but the weather has been so unusually hot and dry they think it's July already."

Carmichael smiled again. "It's nice to meet you, Mrs Heaton," he said before turning back and striding off down the path.

Mavis Heaton kept her eyes firmly fixed on the two officers until they disappeared from view, then as swiftly as she could, she made her way towards the back door of her cottage.

* * *

Carmichael was surprised how far they had to go down the footpath before they met Watson and the uniformed PC, who were taking a breather by the side of a tiny babbling brook when Carmichael and Cooper came upon them.

"How was the walk?" Carmichael enquired with a mischievous smirk. "I take it you've not found any clues?"

Watson's eyes opened widely. "As it happens, we think we have," he replied rather self-righteously and with a wry, triumphant look to the PC stood next to him. "Hawkeye Hill here spotted some dried blood on the handgrip on the first stile we went over. That's why it's taken us so long. We've got one of the other PCs to stand guard until someone from the SOCO team arrives."

"Really?" replied Carmichael. "Then maybe he did come this way."

"I take it there was no sign of anyone down at the other end?" Watson remarked.

"No," replied Carmichael. "We've seen nothing. The only person we've come across is the little old dear who lives in the cottage at the far end of the footpath."

"And she swore blind that she's seen nobody come past," interjected Cooper.

PC Hill smiled. "That will be old Mavis Heaton," he remarked.

"Do you know her?" Carmichael asked.

"We know her son-in-law quite well," PC Hill replied. "Her daughter married a guy called Attwood, Sean Attwood. Over the years he's been the cause of at least half the minor crimes in the villages around here."

Carmichael frowned and nodded knowingly. "Yes, I've come across Sean Attwood a few times," he replied, "but as I recall, it's all low-level stuff he's involved in."

Watson tutted and raised his eyes skyward. "Yes," he concurred, "it's all minor, but if something dodgy is going on

27

in these villages, you can be sure Sean's up to his neck in it somewhere along the line."

Carmichael shrugged his shoulders. "Well that may be so, but as we've no evidence that a crime has been committed in this one, I think we can leave Mr Attwood in peace, for now," he remarked. "Let's get ourselves back to the church and find out how the others have been getting on."

Carmichael turned and started to walk back in the direction he'd come from, followed by Cooper, PC Hill, and a hot and very tired Watson.

Chapter 9

Rachel relished driving the boss's car. Compared to her little Clio, the 3 series BMW, with its dark, comfortable leather seats and tinted windows, seemed the height of luxury.

"I'm going to have one of these," she said out loud as she glided down the narrow country roads en route to the *Observer* offices and her appointment with Norfolk George. "As soon as I make sergeant, I'm having one."

As the car crossed the bridge over the Leeds-to-Liverpool canal, out of the corner of her eye, Rachel noticed a young schoolgirl walking alone along the towpath. The image was fleeting and, with the individual being twenty yards away and some ten metres below her, it was unclear; however, Rachel could have sworn it was Carmichael's youngest daughter.

"Bugger!" Rachel exclaimed as her eyes returned to the road ahead and she realised that the lorry in front had stopped suddenly no more than three car lengths in front of her.

With her brakes screeching and the pungent smell of burning rubber already thick in the air, Carmichael's precious black BMW eventually came to a halt inches away from the intimidating rusty steel bar at the back of the lorry.

Rachel exhaled deeply as the realisation of how close a call that had been suddenly registered.

Seemingly oblivious to what had just occurred behind him, the lorry turned right, leaving the road ahead clear.

Not realising the person responsible for the emergency stop was a policewoman, the driver of the white van behind, who'd also had to brake heavily, sounded his horn loudly and gesticulated in a way he'd certainly not have done had he known who was behind the wheel of the offending car.

Badly shaken, Rachel had no desire to take matters further with the animated lout in the vehicle behind and, after starting her stalled engine, made her way slowly towards her appointment with Norfolk George.

* * *

Barney Green was still at the church when Carmichael, Watson, Cooper and PC Hill entered through the large front door. The young vicar had sent Lindsay Carter and Kerry Gillespie home and had spent the last hour busying himself, tinkering around with Sunday's sermon and reading some of his correspondence.

"Any luck?" he enquired eagerly as he caught sight of Carmichael.

Carmichael shook his head. "As yet, we've no sighting of your mystery man," he replied. "However, in addition to the fragment of trouser material we found on the fence, Sergeant Watson and PC Hill think they've found some traces of blood on a stile on the footpath leading towards Stoney Lane, so we may be making a little bit of progress."

"Do you want some tea?" Barney asked, his expression suggesting he'd appreciate them staying.

Carmichael looked at his watch before turning to face his colleagues. "Why don't you three get back out there for an hour or so to see if the others have found anything else," he remarked. "Then let's all head off back to Kirkwood and get together for a debrief."

The three officers nodded and started to make their way out of the church.

"Don't forget I'll need a lift back, too," Carmichael shouted over at them before they were out of earshot, "as Rachel took my car."

"No problem, sir," replied Cooper, "you can come with me."

As soon as the three colleagues had left the church, Carmichael looked directly at Barney Green and smiled.

"I'd love to have that drink with you," he remarked.

Chapter 10

Having hand-delivered a copy of the artist's sketch to Norfolk George at the *Observer*, Rachel headed off to Kirkwood police station, carefully observing the speed limits to ensure her earlier close shave would not be repeated.

When she arrived at the station, satisfied that the picture would be prominently displayed on the front page of this week's paper, Rachel made her way to her desk. With just two further tasks to complete, she took a large swig of coffee and gently eased herself back into her chair.

* * *

Mavis Heaton picked up the telephone. "Hello, Mavis speaking," she said, her normal greeting to incoming calls.

"Mavis, it's Sean," announced her son-in-law, his voice gruff and his words hurried, as if he was anxious. "I got your voice message. Whatever you do, don't mention to anyone anything about what you saw," he continued.

"What's wrong, Sean?" Mavis enquired, "Was it Brookie that I saw?"

"The less you know the better," replied Sean Attwood, "but if the police or anyone else ask you any more questions, tell them you saw nothing and spoke to nobody."

"Is everything all right, Sean?" Mavis asked, her tone indicating her heightened concern.

"Everything's fine," Attwood reassured her. "Well it will be, as long as you keep schtum."

"If you say so, Sean," replied Mavis, her voice trembling. "I'll not say anything, I promise."

"That's great, Mavis," continued Attwood, his voice sounding noticeably calmer. "I'm going to have to go. I'll see you tomorrow."

Without bothering to get any reply, Sean Attwood ended the call, leaving Mavis Heaton perplexed and anxious about what her son-in-law may be involved in.

* * *

"So, he's just disappeared?" remarked Barney Green as he handed Carmichael a steaming mug of coffee.

"Well, he won't have vanished," replied Carmichael. "It would seem he made his hasty escape over the fence in the graveyard, then down the footpath that heads north to Stoney Lane, but as yet, we can't find anyone who saw him after he left the church."

"What about Mavis Heaton?" enquired the vicar.

Carmichael was surprised the cleric knew her.

He shook his head. "No, we did talk with her and she maintained that she'd been in her garden all morning but saw nobody pass that way."

Barney Green took a sip of his tea. "Well, he must have made off across the fields before he got to Mavis's," he remarked, "as Mavis Heaton is the most observant person around these parts. She misses nothing."

"Really," replied Carmichael. "That's interesting to know."

* * *

33

It was another forty minutes before Cooper, Watson, PC Hill and the other officers entered the church.

"Any luck?" Carmichael enquired.

Watson shook his head. "Forensics have left with that blood sample from the stile and the fragment of fabric we found," he remarked. "They reckon they'll be able to get back to us with some news on the blood type in a matter of hours, but they say it may take a bit longer to discover what trousers he was wearing."

"But I take it there were no sightings of our guy either arriving or leaving from the café at the top of the hill?" Carmichael asked.

Watson shook his head. "Nothing," he replied.

Carmichael drained his mug, placed it down on the small table next to his chair and stood up.

"OK," he remarked, "let's get back to Kirkwood and see how Rachel's got on. With a bit of luck, she may have had some positive responses from other police stations to the description she's circulated."

"Or discovered a crime that's been logged somewhere that matches his confession," added Cooper.

"I do hope you find him," remarked Barney Green with an anxious expression on his face, "and his admission to me proves to be false. The thought that he may have murdered someone is quite frankly horrendous."

Carmichael put on a forced smile, his attempt to try and reassure the vicar.

"I'd not jump to that conclusion yet," he remarked. "My guess is that this is a hoax, but we do have to treat it seriously and we'll be doing all we can to find your mystery confessor."

After shaking Barney Green firmly by the hand, Carmichael ushered his colleagues out of the church and, within a matter of minutes, the officers had all departed, leaving the trendy village vicar alone with his thoughts.

Chapter 11

3:45pm couldn't come quickly enough for Natalie. She'd left her hideaway under the bridge a few hours earlier and, with the day being so warm and dry, had wandered east down the towpath of the Leeds-to-Liverpool canal. She'd travelled about two miles before she turned back on herself, then spent an hour in the library.

From 8:20am that morning, when she'd slipped away and smuggled herself under the bridge, until she emerged back into civilisation at roughly 2:25pm, Natalie had only come across one person: a man walking his dog at about 1pm, whose frown suggested he was at first very suspicious at coming across a girl in school uniform, but when she smiled at him he'd just smiled back and walked on.

She'd opted to spend the last hour before she went home in the library. Natalie felt safe there knowing that she would not be spotted by anyone else from school. She also figured that any adults in there would not turn a hair at a schoolgirl reading quietly, so it seemed as good a place as any to hide out until it was time to return home.

As she correctly calculated, the librarian saw nothing amiss in a girl in school uniform sitting in the reference section reading a book on twentieth-century poets. And, before the hordes of children came piling down the road, any of whom may have recognised her, Natalie had quickly gathered her things and made her way home.

"You're early," announced her mother as Natalie walked through the door and headed up the stairs.

"Yes," replied Natalie as she reached halfway. "I had a free period at the end of the day, so I dashed out as soon as the bell rang."

Although it wasn't unusual for her daughter to go to her room and get changed as soon as she came home from school, for some reason Penny Carmichael sensed something wasn't quite right, but decided now was maybe not the right time to interrogate her.

* * *

Carmichael was in his office, engrossed in the email message sent to all the inspectors at Kirkwood from Chief Inspector Hewitt regarding ensuring expense forms were completed promptly and in line with the framework set down by the Chief Constable's office, when Watson appeared at the door.

"We've got the results back on the blood found on the stile," Watson announced.

Carmichael looked up from his screen. "And what does it tell us?" he enquired.

Watson shrugged his shoulders. "Well, if the blood was from the hands of the vicar's mystery visitor, the only thing he's killed is a pig."

Long frown marks appeared on Carmichael's forehead. "Say that again?" he remarked.

"The blood isn't human," replied Watson, "it's from a pig."

Carmichael sat back in his chair and brushed his fingers through his hair.

"Well, I suppose we've no definitive proof that the blood came from Barney Green's visitor," he remarked, "however, this is starting to look like some sort of ridiculous prank."

Watson nodded. "Do you want us to cancel the request for information that Rachel sent out to the other police stations and call Norfolk George about removing that piece on the front cover of this week's *Observer*?"

Carmichael considered Watson's question for a few seconds.

"With regards to the message Rachel sent out to other police stations, don't do anything yet," he replied. "Let's see what we get back. After all, we're still not certain it's a hoax."

Watson nodded back to show he'd understood and agreed.

"As for the *Observer* article," continued Carmichael, "call Norfolk George and tell him to couch the piece so it comes across as less serious than I previously led him to believe. I'd still like it run though, as I want to identify this person, whether he has killed someone or not. Even if this is an annoying wind-up, he's got some serious explaining to do."

"Right you are, sir," replied Watson before disappearing back into the main office. Carmichael picked up the phone on his desk.

"In the meantime," he muttered to himself, "I'll let Barney Green know what's happening."

* * *

It was just after 7:30pm when Carmichael arrived home, where he found Penny lounging in the garden on her recliner; a present he'd bought for her a few birthdays ago.

"All right for some," he teased as he approached her and planted an affectionate kiss on her forehead.

Penny smiled up at her husband.

"I didn't hear you come in," she remarked. "I was miles away."

Carmichael's eyes widened and staring at the half-empty glass of wine by her side, he shook his head gently from side to side.

"Been on the pop again, I see," he remarked with a cheeky smirk.

"This is my first and only drink for tonight," replied Penny defensively. "To be honest, I've only just sat down. I've been on my feet all day."

"Really," replied Carmichael. "What have you been up to?"

"Oh, the usual," remarked Penny, "washing, ironing, tidying up after everyone. You know, all those incidental little jobs everyone here takes for granted that go unseen."

"So, have you eaten?" Carmichael asked, knowing the conversation was entering dangerous territory and wanting to move on.

Penny shook her head. "Not yet," she replied rather sheepishly. "I had a casserole for us, but I hadn't bargained on Jemma wanting tea. I knew she and Spot On – I mean Chris – were going out tonight, but they decided to eat here first."

Carmichael's resigned nod conveyed his full understanding of what his wife was saying. Spot On, his eldest daughter's long-time boyfriend, had an unrivalled appetite, so he could well imagine the scenario.

"And, to make matters even worse," continued Penny, "Natalie was almost as hungry as Chris. I'm not sure what she ate today, but she demolished two platefuls and a huge piece of chocolate cake."

"What about Robbie?" Carmichael enquired, the absence of any mention of his son not having gone unnoticed.

"He's out with his friends somewhere this evening," Penny replied rather vaguely. "I think they've gone to Southport."

"I see," remarked Carmichael. "It could be a takeaway for us then."

Penny swivelled her legs around on the recliner and sat up.

"I'm afraid so," she replied. "Would that be too much for you to bear?"

Carmichael smiled broadly. "I suspect I'll manage," he announced.

* * *

When their takeaway arrived, it was still light, so Carmichael and Penny made themselves comfortable on the wrought-iron table outside on their brick-paved patio.

"So how was your day?" Penny enquired as she spooned half the contents of the special fried rice from the foil dish onto her plate.

"Very weird," replied Carmichael. "Barney Green called us this morning to say that he'd a visitor in the church with his hands soaked in blood, claiming he'd just killed someone. By the time we got there, the man had vanished and we have no idea where he went, or who he was."

Penny looked back at her husband in amazement. "That is weird," she agreed.

"It gets more bizarre," continued Carmichael. "The only clues we have are a fragment of material found on a fence in the churchyard, which we believe is from the trousers the man was wearing, and some blood we found on a stile along a footpath we think he used to make his escape. However, it turns out the blood is pig blood and we've not been able to identify anything yet that suggests there's been a killing recently in a hundred-mile radius of Moulton Bank."

"So, do you think this is just some joker?" Penny enquired.

Carmichael shrugged his shoulders.

"It's certainly starting to look that way," he remarked. "However, I've got an uneasy feeling about this case. I think there may be something more sinister behind all this."

Penny didn't reply, but her eyes remained fixed on her husband as she tried to absorb the details, he'd just shared with her.

"Have you finished with the rice?" Carmichael enquired, his mind now clearly more focused on his stomach than on the case.

* * *

Sajid Hanif sat bolt upright in bed, his head and chest soaked in sweat.

His muscles taut and eyes bulging in their sockets, he gasped for breath.

"Oh Sajid, you'll wake the baby," his wife, Sonja, remarked as she fidgeted in bed before finally managing to organise herself, so she was sitting next to her trembling husband. "Is it the same dream again?"

Sajid nodded. "Yes," he replied, his voice quivering. "But it's more vivid."

"Maybe you should see someone and talk about it," suggested Sonja, her head bent around his chest, so she could make eye contact. "These dreams are happening more and more."

"I know," replied Sajid, "but nobody can help anymore. It's my punishment, I'll have this forever." From down the corridor the sound of a baby crying pierced the air.

Sonja rolled her eyes and eased herself out of bed.

"We're going to have to do something, Sajid," she remarked. "All this every other night is exhausting for all of us."

Once his wife was out of the room, Sajid lay back on his pillow, his eyes wide open, staring aimlessly into the darkness.

"There's nothing we can do," he muttered out loud. "You can't change what's done."

Chapter 12

Wednesday 1st July

Carmichael sat alone at the kitchen table, a half-full mug of coffee at his side, reading the headline article in the newspaper about a so-called leaked plan claiming the government was about to revamp taxes once again.

He didn't notice Natalie enter the room until he heard the fridge door open.

"Morning," he remarked cheerily, his eye line raised from the paper to his daughter.

Natalie half turned and stared back at her father, her face showing little sign of any reciprocal cheer.

"Morning, Dad," she mumbled before grabbing a carton of milk and heading over to the cupboard to extract a bowl.

"I'm in no great rush this morning," announced Carmichael, "so if you'd like a lift to school, I could drop you off on my way to the station."

"Thanks, Dad," Natalie replied without bothering to turn and face her father, "but I'll walk."

Carmichael couldn't remember any of his children ever declining a lift to school, so he immediately suspected something wasn't right.

"Are you OK?" he enquired. "You don't seem yourself this morning."

Natalie turned, walked over to her dad, smiled and then kissed him on his cheek.

"I'm fine, Dad," she assured him. "I've just got a lot on my mind with exams coming up, that's all."

She again smiled at her father, picked up the cereal packet and started to pour herself a large portion.

"Don't worry about them," remarked Carmichael, "they're just to assess your progress. It's not like they're GCSEs; you've still got a few years before you have to take them."

"I know I'm being stupid," replied Natalie, "but exams always make me nervous."

Carmichael was about to reassure her about her anxieties when his mobile rang.

Looking down at the small screen he could see the name Paul Cooper highlighted in bold lettering.

"Morning Paul," he remarked as he put the mobile to his ear.

Natalie could hear the voice of the caller but could not make out what he was saying. However, from the way her father intently listened, she guessed it was important.

"I'll be over there in ten minutes," remarked Carmichael.

"Is there a problem?" Natalie enquired.

Carmichael forced a smile, walked over to his daughter, placed a kiss on her cheek and walked towards the door.

"Good job you didn't want a lift," he remarked, "as I've got to shoot off."

As he disappeared from her sight and made his way down the hallway, he shouted back, "Don't fret about your exams, you'll do fine."

Natalie puffed out her cheeks before walking over to the cupboard where she grabbed a packet of biscuits and two cans of cola, which she hurriedly stashed in her school bag.

* * *

"So, what have we got here?" Carmichael enquired as he walked from his car towards the cordoned-off area down Wood Lane, the quiet country road on the outskirts of Moulton Bank.

Cooper shrugged his shoulders. "The car was found here early this morning with the doors wide open," he replied, pointing at the maroon 1960s Bentley abandoned in a small lay-by. "A man out walking his dog saw it and, with its doors open, thought it looked suspicious, so called it in when he got home at around seven thirty."

"And the body's in the boot?" Carmichael asked as he and Cooper arrived where Dr Stock, Rachel Dalton and Watson were standing.

"It's easy to see how you made inspector, Carmichael," remarked Stock in his customary manner, not bothering to divert his eyes from the contents of the boot.

Without saying anything, Rachel and Watson stood aside to allow Carmichael to peer into the boot and see the victim.

"Respectable-looking man with dark hair, aged about forty-five," remarked Carmichael, recalling the description Rachel had gleaned the day before from Lindsay Carter and Kerry Gillespie at the church. "Height approximately six foot, smartly dressed in an expensive-looking navy blazer with brass buttons, white open-necked shirt, dark grey trousers with a hole in the seat, brown Derby shoes and an expensive-looking watch."

"He's also got what looks like blood on his hands, sir," added Rachel.

Carmichael glanced at the palms of the dead man's hands, which were indeed bloodstained.

"And he's got a seriously large laceration to his throat," remarked Dr Stock, who this time turned his head and made eye contact with Carmichael.

"How long since he died?" Carmichael asked Stock.

"Between twelve and twenty-four hours, is my considered view," replied Stock. "But I'll need to get him to the lab before I can be more specific."

Carmichael thought for a few seconds before commenting further.

"We need to get Barney Green to view the body, so that we're sure this is the man he saw yesterday," Carmichael announced, "but I reckon that's going to be just be a formality."

"The church is no more than ten minutes' walk away from here," Watson remarked. "There's a footpath twenty yards down the lane that takes you across the fields and comes out almost opposite the church. If you want, I'll walk over now and see if he's there."

Carmichael nodded. "Good idea, Marc," he replied. "Why don't you do that?"

"Do you think the dead man came here straight from the church?" Rachel enquired, as Watson started to wander off down the lane.

Before Carmichael could reply, Cooper interjected. "I very much doubt it," he remarked. "The footpath from the church, where he ripped his trousers, and the stile with the pig blood on are both heading in the opposite direction."

"Paul's right," Carmichael concurred. "I reckon it's more likely he came here afterwards or was driven here and abandoned."

After a brief pause, Carmichael turned to face Cooper. "Is there anything on him or in the car that can tell us who this man is?"

Cooper shook his head. "So far nothing," he replied. "I've done a PNC check on the car and the number plate's not coming up, so it looks like it's got false plates, too."

"Well, it's a beauty of a car and I can't believe there are that many maroon 1960s Bentleys knocking about," Carmichael remarked, "so I'd imagine we'll be able to get this traced fairly easily when Dr Stock's team start looking more closely at the chassis number."

Stock gently shook his head. "It's a good job you have us, Carmichael," he remarked. "God only knows what you'd do without my team."

Carmichael turned to face Rachel Dalton and Cooper and rolled his eyes.

"You're worth your considerable weight in gold, Stock," he replied sarcastically, before turning away and walking around the side of the car.

After spending a good five minutes looking at the car, taking a few photos on his mobile phone and surveying the surroundings, Carmichael made a gesture with his head to Rachel Dalton indicating that he wanted the DS to join him.

"Paul," he remarked to his able sergeant. "I'll leave you here to wait for Marc and Barney Green. Then, once you've established whether this is the man he met yesterday, get yourself back to the station. Tell Marc to go with Dr Stock and his team and report back as soon as they've established the time of death and whether the blood on our dead man's hands is human or pig."

Cooper nodded. "Will do, sir," he replied.

"And what are we doing?" Rachel asked as she followed Carmichael to his car.

"I'd like to go and visit Mavis Heaton again," he replied. "I want to show her the photos I've just taken of the car. I'm hoping they'll register with her as, if our man did walk down that footpath, he may well have parked up near Mavis's house. It's a very distinctive car so there's a chance she may remember it."

Chapter 13

"It looks like it's going to be another hot one today," Carmichael announced as he carefully placed his jacket on the hanger and shut the car door behind the driver's seat. "Not the sort of weather to be wearing a shirt and tie."

Rachel nodded. "Twenty-eight degrees they reckon it will be today," she replied.

"Practically tropical for this part of the world," remarked Carmichael with a wry smile.

"The hotter the better for me," continued Rachel. "That's the only downside for me of living in Lancashire, these sorts of days are few and far between."

Carmichael glanced sideways at Rachel as he fastened his seat belt and started the engine.

"I'll not disagree with you on that one," he remarked. "I reckon it's always a good two to three degrees colder up here than it was in Watford where I grew up. That's for sure."

Carmichael's black BMW sped off quickly down the dry sandy road, sending clouds of dust high into the early morning sky.

* * *

Penny was still sitting at the breakfast table reading the G2 pull-out pages of the *Guardian*, an article on cottage weavers in Britain, when the phone rang.

Abandoning the paper, she sauntered down the hallway and picked up the phone.

"Moulton Bank 645383," Penny said in the voice she only ever used when she answered the landline.

Her children were forever teasing her about the way she answered the phone, but Penny took no heed. She'd always answered the phone like that, and, in her eyes, it was far more courteous than the gruff hello which greeted callers when either Steve or any of her three children picked up the receiver.

"Mrs Carmichael?" enquired the very well-spoken lady on the other end.

"Yes," replied Penny, who thought she recognised the voice, but couldn't work out who it was.

"It's Mrs Rumburgh, from Mid-Lancashire Academy," continued the caller.

In an instant two things flashed up in Penny's mind. The first was the image of Brenda Rumburgh, the frumpy, prim and proper deputy head at Natalie's school, clad in her trademark smart school outfit, most probably purchased from either M&S or the Edinburgh Wool shop. The second, and most alarming for Penny, was that a call from the school could only mean one thing: that something had happened to Natalie.

Penny's throat went dry as she waited for the reason for the call to become apparent.

"I hope you don't mind me calling you, but we were concerned about Natalie," continued Mrs Rumburgh. "With her not being in at all this week, we were wondering if there was anything wrong."

Penny couldn't believe what she was hearing.

"There must be some mistake," she replied, her voice echoing the confusion in her head. "Natalie's been at school."

There was a brief silence before Mrs Rumburgh spoke again.

"I can assure you, Mrs Carmichael," she continued, "Natalie hasn't registered at all this week. That's the reason why I called, as it seemed very unusual. Natalie's rarely off, and when she is you're always very quick to let us know, in keeping with our rules about absenteeism."

"I don't understand," Penny remarked.

"We've spoken to her friends," continued Mrs Rumburgh, "Sophie Keenan and Michelle Smith, and they both maintain that Natalie had texted them to say she had a bad cold. However, with us not hearing anything from you I thought I'd give you a call."

Penny could feel her pulse racing and the palms of her hands started to sweat.

"I don't know what to say," she remarked, her voice trembling. "All I know is that Natalie left the house on Monday, on Tuesday and today at the normal time, in her school uniform and for the last two days has returned in the afternoon at her normal time. However, if you're saying she's not been going to school, what she's been doing during the day is a mystery to me."

"Obviously, we take this very seriously," remarked Mrs Rumburgh in a tone lacking any sympathy for the distress her revelation had caused. "May I suggest that tomorrow, you bring Natalie in person and we have a meeting to try and understand why she's not been attending school."

"Yes," Penny heard herself say, her mind still whirring with all sorts of theories as to why her daughter would be behaving in such an uncharacteristic way.

"Shall we say nine forty-five?" suggested Mrs Rumburgh. "By that time the rest of the school will be in lessons, which will give us time to get to the heart of her unauthorised absence."

"Yes, nine forty-five will be fine," replied Penny, who continued to hold the receiver to her ear for several seconds after Mrs Rumburgh had ended the call.

* * *

"What do you make of all this?" Rachel asked as she and Carmichael headed off in the direction of Mavis Heaton's house.

Carmichael glanced briefly at his passenger before shaking his head and exhaling deeply.

"It's a strange one, that's for sure," he remarked. "Assuming Barney Green confirms that this was the man he met yesterday, and I think there's no doubt he will, and if Dr Stock confirms that the blood on his hands is the same pigs' blood that PC Hill found on the stile, then it would appear that our man has confessed to a murder that almost certainly never happened, only to be murdered himself, within hours of him making his admission, in almost exactly the way he maintained he'd carried out his murder. I've never come across anything like this before. It's bizarre."

Rachel nodded. "Maybe our man was really confessing to a murder he was about to commit when he went to see Reverend Green," suggested Rachel, "but when he tried to carry out the act it went wrong, and he ended up being killed."

Carmichael's gaze remained forward on the road ahead.

"That seems a bit far-fetched to me, Rachel," he replied, "but at this moment in time I've not got a better suggestion."

As he finished speaking, the loud ring on the hands-free in his car indicated that a call was coming through; and the name on the screen told him it was Penny.

Carmichael pressed the button on his steering column to accept the call.

"Hi," he said before his wife had a chance to speak. "I'm in the car on hands-free with Rachel at the moment," he quickly added to alert to his wife that their call could be overheard.

"Hi Rachel," said Penny, trying her best to keep her emotions in check. "How are you?"

49

"I'm fine, thank you," replied Rachel, who had always got on well with her boss's wife.

For a split second Penny seriously considered avoiding the subject that she'd called about, but she was worried and wanted to share the news she'd just received with her husband.

"Steve," she said, "it may be nothing to get too concerned about, but I've just had a call from Mrs Rumburgh at Natalie's school."

As she heard the name Mrs Rumburgh, Rachel's eyes opened wider. She, too, had attended the Mid-Lancashire Academy, albeit at a time before it was called an academy, and she remembered Mrs Rumburgh well, the no-nonsense scourge of every teenage girl she ever oversaw, with her outdated view of how they should dress and behave.

"Right," replied Carmichael, alarm bells already starting to ring in his head.

"Well, according to Mrs Rumburgh," continued Penny, "Natalie's not been at school at all this week."

"But that's baloney," replied Carmichael, "she's gone every day."

There was a brief pause before Penny continued.

"That was my first reaction," remarked Penny, "but it looks like she's been leaving in the morning and coming back in the afternoon, at the usual time, but she's not been attending school at all during the day. Mrs Rumburgh has asked to see the three of us tomorrow at nine forty-five to discuss Natalie's absence."

As Carmichael took in what he had just heard, Rachel remembered the sighting she thought she'd made of Natalie the day before along the canal towpath.

"Sorry to interrupt," she said, "I think I may have seen Natalie yesterday. At the time, I wasn't sure as I only caught a fleeting glance, and it seemed bizarre that she'd be where I saw her, but now you've said she's not been at school I think it could well have been her."

Carmichael shot a confused and angry glare in Rachel's direction.

"Why did you not mention this before?" he said, his voice indicating he wasn't happy.

"I'm sorry," replied Rachel, "but it all happened very quickly, I couldn't be certain it was her and then my attention was diverted by something else."

Rachel decided it wouldn't be her smartest move to elaborate on the reason her thoughts had so suddenly moved elsewhere, namely, the near miss she'd had while driving Carmichael's car.

"Where did you see her?" Penny asked.

"It was near the bridge over the canal on the towpath," replied Rachel. "The girl I saw was alone and looked like Natalie, but I couldn't be certain as they all look the same in their school uniforms."

"Do you mean the bridge just down the road from here?" Carmichael enquired.

"Yes," replied Rachel.

"I'll go there now," Carmichael said. "If she's there I'll bring her home."

"OK," replied Penny, "and thanks, Rachel. Hopefully you'll find her and there's a logical reason behind all this."

Given the hostile reaction she'd received from Carmichael, Rachel didn't want to be seen to make light of the situation with Penny on the call, so said nothing.

Carmichael ended the call, and without saying anything more to Rachel, put his foot down hard on the accelerator and headed towards the canal bridge, no more than five hundred yards away.

Chapter 14

It took Marc Watson less than twenty minutes to locate Barney Green and for the two of them to walk down to the crime scene.

Cooper lifted the flimsy blue plastic cordon tape to allow the earnest-faced vicar to duck under and walk solemnly towards the victim's 1960s Bentley.

Cooper gently took hold of the vicar's arm. "It's not a pretty sight," he remarked. "I just thought I'd let you know."

Barney Green smiled and nodded back at Cooper. "I appreciate you letting me know," he replied. "I'll try not to linger too long."

Cooper let go of his arm. "Just a quick confirmation that this is the man who came to see you is all we need," he said. "But of course, if it isn't him or you're not sure, that's fine too."

"I understand," replied Barney Green, who smiled at Cooper before taking a deep breath and continuing towards the car.

The two SOCOs who'd been taking samples from the boot stepped back to allow Reverend Green to inspect the body and, as they did so, Watson sidled up next to Cooper.

"Would be a real bugger if he said this wasn't his man," whispered Watson irreverently.

At first Cooper ignored his colleague's comment; however,

that delay was short-lived, as Barney Green put his hand to his mouth, nodded vigorously and walked a few steps away from the vehicle.

"Based upon that reaction, I think we can safely say that it's him," remarked Cooper.

* * *

Carmichael parked his BMW in Bramble Way, a small road just a matter of yards from the canal bridge.

"Stay here," he ordered Rachel. "I'll only be a few minutes."

Still feeling bruised by her boss's earlier rebuke, with arms folded firmly across her chest and lips pursed tightly shut, she did as she was told.

Carmichael clambered out of the car and walked towards the narrow dusty track that led down to the canal towpath.

Sat alone on her bag, staring at the sunlight as it bounced off the roof of the bridge and the reflections of the surrounding trees as they danced across the water, Natalie didn't see her father until he was a matter of a few feet away from her.

The sudden awareness that someone was there, followed quickly by the realisation that it was her dad, stunned Natalie. She immediately stood up, mouth wide open and cheeks blushing to bright crimson.

Carmichael said nothing as he approached her.

"What are you doing here?" Natalie enquired as he arrived by her side and took hold of her arm.

"Shouldn't it be me asking you that question?" replied Carmichael.

"How did you know I was here?" continued Natalie, tears starting to roll down her face.

"I'm a detective," replied Carmichael with a generous smile, a special smile that can only be shared between a

53

parent and a child. "It's my job to find missing people. And I'm actually quite good at it."

With almost a sense of relief, Natalie allowed herself to be enveloped in the arms of her dad, who asked her no questions as they walked slowly back towards his car.

Penny was in the front room looking out of the window when the car pulled into the drive. She opened the front door and rushed down the few steep steps to meet her daughter before Natalie had the chance to get out of the car.

"I'm going to have to be on my way," Carmichael said to his wife. "It's probably best for you two to talk this through on your own. I'll see you this evening."

As Penny followed Natalie towards the front door, she half turned and looked at Carmichael with an expression on her face suggesting she'd like him to give her some sort of update.

Her husband's wide-eyed response accompanied with a pronounced shrug of his broad shoulders confirmed that he'd nothing to tell her.

"I'll see you later," she replied with a faintly relieved smile, before turning away and following Natalie into the house.

Chapter 15

Rachel was relieved that the journey from Carmichael's house to Mavis Heaton's cottage on Stoney Lane was only a ten-minute drive, as it was clear from his detached, surly demeanour that her boss was still annoyed with her.

Although she didn't like the cool atmosphere in the car, Rachel had no intention of apologising again; after all, in her eyes, she hadn't done anything wrong.

As soon as the car had come to rest outside Mavis Heaton's cottage, Carmichael glanced across at his young DC.

"I'll do the talking," he announced sharply, before clambering quickly out of the car and marching purposefully down the narrow gravel path that lead to Mavis Heaton's front door.

"That's fine by me," mumbled Rachel under her breath as she followed a few paces behind her grumpy boss.

* * *

"Why on earth didn't you tell me about this?" Penny enquired, her tone partially compassionate, but also indicating a degree of disappointment that her daughter couldn't share the fact she'd been bullied.

"I can handle it by myself," replied Natalie.

Penny's eyes opened wide. "Oh, by bunking off school," she remarked scornfully. "That's hardly handling it."

Natalie Carmichael looked tired and crestfallen.

"I know," she replied. "I just wanted time to think."

Penny smiled and threw her arms around her daughter.

"We'll fix it," she replied. "Your father, me and Mrs Rumburgh will get on to this and it'll be sorted."

* * *

Carmichael was surprised when the figure that opened the door of the cottage wasn't that of the diminutive Mavis Heaton, but that of a tall, thickset man in his mid-forties, with faded tattoos festooning his arms. It was a man Carmichael had come across at various times since he'd arrived in Moulton Bank.

"Inspector Carmichael," remarked Sean Attwood, "and the lovely DC Dalton," he added with a leery smirk aimed in Rachel's direction. "Mavis mentioned you'd been sniffing around here yesterday. What brings you back again?"

"Is your mother-in-law in?" Carmichael enquired.

Sean Attwood looked his two visitors up and down for a few seconds before opening the door wide enough for Carmichael and Rachel to enter the lobby.

"If you go through into the lounge I'll fetch her," Attwood replied, the slight movement of his head sideways indicating that he wanted the two officers to go through the door to their left.

Once they were inside Mavis Heaton's small lounge, Attwood closed the door behind them before walking the ten paces that led him to the kitchen.

Mavis Heaton was sitting behind the kitchen table when her son-in-law entered the room.

"It's Carmichael and that young DC that's always not too far away from him," remarked Attwood with glib derision. "Just remember what I told you," he continued, his intimidating eyes staring directly into Mavis's soul. "You saw nothing, you know nothing, and if he mentions anything about me and Brookie, you can't help him."

Mavis Heaton stood up and walked over to where Attwood was standing.

"I'm not going to say anything," she replied firmly, her expression and tone of voice indicating that she was in no way intimidated by her son-in-law. "But once they've gone, I want you to be straight with me. I know you far too well, Sean. I know when you're hiding something."

Attwood shook his head, but moved aside to allow the old lady, who was comfortably less than half his size, to pass him by and walk down the hall towards the lounge.

* * *

Cooper had driven Barney Green to the vicarage and was back at the police station when he finally got news about the maroon 1960s Bentley.

The initial PNC which he'd requested at the scene of the crime had drawn a blank; however, the chassis number that the SOCO team had given him indicated who the car's last owner had been.

Cooper smiled as the officer at the end of the line gave him a name that was already very familiar to him.

* * *

Mavis Heaton stared intently at the pictures of the maroon car on Carmichael's mobile phone.

Shaking her head, she looked up at Carmichael.

"I'm really sorry, Inspector," she said in a quiet but confident voice. "I've never seen this car before."

Before Carmichael had a chance to say anything more, his mobile rang.

Seeing the name Cooper coming up on the screen, he quickly stood up and walked over to the window.

"I'm sorry," he remarked, "I need to take this call."

Mavis Heaton and DC Dalton remained silent and motionless as Carmichael talked with Cooper on the mobile.

Carmichael spoke in a hushed tone, but even if they could pick up his part in the conversation, they would have learned nothing, given that the short call consisted mainly of Cooper talking and Carmichael listening.

"There's no need," remarked Carmichael, his closing remarks to Cooper. "As it happens he's in the next room, so I'll handle that."

When the call had ended, Carmichael sat down again facing Mavis Heaton and once more pointed at a photo of the maroon car.

"Now think very carefully," he said with an intentionally unhurried delivery. "Are you sure you've never seen this car?"

Mavis Heaton shook her head. "I'm sure," she replied, "I've never seen it before in my life."

As she finished her sentence, the door opened and Sean Attwood sauntered in.

"Perfect timing, Sean," remarked Carmichael. "Your mother-in-law has just informed us that she's never seen this car before."

As he spoke, Carmichael held up his phone so that Sean Attwood could see the photo of the car.

"How about you, Sean?" he enquired. "Have you seen this car before?"

Attwood looked at the phone before shaking his head.

"No," he replied, "I can't say I have."

Carmichael, slowly and deliberately, placed the phone on the table.

"Now that is strange, Sean," remarked Carmichael, "as

I've just been informed that you were the last known owner of this car."

"What!" replied Attwood. "There must be some misunderstanding. I don't and have never owned any car with that registration number."

"That may be true," remarked Carmichael, "as we believe those plates are fake. However, the chassis number on the car quite clearly denotes that Sean Attwood was the last known owner."

With a self-righteous grin on his face, Carmichael glanced quickly at Mavis Heaton and Rachel before returning his focus on Sean Attwood.

"Now, what have you to say about that, Sean?" he enquired.

A question that remained unanswered.

Chapter 16

Sean Attwood had been given little choice other than to accompany Carmichael and DC Dalton to Kirkwood police station.

As he'd left Mavis Heaton's cottage, he'd instructed his mother-in-law, in no uncertain terms, to call Jenny, his wife and Mavis's daughter, and get her to contact Arthur Brewster, Attwood's solicitor. They were to make sure Brewster made his way to Kirkwood station without any delay.

Mavis had clearly done as she'd been commanded, as within no more than fifteen minutes of Carmichael, Dalton and Attwood arriving at the station, Mr Brewster, renowned brief of most of the petty criminals in central Lancashire, arrived at the station and was speaking with his client in interview room one.

* * *

Having spent over an hour gleaning as much information as she could from Natalie, Penny suggested it would probably make sense for her daughter to remain at home for the rest of the day. Although Penny was thankful to have Natalie back home and was shocked and worried about her daughter being bullied at school, there was no way she was going to give Natalie even the slightest hint that she condoned or was in any way happy with her daughter's behaviour.

"You've missed three days of lessons," Penny had remarked as her crestfallen daughter slunk up the stairs to her room. "It's probably going to take you a good while to catch up, so the sensible thing would be to use what's left of today to get all your coursework completed."

Under normal circumstances Natalie would have viewed being told to spend the best part of the day doing homework as the most unwelcome chore possible. However, given how understanding her mum had been and compared to the alternative of spending countless hours under the bridge, as she'd done on the two previous days, Natalie had no issue in complying with her mother's instructions.

As soon as she heard Natalie's bedroom door close and she knew her daughter was safely out of hearing range, Penny lifted the phone and dialled the school to advise Mrs Rumburgh that her daughter was safe at home and to share with the school's deputy head the reason Natalie had given for her behaviour.

* * *

Arthur Brewster was a large, imposing man in his late fifties. With close-cut red hair punctuated with silvery-grey patches, a testament to the passing of time, and an ample beard of similar colouring, Carmichael often thought that Brewster could quite easily have earned extra cash playing Santa at the various Christmas fetes he had so hated attending when the kids were small. Not that Brewster needed the cash. His job had made him wealthy enough to own one of the largest houses on The Common, Moulton Banks' most expensive road; and if that wasn't enough, Arthur had a second house in the south of France and a small bolt-hole somewhere on the Norfolk–Suffolk border.

Despite his penchant for defending the dregs of the area, Carmichael rather liked Arthur Brewster and always enjoyed sparring with him, especially when he knew Brewster's client was guilty.

Carmichael had allowed Attwood's brief and his client twenty minutes together before he started the interview. With the tape recorder running and flanked by Rachel Dalton and Cooper, who'd arrived at the station almost an hour earlier, Carmichael went to ask his first question. However, before he could speak, Arthur Brewster started to talk, his voice loud and assured.

"My client would like it to be known that when you showed him the photograph earlier, he'd only looked at the number plate when he denied any knowledge of the car," he announced. "Mr Attwood does not deny that he owns a maroon Bentley similar to the one in the photo you showed him, but his number plate is SEAN 42."

"My name and the age I were when I bought it," remarked Attwood smugly.

"The car in your photo has a different number plate: WTR 1P," continued Brewster, who appeared to be slightly irritated by his client's sudden interruption.

"Thanks for clarifying the mix-up," replied Carmichael with a forced smile. "As you know, your client has not been charged and is not under caution. We'd simply like some answers about the car, which we are now agreed is Mr Attwood's, and how it came to be involved in a serious incident earlier today."

"My client has no issues in helping the police," remarked Brewster, "as a law-abiding citizen he will do everything he can to assist you."

Carmichael smiled. "In that case, Sean," he continued, "perhaps you can tell me how your car came to be found down Wood Lane this morning?"

Sean Attwood was just about to answer when Brewster placed his hand on his client's arm.

"Perhaps it would help if you could share with us the nature of the incident in Wood Lane that you mentioned earlier," he suggested.

Carmichael considered the question for a few seconds before replying.

"Certainly," he said, "if that will help your client be more cooperative, I'll certainly enlighten you both."

Carmichael extracted a copy of the photofit of the dead man drawn by the artist, based upon the descriptions Barney Green, Lindsay Carter and Kerry Gillespie had provided.

"This man was found earlier today in the boot of your car, Sean," announced Carmichael. "He'd been brutally murdered."

As soon as Attwood saw the photofit his shocked expression told Carmichael that he knew the man.

"Who is he, Sean?" Carmichael enquired. "And what's he doing in the boot of a car owned by you, carrying false number plates?"

Chapter 17

Sajid Hanif had just finished with Mrs Pettigrew, his last appointment before lunch, when the postman delivered the parcel he'd been expecting.

He put the package under his arm and headed out to walk the twenty or so paces that would take him to Herbz coffee bar, his normal lunchtime haunt.

"Black coffee and a cheese and tomato panini, Noel," Sajid shouted over to the tall, curly-haired patron as he sat himself down at his usual table in the corner, at the back of the restaurant.

The café owner smiled over, to register he'd received the order, before turning back to prepare lunch for another one of his regulars.

Sajid tore open the end of the brown envelope. Inside he found a second smaller sealed brown envelope and a folded A4 sheet of paper. He placed the sealed brown envelope on the table before opening up the folded A4 paper and reading the message.

He read it three times before folding it up once more and turning his attention to the sealed brown envelope.

At first, he didn't dare open it, but its size and feel suggested to him that its contents were indeed in line with what had been stated in the message.

Using the bread knife on his table, Sajid gently slit the end of the brown paper and carefully peeled some of it back to reveal a wad of purple £20 notes.

Out of the corner of his eye Sajid noticed Noel Herby walking towards him, which prompted him to stuff both the letter and the package of banknotes back into the outer envelope.

"Have you lost more weight?" Sajid remarked as Noel Herby arrived at his table, a comment which brought a broad smile to the café-owner's face. "Those fifty lengths you do each morning are definitely having a positive effect," Sajid continued.

Noel placed Sajid's coffee and panini on the table.

"I wish," he replied with a smile. "Twenty lengths about twice a week is as much as I can achieve at the moment, but I'm getting there."

* * *

"Do you believe him, sir?" enquired Cooper, as he, Rachel Dalton and Carmichael watched Sean Attwood and Arthur Brewster walking away down the corridor from interview room one.

"I don't know what to believe," Carmichael replied. "It sounds too ridiculous to have been made up, so it could well be true, but we need to check it out."

"How do we do that?" Rachel enquired.

Carmichael smiled. "That's going to be your job," he replied. "There have to be CCTV tapes for the car park where Attwood maintains he left the car. I want you to dig them out and verify whether his story holds water."

Rachel nodded. "Will do, sir," she replied. "And what are your next moves?"

"We're going to check out this guy, Geoffrey Brookwell, who Attwood maintains is the dead man," responded Carmichael.

"I want to know more about a man who'd covertly rent a car from an old school friend, paying him a thousand pounds for just one week's rent, then with bloodstained hands confess to a local vicar that he'd killed someone, before being found murdered himself in the very car he'd rented."

Rachel Dalton shrugged her shoulders and rolled her eyes.

"It's certainly a strange one," she remarked.

"You can say that again, Rachel," replied Carmichael before he headed off in the direction of his office with Cooper two paces behind him.

Chapter 18

Marc Watson hated pathology labs. How anyone would want to do that kind of work was a mystery to him. The assorted smells of body parts and chemicals, used to keep everything germ-free, were almost as obnoxious to him as the gruesome examinations the pathologists carried out on the people that lay on the slabs in front of them.

Everything about these places made him squirm, from the clinical sheen that emanated from every surface to most of the people who worked there.

He suspected that Carmichael knew this, and he had long believed that his boss took some sort of warped pleasure in continually assigning him to tasks that meant he'd have to spend time in this cold and hostile environment.

However, given that his brief had been to report back on the estimated time of death and on the exact nature of the dried blood on the dead man's hands, Watson saw no need whatsoever to be present at the autopsy, electing to wait in the reception area where the smells were less distasteful and there was, at least, a decent coffee machine.

It took a full two hours before Dr Stock emerged through the double doors and strode over to where Watson was sitting.

"You can tell Carmichael that his victim died yesterday between twelve noon and two in the afternoon," remarked Stock.

"That's very precise," replied Watson. "How can you be so exact?"

Stock looked back at Watson over his glasses.

"It would take an age to explain precisely how we know," Stock remarked dismissively. "But tell Carmichael that he was killed where he was found and at around the time I've just told you."

"Right," replied Watson.

"It looks like the killer also reversed the car back a few feet after he'd put your dead man in the boot," continued Stock, "as most of the blood the victim lost when his throat was cut, we found under the car."

"Presumably he did that to cover up the bloodstains," remarked Watson.

Stock returned a blank stare and gave a faint shrug of his shoulders.

"It's up to you and Carmichael to work out why the killer did that," he replied. "My job is to provide you with the facts."

Despite being irritated by the disdain in Dr Stock's remarks, Watson bit his tongue.

"And what about the blood on his hands?" he enquired.

Dr Stock nodded. "It's pig blood," he confirmed, "the same type as was found on the stile."

"Pigs have blood types?" remarked Watson, the surprise evident in his voice.

"Oh yes," replied Stock. "Just like you and me, although they only have two types, A and O. Both the blood sample from the stile and the blood on the dead man's hands are type O."

"Well, Dr Stock, I've certainly learnt something new today," Watson announced.

"Always glad to help expand your knowledge," replied Stock before turning away and walking back towards the double doors. "Tell Carmichael I'll email over my report in a couple of hours," Stock shouted back as he reached the doors and passed through and out of sight.

"I certainly will," remarked Watson under his breath, before draining the last dregs from his coffee cup.

* * *

"I think I may have found our man," announced Cooper from behind his computer screen.

"That's quick," replied Carmichael. "What have you got?"

Cooper swivelled around his screen to reveal the Facebook page owned by a man called Geoffrey Brookwell, whose profile picture looked exactly like the man they'd found dead in Wood Lane that morning.

"What on earth did we do to locate people before Facebook?" remarked Carmichael sarcastically.

Cooper smiled. "It says here he's an actor and that he lives in Knott End."

"An actor," repeated Carmichael. "Can't be a famous one as I've never heard of him. And where the hell's Knott End?"

Cooper smiled. "Can't say I've ever heard of him either," he remarked, "but I know Knott End, we used to go there as kids. It's about forty minutes north of here, not far from Blackpool, on the mouth of the river Wyre. They used to have a small ferry boat that took you over to Fleetwood, we used to…"

"Interesting though I'm sure your childhood recollections are, Paul," interrupted Carmichael, "let's try and focus on Geoffrey Brookwell, rather than waste any time meandering down memory lane."

Without responding, Cooper turned the screen back to face him and started to look again at the details and posts on Geoffrey Brookwell's Facebook page.

69

Feeling slightly guilty about cutting Cooper short so abruptly, Carmichael walked behind his sergeant to look more closely at the detail on his screen.

"No question about it," Carmichael announced, "he's our man. Well done."

Carmichael's praise seemed to have the desired effect, and Cooper started to read aloud from the intro page.

"Geoffrey Brookwell, actor, studied drama and theatre at York St John University, went to Dame Eve Turner Comprehensive School, lives in Knott End, from Moulton Bank."

Carmichael returned to his desk and sat down.

"See if you can find an address for him," he remarked, "and find out if he's married or in a relationship. I'm going to call Marc and see how he's getting on with Stock."

"Will do," replied Cooper.

"Actually," added Carmichael, "if he's an actor, he must have an agent. See if you can locate who that is, too."

As he finished speaking, Rachel entered the room.

"It's all there on the CCTV footage," she remarked.

"That was quick," replied Carmichael.

Rachel Dalton smiled. "It was easy," she remarked. "There's been a fair amount of vandalism lately on cars left in that car park, so the images are already sent directly here. It was a doddle to find what we needed. Especially as Sean Attwood was quite specific about the time."

"So, what have you discovered?" Carmichael enquired.

"Everything," replied Rachel. "Attwood leaving the Bentley parked in the multi-storey car park with the keys behind the back wheel, just as he said. Then, ten minutes later, the dead man arrives, collects the keys and drives off."

"So, Attwood was telling the truth," Carmichael remarked, with more than a hint of surprise in his voice.

"Yes, he was," Rachel replied. "And, what's more, the number plate hadn't been changed when the Bentley was

70

collected, just as Attwood claimed. It was 'SEAN 42' when Attwood left the car and Brookwell drove it away."

Carmichael took a few seconds to think.

"I have to admit I wasn't expecting that," he remarked.

"What do you want me to do now?" Rachel enquired.

"Go and help Cooper," Carmichael replied. "He'll brief you on what he's doing. I'm going to call Marc."

"There's no need," replied Rachel, her gaze directed out of the window, "his car's just pulled into the car park."

Chapter 19

Eager to hear what news Watson had from the autopsy on Geoffrey Brookwell, Carmichael left Cooper and Dalton and hastily made his way downstairs to meet his colleague.

"What's Stock saying?" Carmichael enquired as the two men met on the stairwell.

"He reckons the dead man was killed between noon and two yesterday," Watson replied. "He also maintains that after the killer had put him in the boot of the car, he backed the car up a few metres, presumably to cover the massive bloodstains on the ground from the dead man's injuries."

"Really," remarked Carmichael. "Did he say anything else?"

"Stock also confirmed that the blood on the dead man's hands matches the blood we found on the stile. Pig blood, type O."

Carmichael's look of incredulity made Watson smile.

"Apparently pigs have blood types just like humans," Watson remarked. "I was surprised, too."

Carmichael shrugged his shoulders. "I guess it makes sense," he said, "although I have to admit it's not something I'd ever thought about. Did Stock say anything else?"

Watson shook his head. "No, nothing more," he replied, "only that you'll get his report later today."

"Well, we've now got a name for our dead man," announced Carmichael. "He's Geoffrey Brookwell, a not-so-well-known actor who was brought up in Moulton Bank and was an old school friend of Sean Attwood's. According to Attwood, out of the blue he was sent a thousand pounds in cash over the weekend to rent the Bentley out for just a week."

"Sounds a bit dodgy to me," remarked Watson. "Mind you, anything Sean Attwood gets involved in is usually a bit suspect."

Carmichael nodded. "I agree," he replied, "and even more bizarrely, according to Attwood, at the time he didn't know it was Brookwell. He'd been instructed to leave the car in the multi-storey car park, with the keys behind the wheel, and was told he'd get another thousand pounds when it was returned."

"But you say he didn't know it was the dead man who'd sent him the money?" Watson attempted to clarify.

"No," replied Carmichael. "He says not. He maintains he only found out as he loitered about by the car park exit and saw it was Brookwell behind the wheel."

"And do you believe Attwood?" Watson asked.

"I wasn't sure," replied Carmichael, "but Rachel's checked the CCTV for Saturday and it confirms what Attwood told us. Attwood also claims he never changed the number plates, which the CCTV footage confirms as well."

Watson's forehead creased as he listened to his boss. "I'd lay money on Attwood being more involved in this than he's making out," he remarked. "He may not be our killer, but Sean Attwood's as dishonest as they come."

Carmichael gave a small shrug of his shoulders. "You may be right, Marc," he replied, "but his story checks out and although we shouldn't exclude him from our enquiries, our prime focus now needs to be on finding out more about Geoffrey Brookwell. We need to know why he hired the car then changed the number plates, what he was doing when he entered the church yesterday morning and put the fear of

God into Barney Green, and where he went between doing his disappearing act from the church and being murdered down Wood Lane."

"Sounds like a plan, sir," remarked Watson.

"I'm glad you agree," replied Carmichael, who started to make his way back up the stairs, "as that's what Rachel and Paul are on to right now. Let's go and see how they're getting along."

* * *

Mrs Pettigrew was shocked when Sajid Hanif returned from his lunch break. In all the years he'd worked at Mumford's Opticians, he'd never once taken his full hour's lunch break, so when he emerged looking rather flustered through the door of the practice after almost two hours, she automatically assumed there was something wrong.

"Is everything OK, Sajid?" she enquired, the way she asked the question showing a mixture of genuine concern but also unashamed nosiness.

"Everything's good, Mrs Pettigrew," Sajid replied curtly. Despite being a well-established member of Calvin Mumford's team, having worked there for almost twenty years, Sajid still found it difficult to address the elderly receptionist, who'd been a fixture behind the counter since the practice was established and who assumed a level of importance that far exceeded her pay grade, in any other way.

"I was detained unexpectedly. An unforeseen family matter, but it's nothing serious," he continued. "I don't think I've another appointment until three, so I knew there wouldn't be a major issue."

Sajid knew Mrs Pettigrew would ensure that Calvin Mumford was made aware of his extended lunch break, so after flashing one of his best smiles and just before he disappeared upstairs, he added, "I'll let Calvin know when I see him later. I'm sure he won't mind."

There was, of course, no way Mrs Pettigrew could have known the real reason for Sajid's extended lunch break, namely, to pay the £1000 he'd received in the package into his Mid-Lancashire Building Society account and to rush home to his desktop to check out what had been written in the message that had accompanied the money.

Chapter 20

"We've found an address," announced Cooper, as Carmichael and Watson entered the office. "According to the electoral roll, he's registered as living in an apartment on the Esplanade overlooking Morecambe Bay."

"How far away is Knott End?" Carmichael enquired.

"Depending upon the traffic, about forty minutes to an hour," replied Cooper rather vaguely.

"What about his agent?" Carmichael asked. "Any luck with that yet?"

Rachel looked up from her computer screen. "There's nothing on his Facebook page," she announced, "so I'm checking the agencies in Manchester to see if he's with any of them. No luck so far, but there's not that many so hopefully it won't take long."

"OK, keep looking, Rachel," Carmichael replied, "and while you're doing that, Paul and I'll get ourselves up to Knott End and check out Brookwell's apartment."

Suitably pleased with this announcement, Cooper immediately stood up, grabbed his jacket and headed towards the door.

"What do you want me to do?" Watson enquired.

"You can alert Fylde police that we're going up to Brookwell's apartment," he replied. "They may want one of their team to meet us there. Then, once you've done that, help

Rachel find his agent, if he has one. And, when you find them, if they're reasonably local get over and interview them. I'd like to know how busy Geoffrey Brookwell was and whether he was currently working on anything."

Watson nodded. "Right you are, sir," he replied.

"Shall we take my car?" Cooper enquired.

Carmichael smiled. "No, I think I'll drive," he replied. "I'm never confident about your car surviving a journey for more than twenty miles, so I'd rather err on the safe side."

* * *

Penny knocked gently on her daughter's bedroom door.

"Can I come in?" she asked in a friendly, non-threatening way.

"Yes," replied Natalie, who immediately stopped staring out of her bedroom window and half turned in her chair in order to make eye contact with her mother as she entered the room.

Penny gingerly pushed open the door and walked in, a mug of tea in one hand and her best cheery smile on her face.

"Why do you think they don't like me?" Natalie enquired before her mother had a chance to take more than a couple of steps into the room.

Penny's heart sank as she heard her daughter's words.

Slowly, Penny moved over to where her daughter was sitting, knelt down and put her arms around her shoulders.

"I'm not sure why they're being so nasty to you, dear," she replied, "but I know we're going to get it stopped."

"But why me?" enquired Natalie. "Why are they being so cruel and horrible to me? I've done nothing to them."

Penny hugged her daughter even more tightly, before releasing her grip and looking into her sad, frightened eyes.

"I don't know," Penny said, "maybe they don't really hate

you. Maybe they really hate themselves and their own lives, and they are so scared of this self-hatred that they redirect their anger towards others."

"But why me?" Natalie asked again.

"Maybe they would secretly like to have your life, your friends, your popularity and because they feel they can't, they just want to hurt you."

"And they've succeeded," replied Natalie.

Penny kissed her daughter's forehead and smiled. "Maybe so far, they have," she admitted, "but from here on in that's all going to change, you'll see. We'll get this sorted, your dad, Mrs Rumburgh and me. All this bullying stops as from today."

For the first time since her dad had brought her home, Natalie smiled.

"I really hope so, Mum," she replied. "I just want it all to go away."

Chapter 21

Rachel looked up from her computer screen, her expression one of frustration and incredulity, given that her colleague had, for the whole of the ten minutes since Carmichael and Cooper left the station, remained staring aimlessly out of the first-floor window.

"Are you going to call Fylde police?" Rachel asked.

"I've been thinking," replied Watson without bothering to turn around to face her, "surely we should be asking ourselves where someone would get hold of pig blood?"

Frequently during cases, Carmichael would make a comment or pose a question that Rachel didn't see coming and occasionally Cooper would do the same. However, it was rare for Watson to do so, which made the avenue he was following seem even more insightful than it would have, had it been uttered from the mouths of either of the other two members of the team.

"Do you think there are many pig farms in the area?" Watson asked, this time turning to face Rachel as he spoke.

Rachel shrugged her shoulders. "I guess there will be quite a few," she replied, "but surely, it's local abattoirs we need to be looking for. Farmers will rear the pigs and butchers will sell the meat, but if we're looking for places that will have access to their blood, you'd need to check out slaughterhouses in the area."

Watson nodded. "You're right," he replied enthusiastically. "I think Carmichael's missed a trick here. I'm going to get on to that."

With uncharacteristic vigour, Watson rushed over to his desktop and started to tap furiously on the keyboard.

"What about contacting Fylde police?" Rachel remarked, "and helping me find Geoffrey Brookwell's agent?"

"You'll have to handle finding his agent on your own," replied Watson, "and if you could also make that call to Fylde police, that would be brilliant, too."

Eyebrows raised and mouth wide open, Rachel shook her head gently from side to side, dumbstruck by her colleague's disrespect for her and the lack of regard for the instructions he'd been given by Carmichael less than fifteen minutes earlier.

* * *

The thirty-eight-mile journey from Kirkwood police station to Geoffrey Brookwell's modern, shiny apartment overlooking the sea, at a decidedly windy Knott End, took fifty minutes. For most of the journey, Carmichael tried to fathom out what would motivate someone to hire a prestigious car anonymously from an old school friend, paying a thousand pounds in cash up front; change the number plates; fabricate a story about killing someone, using pig blood to emphasise the lie and then disappear. What was he hoping to achieve?

Having been unable to reach any logical conclusion, he was relieved when the car eventually arrived at its destination.

Waiting outside the property was the unmistakable sight of a small police vehicle with the livery of Fylde police on the side.

"Looks like the local plod want to join us," remarked Carmichael with a wry smile in Cooper's direction, before clambering out of the car.

Cooper chuckled. "Which is exactly what we would have done if the boot was on the other foot," he muttered to himself, before opening the door and following his boss along the pavement.

* * *

After an hour of searching, punctuated only by the three-minute call she made to Fylde police station in Fleetwood, Rachel Dalton finally found the agency that Geoffrey Brookwell was signed up to.

Top Notch Acting Agency was a small business based in the centre of Manchester and, according to its website, was just five minutes' walk from Piccadilly train station.

Elated with her discovery and the fact that she now had Geoffrey Brookwell's picture and career to date, such that it was, on the screen in front of her, Rachel dialled the number emblazoned at the top of the website.

* * *

"Thank heavens for warden-assisted apartments," remarked Carmichael as the doorman departed, leaving him, Cooper and the two officers from Fylde police alone in the small-but-fashionable-looking flat.

Cooper smiled. "He can't have been doing too badly," he remarked. "This place looks pretty plush."

"For this area it's quite an expensive place to live," remarked one of the officers. "This apartment probably sets him back around eight hundred pounds a month."

"Really," replied Carmichael who, in truth, didn't consider eight hundred pounds to be particularly expensive. "Was Geoffrey Brookwell well known in the area?" he enquired.

The two officers exchanged a brief look before both shrugging their shoulders.

"Never heard of him," replied the second officer, in his broad, distinctive local dialect. "He can't have been very successful as we get little news around here, so if we had a celebrity in our midst, we'd know about it."

Carmichael scanned the room.

"OK," he remarked, "let's get looking for anything that could help us understand why Brookwell came back to Moulton Bank and who might have killed him."

* * *

Rachel was hanging on for almost five minutes before Anna Montgomery finally came to the line.

"Anna," she remarked tersely, as if her forename was all anyone needed to be told.

"Good afternoon, Miss Montgomery, I'm DC Dalton from Mid-Lancashire police. I wonder whether you could spare me a few moments of your time this afternoon to talk about Geoffrey Brookwell?"

"Why, what's he done?" replied Anna Montgomery, her brusque manner still to the fore.

"He's not done anything," replied Rachel, "but I'm sorry to have to tell you that we have reason to believe a man we found dead, earlier today, may be Mr Brookwell."

There was a short silence from the other end of the line before Anna Montgomery spoke again.

"Good gracious," she said, her voice still very business-like, but less aggressive. "Do you want me to come over to identify the body?"

Rachel hadn't expected this response. "Does Mr Brookwell have any relatives?" she enquired, trying to give herself a few moments to think.

"Nobody that I know of," replied Anna. "His father died a few years ago and, to my knowledge, he's no siblings and I can't ever remember him mentioning his mother. I think she must have died many, many years ago."

Rachel didn't relish the thought of driving over to Manchester, so decided to accept Anna Montgomery's suggestion.

"If you could come over this afternoon, that would be really helpful," she remarked. "We're based in Kirkwood."

"I've a few things to get done here today," remarked Anna, "so this afternoon is out of the question. However, I could be with you at, say, eleven o'clock tomorrow morning."

"That would be fine," replied Rachel. "I look forward to seeing you in the morning."

Without any further comments or any attempt to prolong the conversation, Anna Montgomery ended the call abruptly and without even saying goodbye.

Chapter 22

Sajid Hanif sat quietly, alone at the back of the tiny half-lit retinal photography room, his head bent down low behind the expensive new instrument Calvin Mumford had only recently installed.

"Hello," he said in a whisper, as the hotel receptionist answered his call. "I'd like to book a room, for the day, tomorrow, if possible. I understand you do day rates."

"Yes," replied the receptionist, "we have rooms available. What name shall I book it under?"

"Hanif," Sajid replied. "And I know it sounds very strange, but if you could allocate me room seven, that would be much appreciated."

The receptionist paused for a second while she checked whether this end room of the outside apartments was going to be free the next day.

"Yes, that's possible," she replied. "Would you like it set up meeting-style?"

"Erm, no," replied Hanif. "It will be fine as it is."

Assuming the purpose of the caller's booking was more pleasure- than business-related, the receptionist didn't ask any further questions. "It will be available from 9am tomorrow morning until 5pm," she announced, "and excluding any refreshments, the cost will be seventy pounds which I'll need you to pay by card today, and which is non-cancellable."

"That's perfect," replied Hanif, who extracted his credit card ready to provide the necessary details the hotel required.

* * *

To Watson's amazement, there were only two abattoirs within a fifty-mile radius of Moulton Bank; and with only one of them being responsible for slaughtering pigs, his newly acquired desire to locate the source of the blood found on Geoffrey Brookwell's hands appeared to be pointing him in the direction of Thomas Crown's establishment, just fifteen miles north of Moulton Bank.

Watson didn't go directly to the abattoir. Instead he dropped in at home to change into more appropriate shoes and an old pair of trousers; clothes he felt more suitable for a visit to a slaughterhouse. However, his detour ended up taking him over an hour as he also took the opportunity, while he was at home, to make himself a sandwich and a cup of tea before leaving.

If Watson had checked the working hours of Thomas Crown's abattoir or had simply not gone home at all he'd have almost certainly been able to arrive well before closing time. However, he hadn't checked the opening times and he had gone home, so when he arrived, at 3:45pm, he found that the slaughterhouse had already shut for the day. Despite knocking hard on the iron-plated door, which had a large notice signifying the company's opening hours as being 6:30am to 3:30pm every weekday, there was no answer.

"Bugger," he muttered under his breath, as he imagined the reception he was likely to get from Carmichael, having not only ignored his directive, but, having done so, not been able to make any tangible progress in his quest to identify the source of the pig blood.

Despondently, Watson made his way back to his car and, with a loud screech of his wheels, shot off back in the direction of Kirkwood police station.

***

Carmichael spent almost fifteen minutes in Brookwell's bedroom carefully rifling through his drawers, reading any letters and notes that laid there. Then, just as meticulously, he rummaged about in the dead man's numerous jackets and trousers hanging neatly behind the mirrored doors of his built-in wardrobe.

There was no doubt that Geoffrey Brookwell was fastidiously tidy: by the looks of it, verging on the obsessive. However, his bedroom revealed no clues as to the reason why he'd gone back to Moulton Bank the day before, why he'd acted so peculiarly, and why someone might have wanted to kill him.

It was in the last jacket pocket that Carmichael found the envelope, a small dog-eared envelope which looked like it had been around for years.

Carmichael took it out and emptied the contents onto Brookwell's bed.

There were four photographs, all of young girls; one a toddler, one a child of about six years old, then two aged about thirteen.

Carmichael looked at them carefully. He couldn't be certain they were of the same girl, but he suspected so. He turned them over to see if anything had been written on the back, but nothing had.

Carmichael had just put the photos back in the envelope when Cooper entered the room holding a torn and food-stained Jiffy bag.

"I think we may have something," Cooper announced as he moved hastily towards where Carmichael was standing, followed closely by the two local uniformed officers.

"What's that?" Carmichael enquired.

"We've found this in the recycling bin," Cooper replied,

holding up the empty padded envelope.

Using just two fingers, Carmichael carefully took the envelope out of Cooper's hand and looked closely at the address and postmark.

"Postmarked last Wednesday from Kirkwood," Cooper remarked. "It could be significant."

Carmichael nodded. "Have you found any letter that could have been inside this?" he enquired.

Cooper shook his head. "There was nothing in the bin," he replied.

Carmichael looked again at the address which had been typed onto a sheet of paper and then attached to the Jiffy bag with clear tape.

"Let's bag this up and get it to forensics," Carmichael instructed. "You never know, there may be a fingerprint somewhere that will help us."

Cooper opened a large plastic bag, holding it so Carmichael could drop in the white Jiffy-bag.

"Look what I found," Carmichael said, while at the same time handing the envelope containing the photographs to Cooper.

Cooper carefully pulled the photos out and looked at them one by one.

"His daughter, maybe?" Cooper remarked.

Carmichael shrugged his shoulders. "They all look like they've been taken when the child wasn't aware," he remarked. "So, if it is a daughter, I'd guess that he's not supposed to be taking pictures."

Cooper nodded, returned the photos to the envelope and handed it back to Carmichael.

"Keep digging around," Carmichael continued, "I'd like to find the letter that was inside the Jiffy bag you found."

He then looked at his watch. "Let's give ourselves another twenty minutes here, then get back to the station and see what the other two have achieved this afternoon."

Cooper nodded, sealed the bag, then headed back into Brookwell's living room.

Chapter 23

It was 5:15pm when the four officers gathered together at Kirkwood police station.

"Did you find anything interesting at Brookwell's flat?" Rachel enquired, her enthusiastic eyes looking keenly in the direction of her boss.

"Nothing earth-shattering," Carmichael replied. "It's a nice apartment, looking out over the sea, and looking at the decor and the clothes he had hanging in his wardrobe, I'd say our victim wasn't short of a penny or two. Also, the place was spotless and incredibly tidy, almost obsessively so."

"So, a rich neat-freak," replied Watson.

Carmichael smiled and shook his head. "I'm not sure I'd say he was necessarily rich, but his lifestyle suggests he was reasonably well off."

"But I take it you found nothing that might help us with the case," Rachel remarked.

"Well, we might have," replied Carmichael, who took out the envelope he'd found in one of Brookwell's jacket pockets. "We found these."

Carmichael laid the four photographs on the desk for the team to look at.

"Do you think it's the same girl?" Watson asked.

"I'd say so," interjected Rachel. "Taken years apart, but they're not very clear."

"No, they're not," agreed Carmichael, "which suggests to me they were taken without the girl's or her parents' consent."

The team fell silent as they studied the images and tried to make some sense of who the child could be.

"We found something else," remarked Cooper after a few seconds had passed, holding up the evidence bag which now housed the Jiffy bag they'd found. "We discovered this in the bin."

He placed the bag on the table in front of his two colleagues, so they could read the address and postmark.

"Postmarked Kirkwood on Wednesday 24th June," Watson read out aloud.

"Do you think Brookwell might have received this from whoever killed him?" Rachel asked.

"I've no idea," replied Carmichael candidly, "but with the postmark being in Moulton Bank, it's quite possible that whatever was in this envelope might have been the reason why Brookwell was in Moulton Bank yesterday and the sender may be involved in some way."

"I'd say it's highly likely," Watson remarked.

Carmichael nodded. "Perhaps, Marc," he replied, "but let's not jump too far ahead of ourselves. Let's see what forensics can come up with and go from there."

"I take it you didn't find what was in the Jiffy bag?" Rachel enquired.

Cooper shook his head. "We didn't find a letter."

Rachel's eyes widened. "Well, there must have been more than a letter," she observed, "otherwise the sender would have just sent it in a normal envelope."

"You're right," Carmichael remarked. "I'm sure there was, but at this stage it's impossible to say what."

"Maybe it was the cash Attwood claims he received to pay for the hire of his Bentley?" Watson suggested.

"Maybe," replied Carmichael, "but as I said just now, let's not make any rash assumptions, it might have been something else completely."

"If it was the cash," Rachel remarked, "then Brookwell would have had to have been pretty quick off the mark."

"What do you mean?" Cooper asked.

"Well this postmark is Wednesday 24th," Rachel replied, "so the very earliest Brookwell would have received it is Thursday 25th. But didn't Attwood say he received the thousand pounds in an envelope on Friday 26th? So, for the package Brookwell received to have contained the thousand pounds, he would have to have posted it on to Attwood on Thursday, too. It's possible, but it's cutting it fine, given the car was required to be collected on Saturday 27th. I reckon it's more likely that whoever sent Brookwell the Jiffy also sent Attwood the money in another parcel, at about the same time, rather than it being Brookwell who reposted the cash."

"That does make sense," remarked Cooper, who was clearly impressed by Rachel's logic.

"Assuming that Attwood is telling us the truth," remarked Watson sceptically. "I'd not be surprised if what he's told us isn't totally kosher."

Carmichael considered all that had been said for a few seconds, before trying to get the conversation to move on. "What's clear," he remarked, "is that we just don't know what was in the Jiffy bag that Brookwell received. It may have been cash, it may have been something else. It may be relevant to his death, then again it may have nothing to do with the strange events from yesterday, or his murder. What is clear, however, is that we need to do whatever we can to get some answers here."

Cooper nodded. "Shall I pick that one up?" he enquired.

Carmichael nodded. "Yes, get on to it first thing in the morning," he replied. "Get the Jiffy you found down to forensics, try and see if you can trace where and when exactly it was posted, and get over and talk with Attwood again. See if he still has the packaging and the letter he maintains he received with the cash on Friday."

Cooper nodded. "Will do, sir," he replied.

Having exhausted the discussion for now on the Jiffy bag, Carmichael turned to face Rachel Dalton and Watson.

"So, how did you two get on trying to trace Brookwell's agent?" he enquired.

Rachel smiled. "I found her and she's coming into the station tomorrow," she replied. "She's offered to identify the body, too."

"Good work," replied Carmichael. "Did she say anything about Brookwell?"

Rachel shook her head. "We didn't speak for long," she confessed, "but her name is Anna Montgomery and the agency's called the Top Notch Acting Agency. According to Anna, Brookwell was single, had never married, and his father died a few years ago. To her knowledge he was an only child, and she reckoned his mother must have died years ago, as he never mentioned her."

"And what time is she coming in?" Carmichael enquired.

"Eleven," replied Rachel.

"Excellent," remarked Carmichael. "When she gets here tomorrow, get her down to the morgue to identify the body and I'll meet you back here afterwards. I'd like to speak to her myself."

"Will do, sir," replied Rachel with gusto.

"And before she arrives," continued Carmichael, "see if you can get a check done on Brookwell's calls, landline and mobile, for the week leading up to his death. I want to know who he talked to."

Rachel nodded. "Will do, sir," she replied again with equal enthusiasm.

Carmichael then turned to face Watson.

"I assume from your silence that you weren't involved much in tracking down Brookwell's agent?" he suggested.

Watson shook his head.

"No, Rachel was on the case on that one," he replied nonchalantly, "I decided to follow an idea of my own."

"Really," remarked Carmichael, "and what was that?"

"I thought it might be a good idea to try and find out where Brookwell got the pig blood from," Watson replied. "The best bet, we thought," his head turning to face Rachel as he spoke, "was an abattoir. So, I've spent most of the afternoon trying to locate the most likely one he'd have used."

Carmichael nodded. "Good thinking, Marc," he replied. "And that would explain your change of clothes. I was wondering why you'd changed." As he spoke, Carmichael eyed his sergeant up and down, a wry smile on his face.

"I figured it might be a bit messy in there," replied Watson.

"And what did you come up with?" Carmichael asked.

"Surprisingly, there's actually only one in this area that slaughters pigs," Watson replied. "A place called Thomas Crown. However, unfortunately, that shuts at three thirty, so I wasn't able to get in to see them."

As he spoke, a puzzled expression came over Rachel's face as she calculated in her head how long it should have taken her colleague to get to the abattoir. Based upon the time he'd left the station, she couldn't see how he wouldn't have been able to arrive well before it closed for the day.

Although she said nothing, her bewildered look wasn't lost on Carmichael, who sensed all was not as straightforward as Watson was telling him.

"So where is this abattoir?" Carmichael enquired.

"It's way out in the sticks, about fifteen miles north of Moulton Bank," Watson replied.

It was now Carmichael's turn to look confused.

"So why did you look around here?" he said. "Surely if Brookwell used an abattoir to obtain the blood, he'd have gone to one nearer his home in Knott End rather than around here."

Although, once said, it seemed obvious, this had never crossed Watson's mind and, for once, he was lost for a suitable response.

"I certainly think it's a line we need to investigate," Carmichael continued, "but broaden your area of interest to include abattoirs in the Knott End area."

Watson nodded. "Will do, sir," he replied, his demeanour less self-assured than it had been just moments earlier.

"I expect those sorts of places open really early in the morning," added Carmichael, "so I suggest you set your alarm quite early tomorrow and see if you can get around all the potential sources in the morning. If you're quick off the mark, there's no reason why you can't get that line of investigation all wrapped up and be back here by lunchtime. Do you agree?"

"I'll do my best," Watson replied, his expression suggesting an early start was not something he was relishing.

Carmichael looked up at the clock, which indicated it was nearly six.

"I better go and brief Chief Inspector Hewitt," he remarked, standing up and making a move towards the exit. "I'll leave you all to it. Let's get back together for another team briefing at twelve thirty tomorrow. By then we'll hopefully be a lot more clued up as to what Brookwell was up to yesterday and, with a bit of luck, who it was that might have killed him."

Chapter 24

Since he arrived at Kirkwood police station, Carmichael's opinion of Chief Inspector Hewitt had changed very little.

It was fair to say that he continued to find his superior stuffy and pompous. Too many times he saw Hewitt's motivation driven more by a desire to protect or enhance his own personal standing with his superiors, rather than to get to the truth, a trait that continually frustrated and annoyed Carmichael.

However, there was no doubt that Hewitt was a sharp and intelligent man, and on occasions the conversations he'd had with his boss, regarding his ongoing cases, had been helpful. Therefore, although if given the choice Carmichael would prefer to "plough his own furrow" (as his father used to tell him), his briefing sessions with Hewitt were not always without benefit.

When Carmichael arrived at Hewitt's office, his door was open and, as soon as the chief inspector saw him approaching, he ushered Carmichael in with a flamboyant sweep of his long, wiry arm. Once inside, Hewitt closed the door behind them and summoned Angela, his PA, on the intercom.

"Two teas please, Angela," he announced, "and no interruptions."

Carmichael sat himself down on the chair facing his boss; the chair was slightly lower to the ground, giving the occupier no choice other than to look up at the immaculately turned out senior officer opposite, with his sharply pressed uniform and gleaming, polished buttons.

"So, what can you tell me about the case, so far?" Hewitt enquired.

Carmichael eased himself back in the chair.

"The dead man is believed to be Geoffrey Brookwell, an actor who grew up in Moulton Bank, but now lives in Knott End," Carmichael replied.

"And is he the man that went into the church yesterday and confessed to a murder?" Hewitt asked.

"We showed Reverend Green the body this morning and he's confirmed that it is the same man," replied Carmichael. "And, from Stock's report, it sounds like he was killed within a few hours of leaving the church."

"Are you any clearer about the motive for his murder?" Hewitt enquired, just as the door opened and Angela appeared with a tray of drinks and biscuits, which she sat on the desk between the two officers before directing a friendly smile in Carmichael's direction and making her exit.

"So far, no," replied Carmichael, "we've no motive or any obvious candidates for his murder. The only person we have who's linked to the events of the last few days is a low-level criminal called Sean Attwood. He's well known to us for petty criminal activity, but I think it's unlikely he'd be involved in a murder. It was his car that Brookwell hired and they were at school together years ago, but that's about all we have on him."

"I take it you've interviewed this Attwood character?" Hewitt asked, while at the same time picking up one of the cups from the tray and moving it slowly towards his lips.

Carmichael nodded. "According to Attwood," he said, "he maintains that he was sent a thousand pounds in cash, unexpectedly, to pay for the rental of his Bentley for a week, with a promise of a further thousand pounds once the car had been returned. He also reckons that, at the time, he didn't know it was Brookwell."

"Sounds very strange," remarked Hewitt. "Two thousand pounds is a hell of a lot of money for a week's car hire, even for a Bentley."

"I agree," Carmichael replied, "but what makes the story even more unusual is that, according to Attwood, he was told to leave the car in the multi-storey car park with the keys behind one of the wheels."

"Have you verified his story?" Hewitt enquired.

"Yes," replied Carmichael. "Rachel's checked the CCTV for Saturday and it confirmed what Attwood told us was correct. Attwood can be clearly seen in the car park leaving the keys behind the wheel, only for Brookwell to arrive ten minutes later and drive away in the Bentley."

"Very strange indeed," observed Hewitt, who took a large gulp of tea. "So, what is your strategy?" he continued, once his lips had parted from the cup.

"We're following up a few avenues of enquiry," replied Carmichael deliberately vaguely, "and tomorrow, we've got Brookwell's agent in to officially identify his body. I'm hoping she can also help us understand why Brookwell would have been behaving like he was yesterday."

Hewitt gently nodded.

"Well, as always, keep me in the loop, Inspector," he remarked.

Taking this as a signal that the meeting was over, Carmichael rose from his seat and, leaving his tea untouched, nodded at Hewitt.

"I certainly will, sir," he replied before turning and making his way towards the door.

He'd taken only a few steps when he abruptly came to a halt.

"There was one other thing," Hewitt had remarked. "I've had a request from the commissioner's office regarding us possibly taking back an old colleague of ours who appears to have made quite a name for herself since leaving us."

Carmichael did not need to be told who Hewitt was talking about; he knew straight away.

"Really," he replied, turning slowly around as he spoke.

"Yes," continued Hewitt, "Lucy Clark. I'm sure you remember her, she was under you when you first arrived."

"Yes, I remember Lucy," replied Carmichael.

"Well, she's been on the fast-track programme since she left us," continued Hewitt. "She's currently a sergeant and by all accounts, should make DI in the next year or so."

"Good for her," remarked Carmichael.

"Well," said Hewitt, "do you think she'd make a useful addition to your team?"

Carmichael cleared his throat. "Lucy was a very capable officer," he replied. "However, I've two sergeants already working in my team and DC Dalton is doing a great job. Being in a team of four works well for me. I'd not want to lose any of the three people I have already just to make way for Lucy, particularly if her secondment is only ever going to be until she makes DI."

Hewitt looked genuinely shocked by Carmichael's rebuff, but was clearly in no mood to push his DI into agreeing to something he wasn't keen on.

"We don't need to respond straight away," Hewitt remarked. "Why don't you think about it over the next few days?"

Carmichael forced a smile. "I'll do that," he replied, before turning again and making a hasty exit from Hewitt's office.

Chapter 25

Under normal circumstances, Carmichael's thirty-five-minute journey home was a time he'd spend going over the case he was working on, as when he was involved in a case, his mind rarely strayed from the details of the job in hand. However, on this evening it was different.

It had been four years since Lucy Clark had left his team and over three since she'd moved to a force nearer her home town in the North East.

Although occasionally he'd thought of her and the massive mistake he'd made in North Carolina, he'd never considered that she'd ever come back to Kirkwood. The idea of her being parachuted into his team and, even worse, the thought of her potentially being made up to the same rank as him in the near future, were of equal concern to him.

Not that Lucy had done anything wrong. In his mind the events that had taken place in his hotel room in Greensboro were his fault and his alone. He was the one that was married, and he was the one that was Lucy's senior officer.

His mind was so preoccupied with the alarming prospect of Lucy Clark's return that it seemed like no time at all before Carmichael's BMW pulled up on the driveway outside his house. He switched off the engine, took a deep breath and clambered out of the car.

* * *

By 7:20 pm, Sajid Hanif had already spent over two hours researching as much as he could about Suresight UK Ltd, the West Country opticians with practices in Bristol, Barnstable, Bude, Helston, Penzance, Exeter and Truro, who were now looking to open an addition to their empire in Kirkwood, hopefully with Sajid at the helm.

Their website was impressive, showcasing what looked like a very modern chain of opticians with state-of-the-art equipment and staffed by young and dynamic-looking individuals.

Sajid hardly gave a second thought to the story he'd concocted regarding his uncle Vivek's condition suddenly worsening: his excuse for having the following day off and a lie that Calvin Mumford had swallowed without question. His thoughts were focused entirely on the meeting he'd be having in the morning with Philip Dobson, Suresight's senior partner, who'd initially contacted him the week before by phone and had now sent him the parcel which almost guaranteed him the position, subject to a successful meeting the next day.

Sajid leaned back for a moment, his thoughts now turning to money and the sort of salary he could negotiate for himself as Suresight's practice manager for its first branch outside the West Country.

He allowed himself a small satisfied smile as he contemplated how much better life was going to be for him, his wife and their new baby moving forward.

* * *

"Are you listening to me?" Penny enquired, her voice stern and slightly irritated by her husband's apparent lack of attention.

100

Carmichael looked up from his large glass of pinotage.

"Yes," he replied, "she's been bullied by those girls and she's worried what they'll do if she's honest and open about it when we meet with Mrs Rumburgh."

Carmichael's brief but accurate summary of the many words Penny had uttered in the previous ten minutes served only to make her even more agitated.

"I don't understand how you can be so relaxed about all this," she remarked in a hushed but forthright manner. "This is Natalie we're talking about, our daughter."

Carmichael stopped thinking about the potential implications of Lucy Clark returning to Kirkwood and forced himself to give his wife his full attention.

"I'll talk with her in the morning before we leave to see Mrs Rumburgh," he replied. "I get why she's anxious, that's the impact bullies can have on their victims; however, now she's told you who they are and what they've been doing, she'll feel better. It's natural for her to be apprehensive about giving the school their names, but if she doesn't feel she can, then we'll just tell Mrs Rumburgh. To be honest, it might help Natalie if it's us who mentions their names first."

Penny, although clearly anxious, seemed reasonably reassured by her husband's words, so much so that she found herself able to stop pacing around the kitchen and sit down across the table from him.

"Anyway, what are their names?" Carmichael enquired.

"Apparently there are three of them," replied Penny, "all in the year above Natalie. I'd never heard her mention any of them before. One's called Chanel Pembroke…"

Carmichael sniggered. "You're joking," he remarked. "Surely nobody calls a child after a perfume?"

Penny shook her head as if to admonish her husband's flippant and inappropriate remark.

"The second one's called Olivia McManus," Penny

continued, "and the other, who Natalie says is the ringleader, is a girl called Jade Attwood."

At the mention of the third instigator of his daughter's misery, Carmichael's eyes widened, and he puffed out his cheeks.

"I'm starting to get sick of hearing the name Attwood," he remarked.

Chapter 26

Thursday 2nd July

Marc Watson's day, for him, had started very early.

He'd checked online, the night before, for additional abattoirs that slaughtered pigs, nearer Knott End, which had revealed that there were two, giving him three businesses to visit that morning.

With there being a reasonable distance between all three slaughterhouses, and with a great desire on his part to conclude all three visits and get back to Kirkwood before lunchtime, Watson had set off from home at 6:35am. He aimed to arrive at Arthur J Bird and Sons, his first chosen call, located midway between Moulton Bank and Knott End, at opening time, which according to its website was 7am.

As he pulled up outside, Watson looked up at the crumbling brick façade with the dilapidated sign reading:

Ar hur J Bir   and   ons

SLAUG   ERERS & WHOLESALE   UTCHERS

SI CE 1924

"Good God," Watson remarked aloud to himself.

Then, with a puff of his cheeks, he clambered out of his car and headed up to make his first call.

* * *

Carmichael sat alone at the kitchen table. It was still over two hours before they'd all have to leave for their meeting with Mrs Rumburgh, but, as always, he'd woken early and had crept downstairs, trying hard not to wake the rest of the family.

As he slowly ate from the cereal bowl in front of him, his mind drifted from the possibility of Lucy Clark returning to his team and all that that may entail, to aspects of the Geoffrey Brookwell case, then on to Natalie and how they were going to help her through this difficult time.

He didn't notice Penny join him until her soft pyjama-clad arms engulfed him from behind.

"Morning," she remarked sleepily, before planting a kiss on his temple. "You're up early."

"I couldn't sleep," replied Carmichael, "I've a lot racing around in my head."

Penny pulled herself tighter to him.

"I didn't ask you last night about your mystery man," she remarked, "any developments on finding him?"

Carmichael nodded gently.

"We've found him all right," he replied. "The only problem is he's been murdered. He was found yesterday morning with his throat cut, in the boot of the car he rented from Sean Attwood. Rachel and I were just leaving the scene yesterday when you called us about Natalie."

Penny released her grip and sat down next to her husband.

"That's dreadful," she replied, her eyes looking up into his. "And do you have any leads as to who killed him?"

Carmichael shook his head.

"Not really," he replied. "Sean Attwood is the most obvious candidate, but we interviewed him yesterday and, while I'm sure he's not being totally honest with us, I don't see him being the killer. He's about as dodgy as they come, but all low-level stuff, not murder."

Penny wandered over towards the kettle.

"A bit like his daughter then," she remarked, removing the lid from the shiny appliance and starting to fill it up from the tap.

"It would appear so," Carmichael replied, shovelling a rather large spoonful of cereal into his mouth.

* * *

Sajid Hanif arrived at the Lindley Hotel at exactly 9:15am. Although his meeting with Philip Dobson, Suresight's senior partner, was not scheduled to start until 9:30am, he was keen to ensure that he arrived in plenty of time to prepare himself for a meeting that would surely prove to be the turning point in his career.

Having collected the large, shiny silver key from reception, Hanif strode confidently back outside the main building to the row of small rooms which were situated to the side of the hotel, tucked out of the way behind large conifer trees.

Hanif placed the key in the lock and with one swift turn, entered the small lobby which led through into the bedroom.

* * *

According to the plaque that had been prominently positioned next to the main entrance, Mid-Lancashire Academy had been established for only seven years, which although technically correct, was at odds with the locally held view that the gleaming new academy was no more than a new building housing the old Dame Eve Turner Comprehensive School, which had been responsible for the education of most of the region's youngsters for decades.

As he'd promised, Carmichael had spoken with Natalie before they left home and, although she had not been too enthusiastic to grass on her three tormentors, he was confident that she'd be candid enough with Mrs Rumburgh to ensure names were disclosed and enough information was forthcoming to prompt the school to commence some form of investigation.

As the three Carmichaels sat outside Mrs Rumburgh's office, Carmichael couldn't help remembering how, in his youth, he'd often been required to wait outside the head of year's office, normally in order to account for some minor misdemeanour he'd been responsible for.

"Are you all right?" he whispered to Natalie, who was sitting in between him and Penny.

Natalie nodded, although it was clear by the pale look on her face that she wasn't.

"It will be fine," Carmichael reassured her, "just tell her what happened, and they'll take over from there. Remember, you've done nothing wrong, you're the victim not the culprit."

"Apart from doing a bunk for a couple of days," Natalie reminded her father.

"Well, yes, that wasn't your smartest-ever decision," Carmichael agreed, "but I'd not worry too much about that."

At exactly 9:45, the door suddenly opened, and the small-but-stocky figure of Mrs Rumburgh appeared from within.

"Mr and Mrs Carmichael," she remarked in a booming, authoritative voice, "do come in."

With a theatrical sweep of her left hand, the aging teacher ushered her visitors into her office.

* * *

It was 9:48am when Sean Attwood's battered pickup truck came to a halt on the gravel driveway of the Lindley Hotel.

Dressed in his best jeans and an open-neck checked shirt, Attwood jumped out of his vehicle and disappeared behind the conifers. He didn't need to go into the main building as he knew exactly where room seven was, having been employed by the hotel six months earlier to help with the refit and decoration of the hotel's outside bedrooms.

When he arrived at room seven, he was surprised to see the door was slightly ajar.

Without bothering to knock, he pushed the door open and confidently entered the lobby.

* * *

Mrs Rumburgh's office was exactly as Carmichael had imagined: dark wooden furniture and an air of a bygone era. Although the school was relatively new, Carmichael could see that the deputy headmistress had tried all she could to preserve the feel of a prior time, a time maybe when Mrs Rumburgh had felt more at home, Carmichael concluded.

Most strange of all to Carmichael was a faded picture of a smiling woman, presumably Mrs Rumburgh some twenty or thirty years before, with a shotgun under her arm and a brace of pheasants in the other hand. Carmichael was intrigued by the photo but decided that now was probably not the right moment to press her for more details.

Having allowed Natalie time to explain why she'd been absent for the past two days, Mrs Rumburgh nodded sagely, looked firstly at Penny sat to Natalie's left, then at Carmichael who was sitting on Natalie's right, before sharing a friendly smile.

"I'm sure I don't have to tell you, Natalie," she said in an authoritative but not unsympathetic tone, "what you did was not only against school rules but was also very foolish. During school hours, you are in our care and to have spent two days wandering around the canal banks on your own places the school in a difficult position."

With a look of remorse on her face, Natalie nodded. "I know," she replied. "I'm sorry."

"However," continued Mrs Rumburgh, "our position on bullying here is very clear. The head has said many times that we will adopt a zero-tolerance approach when it comes to bullying, so I'm sure when I explain the situation to Mr Wisset, he will be very sympathetic toward you."

"Thank you," intervened Penny, "Natalie's very aware that she was wrong to skip school, and I can assure you it won't happen again."

Mrs Rumburgh smiled. "You are indeed very lucky, Natalie, to have such supportive and sensible parents," she remarked, "I only wish all the young people here were so fortunate."

Carmichael's immediate thought was to enquire how Mrs Rumburgh could have possibly come to such a conclusion, given that since entering the room, apart from saying "Good morning" and shaking her hand, he'd said nothing; and Penny could have uttered no more than thirty or forty words. However, things were clearly going Natalie's way, so he decided to remain silent.

"There will, of course, be some consequences to your actions," continued Mrs Rumburgh, "you'll have a great deal of catching up to do on the work you've missed and I'll expect you to apologise in person to your form mistress and to all the teachers whose lessons you missed, but it's unlikely that you'll be punished too severely."

"Thank you, Mrs Rumburgh," replied Natalie with genuine relief.

"Now, tell me again," Mrs Rumburgh remarked, her dark piercing eyes homed in on Natalie, "which girls have been bullying you?"

Natalie glanced first at her father then at her mother before taking a deep breath.

"It was Olivia McManus, Chanel Pembroke and Jade Attwood," Natalie replied.

Mrs Rumburgh nodded as she listened to Natalie. Although her face remained expressionless as she wrote down their names with immaculate script, Carmichael sensed in the elderly lady's eyes that the three names she'd been given came as no great surprise to her.

Chapter 27

With his face drained of colour, Sean Attwood slammed his pickup into reverse, then with the wheel on full lock, swiftly moved a couple of vehicle lengths out into the car park before shoving the gear lever into first and speeding rapidly down the driveway away from the Lindley Hotel.

* * *

"Well, I thought that went quite well," remarked Carmichael as soon as he and Penny were safely within the confines of his black BMW. "Mrs Rumburgh seemed to be fully behind Natalie and, if Mr Wisset is as big on stamping out bullying as she says he is, then I'd not want to be in those three young ladies' shoes."

Penny forced a smile. "I hope so," she replied. "I've yet to be introduced to him, but I'm told he's young and dynamic, and very strict about behaviour. Word is that, in that respect, he and Mrs Rumburgh are of one mind."

"Perfect," remarked Carmichael. "Now let's get you home so I can get back to finding out who killed Geoffrey Brookwell."

As he spoke, Carmichael started the engine and was just about to pull away, when a large blue Nissan Qashqai screeched past them, its wing mirror millimetres from Carmichael's precious BMW.

The driver, a man who looked like he was in his late thirties or early forties, with jet-black hair and a heavy, bushy yet well-groomed beard, dressed in a smart black suit and wearing immaculately shiny shoes, leapt out of the car and rushed towards the school.

"You'd think he'd take more care, being so close to the school," remarked Carmichael angrily. "If I wasn't in such a rush I'd go over and have a quiet word with him."

Penny nodded. "Especially as he's the Head," she replied, with a straight face.

"Really!" remarked Carmichael, his astonishment clear in his voice. "That's Mr Wisset?"

Penny nodded again. "Yes," she confirmed. "And he appears to be late for something."

Carmichael shook his head. "That doesn't inspire me much," he remarked.

Penny smiled. "As I said, I'm told he's a very clever and forward-thinking man," she replied. "By all accounts, he and Mrs Rumburgh are quite a formidable duo who've already really transformed the school and he's only been back about a year."

"Back?" remarked Carmichael.

"Yes," replied Penny. "He's from Lancashire originally, too."

"So, a local lad," remarked Carmichael.

"I'm not sure where in Lancashire," replied Penny vaguely. "It's a big county and I've never come across him before, but he's one of our own, as they say."

Carmichael rolled his eyes. "What is it around here?" he remarked. "Can't people move on?"

Penny shook her head and laughed. "Maybe we locals like it here," she replied. "There's a lot to be said for having roots in an area."

Carmichael, who had no desire to continue the conversation about the pros and cons of staying put in the place you were born versus moving away, eased the car into first gear, checked his wing mirror for traffic and pulled off slowly down the road.

As they moved away, they didn't notice the figure of Harry Bridge, the youthful-looking school caretaker, who had been observing the Carmichaels from behind the bicycle shed at the far end of the car park.

Chapter 28

Marc Watson's expression, as he entered the office at Kirkwood police station, summed up his mood.

"Successful morning?" enquired Cooper, with a sardonic smile etched across his face.

"Total waste of time," retorted Watson before slamming his notebook on the desk and plonking himself in the chair facing his colleague. "Have you ever been to an abattoir?" he then asked Cooper.

Cooper shook his head. "Can't say I have," he replied.

"Grim as hell," announced Watson, "almost as bad as Stock's forensic lab."

Cooper smiled. "I'd have thought they would be all spotlessly clean and tidy places," he remarked.

"In the areas that they process the meat, that's pretty much how it was," conceded Watson. "But they all had this atmosphere about them; and at the last one I went to, I could see them unloading the pigs ready for slaughter. Not a pleasant sight."

Watson paused, his eyes fixed on Cooper, his mouth turned down at the corners and his head slowly shaking from side to side.

"They knew what was coming," he continued, "I swear they could tell."

Cooper laughed. "I'd have never had you down as the

squeamish type when it comes to animals," he announced. "So, will you be abstaining from bacon rolls from now on?"

Watson's expression changed to one of puzzlement.

"Good God, no," he replied. "I'll just try and keep away from slaughterhouses in future."

Cooper chuckled to himself. "Did any of them recognise Brookwell?" he enquired.

Watson shook his head. "No," he replied. "The first two maintain they send all their pig blood to a company who dries it out before sending it on to a black pudding producer in Bury called Huntley. They both reckon it's quite a sought-after commodity. Thomas Crown, the one nearest here, didn't recognise him either. They do the same with their pig blood, but they send it directly to some other black pudding producer in Clitheroe. The guy there did say that they have, in the past, let a few local educational establishments have some, Lancaster University being the main one, but they hadn't done so for a fair few months, as far as he could recall."

"So, a bit of a wasted morning for you, then?" remarked Cooper.

Watson nodded. "Yes," he reluctantly conceded. "I did toy with going to see the drying company, but to be honest, I'm not sure I'm going to get anywhere. How's your morning been?"

"Forensics are looking at the Jiffy bag we found at Brookwell's apartment," he replied, "and I was just about to head off to the local post office to try and see if there's any way they can help me pinpoint where the package was posted."

"What about Attwood?" Watson enquired. "Did you manage to talk with him?"

Cooper shook his head. "I went around to his place," he replied, "but his wife told me he was out, and she had no idea where he was or when he'd be back. I was lucky to get her, as it happens," he continued. "When I arrived, she was just getting into her car. She wasn't very helpful and when I tried to pin her down she just said she hadn't the time to talk with me as she'd been summoned to her daughter's school."

"Do you know how Rachel's getting on?" Watson asked.

"Anna Montgomery, Brookwell's agent, arrived about fifteen minutes ago," Cooper replied. "Rachel's taken her over to the morgue to identify the body. Then she's bringing her back here to interview her with the boss."

Watson puffed out his cheeks. "Well I'm going to get myself a roll and a coffee from the canteen," he remarked before standing up and sauntering over to the door. "No doubt Carmichael will be here pretty soon, so I might not get a chance once he arrives."

Cooper smiled broadly.

"Ham or cheese?" he enquired.

"Both if they have them," replied Watson, his sympathy for the poor animals he'd witnessed entering the slaughterhouse seemingly having deserted him.

"Normality returns," muttered Cooper to himself as he stood up and he, too, made his way towards the exit.

Chapter 29

Cooper was just about to clamber into his beaten-up Volvo to head away to the post office when Watson burst through the swing doors from the station.

"There's been another murder," he shouted over at Cooper.

Just as the panting sergeant arrived at Cooper's side, Carmichael's familiar-looking black BMW entered the car park.

"It's just been called in," continued Watson, his excited voice sounding even worse because the short dash he'd made across the car park had left him out of breath.

"Where?" enquired Cooper as his boss's car pulled into the vacant space next to where they were standing.

Before Watson answered, Carmichael's window lowered. "What's going on?" he asked, his attention stirred by the demeanour of his two sergeants.

"A man's been found at the Lindley Hotel in Moulton Bank," replied Watson. "It looks like a suspicious death."

Carmichael didn't bother to get out of the car.

"Both of you, jump in," he instructed them. "You can fill me in on the way."

* * *

Rachel Dalton emerged from Dr Stock's pathology lab with Geoffrey Brookwell's agent, the flamboyantly garbed, larger-than-life Anna Montgomery.

Despite having just made a positive identification of a man she'd known for the best part of fifteen years, the portly middle-aged woman seemed totally unmoved by the experience.

"Thank you for doing that," Rachel said, deliberately ignoring Anna Montgomery's apparent lack of concern. "These things are not easy."

Anna looked directly into Rachel's eyes.

"I'm, of course, very sad for Geoffrey," she replied. "but we weren't close friends; and his passing, whilst unfortunate, isn't going to cause me any distress. So please don't worry on my account, Ms Dalton."

"Right," replied Rachel, before forcing a smile and ushering the dead man's agent towards her car. "Inspector Carmichael, my boss, would like a quick word with you back at the station, if that's OK."

Anna Montgomery nodded. "I need to be back at the office for a meeting at two thirty," she announced. "So, as long as it doesn't take more than an hour or so, that should be fine."

"I doubt it will take that long," replied Rachel. "The station's only ten minutes away and I suspect he'll already be there when we arrive."

* * *

It took Carmichael almost forty minutes to arrive at the Lindley Hotel, by which time the drive had been cordoned off with the customary yellow and black tape, and two large uniformed officers stood guard at the entrance.

Immediately recognising Carmichael's car, the two officers

117

lifted the tape to allow the black BMW to pass underneath and head up the gravel path.

"No one from forensics here yet?" Carmichael asked the solitary uniformed officer who was standing by the open door to room seven.

"They're on their way, sir," replied the officer.

Carmichael shrugged his shoulders as if to signify his frustration at the SOCO's absence, but, saying nothing, pushed past the uniformed officer and walked through the open doorway, with Watson and Cooper a few paces behind him.

On seeing the body, Carmichael stopped abruptly in his tracks.

He hadn't expected the murdered man to be positioned so neatly in the centre of the bed, his head resting on a pillow and his hands cupped together on his chest.

"Has anybody touched the body?" he enquired to the uniformed officer who had followed them in.

"Not to my knowledge, sir," he replied. "The body was found about an hour ago by one of the hotel staff. She maintains it was just like this when she arrived."

Carmichael moved slowly towards the corpse on the bed.

"What's that in his hand?" Carmichael enquired.

"It looks like his tongue," replied the PC. "But I didn't want to disturb anything, so I can't be sure."

"Good God," remarked Watson. "That's gruesome."

Carmichael remained impassive. "By the look of those marks around his neck, I'd guess he was strangled," he remarked, "and with the lack of blood around, I'd say that his tongue, if that's what it is, must have been cut out after he'd been killed. However, I'll let the good Dr Stock be the judge of that, when he decides to grace us with his presence."

"Did I hear my name?" enquired the familiar voice of Stock, whose portly, squat frame dressed in his familiar white overalls entered the room.

"Glad you could join us," replied Carmichael as he half turned and made eye contact with the pathologist. "I'd appreciate your expert opinion on how and when this man was murdered, as soon you are able."

Stock brushed past the standing police officers and crouched down so that his head was a matter of inches from the dead man.

"I'll do my best," he replied curtly. "But if it helps, I can tell you who he is."

Carmichael's eyebrows raised.

"Who is he?" he enquired.

"His name's Sajid Hanif," replied Stock. "He's my optician, he works at Mumford's Opticians in Kirkwood."

Chapter 30

It wasn't until Carmichael had left room seven that he remembered he was supposed to be helping Rachel Dalton interview Geoffrey Brookwell's agent.

He stood on the gravel path in the warm summer sunshine, took out his mobile and dialled Rachel's number.

As he waited for Rachel to answer, he moved his gaze in the direction of a narrow footpath which meandered away from the main hotel building and into some thickly packed, tall shrubs.

"See where that goes, Marc," he instructed Watson.

Watson nodded before slowly making his way down the path and out of sight.

"Rachel," announced Carmichael loudly when his young colleague finally picked up the call. "I'm sorry, but you'll have to interview Anna Montgomery without me. There's been another murder, so I'm with Cooper and Watson at the Lindley Hotel in Moulton Bank."

"Do we have a name for this one, yet?" Rachel enquired.

"He's called Sajid Hanif," Carmichael replied. "According to Stock, he's an optician in Kirkwood."

"Do you think the murders are connected?" Rachel enquired

"No idea," replied Carmichael brusquely. "Other than them both being male and about the same age, there's no obvious link."

"Anna Montgomery has confirmed that the body we have is Geoffrey Brookwell," Rachel announced, "but I've not talked to her yet about him, as I was waiting for you."

Carmichael paused for a few seconds as he gathered his thoughts.

"Find out whether Brookwell mentioned anything to her about his intention to go to the church the other day," Carmichael told her, "and find out what sort of jobs he had on the go just before he died. We're going to be here for an hour or so, but we'll come back over to the station afterwards for a debrief."

"OK," replied Rachel. "After I've finished with Anna Montgomery, is there anything else you'd like me to do?"

Carmichael thought for a few seconds before replying.

"Did you have a chance to look into Geoffrey Brookwell's calls in the days leading up to his death?" he enquired.

"I've requested a statement from his service provider," Rachel replied, "but it's not arrived yet."

"Stay on that, for now," Carmichael continued.

"Will do," replied Rachel, a split second before Carmichael ended the call.

As Carmichael placed the mobile in his pocket, Cooper emerged from room seven with a brown leather wallet in his hand.

"Stock found this in the dead man's back pocket," he announced, handing the wallet to Carmichael.

Carmichael opened it up and started to study the contents.

"It confirms he is Sajid Hanif," Carmichael remarked as he removed the dead man's driving licence from one of the many compartments in the wallet. "And according to this, he lives in Moulton Bank," he continued. "Sixty-six Thornbush Grove. I think that's on that large housing estate behind the Railway Arms."

Cooper nodded. "Yes," he confirmed, "I've a friend who lives down there."

Carmichael then quickly flicked through the banknotes in the back of Sajid's wallet.

"Seventy-five pounds," he announced. "So, I guess we can rule out robbery."

Carmichael extracted a small photograph from inside the wallet and held it up for Cooper to see.

It was a picture of a smiling Sajid with his arm around a pretty young woman holding a small child, no more than a few months old.

"I assume this is his wife," he observed, "and their baby."

Cooper looked closely at the image before nodding his head.

"I guess we'll need to go and see Mrs Hanif," he remarked.

Carmichael nodded, "Leave that to Marc and me," he replied. "I need you to go to the post office and follow up on that letter Brookwell received. Why don't you get one of the uniformed guys to take you back to Kirkwood. I'll stay here with Marc and interview the hotel staff before we head over to see Mrs Hanif."

"Will do," replied Cooper, who was pleased to have been excused the harrowing duty of informing the dead man's wife. "Is there anything else you want me to do?"

Carmichael thought for a few seconds.

"Actually, you could get over to Mumford's Opticians," Carmichael suggested. "See if they knew anything about Sajid being here this morning."

Cooper nodded before making his way down the gravel driveway towards the entrance where the two uniformed officers were standing guard.

He'd covered about half the distance when Watson appeared from behind the large shrubs.

"It goes down to the main road," he remarked, as he approached where Carmichael was standing, commenting on the pathway he'd been sent to explore. "There's a small iron gate there that leads out onto the pavement next to the road."

Carmichael nodded. "Thanks, Marc," he replied, "let's go and have a talk with the staff here and find out what they can tell us."

Carmichael didn't wait for Watson to reach him before heading off in the direction of the front entrance to the hotel.

Chapter 31

Natalie Carmichael sat in the school canteen slowly nibbling on an apple, flanked by Sophie Keenan and Michelle Smith, her two best friends.

Her overriding emotion was one of relief that her plight was now common knowledge and her three, now suspended, persecutors were out of the way for the time being. Nevertheless, Natalie was still nervous. Even if they never came back to school, she knew that she would inevitably come across them again at some point, so her problems may not yet be over.

Sophie and Michelle tried their best to reassure her, but like most victims of bullies, Natalie was still scared and was not ready to believe that she was free from her ordeal.

Her mood remained low for almost the entirety of lunch; however, a glint in her eyes and a hint of a smile did return to her face when, just before the bell went, Harry Bridge, the heart-throb caretaker, swaggered through the canteen and fired a cheeky wink at Natalie, Sophie and Michelle.

"I reckon he fancies one of us," remarked Michelle. "Probably me."

"In your dreams, Michelle Smith," replied Natalie. "He's got to be at least ten years older than us."

"So what?" replied her friend. "Girls are far more mature than boys, so ten years is nothing."

"I'm not sure my dad would see it that way," remarked Sophie, with a frown and a slight shake of her head.

"Mine definitely wouldn't," agreed Natalie, before sharing with her friends the first proper smile she'd produced in days.

* * *

Back at Kirkwood station, Rachel Dalton looked up at the large clock that hung behind where Anna Montgomery was sitting; it read 12:35pm.

"I'm afraid Inspector Carmichael has had to rush off on another case," she explained, "so it will be just me."

The absence of Rachel's superior didn't seem to bother Anna Montgomery, who just gave a faint shrug of her shoulders.

"I'm more worried about the time," she replied. "I've only got about thirty minutes, then I'll have to be off, so I can get back to Manchester for my two-thirty meeting."

Rachel Dalton looked up into Anna Montgomery's eyes and smiled.

"How long have you been Geoffrey Brookwell's agent?" she enquired.

"Just over fifteen years," replied Anna.

"And what sort of actor was he?" continued Rachel.

"A mediocre one," Anna replied immediately and without any hint of remorse. "He had one reasonably long run about ten years ago as Dr Damien Hook in *The Cumbrian Way*, which lasted about three years, but since that ended, he's not done much. A few voice-overs and adverts, but other than that, zilch."

"I see," remarked Rachel, who paused for a few seconds. "And when did you last have any contact with Geoffrey?" continued Rachel.

"I haven't seen him in months," replied Anna, "but we spoke the other evening."

"When was that?" Rachel enquired.

"It was Monday evening," replied Anna. "He called me at about 5:45pm. He was very excited about some big role he reckoned he had in the bag."

"Really," replied Rachel. "Is it normal for actors to get a role without it going through their agent?"

Anna Montgomery shook her head. "It does happen," she conceded, "but it's very unusual, particularly with actors who have low profiles like Geoffrey."

"So, what role was this?" Rachel asked.

"I've no idea," replied Anna. "He was being very guarded about it, but he said that it was a major role with a big producer, that he'd been given an advance, and he was doing an improvisation for one of the scenes with another actor, on location, the next day."

"And what did you make of what he told you?" Rachel enquired.

Anna Montgomery held the palms of her hands upwards, as if to emphasise her bewilderment.

"Geoffrey wasn't one to fabricate things," she remarked, "but it all sounded a bit unusual to me. Which is what I told him."

"But he gave you no more details about this audition or the nature of this big role?" Rachel remarked.

"None whatsoever," replied Anna. "He assured me I'd get my agent fee but refused to elaborate any more."

"I see," replied Rachel. "And that was the last time you spoke with him?"

Anna nodded. "Yes, that's right," she replied.

"Did he mention anything about intending to go to church on Tuesday?" Rachel enquired.

"Church?" replied Anna Montgomery, her shocked voice loud and shrill. "Absolutely not. I know for a fact that, like me, Geoffrey was an atheist. What on earth would he be doing going to church; and on a Tuesday, too? I thought that lot did their thing on Sundays."

Rachel jotted down a few notes in her pocketbook before continuing.

"Did Geoffrey have a partner or any family?" she enquired.

Anna Montgomery shook her head. "He was always single as far as I was aware," she remarked, her words delivered quite slowly as she trawled the depths of her memory. "At least I was never aware of him having a partner, male or female. As I mentioned to you yesterday, on the phone, I think his mother died some time ago and I know his father passed away recently. As far as siblings are concerned I'm pretty sure he was an only child."

Rachel nodded. "You say he didn't have much work of late," she reiterated, "but I'm told by my colleagues that he'd got himself a really nice expensive-looking apartment in Knott End, looking out over the sea. How did he afford that?"

Anna shrugged her shoulders. "I knew he'd recently moved, but I'd never been to his new place. I can only think it was by using money from his father's estate. It was certainly not from any acting work I put his way, that's for sure."

Rachel nodded. "Finally," she said, "do you know of anyone who would have wanted to kill Geoffrey Brookwell?"

Anna shook her head. "Absolutely no one," she replied with certainty. "He was just an ordinary man who wanted to be a big movie star. Based upon his ability, it was sadly always going to be a pipe dream, but he wasn't the sort of person who I'd have expected to have many enemies."

Rachel smiled and stood up.

"You've been really helpful," she remarked, holding out her right hand. "I'll let you get off, so you can get to your appointment."

Anna Montgomery quickly stood up, shook Rachel's hand and made her way to the door.

The reception area of the Lindley Hotel was large and sparkling, with a polished white-tiled floor and a large, shiny marble reception desk.

As Carmichael and Watson walked in through the enormous pine door, they were greeted by two ladies behind the desk. Both in their late twenties or early thirties, with gleaming smiles, their long hair was brushed back into tight ponytails and they wore matching green company suits.

Carmichael's immediate thought was that had one not been blonde and the other brunette, they could have been mistaken for twins.

"I'm Inspector Carmichael," he announced as he flashed his identity card, "and this is my colleague, Sergeant Watson. Can you tell me who it was that found the body?"

"It was Angela, one of the housemaids," replied the brunette. "She's having a few minutes out the back trying to compose herself."

Carmichael smiled. "That's understandable," he remarked. "She must be very distraught."

"She's only eighteen," remarked the blonde receptionist, "such an ordeal for her."

Carmichael turned his head to look at Watson. "Why don't you go and find her and take her statement?" he suggested.

Watson dutifully nodded.

"I'll take you to her," offered the blonde receptionist, with a welcoming smile.

Carmichael remained in front of the reception desk as Watson followed his guide down the corridor.

"Tell me about the booking for room seven," Carmichael asked, as soon as they had disappeared from sight. "When was it made and who made it?"

The receptionist didn't need to check her records.

"It was made over the phone, yesterday," she replied. "I took it myself."

"And was it made by the dead man?" Carmichael asked.

"Yes," replied the receptionist. "He paid with a credit card at the time of booking."

"Is it common for people to book rooms for the day?" he asked.

"It's not that unusual," replied the receptionist. "People often make those sorts of bookings for business meetings. It's quite rare for the booking to be made so late, and I've never heard of anyone demanding that specific room, but it's not that unusual for daytime bookings."

"So, he specifically asked for room seven?" Carmichael remarked, his voice indicating that he was surprised by this revelation.

The receptionist nodded. "Yes," she replied. "We've had people in the past asking for one of our executive rooms inside the main building, but I can't recall a guest ever asking for an outside room. Mind you, they are cheaper, so maybe that was the reason."

Carmichael considered the receptionist's comments for a few seconds before continuing.

"And what time did your guest arrive this morning?" Carmichael enquired, deliberately using the receptionist's terminology of the dead man.

"It was nine fifteen," replied the receptionist with certainty. "I know because Emma was a little late this morning and she walked through the door at the same time as Mr Hanif. I recall checking my watch."

"Emma?" enquired Carmichael.

"My colleague," replied the receptionist, "the one that took your sergeant to find Angela."

"I see," replied Carmichael. "Is Emma often late?"

The receptionist shrugged her shoulders and rolled her eyes skyward.

"Recently, quite a bit," she replied. "She's just moved into a new flat with her boyfriend and since then, she seems to struggle to get in on time."

Carmichael smiled.

"And until Angela went in, had anyone else gone into room seven after Mr Hanif this morning?" he asked.

The receptionist shook her head. "Not to my knowledge," she replied, "but with the room being outside, someone could have gone in without us knowing."

Carmichael nodded once more.

"What about CCTV?" he enquired. "Do you have cameras installed here?"

The receptionist shook her head.

"Only in the bar area, so we can see if there's anyone who needs serving when there's no staff in there," she replied. "There are plans to install more cameras around the place but I'm not sure when that's going to happen."

Carmichael turned his head to look back out of the front door. He could see the entrance to the drive from his position, which was also directly in the eye line of the receptionists' station.

"Did many cars arrive after Mr Hanif had checked in?" he enquired.

The receptionist shook her head. "With guests checking out, a fair few departed," she replied, "but I can't recall any arriving."

"So, nothing suspicious," Carmichael remarked.

The receptionist shook her head. "Nothing," she replied.

"I'd like a list of all the guests who stayed here last night," Carmichael announced. "Their room numbers and, if they checked out, what time they cleared their bills."

The receptionist nodded. "No problem," she replied. "Do you want it now, as it may take me a while?"

"No, but if you can email it to me at the station as soon as you can that would be brilliant," continued Carmichael, who handed the receptionist a card with his details.

As the receptionist took the card from Carmichael's hand, Watson and Emma, the blonde receptionist, came into view walking quickly down the corridor.

Carmichael waited until the pair reached the reception desk before turning to the receptionist and once more giving her a warm smile.

"I didn't ask your name," he remarked.

"It's Diane Matthews," she replied, returning his smile.

"Well, Diane," Carmichael said, "thank you for your help. And if you could get those details sent to me as quickly as possible, that would be much appreciated."

"No problem," replied the receptionist.

Carmichael moved his head slightly in the direction of the exit, an indication to Watson that he was ready for them to go, before turning ninety degrees and starting to walk away.

He'd only gone a few paces when he stopped and turned back to face the reception desk.

"You don't happen to recall seeing anyone arrive this morning, after Mr Hanif checked in?" he enquired, his question aimed at Emma.

The receptionist shook her head.

"No," she replied, "I saw Sean's truck leaving at about tennish," she continued, "but other than that, nothing."

"Sean?" enquired Carmichael. "Who's Sean?"

"Sean Attwood," replied Emma. "He's the builder who did most of the refurbishment here. He's always around doing stuff."

"Really," remarked Carmichael, who shot a quick glance over in Watson's direction. "And when did he arrive?"

It was now the turn of the two receptionists to exchange glances.

"I didn't see him arrive," replied Emma, "I only saw him leave."

"Did you see him at all, Diane?" Carmichael enquired.

The receptionist shook her head. "To be honest, no," she replied, "mind you, I was quite busy between eight thirty and ten, checking people out."

"As far as you can recall," continued Carmichael, his eyes firmly focused on Emma, "was Sean Attwood's truck in the car park when you arrived?"

The blonde receptionist considered the question for a few seconds before replying.

"Not that I can remember," she replied. "But I was a bit late this morning, so I was in a rush when I arrived."

Carmichael again looked over at Watson before returning his gaze to the two receptionists.

"You've both been very helpful," he remarked. "Thank you for your time."

In unison, the two receptionists smiled broadly at Carmichael, which was his cue to turn away and make for the exit.

Chapter 32

Cooper had just arrived back at Kirkwood police station and was clambering out of the marked police car when his mobile rang.

"Hi, sir," he said seeing Carmichael's name illuminated on the small screen.

"Are you back at the station yet?" Carmichael enquired from behind the wheel of his black BMW, still stationary in the car park of the Lindley Hotel.

"Yes," Cooper replied, "I've only this second arrived back. I'm just about to get in my car and head over to Mumford's."

"Drop that for now," continued Carmichael, "and cancel your plans to look into the posting of that package to Geoffrey Brookwell, too. Also, get Rachel to drop everything she's doing. I need you both to find and bring in Sean Attwood. His pickup was seen leaving the car park here around the time Sajid Hanif was murdered."

"Really?" replied Cooper, who'd stopped in his tracks as soon as his boss had suggested he cancel his plans. "I went to his house early this morning and he was out. His wife reckoned she had no idea where he was."

"Well, he was probably here," replied Carmichael.

"I'll find Rachel and get back out to his house straight away," Cooper confirmed.

"If he's not there," continued Carmichael, "head over to his mother-in-law's house up Stoney Lane. He was there the other day."

"Will do, sir," replied Cooper.

"Actually," Carmichael added, "get his registration and a description of his pickup out to all our vehicles. We need every available PC out there looking for him."

"Will do," replied Cooper, just as Carmichael ended the call.

"Right, Marc," Carmichael said as he turned on the car engine, "now comes the most unpleasant part of our job; informing a young wife and mother that her husband has been murdered."

Sombre-faced, Watson nodded gently but said nothing.

* * *

Mrs Rumburgh very rarely ventured into the staffroom; however, she needed to talk with Miss Ramsey, Natalie Carmichael's form mistress. She wanted to find out whether there had been any issues with Natalie, or any of the others in the form, following her return to school and the suspension of the three girls accused of bullying her.

To Mrs Rumburgh's annoyance, Miss Ramsey wasn't in the staffroom. In fact, apart from two members of staff sitting alone in opposite corners of the room, the staffroom was empty: a highly unusual situation given that it was still lunchtime.

"Where is everyone?" Mrs Rumburgh enquired, her question directed at both members of staff within earshot.

Mr Barber, from the history department, looked out over the large book he was reading.

"I think anyone not on duty is probably sitting outside enjoying the sunshine," he remarked, before his head disappeared again behind his book.

Mrs Rumburgh shook her head in desperation. She wasn't the sort of person who liked her plans being disrupted, for any reason.

Turning smartly on her heels, the deputy head strode purposefully towards the exit. As she did so, out of the corner of her eye, she spied a copy of the local newspaper which had been abandoned on one of the threadbare comfy chairs that littered the room.

Mrs Rumburgh didn't normally read newsprint other than, very occasionally, the *Telegraph*, but she stopped in her tracks and picked the paper up. The photofit which took up almost half the front page looked very familiar to her, which prompted her to read Norfolk George's article about the man the police were keen to make contact with. Although the quality was not great, there was no doubt in her mind who the man was.

Placing the newspaper under her arm, Mrs Rumburgh continued her journey out of the staffroom, her heavy footsteps becoming less noisy as she got nearer her office, twenty yards down the corridor.

"Madam wasn't very happy," remarked Mr Barber, who remained hidden behind his book.

"Is she ever?" came the muted response from the other corner of the room where Mr Saunders, from the French faculty, continued to carefully study the runners at Sandown Park that afternoon.

Chapter 33

Number 66, Thornbush Grove was a small, but relatively new, two-bedroom house towards the middle of seven other houses that made a terrace at the end of, what Carmichael considered to be, a largely unremarkable-looking street.

"How soon will those bereavement specialists get here?" Carmichael enquired, referring to the call he'd told Watson to make to family liaison as they were driving over from the Lindley Hotel.

"About fifteen minutes," he replied. "They're already on their way."

"That's good," remarked Carmichael. "We can manage the situation until then."

Watson nodded, his expression indicating he wasn't looking forward to the task they were about to undertake.

"OK, let's get on with it then," remarked Carmichael, "but say as little as possible to his wife about how he was killed, and keep the revelation about his tongue from her, for now."

Before he'd even finished talking, Carmichael was already clambering out of his car.

* * *

"Is Carmichael sure it's Attwood that's our murderer?" Rachel enquired as she and Cooper swiftly exited the car park at Kirkwood station in Cooper's beaten-up Volvo and headed off in the direction of Sean Attwood's house.

"It would appear so," replied Cooper.

"Well let's hope we find him quickly then," Rachel added, "before he can do any further damage."

Cooper nodded and pressed his right foot hard down on the accelerator.

* * *

With the newspaper spread out in front of her on the desk, Mrs Rumburgh waited for her call to be answered.

"Kirkwood police station," announced the person at the end of the line.

"May I speak with Inspector Carmichael?" Mrs Rumburgh enquired.

"I'll see if he's available," replied the person on the other end of the line.

There was a brief pause before the officer spoke again.

"I'm afraid he's not in the station at the moment," he announced. "Can I get anyone else for you, or can I take a message?"

"No," replied Mrs Rumburgh, "I'll call back later."

"Shall I tell him who called?" enquired the officer.

"There's no need," replied Mrs Rumburgh evasively. "As I say, I'll try again later."

Mrs Rumburgh quickly ended the call, then read once again the *Observer*'s front-page lead article.

* * *

Sonja Hanif remained motionless on the sofa, her eyes moist but not tearful as she gazed into space.

With her young baby swaddled in blankets, awake but

content and quiet in her arms, the young, newly widowed wife of Sajid Hanif seemed dumbfounded by the devastating news that she'd just been given.

"But he was just going to an interview," she muttered almost inaudibly. "How can someone be murdered at a job interview?"

Carmichael looked across at Watson before speaking.

"Can you tell us more about this interview he was attending?" he enquired.

"It was with a man called Philip Dobson," replied Sonja. "He works for a company down south called Suresight UK. He'd contacted Sajid and was keen for him to manage a new office they were opening up here."

"How long had Sajid been talking with Suresight?" Carmichael asked.

"They'd initially contacted him last week by phone," Sonja replied, "then, the other day, they sent him a parcel and had almost guaranteed him the position. Sajid just thought this meeting was to agree his package."

"Parcel," repeated Carmichael. "Do you happen to still have this parcel?"

Sonja, who continued to stare into open space, nodded. "I think it's in the kitchen, on the table," she replied.

Carmichael signalled to Watson to go and retrieve it.

"Is there anyone we can contact to come and sit with you?" Carmichael enquired.

Sonja shook her head. "No, there's just me and Amna now."

As she spoke, Sonja looked down at her little girl, who remained tranquil and silent in her arms.

"So, no family at all?" Carmichael remarked.

Sonja lifted her head upwards, her eyes making contact with Carmichael's for the first time since he'd delivered the bombshell.

"There's Sajid's mother and sister," she announced, "they will need to know, but I've no family."

"Are they local?" Carmichael enquired.

Sonja nodded her head.

"Yes, they live in one of those big houses on Tan House Row," replied Sonja.

"I'll get one of our officers to go up there as soon as they arrive," remarked Carmichael. "Do you want them to bring your mother-in-law here?"

"God, no," replied Sonja, without any hesitation and in a tone that suggested the very idea was repugnant to her. "They don't approve of me," she added. "I'm Sajid's second wife and I'm still considered to be the home-wrecker, in their eyes."

Carmichael smiled. "I see," he replied. "My officers will have to tell them both, of course, but if you'd rather they didn't come over, that's fine."

As Carmichael was talking, Watson emerged from the kitchen clutching a large clear plastic evidence bag with what appeared to be the parcel Sajid had received secure inside. As his eyes met Carmichael's he raised the bag slightly and nodded.

Chapter 34

For the second time that day, Cooper arrived at Sean Attwood's house and, for the second time, Sean's wife Jenny answered the door.

The exasperated look on her face when the door flew open indicated immediately to Cooper and Rachel Dalton that Jenny Attwood was not happy to see them.

"What do you want now?" she asked, her measured words delivered in an unmistakably exasperated manner.

"Has Sean come back, Mrs Attwood?" Cooper enquired.

"No," replied Jenny abruptly. "As I told you this morning, he's on a job somewhere; but I've no idea where."

Down the hallway, behind Jenny Attwood, Rachel could see the figure of Jenny's daughter, still dressed in her school uniform.

"No school today?" Rachel enquired, her question aimed at the girl rather than her mother.

Jenny Attwood turned her head slightly to look back at her daughter before quickly returning her angry gaze towards Rachel.

"Not for some," she responded tetchily, "not that it's any business of yours."

"Can you give me Sean's mobile number please, Mrs Attwood?" Cooper asked.

Jenny Attwood sighed and shook her head despondently.

"Jade," she shouted back down the hallway, "bring me my mobile, it's on the kitchen worktop next to the sink."

Within a few seconds, the tall figure of Jade Attwood appeared at the door, her face surrounded in long chestnut-brown hair and her expression as pained as her mother's.

Without exchanging any words, Jade handed her mother the phone before heading back down the hallway.

Upon seeing Jade Attwood up close, Cooper and Rachel exchanged a look of astonishment, as they both realised that Jade was the child in Brookwell's photos.

Jenny Attwood fiddled with her mobile for a few seconds before holding it up so that Cooper could see the number on the screen.

Sean – 07584 222552

Cooper took out his notebook and jotted down the number.

"Thanks," he said, with a forced smile.

"Is that everything?" Jenny Attwood enquired, her sarcastic tone unable to mask her undoubted annoyance.

"No, there is just one other thing," Cooper replied in a hushed voice. "But it's a bit delicate."

With a quick jerk of his head, he signalled to Rachel to walk down the hallway and shut the kitchen door, so Jade could not hear.

"Come in, why don't you," remarked Jenny, as Rachel slid past her.

As soon as the kitchen door was closed, Cooper took out an A4 copy of the four images from his pocket and showed it to Jenny Attwood.

"Do you have any idea why Geoffrey Brookwell would have these images?" he enquired.

Jenny Attwood looked intently at the photos before once more fixing her glare on the two officers.

"I'd like you to leave now," she said firmly.

141

***

Carmichael and Watson remained with Sonja Hanif in her front room until the two officers from family liaison arrived.

"There's a mother-in-law and sister-in-law that will need to be informed," Carmichael whispered to them as they met on the doorstep. "Tread carefully though, as it seems there's not a great deal of love lost between them."

"Will do, sir," replied one of the officers before Carmichael and Watson departed the house and made their way down the path towards Carmichael's BMW.

"Poor woman," Watson remarked as they arrived at the car. "She seemed crushed."

Carmichael nodded. "She is," he concurred, "and although it may not help her get over this, seeing her and that young child makes me more determined that we catch this maniac."

Watson nodded. "So, where to now?" he enquired.

"Back to Kirkwood," replied Carmichael. "But before we do, I want to call into the opticians' practice where Sajid worked. Cooper was supposed to do that, but in fairness to him, I told him to drop that action and focus on finding Attwood. I also want to talk with Philip Dobson from Suresight, who Sajid was supposed to be meeting at the Lindley."

Carmichael tossed his car keys in Watson's direction.

"You drive," he said. "It will give me time to take a good look at the contents of that parcel Sajid received."

"Sounds like a plan to me," remarked Watson as the two officers clambered into Carmichael's car. "And, with a bit of luck, Paul and Rachel may have Sean Attwood apprehended by the time we get back."

Carmichael smiled. "Now that would be a stroke of luck," he replied.

Chapter 35

After over two hours scouring Moulton Bank and the surrounding area, and after several unsuccessful attempts to reach Sean Attwood on the number his wife had given them, Cooper and Dalton decided to call it a day and head back to the station.

When they entered the office, they found Carmichael and Watson already there.

"Any joy?" enquired Carmichael as the pair entered the room.

Rachel Dalton shook her head. "No," she replied. "He's not at home, his wife says she doesn't know where he is and although we've been up and down every road in the village, there's no sign of him."

Despondently, Rachel sat down at her desk.

"What about the uniformed guys?" Carmichael asked. "Any word from them?"

"There's still a few cars out there searching some of the villages close by," replied Cooper, "but as yet, nothing."

"On a positive note though," announced Rachel excitedly, "we think we've discovered the identity of the girl in Brookwell's photos."

With Carmichael's attention now focused on her, Rachel smiled.

"We're certain it's Jenny and Sean Attwood's daughter, Jade," she added.

"Really," replied Carmichael. "And did you put that to Jenny Attwood?"

Cooper nodded. "We did, but she refused to talk about the images. In fact, at that point she basically threw us out."

"Really," remarked Carmichael again, "now that is interesting."

"How have you got on this morning?" Rachel enquired, her face still beaming at finding the identity of the girl.

"We've found out a few things," Carmichael replied, "namely that Sajid Hanif received a parcel similar to the one Geoffrey Brookwell received."

"But the good news with this one is," interrupted Watson, his voice indicating more than a small degree of satisfying triumph, "we've got that package and the message that was in it."

"Really?" remarked Rachel, her excitement at the news barely restrained.

Carmichael smiled broadly. "Marc and I can update you on what it said. We can also fill you in on the discussions we've had with Sajid's wife, his colleagues at Mumford's and Philip Dobson, the person who he thought had sent him the parcel. However, let's try and get some order to our thinking."

As he spoke, Carmichael walked over to the whiteboard.

"Let's review what we know so far, taking things step by step," he continued.

Cooper, Watson and Dalton angled their chairs to face where Carmichael was standing.

Carmichael picked up a red marker and, in bold writing, wrote FACTS on the top left-hand side of the whiteboard.

* * *

It took the team no more than twenty minutes to debate and complete their list of facts.

Standing aside from the whiteboard, Carmichael started to summarise the eleven items on their list.

"Item one," he stated. "At ten thirty on Tuesday morning, Geoffrey Brookwell went into Moulton Bank C of E church with his hands covered in blood and confessed to a murder. He then disappeared. Item two, we now know the blood in question was pig blood."

"Type O," added Watson.

"Exactly," said Carmichael, before continuing to go through his list.

"Item three, his body was found the following morning, that's Wednesday 1st July, in the boot of the car he'd been using, which belonged to an old school friend, Sean Attwood. Item four is that according to Stock, Brookwell died between twelve noon and 2pm on Tuesday, his throat having been cut by his killer."

Carmichael paused for a few seconds to allow any of the team to make comments. When nothing was forthcoming from any of his three officers he resumed his synopsis.

"Item five," he continued. "We know through the CCTV footage that Attwood and Brookwell made the handover of the car at the multi-storey on Saturday 27th June, which was done without them being together. And, that the car, when it was driven away, still had its genuine plates on it, which is in sync with the account Attwood gave us about the car being rented out."

"I'm still not convinced about him not knowing it was Brookwell," remarked Watson. "That may just be Attwood trying to build some sort of story."

Carmichael nodded. "I agree," he remarked, "but the simple fact is that the handover was as he told us. It's quite clear on the CCTV footage."

All three of Carmichael's officers nodded in agreement.

"Item six," continued Carmichael. "Brookwell received a

Jiffy bag, postmarked Wednesday, 24th June from Kirkwood, which we found in his apartment in Knott End. Unfortunately, we can't see any sign of the contents. And finally, item seven, that there were images of a girl presumed to be Jade Attwood in Brookwell's possession. Is that everything we have as facts on the Brookwell murder?"

"I think so," confirmed Rachel, who seemed to be responding for the whole team.

"Now let's focus on this morning's murder," remarked Carmichael. "Item eight on our facts list is that the second dead man, Sajid Hanif, also received a package recently. This was delivered to his work, something the receptionist has confirmed. Also, according to his wife, Sajid received a call a week or so ago from a man purporting to be Philip Dobson, basically offering him a job. Dobson completely denied this, when I spoke with him earlier."

"Looks like both men received bogus job offers," remarked Rachel, "if what Anna Montgomery told me is correct."

"Yes, I wonder if Geoffrey Brookwell received a call, too, about his dream role," added Watson.

"That's a reasonable assumption to make, I'd say," replied Carmichael, "but let's stick to the facts, for now."

"I guess what's different about Hanif's letter," observed Cooper, "is that we have it in its entirety, unlike the package that Brookwell received."

"Exactly," agreed Carmichael. "Having Hanif's letter claiming to be from Philip Dobson, offering him a job, confirming it had a thousand pounds in it and asking him to book room seven at the Lindley Hotel for a meeting the following day, is a massive breakthrough for us."

"And Mrs Pettigrew at Mumford's confirmed that a package did arrive for Sajid Hanif yesterday," added Cooper.

"Absolutely," concurred Carmichael. "Which brings us on to item nine."

The officers looked at the short note in red against item nine.

"Sajid Hanif arrives at the Lindley Hotel at 9:15am and checks into room seven, an outside room facing the car park."

Carmichael looked at his three officers to see if they had any comments to make about that point. When nothing was forthcoming, he continued.

"Item ten, he's murdered between then and 11:30am when the young housekeeper finds his body. He's found laid out neatly on the bed but with his tongue removed and placed in his hands. Obviously, we still need Stock to confirm how he died, but it looks like it was through strangulation."

"Which leaves us with just item eleven," remarked Watson.

"Yes," agreed Carmichael, "that a pickup truck identified by one of the receptionists as belonging to Sean Attwood, was seen leaving the Lindley car park at approximately 10am."

The team all fell silent for a few seconds until Carmichael spoke.

"Not a bad list of facts," he remarked optimistically.

"And the obvious conclusion after reading them is that our one and only suspect has to be Sean Attwood," remarked Watson.

Without hesitation, he then picked up the blue marker and wrote Sean Attwood in bold capital letters.

"But the problem is," remarked Rachel Dalton forlornly, "we don't know where he is."

Chapter 36

Mrs Rumburgh, with the local *Observer*'s front-page lead article on her desk in front of her, glanced at the clock on her office wall. It was 4.05pm.

Carefully picking up the phone on her desk, she redialled the number she'd called earlier that afternoon.

* * *

"Do you want to start a list of unknowns?" enquired Rachel Dalton, referring to Carmichael's well-trodden method of analysing his cases.

Carmichael thought for a few seconds before answering.

"I think we'll have time for that later this evening," he remarked, a comment that prompted his team to realise that it was probably going to be a late one. "I want all our energies to be focused on finding Sean Attwood. If he's not our killer, he's certainly up to his neck in all of this, so the sooner we apprehend him the better."

"Do you think he's done a runner?" Watson enquired.

"It looks highly likely," replied Carmichael. "So, we need to extend our search over a wider area and get his number plate circulated nationally. Can you get on to that, please, Marc?"

Watson nodded but remained stationary.

"Now would be good, Marc," remarked Carmichael.

"Oh, right you are, sir," Watson replied, before making a beeline for his desk on the other side of the room.

"Also, as we have his mobile number," continued Carmichael, "let's see if there's any way we can detect his movements via that."

"I'll get onto that," replied Rachel, who immediately started to head over to her desk.

"No," Carmichael shouted, "let Marc do that, too."

Watson turned and nodded back in Carmichael's direction.

"What about us?" Cooper asked.

"I want you to get back onto trying to track down more about where and when those packages were sent to Brookwell and Hanif," Carmichael replied. "And, if we could get some CCTV footage of the sender, even better."

"Got you," replied Cooper, who quickly grabbed his jacket and the car keys he'd left on his desk and disappeared out of the door.

Carmichael was contemplating what he and Rachel were going to do when the office phone rang.

Rachel was the first to react, picking up the receiver after just two rings.

"It's the desk sergeant, sir," she announced, after having listened for a few seconds. "Apparently, Mrs Rumburgh wants to talk with you."

Carmichael rolled his eyes to the ceiling.

"Get him to put her through to my office," he replied, the tone of his voice suggesting he wasn't at all keen to take the call.

Carmichael made his way to his office and, once inside, closed the door firmly behind him.

"Who's Mrs Rumburgh?" Watson enquired, once he knew Carmichael was safely out of hearing range.

Rachel smiled. "She's the deputy head at the Mid-Lancashire Academy. The boss's youngest daughter goes there."

Watson shrugged his shoulders. "So, nothing to do with the case then?" he remarked.

"I very much doubt it," replied Rachel, not wanting to be drawn into sharing the details of Natalie skipping school with her nosey colleague.

* * *

"Mrs Rumburgh," said Carmichael in his best manufactured positive tone. "Is everything all right with Natalie?"

"My call's not concerning your daughter, Inspector," replied Mrs Rumburgh, her voice clear and projected in her usual authoritative manner. "I'm calling about the sketch of the man on the front of this week's *Observer*," she continued. "It looks very much like Geoffrey Brookwell, a pupil I taught many years ago, and someone who occasionally helped us out here at the Mid-Lancashire Academy."

"I see," remarked Carmichael. "Did you know him well?"

"Did?" remarked Mrs Rumburgh. "Do I take it that something ghastly has happened to poor Geoffrey?"

Carmichael could have kicked himself. He'd have chastised any of his team, no matter how inexperienced they were, for making such a rookie mistake.

"When did you last see Mr Brookwell?" he enquired, deliberately trying to avoid answering her direct question.

"On Thursday last week, at about three thirty," replied Mrs Rumburgh, hurriedly but with frightening precision. "He'd just finished helping out Miss Turner's drama class and I bumped into him in the corridor. But you didn't answer my question."

Carmichael paused for a few seconds.

"I'm afraid I've some bad news for you," he remarked. "Unfortunately, Geoffrey Brookwell was found dead, yesterday."

"Oh, my goodness," remarked Mrs Rumburgh, "how awful. He was in such high spirits, too, when I saw him last. He'd just landed a very big part and was ever so thrilled."

"Yes, I'm sorry to be the bearer of such bad news," continued Carmichael. "Did he tell you much about the part?"

"Not much," replied Mrs Rumburgh. "He said it was all still hush-hush, but he was very excited about it."

"Did you know him well?" Carmichael asked again.

There was a pause for a few seconds, in which Carmichael couldn't work out whether Mrs Rumburgh was trying to compose herself or whether she was simply considering how to answer his question.

"Not really," replied Mrs Rumburgh, although her rather hesitant reply suggested to Carmichael that she may have been downplaying their relationship.

"Would it be possible for us to meet, Mrs Rumburgh?" Carmichael enquired.

"If you think it will help you," replied Mrs Rumburgh, "I'd be more than willing to meet with you."

"If I come over now, would that work for you?" Carmichael asked.

"Yes, of course," replied Mrs Rumburgh. "I'll be in my office for at least three more hours, so come over when you're able."

Carmichael looked up at the clock.

"I'll be with you before five," he said, before ending the call.

Carmichael took a few moments to consider the conversation he'd just had with Mrs Rumburgh, before springing up and rushing to the door.

"What did Brookwell's agent say about him claiming to have been offered this big role?" he shouted over at Rachel Dalton.

"Not a lot," replied Rachel. "She reckoned it wasn't organised through her and that Geoffrey may well have been exaggerating things."

"Grab your coat and come with me," he shouted over to her. "You can tell me all about it in the car."

Watson looked on without uttering a word as Carmichael and Dalton exited the room and rushed away down the corridor.

Chapter 37

Penny had been waiting all afternoon to hear the lock turning in the door to signify her daughter's return from school. So, at 4:15pm precisely, when that familiar sound resonated down the hallway, she exhaled deeply and made her way from the kitchen to greet Natalie.

"How was it?" she asked, eager to hear Natalie confirm that all had gone well at school.

She didn't have to reply. The broad reassuring smile on the teenager's face provided the answer.

* * *

"Tell me about your conversation with Anna Montgomery?" Carmichael asked, as he and Rachel Dalton headed towards the Mid-Lancashire Academy.

Rachel took out her pocketbook and looked at the scribbled notes she'd taken.

"She maintained that she'd known Geoffrey Brookwell for over fifteen years," replied Rachel. "She didn't seem to have much of a relationship with him, describing him as being 'a mediocre actor', although he does appear to have had a long run about ten years ago as a character called Dr Damien Hook, in *The Cumbrian Way*, which lasted about three years."

Carmichael shook his head. "Never heard of it," he replied.

"Me neither," said Rachel. "I'll check it out but suspect it was one of those daytime soaps that few people actually watch."

Carmichael smiled and nodded. "Yes, check it out, Rachel."

"What else has he been in?" Carmichael enquired.

"According to Anna, just a few voice-overs and a few adverts, but other than that, nothing," replied Rachel.

Carmichael took a few seconds to take in what Rachel had just told him.

"Find out whether that sort of job pays much," he remarked. "Geoffrey had a nice expensive-looking apartment, so I'd like to understand how he could afford that."

Rachel smiled. "I thought that, too, and when I put that to Anna, she reckoned his apartment might have been funded using money from his father's estate. He apparently died quite recently, with Geoffrey being his only child."

"In that case," remarked Carmichael, "get on to the probate office and find out how much he inherited."

"Will do," replied Rachel enthusiastically.

"What else did Anna tell you?" Carmichael enquired.

"She said that she'd not seen him in months," replied Rachel, who was still referring to her notes, "but they'd spoken on Monday evening. Apparently, he'd called her at about 5:45pm. She said that he was very eager to tell her about the big role he reckoned he'd got in the bag."

"What more did he tell her about this role?" Carmichael asked.

"Nothing of any consequence," replied Rachel. "He appears to have been very light on detail. He told Anna it was a major role with a big producer, that he'd been given an advance, and he was doing an improvisation for one of the scenes with another actor, on location the next day."

154

"You didn't mention that before," remarked Carmichael. "She definitely said improvisation?"

"Yes," replied Rachel, suddenly realising the significance of what Carmichael was saying. "Do you think his appearance at the church was part of that improvisation?"

"That's what I'm thinking," replied Carmichael.

"If it was," said Rachel, her brow furrowed as she contemplated Carmichael's hypothesis, "that would mean he'd have to have thought Rev Green was also an actor."

"Well, maybe he did," replied Carmichael.

Rachel thought deeply for a few seconds.

"Actually, that would make sense with something else Anna said."

"What was that?" Carmichael enquired.

"Well, when I asked her if she knew anything about Geoffrey planning to go to church the next day, she seemed astounded and said that he was an atheist," Rachel replied. "So, I guess, he's hardly likely to confess to a vicar about killing someone."

"Exactly," remarked Carmichael. "Did Anna Montgomery say anything else of any note?"

"Not really," replied Rachel. "She said he didn't appear to have had any living relatives, to her knowledge, and she was never aware of him ever having a partner at all. She also said that, in her view, Geoffrey wasn't one to fabricate things, but she thought what he'd told her about the big role sounded very suspicious."

"What about enemies?" Carmichael asked.

Rachel Dalton shook her head. "Although she didn't seem to have much of a relationship with Geoffrey, she did describe him as just an ordinary man who wanted to be a big movie star. In her words this was, sadly, always going to be a pipe dream. However, she reckoned he wasn't the sort of person she'd expect to have many enemies."

Carmichael paused for a few seconds before looking over at Rachel.

"You know what this means, don't you?" he remarked.

Rachel looked back at him blankly. "No," she conceded.

"Well, to be able to fabricate two job offers to the two dead men," Carmichael continued, "which are so tempting and appear so perfect for them, I'd suggest that our killer knew both these guys really well."

"Someone like Sean Attwood," added Rachel.

Carmichael shrugged his shoulders. "He's certainly mixed up in all this, but for some reason, I'm not totally convinced he's our man," he replied. "This all sounds like it's been orchestrated by someone really smart. And I'm not sure Attwood fits that bill. Also, those false number plates not being on the car when he handed it over to Brookwell, that's really confusing me."

"Maybe he deliberately did that to throw us off the scent," suggested Rachel.

"Maybe," replied Carmichael pensively, "but I'm not convinced."

"Well, hopefully Mrs Rumburgh should be able to help us put some meat on the bones," continued Rachel.

"From my conversation with her earlier," remarked Carmichael, "it's clear she knew Brookwell pretty well and for a long period of time, so hopefully she'll be able to give us a greater insight into the life of our budding actor and maybe point us in the direction of the killer."

"Let's hope so," remarked Rachel optimistically.

Chapter 38

Carmichael's car had just pulled into the school car park when his mobile rang.

"Top of the class, Carmichael," remarked the instantly recognisable tone of Dr Stock down the line. "Your latest corpse was indeed strangled and as you so correctly conjectured, had his tongue removed post mortem, rather expertly I might add."

"I'm grateful for the accolade," replied Carmichael, his response more sardonic than appreciative. "What else can you tell me?"

"The victim appears to have only had a slice of toast and a coffee for breakfast," informed Stock in his customary monotone voice, "which he'd eaten about an hour before he died."

"And the time of death?" Carmichael enquired.

"I'd put it at between nine and ten this morning," replied Stock with an assurance which surprised Carmichael in its precision.

"Well, we know he checked in at nine fifteen," remarked Carmichael, "so that gives us a forty-five-minute window for Sajid Hanif's murder of between nine fifteen and ten."

"There's more," Stock added, as if the best was yet to come.

Carmichael listened intently as Stock relayed the details of what else he'd uncovered.

* * *

The manager at Kirkwood post office looked closely at the images of the two padded envelopes.

"I can't tell you much, I'm afraid," he remarked. "All I can say for certain is that they both passed through one of our cancelling machines, here in Kirkwood; this one being processed on the evening of Wednesday 24th June and the other, five days later."

As he spoke, he pointed in turn to the images; firstly, to the one they'd found in Geoffrey Brookwell's apartment, then the one addressed to Sajid Hanif.

"So, were they handed in over the counter or simply dropped into a postbox somewhere?" Cooper enquired.

"Could be either," replied the post office manager. "My guess is that they were posted, as they have postage stamps on them rather than the postage stickers we'd apply if they were brought into one of our counters; and they'd easily fit into one of our postboxes. But, I'm afraid it's impossible to say for certain."

"But you're sure they were both processed here, in Kirkwood?" said Cooper.

"A hundred per cent," replied the post office manager.

"From how far away do you collect parcels that are processed here?" Cooper asked.

The post office manager pointed up to the map on the wall to his left.

"Anywhere within that red zone," he replied.

Cooper looked up at the map, which depicted an area stretching almost ten miles in all directions from Kirkwood.

"How many postboxes and post office counters are there in that region?" he enquired.

The post office manager smiled.

"This is the only main post office, but we have eighteen

smaller sub post offices, and I'd have to check on the exact number, but I think we have about seventy-five postboxes in total."

"So, could either of these have been handed into a sub post office?" Cooper enquired.

"No," replied the post office manager. "If they had, they'd have been cancelled on site, which would have given them a slightly different postmark. These were either put into one of our boxes or handed over the counter here."

"What about CCTV," he enquired, "do you have CCTV on your counters here?"

"Absolutely," replied the post office manager.

Cooper's eyes widened as, at last, it appeared he might be getting somewhere.

"Excellent," he remarked. "Could you get the tapes for me, please, for the days when these parcels were posted?"

* * *

"What did Stock say?" Rachel enquired, as she and her boss walked towards the school entrance.

Carmichael smiled broadly. "He's found fibres under Sajid Hanif's fingernails," he replied, "and my guess is that they'll match whatever Sean Attwood was wearing this morning."

Chapter 39

For the second time that day, Carmichael sat in Mrs Rumburgh's office, her imposing antique wooden desk and faded photo of the young Mrs Rumburgh with her gun and pheasants separating him from the stern-looking deputy headmistress.

However, this time it was Rachel sitting next to him, an ex-pupil of Mrs Rumburgh's, whom she'd acknowledged with an affectionate smile when Carmichael had introduced her.

"You mentioned it was last Thursday when you last saw Geoffrey Brookwell," Carmichael remarked. "Can you please elaborate a little on that last meeting?"

"As I informed you on the phone," Mrs Rumburgh replied, "it would have been at about three thirty. Brookie had just finished helping out Miss Turner's drama class, and I bumped into him in the corridor."

"Brookie," remarked Carmichael. "Is that how you referred to him?"

"It was his nickname at school," replied Mrs Rumburgh. "These names tend to stick, I'm afraid, even when the pupil leaves and becomes an adult."

Carmichael smiled. "You mentioned that he'd landed a big part," he continued. "Did he talk much about that?"

Mrs Rumburgh shook her head. "He was clearly excited," she replied, "but was tight-lipped regarding any detail. He said he had to keep it secret until it was officially announced. However, it did sound like it was going to be a breakthrough for him."

Carmichael glanced sideways at DC Dalton before returning his attention to Mrs Rumburgh.

"So, Mr Brookwell was a pupil of yours," he said. "What sort of pupil was he?"

Mrs Rumburgh eased herself back into her large chair.

"Academically an average student," she replied, "but a likeable young man in the main."

"In the main?" enquired Carmichael, instantly seizing upon the implication of Mrs Rumburgh's wording.

Mrs Rumburgh took a few seconds to respond.

"He was from a decent family, with good manners and a pleasant way about him," replied the deputy headmistress, "but he did go a little off the rails when he got to the age of about fifteen. It was short-lived, lasting about a year or so, as I recall, but during that time he was quite a handful."

"What sort of things are we talking about?" Carmichael asked.

"Unruliness in class, a degree of truancy at times and some incidents of bullying," replied Mrs Rumburgh. "But we sorted him out."

Carmichael smiled as the image of Mrs Rumburgh throwing herself into bringing the young Geoffrey Brookwell to task flashed across his mind.

"And was there a specific reason for this abrupt change in behaviour?" Rachel enquired.

Again, Mrs Rumburgh took a moment to consider her response.

"Two factors, probably," she replied. "The sudden breakdown of his parents' marriage was probably the main cause of his behavioural issues; however, he also got involved with a group of boys who led him astray somewhat, for a year or so."

"Really," remarked Carmichael, "anyone we might know?"

"As I recall, there were a few of them in the gang," recounted Mrs Rumburgh, "but the ringleader was Sean Attwood, whose daughter is, coincidentally, one of the young ladies involved in the incident we discussed this morning."

As she spoke, she peered over her glasses, her small dark eyes piercing and unsettling in their intensity.

"Anybody else you remember from the gang?" Carmichael asked.

"Apart from one other boy, whose name temporarily eludes me," replied Mrs Rumburgh, "I'd say the others just blindly followed what Sean Attwood told them. But Attwood and that other boy certainly were a bad influence on Brookie for that tough time in his life."

Carmichael again glanced sideways at Rachel Dalton before responding.

"Would the other boy you're trying to remember be Sajid Hanif, by any chance?" enquired Carmichael.

On hearing the name suggested by Carmichael, Mrs Rumburgh's forehead wrinkled.

"No, no, it wasn't Sajid," replied the deputy headmistress. "Sajid was a few years younger than Brookie and Attwood. He was a good student, never in trouble. Why on earth did you think it would be him?"

Carmichael shrugged his shoulders.

"It's just a name that has come up during our enquiries," he replied.

"Horton!" exclaimed Mrs Rumburgh. "Tim Horton, he was the other boy."

"The owner of Horton's Health Spas?" Rachel enquired, her voice suggesting a degree of surprise.

"Yes," replied Mrs Rumburgh. "Very successful and respectable today, but he was a nightmare as a teenager."

Carmichael knew of Horton's Health Spas as Penny had once been given a day's treatment as a present for Christmas by her mother; an experience that she'd thoroughly enjoyed, as he recalled. However, other than that, he'd no more knowledge about the business or its owner, but from her reaction, suspected his young colleague did.

"Tell me about Geoffrey Brookwell, the adult?" Carmichael asked the deputy headmistress. "Was he someone you knew well?"

"Reasonably well, I suppose," responded Mrs Rumburgh. "He'd been coming into school off and on for a few years. He kindly agreed to help out our drama classes when required."

"I see," Carmichael remarked. "And did he get on with everyone?"

"Absolutely," replied Mrs Rumburgh without hesitation. "The staff and the pupils all liked Brookie. He was always so enthusiastic, constructive and encouraging with our students; a really positive force."

Carmichael eased himself back in his chair before delivering his next question.

"Did Jade Attwood ever have drama lessons while Geoffrey Brookwell was helping out?" he enquired.

Mrs Rumburgh looked puzzled at the question.

"I suspect so," she replied rather vaguely. "Why on earth are you interested in a connection between Brookie and Jade?"

Carmichael shrugged his shoulders, "Just a possible line of enquiry we're following," he replied, as obtusely as he could.

Mrs Rumburgh remained perplexed but said nothing.

"What about Sean Attwood," Carmichael enquired, "have you had any contact with him since he left school?"

Mrs Rumburgh fidgeted in her chair.

"He's had to come in with his wife on a couple of occasions," she replied, "in connection with Jade's behaviour. And he did do some work for me at home."

"What work was that?" Carmichael asked.

"Oh, he decorated my hallway for me, a few years ago," replied Mrs Rumburgh. "And he fitted new locks for me on my front door when my key broke off, a couple of weeks ago."

Throughout their discussion, Carmichael had found himself, as he had been that morning, distracted by the bank of old metal filing cabinets and the fading photograph on Mrs Rumburgh's desk; so much so, that he felt he had to satisfy his inquisitiveness.

"That picture," he remarked, pointing to it with his left hand. "Is that you?"

Mrs Rumburgh smiled, "It was taken many years ago but, yes, it's me."

"Do you still shoot?" Carmichael enquired.

"Alas, no," Mrs Rumburgh confessed, with a degree of sadness in her voice. "I was brought up on a farm, and guns were second nature to me. However, I haven't shot in an age. I've still got my guns at home, all fully licensed and locked away," she continued, "but I haven't fired either of them in years."

"And the filing cabinets?" Carmichael enquired. "They look quite old."

Mrs Rumburgh smiled. "I should actually get the contents archived somewhere as I rarely use them. They are old files of past pupils. I suspect you're still in there somewhere," she remarked, her eyes fixed firmly on Rachel, who Carmichael could see looked ever so slightly perturbed at the prospect of her school years being discussed.

"The oldest ones must go back over thirty years," continued Mrs Rumburgh. "They need to be cleared out really. Maybe a job for me in the summer holidays."

Carmichael smiled. "So, can you think of anyone who would have wanted to harm Brookie?" he asked.

Mrs Rumburgh shook her head.

"Absolutely not," she replied resolutely. "And I can assure you, Inspector, that whoever it was that killed poor Geoffrey, they won't be connected with this school."

Chapter 40

"So, what do you make of that?" Carmichael asked his young colleague, as soon as they'd clambered inside his black BMW.

"I'm impressed she remembered me," replied Rachel. "But other than that I'm not sure we learned that much."

Carmichael nodded. "Other than that Mrs Rumburgh likes shooting, of course," he remarked.

"I guess we may have another potential suspect in Tim Horton," Rachel added. "But I'd suggest him being a bully a few decades ago is hardly a reason for us to get too excited."

Carmichael smiled. "Yes, you're right," he replied, "however there's always the chance that Attwood and Horton are still friends, so I'd say he's worth talking to."

Rachel nodded. "His main health spa is Houghton Hall, it's close to Ruffington, just off the Preston Road."

Carmichael checked his watch; it was 5:30pm.

"That's only about twenty minutes away," he remarked, "so there's a fair chance he's still working. Let's get on over now. If he's not there we can go back in the morning, but if we're sharpish and there's no traffic, I expect he'll still be about."

Rachel wasn't so sure but was happy to go along with her boss's assumption, not that she had any other option as he was the one who was driving.

* * *

Mrs Rumburgh couldn't settle after the visit from Carmichael and Rachel Dalton. Although she didn't know why Carmichael had suggested Sajid Hanif might have been one of Geoffrey Brookwell's old school acquaintances, his name, brought up in the context of poor Geoffrey's murder, now made her feel very uncomfortable.

She wondered whether she should have mentioned that unfortunate incident from all those years ago. Maybe it would be relevant to the inspector. Anxious about what to do, Mrs Rumburgh walked over to the large metal filing cabinet that housed all the records of past students. She took out six files, one from the row with surnames starting with A, one from the row with surnames starting with B, three from the row with surnames starting with H and the last file she extracted was from the row starting with the letter T.

As she pulled out the last file, her eyes became fixated on the picture of the broadly smiling young boy, his face a mass of freckles and his head ablaze with an explosion of fiery ginger hair. It was probably over twenty years since anyone had looked at Billy Taylor's school file, but as soon as she saw his happy face, Mrs Rumburgh's head suddenly became filled with images of the lively young man she'd taught, well over two decades ago.

* * *

"Did you expect Sajid Hanif to be a friend of Attwood and Brookwell?" Rachel enquired, as Carmichael's car headed down the quiet country lanes in the warm evening sun.

"I wasn't overly optimistic she'd say Brookwell and Hanif were friends," he replied, "but their deaths are likely to be linked, and Attwood could well be involved in some way, so I just thought I'd give it a try."

Rachel smiled, "They may not have been chums," she

remarked, "but at least we do know that both murdered men are local boys who went to the same school, so I guess that's progress."

"That's right," replied Carmichael, cheerily. "You make a very good point there, Rachel."

Pleased that her contribution had been so enthusiastically received by her boss, Rachel eased herself back into her seat; she always felt pleased when she knew Carmichael was appreciative of her input.

* * *

Despite it being 5:30pm, Cooper had no intention of calling it a day. Sitting alone in the IT suite, he started the first tape he'd been given by the postmaster. With a large pile of three-hour tapes to pore over, it was going to be a late evening and, even if he managed to rope in some help, he figured it would be a couple of days before he could complete the latest chore assigned to him by his boss.

Watson had also resigned himself to another late night at the station. As he'd been instructed, he'd circulated the details of Sean Attwood's car to a wider police audience and had alerted all ports. He'd also asked if he could be given a report on movement and activity linked to Sean Attwood's mobile; a request that had yet to yield anything.

He was leaning back on two legs of his chair, coffee in hand, when his mobile rang.

"Evening, sir," he remarked cheerily, as he saw who was calling him.

Carmichael, never one for small talk, launched straight in.

"Any developments your end, Marc?" he enquired.

"No luck in locating Sean Attwood, if that's what you mean," replied Watson. "However, I've circulated his number plate to all forces in the North and Midlands and have done an 'all ports'."

"What about his mobile?" Carmichael enquired.

"I'm waiting for a response from his network supplier," replied Watson. "I may not hear until the morning, given it's now after five thirty."

"How about Paul?" Carmichael enquired. "Has he fared any better?"

Although slightly miffed at the insinuation that he'd failed in his tasks, Watson elected wisely to ignore the underlying assumption in Carmichael's question.

"As far as I know, no," replied Watson. "He's back and poring over CCTV tapes from the post office."

Carmichael thought for a few seconds before continuing the conversation.

"Rachel and I have a lead we're following up," he remarked. "And it'll be about an hour and a half to two hours before we're back at the station. Why don't you help Paul until we get back? I'm sure he will welcome another pair of eyes."

Watson rolled his eyes skyward.

"No problem," he replied, with as much forced enthusiasm as he could muster. "I'll go down there straight away."

"Good," replied Carmichael. "There's one other thing. Stock's team have found fibres under Sajid Hanif's fingernails. So, if you do locate Attwood before we get back, bag his clothes and get them to forensics straight away."

"Will do, sir," replied Watson, although the call had been ended by his boss before he'd managed to finish his response.

Chapter 41

Carmichael's hunch proved correct. Tim Horton was still at work when they arrived at just before 6pm and, having dispensed with their introductions, Carmichael and Rachel Dalton sat themselves down at the large glass table in Tim Horton's expensively furnished office.

"How can I help you?" Horton enquired in his thick Lancastrian accent with a broad, confident smile.

"We're investigating the deaths of two people we think you might know," replied Carmichael.

Horton's smile slowly dwindled.

"Two deaths!" he remarked. "I'm aware that poor Brookie had been killed but didn't know there had been anyone else."

Carmichael nodded gently.

"Yes, I'm sorry to have to tell you that not only are we examining the murder of Geoffrey Brookwell, but we are also now investigating the murder of someone else you may have known, Sajid Hanif," replied Carmichael.

"Sajid," repeated Horton. "I remember him from school, but he was a few years below me, so he wasn't a friend, and I've not seen him since I left school, over twenty years ago."

Carmichael smiled. "Well, like you, Mr Hanif stayed in the area after he left school," Carmichael said. "He became an optician."

"Probably why I never bumped into him," remarked Horton, "my eyesight's perfect, twenty-twenty."

Carmichael smiled again, a faint forced smile, the one he often used before launching into an interrogation.

"When did you last see or talk to Geoffrey Brookwell?" he enquired.

Horton leaned back in his chair. "God knows," he replied, "must have been five years ago, maybe even more. There was one of those boring school reunions and God knows why, but I went. He was there, as were loads of others from our year."

"Can you be more specific about when that was?" Carmichael asked.

Tim Horton thought for a few seconds.

"It would have been to mark it being twenty years since we all left school," Horton replied, "so, actually, it would have been just over four years ago. It was in June as I recall, a really hot day, pretty much like today. We went to the races in the afternoon then had a function at the Lindley Hotel in Moulton Bank."

On hearing that the school reunion had chosen the hotel where Sajid Hanif had been murdered that morning, Carmichael and Dalton exchanged a sideways glance. A look that did not go unnoticed by Tim Horton.

"Why didn't you stay in touch after school?" Carmichael enquired. "You both remained in the area, so it's not as if you couldn't have met up, now and then."

Tim Horton started to fidget in his chair.

"What is all this?" he enquired. "Are you trying to suggest I had something to do with Brookie's murder? If so, I think I need to have a solicitor here."

"Absolutely not," replied Carmichael firmly. "We're just trying to get some background on two murders and in the course of our enquiries, your name came up as being a school friend of one of them."

Carmichael's words seemed to pacify Horton, who nodded gently.

"I don't know why we didn't keep in touch," he remarked. "Brookie was a reasonably close mate at school, but we just drifted apart. He went off to do his acting stuff and after a year or so of not knowing what I wanted to do, I started being a personal trainer and have built the business up from there."

"A very successful one, too," added Carmichael, deliberately trying to massage Horton's ego.

It clearly worked; the huge grin on Tim Horton's face after hearing Carmichael's praise was testament to that.

"What about Sean Attwood?" Carmichael enquired. "Did you keep in contact with him?"

Horton looked shocked at the mention of Sean Attwood's name.

"What's Sean got to do with any of this?" he asked, the pitch of his voice raised a few octaves higher.

"I take it from your answer that you're still friends with Sean?" Carmichael probed.

Tim Horton again leant back in his chair.

"Yeah, Sean and I are still mates; what of it?" he said, his words spat out with a mixture of not only indignation and curiosity, but also a degree of hostility.

"When did you last see Sean?" Carmichael enquired.

"Last Sunday," replied Horton. "We had few pints together at the Railway in Moulton Bank."

"That would be the 28th June?" Rachel interjected, to confirm exactly which Sunday Horton was referring to.

"Yeah, I guess so," replied Horton.

"And how was he when you saw him?" Carmichael enquired.

Horton paused for a few seconds.

"In great form, as it happens," he replied. "He said his

building business was good and he'd even hired out his old Bentley to someone for a grand."

Carmichael and Dalton exchanged another sideways glance.

"Did he say who to?" enquired Carmichael.

Horton shook his head.

"No" he replied. "But why are you asking me all these questions about Sean?"

Carmichael looked directly into Horton's eyes.

"Do you know where Sean Attwood is?" he enquired.

"At home I'd guess," replied Horton. "Do you want his address?"

Carmichael shook his head.

"We know where Sean lives, Mr Horton," he remarked. "But the thing is, he's not there and we need to talk with him urgently."

A change came over Tim Horton's face, as if he suddenly realised what this was all about.

"No way," he said loudly. "I've known Sean for years and there's no way he'd get caught up in anything so serious as murder. He sails a bit close to the wind sometimes, as we all do, but murder? No way."

Carmichael stood up.

"We're not saying that Sean's a murderer," he remarked, "but we do need to talk with him urgently. So, if he calls you or pops around to see you, I want you to contact me straight away, Mr Horton. Is that clear?"

Tim Horton remained in his chair looking slightly dazed.

"Of course," he replied.

* * *

Mrs Rumburgh had spent over forty minutes poring over the contents of the six files on her desk, the only interruption being Harry Bridge, the caretaker, who came in briefly to empty her bin.

She was still deeply troubled following her meeting with Inspector Carmichael and DC Dalton. After considering her options, Mrs Rumburgh decided that she needed to contact Carmichael again and inform him of her concerns.

However, before doing so, she wanted to do two other things first.

She flicked through her notebook until she found the number she needed, picked up the phone on her desk and dialled the eleven digits written down in front of her.

Chapter 42

"What did you make of Tim Horton?" Carmichael asked, as he and Rachel Dalton headed back towards Kirkwood police station in his black BMW.

"He's a cocky devil," the young DC replied, "but he didn't give us much, did he?"

Carmichael nodded. "Not even a cup of coffee," he replied.

Rachel Dalton smiled broadly.

"We can obviously check out the alleged last meeting they had in the Railway Tavern, but even if that proves to be true, that doesn't mean they haven't met again since. Anyway, what do you think?"

Carmichael gazed across in Rachel's direction.

"I think our Mr Horton was genuinely surprised to hear about Sajid Hanif's death, and I believe him when he says that he hardly knew him. And, to a degree, I can swallow him not having had much contact with Geoffrey Brookwell since school; however, I don't buy him maintaining that he had no idea who hired the car from Attwood. He knew about the thousand pounds, so he's got to have asked Attwood who'd hired it; and by Sunday, Attwood had seen Brookwell drive off in it."

Rachel nodded. "I agree," she concurred.

"I also don't buy his attempt to make us believe he has no idea where Attwood is now," continued Carmichael. "They're best buddies and Horton has resources at his fingertips. Attwood will have contacted him today, I'm certain; and I'm equally sure Horton is helping him evade capture."

"So, what's our plan of action?" enquired Rachel.

Carmichael considered her question for a few seconds.

"The first thing we need to do is get back to Kirkwood and find out how Marc and Paul are getting along," he replied. "We can decide how we proceed from there. However, one thing's for certain, keeping a close eye on our Mr Horton will be a major element in the strategy, moving forward."

* * *

It was after 9:30pm before Carmichael left Kirkwood police station.

Having spent over an hour with his team, exchanging details of their investigations and agreeing their individual areas of focus for the next day, Carmichael then spent a further ninety minutes in discussions with Chief Inspector Hewitt. His boss was notorious for being one for getting into the minutiae of a case, but even by his renowned, nit-picking standards on this particular evening, in Carmichael's eyes, he'd raised the bar to new heights.

In fairness to Hewitt, Carmichael had to concede that his boss had been very supportive, approving a twenty-four-hour tail being assigned to Tim Horton until Attwood had been located and agreeing to apply for permission from the court for Horton's mobile calls to be monitored. So, although Carmichael could have done without having to provide such a comprehensive account of their progress so far, by the time he'd left Hewitt's office, he had at least secured some tangible support from the fastidious chief inspector.

As his car came to a halt on the gravel drive outside his house, Carmichael noticed the curtains in the front room twitch. It was clear Penny was waiting for him to arrive home, presumably to discuss how Natalie had got on at school that day.

Carmichael was keen to hear all about his youngest daughter, and hopeful of learning that she was OK, but given that it was now ten o'clock and he was bushed, Carmichael prayed the update would be a short one, so he could have a shower and get his head down.

Chapter 43

As soon as he walked through the front door, Penny could see that her husband was exhausted.

"I take it you've had a busy day," she remarked, as she planted a kiss on his lips.

Carmichael put his arm around her waist and smiled. "You could say that," he replied. "How was yours?"

"It's been fine," said Penny. "Natalie seems much happier now that Mrs Rumburgh and Mr Wisset are aware of what was happening, and those girls are suspended."

"That's good," remarked Carmichael. "Did she tell you any more about what was going on?"

Penny nodded. "A little," she replied, her voice breaking up slightly as she spoke, a sign of how angry she still was. "It sounds like that Jade Attwood, Olivia McManus and Chanel Pembroke have been making her life a misery for a long time, poor Natalie."

"What sort of things were they doing?" Carmichael asked.

"Nothing physical," replied Penny, "thank God. But they've been making snide comments about her looks and just generally making her feel self-conscious. She says it's been going on for about two or three months. I don't know why she didn't tell us."

Carmichael shrugged his shoulders. "Well, we know now," he replied, before kissing his wife tenderly on her forehead.

Penny looked up into her husband's piercing blue eyes.

"I'm still fuming about it," she continued.

Carmichael pulled his wife close and kissed her again.

"Me too," he remarked. "But it's being sorted."

Penny nodded and took a deep breath. "Anyway, tell me about your day?" she asked.

Carmichael released his arm from Penny's back and the pair sauntered through into the front room.

"In common with Natalie, one of the Attwood family has figured large in my day," he remarked before plonking himself down in his favourite chair.

"Really," said Penny, her interest enhanced by the mention of that name. "How's that?"

"We've now got two murders, Geoffrey Brookwell and a man called Sajid Hanif, who was murdered this morning at the Lindley Hotel," Carmichael replied. "Although they were a few years apart, both men attended the same school, and both appear to have received packages promising them lucrative jobs, prior to being killed."

"So, how do the Attwoods figure in all of this?" Penny enquired.

Carmichael stroked his chin with the palm of his right hand.

"Attwood's our main... actually our only suspect," he replied. "He was a close friend of Brookwell's when they were at school; he hired out his car to him for an extortionate amount of money, and he was seen fleeing the hotel car park at about the time Hanif was killed."

"And what does he have to say for himself?" Penny asked.

"That's the problem," replied Carmichael wistfully, "we can't find him."

Penny thought for a while.

"So, you've no other suspects?" she remarked.

Carmichael rolled his eyes and his lips tightened.

179

"Well, there's another member of the old school gang we've spoken to," he replied, "but I'm not sure he's directly involved."

"Who's that?" Penny enquired.

"A man called Tim Horton," Carmichael replied. "He's the owner of …"

"I know Tim Horton," Penny interjected. "He's that flash, smug bloke who's always in the local newspaper giving his opinions on all and anything that's happening in the area."

Shocked at his wife's spontaneous condemnation of the man he and Rachel had met earlier that evening, Carmichael looked intently in Penny's direction.

"Not a fan, then," he remarked sarcastically.

"I've never met him, of course, and I did enjoy that day I spent in one of his spas," Penny responded, "but he's not what he seems, in my view."

It was very rare for Penny to offer unsolicited opinions about people, especially if she'd not met them, but, in his experience, his wife was a very good judge of character, so he made a deep mental note of her comments.

"You say Sean Attwood's disappeared," remarked Penny, "do you think he's made run for it?"

Carmichael shrugged his shoulders.

"That's what it looks like," he replied, "but we're on to him and the team all have clear assignments for the morning, so I'm confident we'll find him soon."

"I bet they have," remarked Penny with a faint smile, before pushing herself up from the sofa and walking towards the door. "Anyway, what do you want to eat? I bet you've had nothing since lunchtime."

Carmichael remained in his seat as his wife sauntered away along the hallway.

"A large bacon sandwich and a glass of malt whisky," he replied.

Chapter 44

Friday 3rd July

Carmichael was in the shower when the house telephone rang.

"Hello," Penny said, after rushing downstairs in her pyjamas and picking up the receiver in the hallway.

"Oh," remarked Rachel Dalton on the other end of the phone, "good morning, Mrs Carmichael, is the boss about? I've tried his mobile but he's not answering."

"Morning, Rachel," Penny replied. "He's in the shower, is it urgent?"

"Yes," Rachel replied without hesitation.

"Hang on," Penny replied, before resting the phone on the small table and heading upstairs to retrieve her husband.

* * *

"Three deaths in about as many days," remarked Stock, as they looked down on the forlorn figure of Mrs Rumburgh's limp, motionless body slumped sideways in her small blue Ford Fiesta. "Anyone would think you're going for a mention in the *Guinness Book of Records*, Carmichael."

Flanked by Watson and Rachel Dalton, Carmichael ignored the pathologist's facetious comment.

"Is this suicide?" Carmichael asked.

"Hosepipe attached to the exhaust and fed through the back window, all other windows shut and the engine running," announced Stock. "You'd think so, wouldn't you? However, the severe bruise to the back of this poor lady's right ear suggests to me that she may well have been knocked unconscious before this happened."

"So, we're talking about murder here?" Watson asked.

"I can't be a hundred percent sure, right now," replied Stock, "but from what I can see, I'd say there's a good chance."

After talking to Rachel, it had taken Carmichael less than forty minutes to finish his ablutions, grab a slice of toast (which he'd eaten in his car) and drive the twenty miles to Mrs Rumburgh's small chocolate-box cottage.

Dead bodies were such a common sight in Carmichael's world that he was seldom affected by what he saw at any crime scene. However, the sight of the lifeless body of Mrs Rumburgh, someone he'd seen no more than fifteen hours earlier, had an enormous impact on him.

He tried hard to keep his emotions in check, but inside he could feel his heart racing and his blood boiling.

"We have to find Attwood," Carmichael announced firmly. "And quickly."

* * *

With her husband having not come home last night, her daughter having been suspended from school, and the police forever calling or dropping by trying to locate Sean, the last thing Jenny Attwood needed was to see her mother's stony face on her doorstep at eight o'clock in the morning.

"Did Sean get that message I left him last night on his mobile?" she enquired brusquely.

"I don't know, Mum," replied Jenny, her worried face

indicating all was not well inside her head. "He never came home last night. I don't know where he is."

Mavis Heaton seemed oblivious to her daughter's anguish. "Don't try and cover for him," she said angrily. "I know there's something going on and I want to know, now."

"Come inside," snapped Jenny Attwood, grabbing hold of her mother by the arm and pulling her forcefully into the house.

Chapter 45

Carmichael, Watson and Rachel Dalton left Stock and his team to their work and entered Mrs Rumburgh's neat and tidy kitchen.

"Who found the body?" Carmichael enquired.

"It was the paper boy, this morning," replied Rachel. "He's just fifteen, so he's been taken home by a WPC. She's going to take a statement from him when he's with his parents."

Carmichael nodded. "He probably won't be able to tell us too much," he remarked, "I suspect she'd been dead a good while before he arrived, judging by the amount of smoke in the garage."

Watson nodded. "And if she didn't get a paper, with her house being so remote she could have been here ages before anyone found her," he said.

As Watson finished his sentence, the phone in Mrs Rumburgh's kitchen started to ring.

The three officers looked at each other before Carmichael walked the few short paces to the pine Welsh dresser and picked up the receiver.

"Hello," he said.

"Oh, I must have the wrong number," said the male voice on the other end of the line.

"Maybe not," remarked Carmichael. "Are you trying to speak with Mrs Rumburgh?"

"Yes," replied the voice, sounding a touch perplexed. "This is Nigel Wisset, the headmaster at the academy. Is Mrs Rumburgh there?"

* * *

Back at Kirkwood police station, Cooper, oblivious to what was happening about twenty miles away, continued to wade through the CCTV tapes trying to identify the person who'd posted the packages to Geoffrey Brookwell and Sajid Hanif. Even with three tapes running simultaneously on the large screens in front of him, Cooper figured it would still take him days to go through all the material he'd been given. And so far, he'd not found anything.

* * *

"That was Mrs Rumburgh's headmaster," remarked Carmichael, as soon as he'd finished the call. "He was concerned when she didn't arrive at school this morning. Apparently, they had a meeting scheduled for seven forty-five, and according to Mr Wisset, Mrs Rumburgh's never late for anything."

Rachel Dalton nodded vigorously. "That stacks up with the Mrs Rumburgh I remember from school."

"Well, she's certainly late now," remarked Carmichael.

"I bet he was shocked," Rachel said, her eyes glued to her boss.

Carmichael nodded. "I'd say so," he replied. "Once I'd told him what has happened it was as if he'd been struck dumb."

"So, what do we do now?" Watson enquired.

Carmichael took a few seconds to reflect and decide how to reply.

"With three unexplained deaths, two of them certainly murders," he said, his delivery slow and considered, "and with so many unanswered questions, we need to focus on the key areas for now."

Watson nodded. "I hope you don't mind me saying, but I'd suggest Paul's time may well be better spent doing other things rather than poring over those CCTV tapes."

Carmichael nodded. "Point taken," he replied. "I'll call him and get him to draft in a couple of uniformed officers to do that. And while they're at it they can see if there are CCTV cameras near any of the postboxes that our mystery man might have used and check those images as well."

"So, what do you want us to focus on now?" Rachel enquired.

"I'd like you to take the lead on the first murder," he replied. "I want you to go over every statement we've taken, the pathology report, and if need be, talk to his agent again. Also, you need to talk with that teacher Mrs Rumburgh mentioned when we spoke with her last night."

"Mrs Turner," remarked Rachel, her memory seemingly as keen as ever.

"Yes, Mrs Turner," he concurred, although if the truth was known, he'd forgotten her name. "See if she was close to him. After all, he helped her out enough. I'd imagine she and he would have got quite chummy."

Rachel Dalton nodded. "I'll get on to it right away," she said, before heading for the door.

"Before you do, though," announced Carmichael, "I need you to chase up the mobile phone activity report for Geoffrey Brookwell. That must have come through by now. Once you have that, call me to let me know who he spoke to or was in conversation with by text, in the days before he died. And remember to get on to the probate office to find out how much he inherited when his dad died."

Rachel nodded again. "Got all that, sir," she replied, before disappearing out through the door.

"What about me?" enquired Watson. "Do you want me to continue to focus on finding Attwood?"

Carmichael thought for a few seconds before replying.

"No, I'd like you to concentrate your attention on Sajid Hanif's murder," he replied. "And as I said to Rachel, go back over everything. All the statements we received, and if need be, talk with his wife again. Speak to Mumford's and to Suresight too, if you need to. Also talk with Hanif's mother."

Watson nodded vigorously. "I'm on it, sir," he replied and headed for the front door.

"Run a check on his mobile, too," Carmichael shouted after his sergeant.

Although Watson didn't respond, Carmichael was sure he'd heard him.

For a few seconds Carmichael stood alone in Mrs Rumburgh's tiny kitchen before muttering to himself, "That just leaves Cooper and me. Cooper can take the lead in finding Sean Attwood and turning some heat on Tim Horton. Which leaves me to have a good look around here, then I'll take a trip to see Mr Wisset at the school."

Chapter 46

"I don't know what's going on, Mum," remarked Jenny Attwood. "All I know is that those bloody coppers are at my door constantly, wanting to know where Sean is, and I don't know. I'll tell you what though, I'm bloody worried. He's never stayed out all night before without telling me where he's going."

Mavis Heaton could see her daughter was distraught. They'd never had a particularly affectionate relationship, not since Jenny was a teenager and thought she knew it all, but Mavis was always able to spot when her daughter was anxious and that was certainly now.

"Do you think he's involved in Brookie's death and the murder of that optician yesterday morning?"

"What optician?" Jenny enquired.

"That Asian lad," replied Mavis, giving the appearance of someone who'd forgotten his name. "They found him yesterday morning at the Lindley. It's the talk of the village."

Jenny shrugged her shoulders. Apart from going to school to collect Jade, she'd not been out of the house, so any village gossip had passed her by.

"I don't know what he's been up to," replied Jenny. "But whatever it is, I bet that bloody Tim Horton is mixed up in it. I've told Sean before to have nothing to do with that slimy creep, but Sean never listens."

Mavis thought long and hard about whether she should tell her daughter about seeing Geoffrey Brookwell on Tuesday morning, parking outside her house then walking down the footpath, and how Sean had told her to keep quiet about it. She also wondered whether she should mention the call she'd received from Brenda Rumburgh the evening before, and whether it would make matters worse if she told her daughter the nature of the voice message she'd left on Sean's mobile after talking with the deputy headmistress.

Given the pain that was already clearly etched across Jenny's face, she elected to stay silent about it, for now. Mavis figured it would only make her daughter even more anxious than she was already.

"You mentioned a voice message," remarked Jenny, as if she'd been able to read her mother's mind. "What was that all about?"

"Oh, nothing," replied Mavis. "It was just to find out when he was going to come and fix that gate in the garden. He's been promising to do it for months."

Jenny Attwood shrugged her shoulders. "I think that's probably the last thing on his mind at the moment," she replied, her voice hushed and fearful.

Chapter 47

Carmichael called Cooper to update him about Mrs Rumburgh and advise his sergeant of the new tasks he'd assigned him. In typical Cooper style, he accepted the change of direction he was being given without any comment. After making that call, Carmichael then spent the next twenty minutes going from room to room in Brenda Rumburgh's small but immaculately presented cottage.

Having met the occupant, it came as no surprise to Carmichael to find everything in her house to be orderly and tidy. Her bed was made, with precise hospital corners and pillows as well plumped as any hotel he'd ever stayed in. The kitchen table was clutter-free with its chairs neatly underneath, and the German dishwasher, almost identical to Penny's at home, had the light on indicating that it had finished its cycle. Carmichael opened the dishwasher door, revealing its sparse contents, gleaming brightly but stone cold. A glass tumbler, a large coffee mug, a cereal bowl, a side plate, a teaspoon, a tablespoon and a knife were all that lived in the large, shiny interior; hardly enough to warrant a cycle, he thought.

Carmichael then went to the small pop-up bin in the corner and put his foot on the pedal. The lid shot open to reveal that, like the dishwasher, it was almost empty. Except for some discarded soggy-looking Rice Krispies and the well-done crusts from a couple of slices of toast, the bin revealed nothing of significance.

However, having considered what he had seen in the house, Carmichael was now pretty certain he could predict, within a matter of a few hours, when it was that Mrs Rumburgh's life had been extinguished.

* * *

Rachel Dalton arrived at the Academy at precisely 9am, just as hundreds of children and dozens of teachers were settling down for the first period of the day. Having been escorted to the staffroom door by a rather sullen woman who had met her at reception, Rachel took a few steps inside.

"Is Mrs Turner here?" she enquired, her question a general one aimed at five or six teachers who still occupied the staffroom.

Two slenderly built ladies, who had been deep in conversation, turned their heads to face Rachel. They were both about the same age, mid-thirties. The shorter one of the two smiled in Rachel's direction.

"I'm Miss Turner," she replied, the emphasis clearly on the Miss.

Rachel smiled and presented her identity card.

"I'm from Mid-Lancashire Police," she said, with a friendly smile. "Can we have a few moments alone, please?"

At the mention of Rachel's employer, the whole of the staffroom stopped what they were doing and turned to look at the young DC. Then, almost as if by command, they then turned to face Miss Turner, who looked suitably uncomfortable, her now crimson cheeks signifying her quickly acquired embarrassment.

"I'll leave you to it, Chloe," remarked the second woman, who also smiled at Rachel before turning her attention once more to her friend. "I've got a couple of free periods so I'm just shooting out for a bit. I'll see you later."

Chloe Turner smiled back at her colleague who, in an instant, scurried away and out the door, leaving Miss Turner alone trying to work out what on earth the police would want with her.

* * *

PC Dyer had been on duty for only an hour when he spied Tim Horton leaving the health spa and heading over to his bright-red Jaguar. Dressed in his casual clothes and sat behind the wheel of his less ostentatious dark-blue Renault, he felt confident that if he gave Horton a reasonable head start, and with a couple of cars between them, his task to keep a discreet eye on Horton's movements would not be compromised.

* * *

Watson arrived at Sajid Hanif's mother's grand-looking detached house at 9:05am. Having parked just outside the gates, he strode purposefully up the gravel drive that led to Mrs Hanif's imposing front door.

He was a few paces short of the door when it suddenly opened and the slightly chunky frame of a woman, no older than him, appeared from the house.

"I take it you're police?" the woman remarked, the tone of her voice suggesting she'd had several visits from the police recently.

"Yes," replied Watson, while at the same time displaying his identity card. "My name is Sergeant Watson. May I speak with Mrs Hanif?"

* * *

"I'm sorry, I can't help you," remarked Miss Turner as her short discussion with Rachel was nearing the end. "I really liked and admired Brookie, but we weren't friends."

Rachel got up from the small plastic chair she'd been sitting on and put out her hand to shake Miss Turner's hand and smiled.

"That's absolutely fine," she replied. "You've been very helpful."

As soon as Rachel had turned and was on her way out of the small study room where the two ladies had been talking, Miss Turner's forced smile faded from her face. For months Chloe Turner had secretly hoped that Brookie would take more of an interest in her, but despite the many hints she'd dropped, he never had. Her heart sank to think that now the man for whom she'd entertained thoughts of romance had died and with him the realisation that her fanciful dreams would never be fulfilled.

* * *

For the first ten minutes of his pursuit, PC Dyer was happy with how it was going; two cars between him and the red Jaguar, and Horton was driving at a modest speed.

However, it was when he suddenly turned right off the A47 down the narrow, but very straight, country road that led to Rumford Woods that PC Dyer started to feel uneasy. No longer was there a buffer of two cars between him and Horton. More worryingly, Horton's car had sped up since it had turned onto the B-road and was now travelling at a speed too fast for such a tiny country lane.

PC Dyer had to think quickly. *Do I speed up, too, and risk him twigging that he's being tailed, or do I drop back and risk losing the quarry?*

PC Dyer chose the latter.

* * *

It had been Sajid Hanif's sister, Nora, who had met Watson at the front door and then shown him into a large room, where Sajid's mother was sitting.

"Another policeman with more questions," Nora had said before pointing in the direction of an empty chair, her directive to Watson as to where he should sit.

Despite the frosty greeting, Watson had been relieved to find that Mrs Hanif was much friendlier and willing to talk.

After twenty minutes and with all his questions answered, Watson got up from his chair and gave a faint smile.

"As I said when I arrived," he remarked, "we are doing all we can to find your son's murderer. I can assure you that we will get the person responsible."

Mrs Hanif's eyes shone back in Watson's direction like trace laser beams.

"Be sure you do," she replied. "Sajid was a good boy, he did not deserve this."

Once again Watson forced a faint smile before being ushered out of the room by Nora, who remained as cold and detached as she had when she'd first opened the front door.

Chapter 48

When PC Dyer reached the small crossroads, Horton's car was nowhere to be seen.

"Bugger," he shouted out loud, although nobody could hear him.

He looked up at the signpost.

The sign indicated that Kirkwood was nine miles away to the right; to the left was the small village of Hasselbury, six miles away, and according to the signpost if he carried on straight ahead for five miles he would arrive at Rumford Woods.

Dyer knew these lanes well and realised that if he made the wrong choice, the chances of being able to backtrack later and find Horton's Jag were slim to zero.

His gut feel told him that Horton would be heading for Rumford Woods, so with no other information to guide him and the passing of time now his enemy, he chose to follow his instinct and carry on in the direction of Rumford and the woods.

* * *

Carmichael's arrival at the academy coincided exactly with Rachel's departure.

As the two colleagues met in the school car park, Carmichael grinned.

"Fancy seeing you here," he remarked.

Rachel returned the smile.

"I've spoken with Miss Turner and she couldn't tell me anything we didn't know already," she remarked.

Carmichael sucked on his back teeth for a few seconds before continuing.

"OK," he said. "Well, just crack on and check out other potential leads, most importantly get onto Geoffrey Brookwell's mobile phone records."

"Will do," replied Rachel before climbing into her car.

"Tell the others I want a team briefing at five this evening," Carmichael said, just before Rachel closed the car door.

He knew she'd heard, as she nodded and smiled before starting her engine.

Carmichael remained stationary, watching intently as his young colleague departed the car park. Once she was out of sight, he turned and headed towards the school entrance and a meeting with Mr Wisset.

He didn't notice Harry Bridge, the school caretaker, who had stopped by the bike sheds and had been observing the two officers as they'd been talking.

* * *

Tim Horton took a long look in his rear-view mirror. As soon as he was certain he'd lost the dark car that was tailing him, he allowed himself a small wry smile before continuing his journey towards the tiny hamlet of Hasselbury.

Chapter 49

Mr Wisset sat behind his large desk in his expansive office, ashen-faced, his hands cupped and supporting his bearded chin.

"I can't believe she's dead," he remarked mournfully in his soft Lancashire accent. "Was it a heart attack?"

Carmichael took a few seconds to consider his response before deciding there was no reason why he couldn't share some of the details with the distraught head teacher.

"She was found at home this morning, slumped in the driving seat of her car," he replied slowly and quietly. "The engine was running; a tube had been attached to the exhaust and was then threaded through the window."

Before Carmichael had finished talking he could see Mr Wisset's eyes open wider and his head start to shake, slowly at first, but becoming more vigorous.

"You need to get your forensic team to look carefully into this, Inspector," he announced firmly. "Brenda Rumburgh would never take her own life."

Although momentarily taken aback by Wisset's remark, Carmichael's inquisitive instinct quickly kicked in.

"Why do you say that?" he asked.

"Because Brenda Rumburgh was a very deeply committed Catholic," Wisset replied. "Although this is a predominantly C of E school, she remained a devout Roman Catholic and for her, suicide would have been a mortal sin. There is no way she'd take her own life, believe me."

Carmichael had no intention of sharing any further details of Mrs Rumburgh's death with Wisset. However, inwardly the headmaster's unequivocal, unsolicited remark was reassuring to Carmichael, as it tied in with Stock's initial suspicion and the picture of events that Carmichael was starting to build in his head.

"Tell me about Mrs Rumburgh," Carmichael asked. "What sort of person was she?"

Wisset removed his hands from his chin and shrugged his shoulders. "She was simply the greatest, most professional deputy head I've ever met," he replied. "She had old-fashioned values when it came to teaching methods and standards, but she was right, and the results prove it. I'd have never been able to make the changes we needed to make here without her; she was simply unique and I'm not sure how on earth I'll manage now Brenda's gone."

Upon ending his reply Wisset looked blankly into space, clearly shocked and confused.

"Can you tell me, Mr Wisset, when it was that you last saw or spoke with Mrs Rumburgh?" Carmichael enquired.

"Call me Nigel," replied Wisset, his attention and thoughts still appearing to be miles away.

"So, when was it, Nigel?" Carmichael enquired for a second time.

"I last saw her last night," replied Wisset. "She came into my office at about six fifteen and asked if I'd be free in the morning for a chat about something that was worrying her."

"What was that, Nigel?" Carmichael asked.

Wisset shook his head. "I've no idea," he replied. "She said she needed to do a few things before we talked, but from her demeanour I'd say it was pretty important. That's why I was baffled when she didn't show this morning at the time we agreed."

"Seven forty-five," remarked Carmichael, which was the time Nigel Wisset had given him on the phone earlier.

"Precisely," replied Wisset. "Do you think her murder is linked to what she wanted to talk to me about?"

Carmichael shook his head slowly. "Nigel, at the moment we've no evidence that Mrs Rumburgh was murdered," Carmichael remarked. "Now cast your mind back; was there anything she said that might help us understand what it was that she wanted to talk to you about?"

Nigel Wisset considered Carmichael's question for several seconds, then with the faintest shake of his head replied, "No, nothing that I can recall."

Carmichael forced a smile.

"That's about all I need to ask you at the moment, Nigel," he said, as he stood up from his chair. "However, before I go, can I take a look in Mrs Rumburgh's office?"

"Yes, of course," replied Wisset.

Carmichael shook the headmaster's hand and made his way to the door.

"Are you happy for me to make an announcement to the staff and pupils regarding Brenda?" Wisset enquired.

Carmichael stopped walking, turned and looked into Wisset's pallid face.

"Yes, that would be fine," he replied, "but please don't announce the nature of her death as that's not something I want to be known at the moment."

Nigel Wisset nodded. "I understand," he replied.

"Actually," Carmichael said, "what ever happened to Mr Rumburgh?"

"He died years ago, as I understand," replied Wisset.

"So, to your knowledge there are no living relatives," Carmichael added.

Wisset shook his head. "Not that I'm aware of," he replied. He then put his right hand to his hairy chin as if he'd just remembered something. "Actually, that's not strictly true," he continued. "There's Mavis Heaton. I think she's somehow related to Brenda."

Carmichael's brow furrowed as he heard the name.

"Do you mean the old lady that lives at the top of Stoney Lane?" he enquired.

"Yes," replied Wisset. "She used to be a teaching assistant here, but she retired long before I started. She helped out in the science department, I'm told."

"And what relationship is she to Mrs Rumburgh?" Carmichael asked.

"I'm not totally sure," replied Nigel Wisset, vaguely, "but I think Brenda told me that one of Mavis's husbands was her brother or maybe it's Mavis Heaton who was Brenda's husband's sister."

Looking perplexed, Wisset paused and looked at the ceiling, as if trying to receive some inspiration.

"To be honest," he continued, "I'm not certain of the details, but I'm sure they were related by marriage in some way."

"One of her husbands?" remarked Carmichael, his words spoken as a clear prompt for Nigel Wisset to be more specific.

"As I say, I wasn't here when she worked at the school," replied Wisset. "And I don't know the woman, but I seem to recall that Brenda said she'd been married a few times. I didn't get the opinion Brenda cared for her that much, either."

Carmichael smiled. "How interesting," he said.

"Is there anything else?" Wisset enquired.

"No, Nigel," replied Carmichael, as he rose to his feet. "You've been most helpful."

Carmichael sauntered towards the door, then abruptly stopped and turned back to face the headmaster.

"Are you originally from this area?" he enquired. "I'm

a southerner myself, so I'm still not able to distinguish the difference between local dialects."

Wisset shook his head. "I'm an outsider, too," he replied with a forced grin. "I'm from Ramsbottom; as the crow flies, about forty miles north-east of here."

"That's still fairly local though, isn't it?" remarked Carmichael.

Wisset looked back at Carmichael and smiled. "You're a foreigner here if you're from more than a few miles away, Inspector. It takes generations for incomers to be totally accepted in these parts."

"Maybe I shouldn't feel so bad then after all," replied Carmichael, with a faint smile. "I thought I was the only unwelcome outsider around here."

Chapter 50

WPC Twamley's face lit up as soon as she saw the image on her screen.

She had no idea who the person was in the CCTV footage, but what was for certain was that it was a young, smartly dressed female who appeared to be posting not just a Jiffy bag that was about the size of the one received by Geoffrey Brookwell, but several other letters, too. Her immediate thought was that the woman on the tape was most likely an office junior dropping the post into the postbox on her way home from work.

WPC Twamley froze the image, then enlarged it and, with an enormous sense of pride in her achievement, picked up the phone and started to dial Sergeant Cooper.

* * *

PC Dyer's mood could not have been more different, his Renault now stationary in the small pull-in point at the far end of Rumford Woods.

Having not had eye contact with Horton's car for over thirty minutes and with there being no trace of it in any of the small lanes that came off the narrow country road that ran through the woods, Dyer knew he'd chosen the wrong direction at the crossroads, five miles back down the road.

"Blast it," he muttered, before dialling Carmichael's number.

* * *

For the third time in two days, Carmichael found himself in Mrs Rumburgh's office, only this time he was alone.

He picked up the photo frame of the young Mrs Rumburgh and her shotgun which, despite being behind glass, looked faded and dated. He wondered what sort of young woman she'd been.

As he looked at the photo a thought suddenly came to him. *"I've still got my guns at home, all fully licensed and locked away,"* she'd told him, but he hadn't seen any guns at her house or, for that matter, any cupboard that could have housed them. He made a mental note to get someone to check that out.

After he placed the frame back on Mrs Rumburgh's desk, Carmichael's mobile rang.

"Carmichael," he remarked, his normal greeting to incoming work calls.

As he listened intently to the apologetic story from PC Dyer, he eased himself into Mrs Rumburgh's chair, a wide leather armchair which swivelled on three large castors.

Out of the corner of his eye, he noticed a small green triangle of card on the surface in front of him, ripped along its longest side and no bigger than four or five millimetres in length.

Other than that, the desk was neat and tidy, with no papers. And apart from her photo frame, a telephone and a large desk pad encased in a leather surround, there were no other objects.

"Just get yourself back to the spa," remarked Carmichael, his words delivered without any attempt to disguise his frustration at PC Dyer's failure. "I suspect he'll be back at some stage today, but in future stay closer to him."

Carmichael cut short the call, picked up the fragment of card and studied it for a few seconds before then putting it in the breast pocket of his shirt.

Sitting on his own in Mrs Rumburgh's lonely office, Carmichael couldn't help feeling that they were getting nowhere fast.

He remained in Mrs Rumburgh's chair for a further ten minutes, mulling over the case in his head, an activity which did little to lighten his mood as it only served to confirm to him just how little progress they were making.

Suddenly his attention was drawn to the telephone, an old model which, when he lifted the receiver, gave out a dialling tone suggesting it was a private line.

Carmichael replaced the receiver and exited the room.

* * *

"Fantastic work," remarked Cooper when WPC Twamley informed him about the image she'd found on the CCTV. "We've a debrief with Carmichael this evening, can you get four copies printed so I can show the others?"

"Of course," replied PC Twamley, "where do you want me to leave them?"

Cooper was speaking from his car which was parked outside Sean Attwood's house.

"I'm just about to interview someone," he replied. "I don't expect to be that long, so should be back at the office within a couple of hours. If you can put them on my desk then keep looking to see if you can find who posted the parcel to Sajid Hanif, I'll take a look at them when I return."

"Will do," remarked WPC Twamley cheerily. She liked working with CID, particularly DC Dalton and Sergeant Cooper; their work was always far more interesting than the normal run-of-the-mill work she was asked to do and DC

Dalton and Sergeant Cooper were always friendly towards her.

* * *

Carmichael smiled politely at the school admin lady behind the glass window.

"Is it possible to see if any calls were made from one of the telephone lines going out from here yesterday evening?" he enquired.

The sullen-looking woman with short cropped black hair and a gaunt thin face eyed Carmichael up and down for a few seconds before replying.

"Yes, we can," she confirmed, "but private calls are not allowed, and I'll have to confirm with either Mr Wisset or Mrs Rumburgh that it's OK first."

Carmichael showed the receptionist his identity card.

"Well, would you be so kind as to do that right away, please?" he said. "Ask Mr Wisset and tell him it's Mrs Rumburgh's phone I'm interested in."

Although the receptionist looked even more unhappy than she had before, she nevertheless picked up the phone by her right-hand side and pressed the three digits that would connect her to the headmaster's office.

Chapter 51

What the school admin lady lacked in charisma and cordiality she more than made up for in results as, within two minutes of getting Mr Wisset's approval to provide Carmichael with the information he wanted, an A4 sheet of paper spewed out of the printer and was handed over to him.

"Thank you," remarked Carmichael, smiling broadly at the inimical face on the other side of the hatch.

"Is that everything?" she responded offhandedly.

"Yes, thanks," replied Carmichael, a split second before the hatch was shut firmly in his face.

Carmichael allowed himself a wry smile before making his exit from the academy.

* * *

Cooper hadn't expected to be greeted by three generations of the Heaton/Attwood clan, but when Jenny Attwood ushered him into the large lounge he saw Jenny's daughter, Jade, and her mother, Mavis Heaton, sat anxiously side by side on the mammoth sofa.

"Before you ask, we've no idea where Sean is," remarked Jenny, as she took a seat next to her mother. "I've not seen him since he left for work yesterday morning, he hasn't called or texted and we're all bloody worried."

Cooper nodded sympathetically before taking out his notebook.

"I realise you've gone over a lot of this before," he said, "but I'd like to ask you some more questions."

* * *

As soon as he was safely inside his black BMW, Carmichael took out the A4 sheet of paper he'd been given by the admin lady and looked at the most recent calls made from Mrs Rumburgh's line.

The report clearly showed that after 5pm there'd only been one call made, at 6:17pm, to a local number.

Carmichael pulled out his mobile and dialled the eleven digits to connect him to Brenda Rumburgh's last known call.

The phone at the other end rang ten times before it kicked into voicemail.

"Hello, this is Mavis Heaton," came the recorded message, "I'm sorry but I'm not able to…"

Carmichael aborted the call, placed his mobile gently onto the passenger seat and fixed his gaze through the front windscreen.

As he considered his next move, Carmichael's attention was drawn to the figure of a young man in blue dungarees taking out a black bin liner from the bin on the other side of the car park, then replacing it with a fresh bag. A smile came to his face as he watched the man, whom he assumed to be the school caretaker, struggle firstly to find the right end of the new bin bag, then struggle even more to try and get the plastic to separate so he could get it open; a frustrating predicament that Carmichael had encountered himself at home on more than one occasion.

* * *

Hotfoot from his encounter with Mrs Hanif Senior and her daughter Nora, Watson entered the office at Kirkwood police station and spied Rachel Dalton's head poking just above her computer screen.

"How's it going, Rachel?" he enquired chirpily.

"Not brilliantly," she replied. "I've got Geoffrey Brookwell's mobile phone report from his service provider, but it doesn't show anything that's particularly interesting, and I'm just plodding through the statements we took and Stock's forensic report."

"What about the inheritance from his dad's estate?" Watson asked. "Any word on how much he got?"

Rachel shook her head. "Not yet," she replied. "But the probate people said they'd check and get back to me."

"I still reckon we're missing a trick not following up more on the pig blood," Watson remarked. "And what about those number plates? Someone must have changed them. And we should be asking ourselves why they were changed."

Rachel thought Watson's comments were valid and that both avenues warranted consideration, but how they were going to go about finding answers to either of those conundrums was a mystery to her.

"Oh, the mobile reports for Sean Attwood and Sajid Hanif are through, too," she remarked, pointing to the papers she'd deposited on Cooper's and Watson's desks. "I've not looked at them; I thought I'd leave that pleasure for you and Paul."

"Well I hope his mobile report proves more helpful than Sajid's mum and sister," Watson replied.

"Why's that?" Rachel asked.

"Because," he replied, as he reached his desk and started to look at the two A4 sheets of paper, "Mrs Hanif wasn't able to help at all. She's still numb with shock, poor lady, so I guess it's understandable. As for his sister, she's a right miserable cow. Plain rude and totally unhelpful. Anyone would think we're the enemy."

"And I thought you had a gift with the ladies," she remarked sarcastically.

"George Clooney's charms would be useless on that one," muttered Watson.

Rachel smiled wryly to herself, but kept her eyes focused on her computer screen.

* * *

Carmichael, still seated in his stationary car, watched the caretaker disappear around the corner. He was just about to start his engine when his mobile rang. "It's Stock," came the familiar voice.

"What have you got for me?" Carmichael enquired.

"Mrs Rumburgh died from the fumes she ingested," Stock announced, "but she was almost certainly unconscious before she inhaled anything that was kicked out from her car engine. That bruise I mentioned was the result of a hefty blow from behind by a very heavy object. If her skull had not been so strong it could have killed her on its own."

"So, it was murder," remarked Carmichael.

"Yes, in my humble opinion her death was most certainly not of her own making," he replied rather obtusely.

"Thanks, Stock," replied Carmichael. "Anything else?"

"I can tell you quite specifically the time she died," Stock continued.

"Between seven and nine last night, I'd guess," replied Carmichael without hesitating.

"I'm impressed," replied Stock. "How did you come to that conclusion?"

Carmichael allowed himself a smug smirk.

"It was based upon the contents of her bin and the items

in her dishwasher," he replied. "All breakfast items, which suggests to me that she got home yesterday evening and was killed prior to having anything to eat or drink."

"You're not as dumb as you look, Carmichael," Stock remarked. "My altogether more scientific conclusion gives a slightly wider timeline but is broadly in keeping with yours. I'd say the unfortunate lady died between six and nine o'clock yesterday evening."

Feeling pleased with himself, Carmichael smiled again.

"We know she made a call from her office at six seventeen last night, and to get from the school to her house must be at least twenty to thirty minutes, so I think we can safely revise your time to between seven and nine," Carmichael said. "Exactly what I said."

Stock didn't like being outsmarted, especially by unscientifically based claims. "I'm sticking to my three-hour window," he said firmly. "If you want to amend that to suit your needs that's up to you, but my conclusion, which will be in my report, will be between six and nine."

Carmichael could sense Dr Stock was becoming a little agitated, and although that always amused him, he still needed Stock's team to help him, so he decided not to pursue the time-of-death conversation any further.

"One other thing, Stock," he remarked.

"What's that?" replied Stock.

"Did any of your team locate any shotguns in Mrs Rumburgh's house, or a locked cupboard where there may be guns inside?"

On the other end of the line, Stock scowled and took a few seconds to take in what Carmichael was asking.

"No," he replied, "not to my knowledge, but I'll ask the guys who are still down there to see if they can find anything. Is it important?"

Carmichael took a deep intake of breath.

"Probably not," he replied, candidly, "but according to Mrs Rumburgh, when I spoke with her yesterday, she said she had shotguns at home under lock and key. I don't see why she'd lie to us."

"As I say, I'll check it out," said Stock. "I'll get back to you later."

"Thanks, Stock," replied Carmichael, before ending the call.

Chapter 52

Cooper was just leaving Sean Attwood's house when his mobile rang.

He quickly took the phone out of his pocket and looked at the small screen; it indicated that Carmichael was trying to talk to him.

"Thanks for your time, Mrs Attwood," he said quickly. "I'll be in touch if there are any developments."

The expressionless Jenny Attwood closed the door behind her, and Cooper, turning his back to the door, took the call.

"How's it going, Paul?" Carmichael enquired. "Any new developments with Attwood?"

"Not really," replied Cooper. "I'm just leaving his house now. None of them could help and, for what it's worth, if they do know where he's hiding they're all unbelievable actors. If you want my opinion, they're genuinely worried. I don't think they have any idea where he is."

"They?" remarked Carmichael. "Who are they?"

Cooper sniggered. "I had three generations in there," he replied. "His wife, his daughter and his mother-in-law."

"Mavis Heaton!" exclaimed Carmichael. "Is she still there?"

"Yes," replied Cooper. "Why do you ask?"

"Because," said Carmichael, "she was the last person Mrs Rumburgh called last night before she died. She called her at six seventeen from her office at the academy."

"Really?" replied Cooper. "She never mentioned the call, but in fairness I never mentioned that Mrs Rumburgh was dead."

Carmichael thought for a few seconds.

"Go back in there and find out about that call," he instructed his loyal sergeant. "I want to know why Mrs Rumburgh called her."

"Will do," replied Cooper.

"Also, Mr Wisset, the headmaster, told me that Mrs Rumburgh and Mavis Heaton are related by marriage. See if that's true and if so, how they're related. See if you can find out how close they were."

"Really?" replied Cooper. "That's a bit of a surprise."

"Also, get Jenny Attwood on her own and quiz her again; this time more forcefully if need be, about those photos we found at Brookwell's apartment," continued Carmichael. "If they are Jade, I want to know what Jenny has to say about Brookwell having pictures of her daughter."

"Understood," replied Cooper.

"Then head straight back to the station," continued Carmichael. "I know we were all going to meet up at five, but I think we should pull that forward as I want to recap on everything that we've learned as a team so far today, before we do anything more."

"Right you are, sir," replied Cooper, the last two words unheard by Carmichael, who had already ended the call.

* * *

"Bingo!" exclaimed WPC Twamley excitedly, as CCTV footage she was watching revealed the figure of the same young woman depositing what looked like another Jiffy bag into the same postbox.

WPC Twamley froze the tape and enlarged the image.

There was no doubt about it: it was definitely the same person who posted the Jiffy bag in the footage she'd spotted earlier from Wednesday 24th June, but this image was much, much clearer and far more of the woman's face was visible.

She sent the latest image with the date and time, Tuesday 30th June 16:59:37, to the printer. She ordered four copies to be printed.

* * *

After forty-five minutes more inside the Attwood house, Cooper emerged with a contented, self-righteous smile on his face. Mavis Heaton and Jenny Attwood, once he'd got them alone, had both been extremely helpful.

Keen to share the information he'd gleaned from the two women, Cooper quickened his step as he purposefully strode towards his beaten-up Volvo at the end of the driveway.

Chapter 53

It was precisely 12:30 when Carmichael started the team debrief.

"Who'd like to kick off?" he asked.

"It may as well be me," replied Rachel, "as I've been looking into the first murder."

"Makes sense," replied Carmichael.

Rachel took out her notebook.

"Geoffrey Brookwell, an actor living in Knott End, receives a Jiffy bag containing a message and presumably a thousand pounds in cash, on around Thursday 25th June," she announced, "WPC Twamley has identified someone who we think may have posted the package in Southport Road, Kirkwood on Wednesday 24th June, at five past five."

Rachel passed around the image that WPC Twamley had downloaded.

"Although the picture's not that good," continued Rachel, "WPC Twamley also found another image, this one of the same woman posting the package to Sajid Hanif, on Tuesday 30th June, which is a lot clearer."

Again, Rachel provided everyone with an A4 print of the young woman, with long dark hair, posting items into the same Southport Road postbox.

"This one's much clearer," Watson remarked. "I'd be amazed if we don't manage to trace her from this."

"She looks like the office junior," remarked Rachel, "possibly posting the day's mail on her way home from work."

Carmichael looked at the times posted on the two printouts and nodded sagely.

"That's a job for you this afternoon, Rachel," remarked Carmichael.

Rachel frowned. "What's that?" she enquired, her expression showing she was a little puzzled.

"Get yourself to this postbox on Southport Road at around five," he replied. "My guess is that our mysterious poster will be there posting the mail again, as normal."

Rachel nodded. "Of course," she remarked. "Not sure why I didn't think of that."

Carmichael smiled. "That's why I'm an inspector," he remarked.

Rachel gazed back down at her notes.

"I've checked the statements from Reverend Green, Mrs Carter, Mrs Gillespie and Geoffrey's agent, Anna Montgomery; I've also talked with Miss Turner, the drama teacher he worked with at the academy and I can't find anything that we've missed," Rachel remarked. "It's as we have known for a while, he is offered this fantastic job, he appears to be hoodwinked into carrying out a bizarre role play at the church claiming to have murdered someone, only to disappear in the hired Bentley with false number plates."

"I'm still sure that the pig blood on his hands may help us find out who the killer is," interjected Watson. "If we can find out where he got it, that should provide us with a fresh avenue to pursue."

Carmichael shrugged his shoulders. "Maybe," he replied tentatively, "but I've been thinking about that, and my guess is that Brookwell was told to get the pig blood in that message he received. I can't see him being given it by his killer."

Watson hadn't thought of that but wasn't about to tell his boss and give Carmichael a second opportunity to brag about his superior brain, so said nothing.

"So, let's go over the murder scene again," Carmichael said.

Rachel nodded.

"Geoffrey's body was found in the boot of the Bentley, down Wood Lane on the morning of Wednesday 1st July," continued Rachel. "According to Dr Stock, he was killed the day before, between twelve and two in the afternoon. His throat was cut, then he was lifted into the car and the car was reversed to cover the large pool of blood on the floor."

"With no witnesses and no fingerprints on the car," remarked Carmichael.

"That's correct, sir," replied Rachel. "Wood Lane is a dead end and the body was found well past the last house; hardly anyone ever goes that far down."

"There's a cut-through which leads through the fields and down to the canal," interjected Watson. "Maybe the killer came and went that way."

"I'd guess that Brookwell must have weighed about ninety to a hundred kilograms," Cooper remarked, "so whoever killed him must have been strong to lift him from the floor to the boot."

Rachel Dalton flicked through Dr Stock's report. "Eighty-seven kilograms," she remarked, as soon as she found the information.

"Good point, Paul," remarked Carmichael. "And you'd expect him to be covered in Brookwell's blood, too."

"As you said, Rachel," remarked Watson, assuming she'd finished, "other than finding the young woman who appears to have posted the Jiffy bag to Geoffrey, we're not much further on than we were a few days ago."

"I know," Rachel concurred. "I've nothing more to add to what we already know about the handover of the car in Kirkwood multi-storey on Saturday, and of course, there are the photos of the young girl that you found at his apartment."

"Which are of Jade Attwood," interjected Cooper, "that's now been confirmed by her mum."

"But, as you say, Rachel," remarked Carmichael, "we've really nothing more than we had yesterday."

"Well, there were a couple of other things," Rachel announced. "Firstly, the probate people have just got back to me with the amount he inherited when his dad died."

"How much was it?" Carmichael enquired.

"A fairly sizable amount," replied Rachel, who checked her notes, so she had the exact figure. "Two hundred and seventy-three thousand, eight hundred and ninety-three pounds."

"That would pay for his apartment in Knott End, that's for sure," remarked Cooper.

"I'm sure it would," Rachel added. "But I'm not sure it will help us find his killer."

Carmichael nodded. "Good to know," he remarked, "even if it's not of paramount importance to the case."

"What was the other thing you found out?" Cooper asked.

"It may also be nothing," Rachel replied, "but in the activity report on Geoffrey's mobile phone, I found a record of an incoming call at four thirty-five on the evening of Tuesday 23rd June, which went on for almost thirty minutes. It could have been from his killer as it's the only one he received in the last three months from that number."

"A bit of a wild assumption," remarked Watson. "Did you manage to trace who it came from?"

Rachel shook her head. "That's the issue. It's from a pay-as-you-go phone, so I couldn't get a trace on it. I called it a few times and it's coming up as unobtainable."

Carmichael thought for a few seconds.

"Marc's right," he said, "the chances are it's not the killer, but thirty minutes does seem a long time to be speaking, so it may be a burner that the killer used. Write the number up on the whiteboard, just in case we come across it again."

Rachel stood up, walked over to the board and started writing the number as she was told.

She'd written just seven of the eleven digits when Cooper shouted, "Stop! Are the last four digits 'eight three seven two'?" he enquired.

Rachel stopped writing and turned around, her face a picture of astonishment.

"Yes, they are," she replied. "How did you know that?"

Cooper grinned and held up the call record of Sean Attwood's mobile, that he'd picked up from his desk. "Because that number called Sean Attwood at nine thirty-five yesterday morning, about twenty minutes before Attwood was seen leaving the Lindley Hotel."

As Cooper was talking, Watson started looking at the call record he had for Sajid Hanif. Suddenly he stopped and held up his report.

"Sajid too," he said enthusiastically, "someone using that number called him at six thirty-two on Thursday 25th June, a call that lasted twenty-three minutes."

"Maybe that's the call he thought was from Philip Dobson at Suresight," suggested Cooper.

"Could be, Paul," replied Carmichael. "The date certainly ties in with what Sonja told us."

The room fell silent again for a few seconds, as the team absorbed what had just been discussed.

"With Attwood having received a call from that number," Cooper suddenly remarked, "doesn't that suggest he's not the killer? In fact, isn't it more likely that he's going to be another victim?"

219

"If he isn't already," added Rachel, who was nodding in agreement with Cooper's observation.

Carmichael thought for a few seconds before responding.

"Maybe," he replied, "but whoever is behind this is certainly cunning enough to try and throw us off the scent by calling himself on the burner, just to make us think he's not our man."

"I agree," interjected Watson, "I still think Attwood's our prime suspect."

Chapter 54

"I think I've found the gun cupboard," remarked Stock's forensic assistant, who was crouching in his white head-to-toe overalls, peering into the small recess under Mrs Rumburgh's stairs. "It appears to have been forced open."

"I take it it's empty?" remarked Stock.

"Yes," replied the forensic assistant, who shone his torch on the broken-open door. "There are spaces for two guns, but you're right, it's empty."

Stock listened intently.

"Photograph the area thoroughly and check for prints," he replied. "Carmichael enquired about this specifically, so make sure you do an exhaustive job. I don't want him complaining that we've missed anything."

* * *

"Shall I go next?" remarked Watson.

Carmichael nodded. "Yes, let's go over Sajid Hanif's murder."

"I went to see Sajid's mum and sister, earlier," Watson remarked. "Neither were particularly helpful; Mrs Hanif because, in my view, there's not a lot she can tell us; the sister, Nora, was just unwilling to help. I doubt she knows anything either, but that woman certainly isn't a fan of the police."

"So again, apart from the mystery caller we've just identified, you've nothing more to add to what we knew before," remarked Carmichael, his words delivered in an aggressive, disappointed tone.

Watson shook his head. "No," he replied rather meekly.

Carmichael swung around to face Cooper.

"What about you, Paul?" he enquired. "You've had an expression on your face since you arrived back that suggests you've made a breakthrough."

Cooper smiled, "It may not prove to be important, but I do have some information from Jenny Attwood and Mavis Heaton that's new and I think, may be relevant."

"We're all ears, Paul," remarked Carmichael. "What is it that you've discovered?"

Cooper smiled. "First of all," he said, "as I told the boss earlier, in my view none of the women appear to know where Sean is. They could be lying, but I'm convinced they're no wiser than us about his whereabouts and why he's gone missing."

"Do they look worried?" Rachel enquired.

Cooper nodded his head vigorously. "They look very concerned," he confirmed.

"So, what do they think happened to him?" Carmichael enquired.

Cooper shrugged his shoulders. "They don't know," he replied, "but I think they're starting to fear the worst."

Carmichael nodded. "Go on then, what did you find? The suspense is killing me."

Cooper smiled and looked down at his notebook. "When I showed Jenny the photos again and asked her to tell me why Geoffrey Brookwell had pictures of her daughter, she eventually admitted that she'd had a brief drunken dalliance with him at about the time she fell pregnant with Jade."

"So, Jade's his!" exclaimed Rachel.

Cooper shrugged his shoulders.

"Jenny says not," he replied. "She described the event as a disastrous, alcohol-induced fumble that lasted seconds and she swears blind that Jade is Sean's."

"Drunken fumble it may have been," remarked Carmichael, "but it looks like Brookwell certainly seemed to have thought Jade was his."

Cooper nodded. "Yes," he replied, "but Jenny says she told him, just after Jade was born, that she wasn't his and told him to stay away. She maintains that he never mentioned it again and she's adamant that she never knew about the photos."

"That would tie in with them looking as if they'd been taken without anyone knowing," added Watson.

"Yes," Cooper agreed, "Jenny maintains that, as far as she knew, Brookwell had accepted what she'd told him when Jade was small and had moved on."

"Apparently not," Carmichael remarked.

"Jenny says that nobody knows about her fling with Brookwell," continued Cooper, "and she says that neither Jade nor Sean have any inkling about Brookwell and her."

"And do you believe her?" Carmichael asked.

Cooper shrugged his shoulders. "I'm not sure," he replied. "However, she's certainly terrified that it might get out and begged me to keep quiet about it."

"We may well have just found our motive," suggested Watson. "Sean finds out about his wife and Brookwell and kills him."

Carmichael's expression suggested he wasn't altogether sure about Watson's idea.

"It could be," he replied sceptically, "but that wouldn't account for Sajid Hanif's death or that of Mrs Rumburgh. If Brookwell was our only victim and the way he'd been killed had been more straightforward then yes, I'd be inclined to agree with you, but these murders are far more complicated.

Sean Attwood may well be our murderer, but I don't think he killed Brookwell because of Jade. I imagine he still doesn't know anything about his wife's drunken romance all those years ago."

It was clear from the expression on Watson's face that he didn't agree with his boss, but he chose not to argue his point any further.

"What about Mavis Heaton?" enquired Carmichael. "What did she have to say for herself?"

Cooper looked again at his notes.

"She confirmed that she received a call on her mobile from Mrs Rumburgh," he remarked. "She reckons it was at about six twenty."

"Why did Mrs Rumburgh call her?" Carmichael asked, eager for Cooper to speed up in providing the team with his findings.

"Mavis Heaton said that Mrs Rumburgh seemed very apprehensive. She first asked if Mavis knew where Sean was, and when she told her that she didn't know, Mrs Rumburgh then asked her if she had any idea where the family of a boy called Billy Taylor lived."

Carmichael looked perplexed. "Who's Billy Taylor and why is she asking Mavis Heaton about him? Also, she must have Sean Attwood's phone number as he did some work for her, and Jade's home number must be on redial with the school, she's in trouble so much. Why get Mavis Heaton involved?"

Cooper smiled. "All good questions, sir, and ones I asked Mavis, too," he replied. "She told me that Billy Taylor was a pupil at the school about twenty or thirty years ago. A nice young man by all accounts," Cooper remarked, "but sadly he tragically died in an accident in the canal."

"I remember that," remarked Watson. "It was a case my dad investigated when he was the local bobby in Moulton

Bank. I was only about seven or eight, but I remember it was a big thing in the village at the time."

"Really?" remarked Carmichael, who wondered whether Penny would have remembered it or even known the boy.

"Do you want me to ask my dad about it?" Watson enquired.

"Yes," replied Carmichael instantly. "If you could please, Marc. And see if you can locate the whereabouts of any living family members of the poor boy. So, what else did Mavis have to say?" Carmichael asked, turning his attention back to Cooper.

"This is where it all gets quite complicated," replied his sergeant.

Chapter 55

Having listened intently for almost twenty minutes as Cooper outlined Mavis Heaton's complex family relationships, Carmichael, Watson and Rachel Dalton sat in silence as they tried to absorb what they'd just heard.

They would have probably been quiet for a good few more seconds, too, had Carmichael's mobile not rung.

"Stock," Carmichael said as he saw who it was on the small screen, "what have you got for me?"

"We've found what looks like the gun cabinet," remarked Stock. "It was under the stairs and has been broken open."

"I take it the cabinet is now empty," Carmichael said.

"Yes," replied Stock. "According to my information, that's correct."

"Anything else?" enquired Carmichael.

There was an audible sigh from the other end of the line.

"No, that's it," replied Stock, "I just thought you'd like to know. You'll have my full report later today."

Before Carmichael had a chance to thank the efficient chief pathologist, the line went dead.

"Looks like I've upset him, somehow," remarked Carmichael as he put his mobile back on his desk.

"What did he have to say?" Watson enquired.

"His team have located a cabinet in Mrs Rumburgh's house where we think she kept her shotguns," replied

Carmichael. "The problem is that it's been broken into and is now empty."

"Do you think Mrs Rumburgh's killer has them?" Rachel asked.

Carmichael nodded. "That would be my guess, Rachel," he replied. "And if so, I'm concerned about what else he will do now he has at least one firearm."

After another brief pause Carmichael continued.

"We can talk about Mrs Rumburgh in a minute," he said, "but let's just make sure we all understand what Paul has just told us before we move on."

The team all nodded.

"So, you're saying that Mavis Heaton has been married twice and is essentially Sean Attwood's stepmother?" Watson said.

"Sort of," replied Cooper. "She actually never married Sean's dad, Martin, but they did live together for over ten years and she maintains that she was basically Sean's mum in all but name."

"Run through it again, please," Rachel asked, who looked thoroughly confused.

Cooper smiled and looked at his notes so that he got everything right.

"When Mavis was eighteen, she married Dennis Hampton, Mrs Rumburgh's older brother; Mrs Rumburgh's maiden name was Hampton. It was a big scandal at the time, as he was in his late thirties and had been her teacher at school. She maintains that nothing untoward happened between them while he was her teacher but says that tongues wagged at the time and he was forced to leave teaching: something he never recovered from and which led to their marriage breaking up. They split up when Mavis was in her mid-twenties."

"So where is he now?" Carmichael enquired.

"And where's their son that you mentioned?" Rachel added.

"According to Mavis, Dennis Hampton died about fifteen years ago," Cooper replied. "And she reckoned that she's not seen James, her son, in well over twenty years. He apparently went to live with his father when they separated, and they drifted apart."

"But he'd have been just a very young child when they parted," Rachel remarked. "He wouldn't have had a choice of who he went with; that must have been decided between them."

"Or through a court," interjected Carmichael.

"What sort of mother would abandon her child like that?" Watson remarked.

Cooper shook his head. "I don't know," he replied. "Maybe Mavis was a bit immature when she was younger, but I admit it did strike me as strange that she'd agree to let her child go to the father."

"Maybe her new man told her he wouldn't take on the child," suggested Rachel.

Cooper shook his head again. "She only started seeing him after the marriage broke up," he said.

"That's what she says," remarked Watson. "I think she may have been telling you a modified version of events, to put herself in a better light."

"I wonder what Mrs Rumburgh thought about all this?" Carmichael remarked.

Cooper shrugged his shoulders. "I asked Mavis and she maintained that Mrs Rumburgh bore no ill will towards her, but I guess we'll never know."

"And then she marries Ronald Heaton," said Carmichael, keen to get the story repeated by Cooper in a more timely manner.

"Yes," continued Cooper, "she fell pregnant with Jenny

by Heaton and she and he married six months before Jenny was born."

"Then she leaves him, too," added Rachel.

Cooper nodded. "That marriage only lasted two years," he said. "That's when Mavis left Ronald and started living with Martin Attwood, who already had a young boy, Sean, who Mavis took on as her own; Sean's mother had died before she took up with Martin."

"So, Sean and Jenny are brought up together, as brother and sister, but eventually marry," said Rachel.

"All sounds a bit weird to me," interjected Watson.

"Weird it may be, but they're not blood-related and there's only about seven or eight years' difference in their ages, so I guess it's fine," Cooper replied.

"So, where's Ronald Heaton and Martin Attwood now?" Carmichael enquired. "And were there any other children involved with any of the various relationships?"

"Martin Attwood's dead," replied Cooper, "he also died about fifteen years ago, but Ronald Heaton's still alive, apparently. He's somewhere in the Salford area of Manchester according to Mavis. She says her daughter and he talk occasionally on the phone, but she reckons it's well over five years since he and Jenny last met up; and other than on one occasion, at Jade's christening, Mavis hasn't seen or spoken to him since she walked out on him."

"Any other siblings of either Sean or Jenny?" Carmichael asked.

"No," replied Cooper. "She maintains that Sean is an only child and she's just had two children, James Hampton and Jenny Attwood."

"And we don't know where James is?" Carmichael asked.

Cooper shook his head. "Mavis says she has no idea," he replied.

Carmichael thought for a few moments.

"Something for you to do, Rachel, before you go over to that postbox at five this evening. See if you can find Ronald Heaton and James Hampton," he said.

"Will do, sir," replied Rachel.

"Don't you want me to do that?" Cooper enquired.

Carmichael shook his head.

"No, Paul, I'd like you to go over and help PC Dyer with the surveillance on Tim Horton. "I don't want him giving us the slip again."

"OK, sir," replied Cooper, who shut his notebook indicating he had no more information to share with the team.

Chapter 56

It was ten minutes after one when shotgun fire echoed across the valley between Ambient Hill and Ashurst Point.

It was impossible to tell exactly where it came from, and in truth few who heard it even batted an eyelid, as gunfire or the sound of bird scarers, was so commonplace in that sleepy part of Mid-Lancashire.

* * *

"I suppose I need to update everyone on my findings this morning," Carmichael remarked, the team of four all still absorbed in their briefing.

"First of all, Stock has confirmed the time of Mrs Rumburgh's death to have been between six and nine last night," he continued. "And he's saying that she was knocked unconscious by what he describes as 'a hefty blow to the head', before she inhaled the exhaust fumes from her car. We know she made that call to Mavis Heaton at six seventeen from her office, and it would take her the best part of thirty minutes to drive home. So, based on that we can quite accurately say Mrs Rumburgh died between seven and nine last night."

"And she was murdered," interjected Watson.

"Yes, Marc," replied Carmichael. "She, too, was murdered."

"Has Stock's team uncovered anything else?" Rachel asked.

Carmichael shook his head. "Nothing more, other than finding the empty gun cabinet," he replied.

"And how did your meeting with the headmaster go?" Cooper enquired.

Carmichael nodded his head. "It was interesting," he replied. "Mr Wisset's very upset. He appears to have been a big admirer of Mrs Rumburgh's. In fact, I got the impression that she was almost like a mentor to him, even though she was his understudy at the school."

"Do you think he could be involved?" Watson asked.

Carmichael shook his head. "I very much doubt it," he replied. "I hadn't even finished telling him about how we found Mrs Rumburgh when he was telling me that she must have been killed. If he were the killer, I don't think he'd be saying that."

Watson nodded. "I guess that's true," he concurred.

"But what made him say that?" Cooper asked.

"Well, in his view," replied Carmichael, "she'd never have taken her own life."

"Why was he so sure of that?" Rachel enquired.

"Because, apparently, Mrs Rumburgh was a devout Catholic," continued Carmichael. "In Wisset's view, suicide would never have crossed her mind."

Cooper, Watson and Rachel Dalton exchanged brief looks before nodding gently to each other, as if to signal their acceptance of what their boss was telling them.

"So, what else did he tell you?" continued Watson.

"Well, apart from alerting me to Mrs Rumburgh and Mavis Heaton being related by marriage, although he was quite vague about that, and being adamant about her inability to take her own life, nothing much," responded Carmichael. "He did say that Mrs Rumburgh came to see him at about six

232

fifteen yesterday evening, saying that she wanted to talk to him about something that was worrying her. Which is why they arranged to meet up this morning."

"The seven forty-five meeting," remarked Rachel.

"Yes," replied Carmichael. "According to Mr Wisset, he said she told him that she needed to do a few things before they talked."

"Making that call to Mavis Heaton being one of them, I'd say," interjected Cooper.

Carmichael nodded. "I reckon that's a safe bet, Paul."

"And Wisset has no idea what the subject matter was," added Watson.

Carmichael shook his head. "That's what he told me," he replied.

"Do you believe him, sir?" Rachel enquired.

Carmichael considered the question carefully before answering. "Actually, I do," he replied.

* * *

PC Dyer, sat quietly in his car outside the spa entrance, had just about given up hope of seeing Tim Horton again that afternoon. Then suddenly he noticed Horton's car approaching in his wing mirror.

He slid down a few inches in his seat until the man he'd been ordered to follow drove past him and turned up the drive leading to his grand-looking health spa.

He looked at the clock on the dashboard of the car; it read 1:37pm.

Chapter 57

Carmichael glanced up at the clock on the office wall.

"We've been here well over an hour," he remarked, as if that fact was cause for calamity. "We need to get our thoughts and findings documented and then get out there and find our killer."

Ever since he'd arrived at Kirkwood police station, Carmichael's modus operandi for solving cases had remained consistent: frequent team updates to share information followed by his, now infamous, three lists, of knowns, assumptions and finally, questions that need answering.

Rachel Dalton was so used to this method of working and was so frequently the person chosen to write down their observations and opinions on the whiteboard that, without needing to be asked, she picked up a green marker and stood by the list of knowns that they'd written the day before. She underlined the word "known" with two thick green lines.

* * *

Nigel Wisset had spent the morning ensuring everyone that needed to know was made aware of the sudden death of Mrs Rumburgh. Despite being asked several times about how he was feeling following the death of his friend and mentor, Nigel ploughed on with the responsibility that now fell on his shoulders as head, to ensure the communications were clear and appropriate.

"He looks in shock himself," Mr Barlow, the head of year nine had muttered to Miss Lomax, the normally ebullient head of science; the latter just nodded, head down, trying to hold back her tears.

With the governors, the department heads and finally the rest of the teaching staff all now fully aware of the sad news, Nigel Wisset felt able to inform the whole school, a task which he had scheduled for 2:15 pm in the school hall.

Rumours had already been circulating amongst the children about the reason for a sudden afternoon assembly being called; something that had not happened before under the headship of Mr Wisset.

Although most of the speculation was way off the mark, the fact that Mrs Rumburgh had not been seen that day had prompted some bright pupils to work out that the announcement would have something to do with the member of staff the majority of the school's students revered the most.

Mr Wisset clambered sombrely up the five wooden steps that led to the stage to deliver the tragic news to the school.

* * *

It was 2:20pm when Carmichael and his team finished documenting their thoughts.

Standing back with his arms folded tightly to his chest, Carmichael looked at the forty bullet points he and his team had documented in the three lists.

"Is that everything?" he enquired, his question aimed at all three of his officers.

"I think that's about it," responded Cooper, his voice seemingly speaking for the whole team.

Knowns:

- On Tuesday 30th June 10:30am, Geoffrey Brookwell went into Moulton Bank C of E church with his hands covered in blood and confessed to a murder. He then disappeared.
- We know the blood in question was pig blood. Type O.
- Brookwell's body was found on Wednesday 1st July in the boot of the car he'd been using, which belonged to an old school friend, Sean Attwood. Car had false plates.
- SOCO indicate that Brookwell died between 12 noon and 2pm on Tuesday, his throat having been cut by his killer.
- Attwood and Brookwell made the handover of the car at the multi-storey on Saturday 27th June, which was done without them being together. The car, when it was driven away, still had its genuine plates on it.
- Brookwell received a Jiffy bag, postmarked Wednesday 24th June in Kirkwood, which we found in his apartment in Knott End. No contents found yet.
- There were images of a girl confirmed as Jade Attwood in Brookwell's possession.
- The second dead man is Sajid Hanif, he also received a package recently. This was delivered to his work on 1st July, something the receptionist has confirmed. In that letter he is offered a job, given a thousand pounds and asked to book room seven at the Lindley Hotel for a meeting the following day (2nd July).
- According to his wife, Sajid received a call the week before from a man purporting to be Philip Dobson, basically offering him a job, which Dobson completely denies making.
- Sajid Hanif arrives at the Lindley Hotel at 9:15am and checks into room seven, an outside room facing the car park.
- Sajid is murdered between 9:15am and 11:30am when the young housekeeper finds his body.

- A pickup truck identified by one of the receptionists as belonging to Sean Attwood was seen leaving the Lindley car park at approximately 10am.
- The same pay-as-you-go burner appears to have been used to contact Attwood, Hanif and Brookwell.
- A young woman has been identified on CCTV footage posting Jiffy bags at the same postbox at around 5pm on the two days we believe the parcels were posted to Brookwell and Hanif.
- Sean Attwood has not been seen since his pickup left the Lindley Hotel on 2nd July.
- Mrs Rumburgh died of carbon monoxide poisoning between 7pm and 9pm on Thursday 2nd July. Murder was staged to look like suicide.
- Mrs Rumburgh's guns have been taken from her house.
- Mrs Rumburgh called Mavis Heaton on the evening she died.
- According to Mavis Heaton she mentioned a boy called Billy Taylor and was keen to locate Sean Attwood.
- Sean Attwood, Geoffrey Brookwell and Tim Horton were all friends at school. Tim Horton still sees Attwood.
- Geoffrey Brookwell believed Jade Attwood was his daughter, Jenny Attwood denies this.
- According to Mr Wisset, Mrs Rumburgh wanted to see him about something urgent. They'd arranged to meet on Friday 3rd July.
- Mavis Heaton and Mrs Rumburgh were related by marriage.
- Mavis Heaton had been the long-term partner of Sean Attwood's father and brought Sean up as her own son.

Assumptions:

- There is a single killer.
- The three murders are linked – not random acts.

- Whoever murdered the three people now has Mrs Rumburgh's guns.
- The young woman in the CCTV posting the Jiffy bags knows the killer.
- Mrs Rumburgh was killed because of something she knew or had worked out.
- Sean Attwood knows more than he has been saying.
- Tim Horton knows where Sean Attwood is.
- The killer can afford to lavish multiple thousands of pounds to lure Brookwell and Hanif to their deaths.

Questions:

- Who killed Brookwell, Hanif and Mrs Rumburgh?
- Why has the killer spent time and money making Brookwell and Hanif believe they have new jobs before killing them?
- Who changed the plates on the Bentley – and why?
- What did Mrs Rumburgh want to talk to Sean about?
- What did Mrs Rumburgh want to talk to Mr Wisset about?
- What has Billy Taylor's death got to do with the killings?
- Who is the mystery young woman who posted the Jiffy bags?
- Where is Sean Attwood?

"We've lots to do," Carmichael remarked ruefully, before sending his team away to carry out their latest instructions.

Once he was alone in the office, Carmichael sat down in front of the whiteboard and again read through the forty points.

"I'm sure we're missing something obvious," he muttered to himself.

238

Chapter 58

The stunned school remained silent as Mr Wisset departed the hall, leaving the form teachers to have more intimate conversations with their classes, many of whom were in tears at the news.

"I bet your dad's in charge of the investigation," one of the boys in Natalie's class said to her.

"Only if it's a suspicious death," replied Natalie calmly. "If it was just a heart attack or something like that he wouldn't get involved."

This seemed to placate her classmate who sauntered away, seemingly content with the response he'd received from the inspector's daughter.

True to the promise he'd made to Carmichael, Mr Wisset hadn't mentioned how Mrs Rumburgh had died, which remained unclear to teachers and pupils alike. However, Natalie had seen her father's car in the car park of the school that morning, so although she wasn't about to let on, she was pretty sure Mrs Rumburgh's death was being investigated by her dad, so in her view it was unlikely to be down to natural causes.

* * *

Carmichael spent almost twenty minutes alone in the office at Kirkwood, going over the points he and the team had documented on the screen, before pressing print and obtaining a hard copy. Grabbing the copy and the images WPC Twamley had taken from the CCTV footage, Carmichael stuffed them all into the large green loose-leaf folder and, case file in hand, headed towards the door.

* * *

Since arriving back at the health spa, Tim Horton had remained in his office with strict instructions to his staff that he was not to be disturbed.

It therefore came as a major surprise to him when his secretary, Lynn, knocked on the door and sheepishly entered the room.

"Sorry to trouble you, Mr Horton," she said nervously, "but there's a lady here who is adamant that she should speak with you."

"Who?" shouted Horton, clearly agitated at being troubled by a visitor.

"She says her name is Jenny Attwood," replied the edgy-sounding PA. "She maintains that you'll see her because you're her daughter's father."

The look of amazement on Tim Horton's face indicated to his PA that there might be something in what she'd been told.

"Shall I show her in?" Lynn asked.

Before Horton could reply, Jenny Attwood marched into his office and plonked herself opposite the owner.

"What on earth are you doing telling Lynn that I'm Jade's dad?" he enquired, his voice loud and full of anger.

"Did I say father?" replied Jenny Attwood, with a smug grin aimed at the quivering PA. "I meant godfather."

* * *

Marc Watson's dad, Wally, had been the village policeman in Moulton Bank for over thirty-five years. Although he'd retired over two decades before and now found it very difficult to get around, Wally Watson's mind was still agile, and his memory had not diminished one iota with the passing of time.

"Do you remember the case of that schoolboy, Billy Taylor, who died when you were the bobby in Moulton Bank?" Marc asked.

His father thought for a moment.

"Aye," he replied, "the ginger-haired lad who drowned in the canal."

"That's right, Dad," said Marc. "Can you recall whether there were any suspicious circumstances with his death?"

With a shake of his head and a perplexed expression, Wally Watson clearly didn't.

"No," he remarked. "It was a sad case of a young lad who couldn't swim that well, falling into the canal on his way home. The forensic guys did a very thorough job, as I remember, and there were no signs of foul play. The lad just slipped and fell into the water. He couldn't get himself out and, being alone, he drowned. All very tragic, but a pure accident."

"So, at no stage did you feel it could have been more sinister?" Marc enquired.

"Well at first, when the body was found, we had an open mind," replied Wally. "But there was no evidence that pointed to anything sinister, as you put it, son."

"So, who was it that found the body?" Marc asked.

The old man squinted, his focus directed at a point behind his son's left shoulder for almost thirty seconds as he tried to recall a name.

"It was a classmate of his," Wally replied eventually. "A lad called …"

Wally stopped as he again tried hard to remember the classmate's name.

" … The Asian lad," he said after a few minutes. "Nice boy whose family owned the village store, back in the day."

"Sajid Hanif?" suggested Marc.

"That's it, Sajid Hanif," replied Wally, his face brought to life by the name being identified. "He'd stayed behind in class and followed down the path after Billy Taylor about twenty minutes later. He found his friend face down in the water and fished him out, but it was too late. The poor lad was already dead."

* * *

"What's your game?" Tim Horton shouted as soon as he and Jenny Attwood were alone. "Lynn's always talking with Carol. I don't want her or Hayley, for that matter, getting the wrong end of the stick about Jade; especially after we had all that nonsense with Brookie when she was born."

Jenny Attwood stared back at Horton.

"Tough," she replied, "I don't give a damn. What I want to know is, where's my husband and why was Brookie still carrying photos of Jade?"

Tim Horton leaned forward in his chair. "I'm telling you, Jenny, whatever your game is, you can keep Hayley out of it," he shouted.

"You get quite prickly when there's a chance precious Hayley might think badly of you, don't you, Tim?" retorted Jenny, who was in no mood to back down.

Tim Horton recoiled back into his chair.

"Jenny," he said firmly, but as calmly as he could, "I have absolutely no idea where Sean is, and I've not spoken with Brookie in years. I have no idea why he still had Jade's photos. I thought he got the message years ago. I promise you, I'm as baffled by all this as you are."

Jenny took a deep intake of breath.

"Do you think Sean may have got wind of me and Brookie, and actually thinks that Brookie is Jade's dad?" she enquired.

Tim Horton considered the question for a few seconds before shaking his head.

"Only you, me and Brookie ever knew about your little fling," he remarked. "And as far as I was aware, we'd successfully convinced Brookie that he wasn't Jade's dad. Unless Brookie told Sean, I don't see how he would have known. All I can say is that I certainly haven't told Sean anything."

Seeing that his words appeared to placate Jenny, Horton became more relaxed.

"You don't think Sean killed Brookie because he found out about the two of you, do you?" he said, his tone indicating the mere notion was fanciful.

Jenny Attwood shrugged her shoulders. "I don't know what to believe, Tim," she replied.

Chapter 59

With his team all assigned their latest duties, Carmichael decided to revisit the spot down Wood Lane, where Geoffrey Brookwell's body had been found on Wednesday.

This wasn't an uncommon tactic for Carmichael; he often returned to crime scenes on his own when he wanted to think, as he somehow found it easier to make sense of the information he'd acquired when he was in the place an event had occurred. For no other reason than Wood Lane being closer, he decided to go there rather than any of the other two murder scenes.

Carmichael parked his BMW about ten metres from where the Bentley with Geoffrey's body had been found. He clambered out of the car and walked slowly towards the precise spot where Geoffrey Brookwell's throat had been cut.

Without the blue and white cordon, the myriad of police cars, the Bentley and the SOCOs in their white overalls, all looked normal; a quiet country lane shrouded in tall trees with just the birdsong and the rustling of leaves to break the silence. That was until Carmichael's mobile started to ring.

"Hi Paul," Carmichael remarked as he took the call. "What have you got for me?"

"An interesting one," replied Cooper. "I'm with PC Dyer outside Horton's Health Spa. Guess who's just come out?"

Carmichael had never been that keen on guessing games.

"I've no idea, Paul. But do enlighten me," he responded.

"Jenny Attwood," replied Cooper, clearly delighted at what they'd just seen. "Do you want me to tail her?"

Carmichael thought for a few seconds.

"No," he replied. "Stay with Horton. I can't think what Jenny wanted with him, but the fact that she went to see him strongly suggests he's involved in some way, or at least she thinks he is. Stick with him for now, and if he leaves make sure you see where he's going."

* * *

To her surprise, it took Rachel no time at all to locate the first of the two men she'd been tasked to find.

As Cooper had said at the briefing, Ronald Heaton lived in Salford, and after looking at the current electoral role, Rachel was able to find an address which then helped her locate Mavis's second husband's telephone number.

Within an hour of starting her search for Ronald Heaton, Rachel was on the phone talking to him.

However, that's as far as her good fortune stretched, as Ronald confirmed he'd not seen or spoken to Mavis since Jade's christening, fifteen years earlier; and it appeared that even his contact with Jenny, his daughter with Mavis, was sporadic to say the least; Christmas cards, birthday cards and maybe a couple of texts or calls a year was the sum total of their relationship.

Rachel put down the phone, puffed out her cheeks and glanced at her watch.

Wanting to make sure she was in a good position at the postbox in plenty of time before the young woman's normal arrival at 5pm, Rachel figured she had about thirty minutes to start trying to find James Hampton, Mavis's first child from her marriage to Mrs Rumburgh's older brother.

Rachel knew the chances of locating him before she had to leave were, at best, slight but thought she should still make a start.

* * *

Carmichael stood alone in Wood Lane, just by where the car had been parked. Although the SOCOs had tried to clear the pool of blood they'd found under the car, the ground still bore the marks of where Geoffrey Brookwell had drawn his last breath.

Carmichael's mind raced as he thought about the poor man's last seconds on earth. He clearly knew his murderer, Carmichael decided; he also would have arranged to meet at that spot, probably an instruction in the letter or in the mystery call he'd received.

Then there was the pig blood. *What was that about?* he asked himself. And the false number plates. *Why go to all that trouble?*

Carmichael opened the folder to look at the photos from the crime scene again. It was a green folder, in a shade not too dissimilar to the fragment of green card he'd found on Mrs Rumburgh's desk.

Painstakingly slowly, Carmichael looked at the photos taken from each of the three murder scenes before carefully placing them back in the folder.

"Of course," he muttered to himself.

Chapter 60

Carmichael's car had just pulled into the car park of the academy when his mobile rang. It was Watson.

"Have you finished talking with your dad?" Carmichael enquired.

"Yes," replied Watson, "although there's not much to tell."

Carmichael looked at his watch; it was 4pm.

"I'll tell you what," Carmichael said, "rather than tell me now, why don't you come over to the academy right away and we can talk here. An extra pair of hands would be useful."

Despite being unsure what Carmichael had in mind for him, Watson decided to just do as he was told.

"Right you are, sir," he replied. "I'll be with you in about twenty minutes."

* * *

"Where do you think Horton went when he gave you the slip?" Cooper asked DC Dyer.

Dyer shrugged his shoulders. "He lost me at the crossroads on the way to Rumford Woods," he replied. "I guessed he'd gone straight over, but he must have turned."

"So, he headed either right towards Kirkwood or left towards Hasselbury," Cooper remarked.

Dyer nodded.

Cooper thought for a few seconds. "If I was going from here to Kirkwood, I'd not go anywhere near that road," he remarked. "It's a narrow, twisting road. Unless he was deliberately trying to give you the slip, my guess is it was somewhere in Hasselbury he was going."

"Makes sense," replied Dyer, who couldn't fault the sergeant's logic.

"And as there's only a few dwellings down there I'd imagine it won't take long to pinpoint where he went."

* * *

It was no surprise to Rachel that, by the time she needed to leave the station, she'd made no progress at all in finding James Hampton. She'd checked the police records and drawn a blank; she'd then looked at the last local census records but there was nobody of that name in the area. As a last effort to try and make some headway, she'd checked out how many people had social media accounts under the name James Hampton in the UK.

Her desktop had reached twenty-three accounts when she decided she'd have to go, and worryingly, it hadn't finished.

"This isn't going to be easy," she muttered to herself as she grabbed her bag and headed towards the exit.

* * *

Mr Wisset looked shocked when he came from his office to meet Carmichael in the corridor.

"Have you caught Mrs Rumburgh's killer?" he enquired in a whisper, his eyes staring intently at Carmichael in anticipation of receiving a big announcement.

Looking beyond the headmaster, through the open office door, Carmichael's gaze became fixed on a large framed certificate; probably Wisset's degree, he thought, although it was from an institution that Carmichael had never heard of before called Alsager College.

"We're not certain it was murder," Carmichael replied, not wishing to reveal any information at this stage. "We are still awaiting the pathologist's full report."

"It was murder," remarked Wisset firmly. "I'm certain of it, and the fact you're here suggests to me you're sure of it, too."

Carmichael couldn't fault the headmaster's logic but wasn't prepared to confirm anything to Wisset at this stage.

"I'm here to have another look in Mrs Rumburgh's office," he remarked. "Is that OK with you?"

"Of course," Wisset replied. "You know where it is, please go ahead."

As he spoke, the headmaster made a sweeping motion with his right hand, indicating he was happy for Carmichael to walk past him and go into the dead woman's office.

Carmichael smiled and walked by the headmaster, who started to follow. However, Wisset had only taken a couple of paces when Carmichael turned around and looked him fully in the eyes.

"I'll be all right on my own for now, thank you," he said firmly. "My sergeant is on his way and between the two of us we'll be able to do everything we need to."

"Oh, right, no problem," replied Wisset, who was clearly a little taken aback by Carmichael's rebuttal. "I'll be in my office until about seven this evening if you need me; and tomorrow I'm likely to be in here for most of the day, too."

"That's good to know," replied Carmichael.

The two men then exchanged forced smiles before making their separate ways into the two neighbouring offices.

Chapter 61

Rachel Dalton arrived at the red postbox at precisely 4:30pm. She reckoned that would give her plenty of time to find a good vantage point to watch out for the young woman WPC Twamley had spotted on CCTV, posting the two Jiffy bags they believed were destined for Geoffrey Brookwell and Sajid Hanif.

She first checked the notice on the postbox, which indicated that the next collection was due at 5:30pm, before turning her head firstly ninety degrees to the left, then ninety degrees in the other direction.

"That will do," she muttered to herself, as she spied a small arched alleyway a matter of feet away from the postbox.

As Rachel arrived at the brick arch, she could see that it led to a small car park which housed six cars, presumably for the solicitors' practice of Montgomery & Pilkington, the only building behind the archway. She chose the shaded side of the arch, which was nicely out of sight, but had full vision of the postbox.

Rachel checked to make sure there was nothing on the wall that would mark her jacket before leaning herself against the brickwork, a post she figured she'd be occupying for at least the next half-hour.

* * *

Carmichael had already been inside Mrs Rumburgh's office for thirty minutes when Watson arrived.

"Sorry it took me so long to get over here," remarked the sergeant apologetically, "the traffic is awful."

Carmichael, who had spent the last twenty minutes looking through the files in Mrs Rumburgh's large metal filing cabinets, half turned so he was facing Watson.

"No problem, Marc," he replied. "Can you go through those cabinets and take out any files that are in there for people connected to the case, but more importantly, any file that's missing that corner."

As he spoke, Carmichael pointed to the small triangle of green card, the fragment of a file he'd spotted that morning.

Without asking for any further clarification, Watson strolled over to the last of the six cabinets, the one marked V to Z.

"This may take a while," remarked Carmichael, with a wry smile. "I've been at it twenty minutes and I've only just finished A to D."

As Watson reached the filing cabinet, he noticed that his boss had already extracted two files and placed them on the top of cabinet marked I to L, which was located midway between the two officers.

"Whose are those?" he enquired.

"They're Sean Attwood's and Geoffrey Brookwell's," replied Carmichael. "Take a look at them, there's nothing in there that we don't already know; both seem to have been less than model students, but Attwood has the larger list of crimes against humanity."

As he spoke, Carmichael smiled as if he was pleased with his flippant, exaggerated character assassination.

Watson picked up Sean Attwood's file and peered inside.

The first thing that struck him was the photo; a full-face picture taken probably when Attwood was about sixteen, of a gaunt-looking, spotty-faced boy, sporting a scowl under a mass of unkempt blonde locks which half covered his eyes.

"I see what you mean, sir," remarked Watson, "a villain if ever I saw one."

* * *

Cooper looked at the clock on PC Dyer's dashboard; it read 16:37 in bright, flashing white lights.

"I wonder what time he's planning on clocking off tonight," he remarked, the monotony of sitting in wait clear in his voice.

PC Dyer shook his head. "No idea, Sarge," he replied, his eyes fixed on the entrance to Horton's Health Spa.

"I'm going to wait in my car," continued Cooper, "as he could be coming out any time now, I'd guess, and we both need to be ready to follow him."

"I understand," replied PC Dyer.

"And when he does leave, let's keep in contact so we can agree a strategy," Cooper added.

"Right you are, Sarge," replied PC Dyer as Cooper clambered out of the car and started to walk the twenty or so paces to his beaten-up Volvo.

"I hope it's not a high-speed chase," muttered PC Dyer to himself, "as that old thing's no match for Horton's sporty motor."

* * *

"So, what did your dad tell you about Billy Taylor's death?" Carmichael enquired, as he reached letter G in the second of Mrs Rumburgh's ancient cabinets.

"Not much, I'm afraid," replied Watson, who was up to letter W, working back from the end of the alphabetically sorted files. "Billy's death wasn't seen as being suspicious, just a very unfortunate accident by all accounts. He appears to have slipped by the canal and drowned when on his way home from school. No witnesses came forward at the time, so the police and coroner concluded that it was just a tragic accident."

"And your dad still believes that?" Carmichael asked.

"Yes, he does," replied Watson.

"So, we're no further forward," Carmichael remarked, just as his fingers reached the files starting with the letter H.

"Well, there was one thing Dad told me which is interesting," remarked Watson.

"What's that?" enquired Carmichael.

"Well, it would appear that the person who discovered Billy's body was Sajid Hanif," replied Watson. "He and Billy were good friends, according to Dad."

"Really," remarked Carmichael, "that is interesting; and so is this."

As he spoke, Carmichael pulled out three files from his cabinet, which had been put away together.

"What's that?" Watson asked.

"Sajid Hanif, James Hampton and Tim Horton's files are all next to each other," replied Carmichael, who was clearly excited by his finding.

"Well, they are all aitches," replied Watson.

Carmichael smiled. "They are, Marc," he concurred, "but after Sajid Hanif it should be Michael Hanscomb. But here that file is before Sajid Hanif, and there are another three files that should have been between Sajid Hanif and Tim Horton, but they've been put back behind Tim Horton."

"Maybe Mrs Rumburgh was in a hurry and just filed them incorrectly," remarked Watson.

"That's maybe what's happened," replied Carmichael slowly as he thought. "I'd certainly say that whoever did put them back did so in haste."

"I'd agree with that," replied Watson.

"But whether that person was Mrs Rumburgh or someone else is the big question," continued Carmichael.

Watson nodded. "I suppose it is," he concurred.

"But, more importantly," continued Carmichael, "what it does tells us is that she had them all out together; and my bet is, she did that last night."

Watson nodded again.

"Which begs the question," Carmichael continued, "why did Mrs Rumburgh want to look at Sajid Hanif, James Hampton and Tim Horton's files after Rachel and I spoke with her yesterday evening?"

Chapter 62

For over twenty minutes Rachel Dalton had kept her vigil under the archway. In all that time nobody had posted so much as a single letter into the postbox.

She checked her watch; it was 4:53pm, about the time the mystery young woman had been caught on the CCTV footage posting what they believed to be the all-important packages to Geoffrey Brookwell and Sajid Hanif.

"Any moment now," Rachel said to herself.

* * *

With just one filing cabinet to go through, Carmichael and Watson had, between them, extracted eight files by the time they turned their attention to the last cabinet: the one housing files for old students with surnames from M to P. The faded green folders carrying the school records of S A Attwood, G P Brookwell, J S Hampton, S Hanif, J A Heaton, T Horton and W Taylor had been carefully stacked on top of the metal cabinets. The eighth, that of a P E Lathom, had been extracted by Carmichael and placed next to the binder of documents relating to the case which he'd brought from the station.

"I'll leave that last cabinet to you, Marc," Carmichael remarked. "I'm going to go through these folders and see if there's anything in here that can help us. Particularly the one for Tim Horton, which has the missing corner that matches the piece of folder I found earlier."

As he spoke, Carmichael placed the fragment of green card he'd found on Mrs Rumburgh's desk next to Tim Horton's school folder. It was a definite match.

Watson nodded. "No problem," he replied.

* * *

PC Dyer had momentarily lost concentration and found himself staring at a group of young lads, larking about on their bikes some thirty metres down the road, when the radio sprang into life.

"We're on!" exclaimed Cooper's voice. "Horton's on the move."

"Do you want me to lead the way or will you?" enquired Dyer.

"You go first," replied Cooper. "Stay close to him. If he goes the same way as before, break off at the crossroads where you lost him last time and tell me which way he goes so I can take over. Make sure he sees you go another way, then double-back and follow on behind me, but stay out of sight of his rear-view mirror."

"Will do," remarked Dyer, who pulled out as soon as Horton's bright-red car flashed past him.

Cooper allowed two cars to get behind Dyer's car before he pulled out and joined the pursuit.

* * *

"Have you heard anything from the others?" Watson enquired, as he ploughed his way through the final cabinet.

Carmichael remained focused on the files they'd extracted but shook his head. "No," he replied, "which suggests that

Horton is still in the health spa and Rachel's not yet accosted our mystery Jiffy bag poster."

"Right," remarked Watson, who could see Carmichael was preoccupied with the files.

"I think I've made one breakthrough though," continued Carmichael, his attention still firmly on the folders in front of him.

"Really," replied Watson. "What's that?"

"I've been puzzled by the reason for changing the number plates on the Bentley," he said. "I went up to Wood Lane earlier and when I was there it suddenly came to me. The false plate has a meaning."

Watson stopped his ferreting in the cabinet and turned to face his boss.

Seeing that Watson was still perplexed, Carmichael smiled and pulled out a photograph of the number plate, one that was taken at the murder scene down Wood Lane on Wednesday.

Carmichael passed over the photo to Watson. "What do you see?" he asked his sergeant.

"I see WTR 1P," replied Watson.

Feeling suitably pleased that Watson still hadn't got it, Carmichael smiled again then shook his head.

"That's how it looks, but if you were to move the spacing, it could read WT R1P," suggested Carmichael. "William Taylor Rest in Peace."

Chapter 63

Horton's flash red car sped rapidly down the winding country roads in the same direction it had done earlier in the day. However, this time PC Dyer didn't give him any sort of gap, remaining about twenty metres behind his quarry.

Three cars back and moving significantly slower, Cooper had lost sight of Horton and Dyer.

"What's happening?" Cooper enquired over their radio link.

"He's just coming up to the crossroads now," replied PC Dyer. "He's not indicating so I'm not sure which way he's going."

"Keep talking, Dyer," replied Cooper, "I need to know which way he goes."

"Left, left!" exclaimed Dyer. "Horton's on the road to Hasselbury. I'm going to turn right."

"That's fine," replied Cooper. "I'll try and get behind him now."

PC Dyer's car turned right, followed by the cars that had separated him from Cooper's Volvo.

There was no sign of Horton when Cooper reached the crossroads but knowing where he was heading, Cooper turned left towards Hasselbury.

* * *

Rachel Dalton looked at her watch; it was 5:13pm.

For the first time since she'd taken up her position and kept her eyes keenly focused on the postbox, Rachel started to consider the possibility of the woman not showing. She'd certainly not presented herself so far. In fact, only three letters had been posted while she'd been there, all by different people, none of whom bore the slightest resemblance to the woman in the CCTV footage.

* * *

Cooper put his foot down hard on the accelerator and sped quickly down the road after Horton.

"I've lost sight of him," he remarked to Dyer. "He must be hammering it down here."

Horton grinned to himself. He knew he'd once again shaken off the Renault that had been tailing him for the second time that day. Feeling smug, he looked momentarily down at the radio to change channels.

* * *

It was precisely 5:15pm when Watson finished going through the final cabinet.

"That's the lot," he remarked. "So, we've just got those files in your pile."

Carmichael nodded. "I'm not really sure they tell us that much," he conceded. "They confirm that Horton and Attwood were tearaways, even as teenagers, but not much more than that."

"What about the others?" Watson enquired.

Carmichael shrugged his shoulders. "Billy Taylor, Jenny Heaton, James Hampton, Sajid Hanif and Geoffrey Brookwell all seem like good students. As Mrs Rumburgh did mention,

Geoffrey appears to have gone off the rails a little when he was about sixteen, but to be honest, there's nothing in any of them that jumps out at me as being helpful to us."

"What about the other file you took out?" enquired Watson, having seen his boss put a file with his papers.

"Oh, that's not relevant to the case at all," Carmichael replied.

* * *

There was already a grey Nissan parked between him and Tim Horton's steaming wreck of a car, when Cooper's Volvo turned the corner. Cooper was going so fast himself that he almost caused a second incident, however his trusty old car managed to come to a halt inches away from the parked vehicle.

A man in his mid-thirties was tugging hard at the driver's door of Horton's vehicle, but was clearly struggling to get it open.

"There's been an accident," Cooper barked down the radio at Dyer. "Get an ambulance and the fire brigade here. It looks like Horton may need cutting out."

Cooper didn't wait for a response, jumping out of his car and rushing over to where the crumpled red sports car had become embedded in the oncoming white transit van.

With smoke billowing from the bonnet of Horton's car, Cooper arrived beside the driver of the Nissan, who was heaving with all his might on the door handle.

"Bloody idiot," the man shouted, the strain of his efforts clearly evident from the protruding veins on his bulging neck. "I'm not surprised he's had a prang. He was doing at least fifty down these tiny lanes. Anyone would think he was in a bloody race."

"The services are on their way," announced Cooper, as he peered through the side window at the motionless figure of Horton slumped sideways over the passenger seat.

Chapter 64

At 5:37pm, when the postman arrived to transfer the letters from the rigid old red postbox into his sack, Rachel Dalton knew the young woman wasn't going to show.

"Damn," she muttered under her breath. "Carmichael's not going to be happy."

Before Rachel had a chance to think about her next move, her mobile rang; it was Carmichael.

"Evening, sir," she said.

"Did you apprehend the woman?" Carmichael enquired.

"No," replied Rachel. "She didn't show."

Rachel could hear Carmichael sucking in breath through his teeth, a sure sign he was annoyed.

"I've been here over an hour, sir," Rachel continued. "I didn't miss her, she just didn't show up."

Rachel could tell that Carmichael was in the car, the sound of the engine and rushing wind a clear giveaway.

"Look, there's been a development," announced Carmichael. "Horton's had a car accident while Cooper and PC Dyer were tailing him. I'd like you to get yourself over to Horton's house and tell his wife, then when you're done, get yourself over to the A & E department at Southport Royal. According to Cooper they're taking him over there in an ambulance. Marc and I need to see someone first, but we'll meet you and Cooper there later."

"Is Horton in a bad way?" Rachel enquired.

"I don't have all the details," replied Carmichael vaguely, "but Cooper reckons he's still unconscious and it looks pretty serious."

"OK, sir" said Rachel. "Do we have Horton's address?"

"No," replied Carmichael. "You're a detective, you'll need to detect it yourself. I'm sure if you phone either the health spa or get the station to check records, you should get it pretty easily."

"No worries," replied Rachel, who in truth didn't need to be told how to find an address, she was simply trying to verify whether that information was already known to Carmichael and maybe save herself some time.

* * *

As soon as they'd received the call from Cooper about Horton's accident, Carmichael and Watson made a quiet exit from the academy, taking the files with them. Carmichael didn't bother telling Mr Wisset they were leaving as he didn't think there was anything more to discuss with the mournful headmaster.

Telling Watson to leave his car in the school car park, the two officers made their way together to 66, Thornbush Grove to pay another visit to Sajid Hanif's grieving widow.

* * *

Cooper had been amazed at just how quickly first the paramedics, then the fire brigade had arrived at the scene; and within the space of half an hour, Tim Horton was on his way to Southport Royal, a journey of just over twenty minutes.

Having already called Carmichael to let him know what was happening, Cooper left PC Dyer at the scene to take statements and was following close behind the ambulance, its blue lights flashing and siren screeching as it sped down the twisting, narrow country lanes.

* * *

"Why do you want to talk to Sajid's widow again?" Watson enquired as they made their way towards Moulton Bank.

"I want to know if Sajid ever talked about that day at the canal, when he found Billy Taylor's body," replied Carmichael. "I'm thinking that maybe there was more he knew than he told your dad and his colleagues at the time."

"Wouldn't his mother and sister be more likely to be able to help us more with that?" remarked Watson. "After all, this all happened years before Sajid married Sonja."

Carmichael took a few seconds to consider his sergeant's question.

"You may be right," he replied, "but if Sajid did know more than he told the police at the time, I'd wager he is more likely to have unburdened himself of the details to his wife, years later, than to his sister and parents."

Watson wasn't so sure but accepted his boss's logic as at least possible, so said nothing more.

"Why don't you occupy yourself with those files while we're driving?" suggested Carmichael. "See if there's anything in there that leaps out at you as being relevant to the case."

Watson stretched his right arm back through the gap between the seats and grabbed the pile of green folders that Carmichael had left on the back seat. Placing the seven files on his lap, he opened the first, the one marked S A Attwood in faded blue ink, and started to read.

* * *

Tim Horton's beautiful mansion was located no more than five miles from the postbox where Rachel had been lying in wait, in vain, to apprehend the mystery young woman.

After her call ended with Carmichael, she remembered that her parents had once been to a lavish dinner party there, so a quick call to her mum enabled Rachel to discover the address.

As soon as she arrived Rachel got the impression that nobody was at home, there being no cars in the wide gravelled driveway and all the windows to the house being shut tight. She rang the doorbell twice, with no answer. She peered through the windows at the front of the house; all looked quiet and still inside. After a few seconds, she went around the back. It was then that she spied a figure in the middle of the rear lawn, raking up grass cuttings.

Rachel walked over to the man, an elderly gentleman who looked like he was in his late sixties or seventies.

"Hello," she said in a friendly manner. "Is anyone at home here?"

The old man looked guarded.

"Who's asking?" he enquired in a thick Lancashire accent.

Rachel held out her identity card. "I'm with the police," she replied.

After carefully studying the card the old man became more cooperative.

"They're at their villa in Spain," he replied, "flew out this morning; well Mrs Horton did and Hayley. I think Mr Horton's going over early next week. He'll probably be at the health spa."

Rachel smiled. "Right," she said. "Do you happen to have Mrs Horton's mobile number?"

The old man wrinkled his forehead and shrugged his shoulders.

"What would I be wanting that for?" he replied rather

obtusely. "I cut the grass and weed the lawns two days a week. I'm not a friend of theirs."

Rachel smiled again. "Of course," she replied, before striding away.

* * *

"Find anything?" Carmichael enquired as his black BMW arrived at Sajid Hanif's house.

"Not really," replied Watson. "The only thing that's a bit surprising is that all the folders have a photograph attached; in fact all the ones I looked at, as far as I can recall, had photographs."

"What's so surprising about that?" remarked Carmichael, who appeared mystified by what Watson had said.

"Well James Hampton's doesn't," he continued.

Amazed he hadn't spotted that himself, Carmichael took the folder for James Hampton out of Watson's hand and opened it up.

"You're right," Carmichael remarked.

"Maybe there wasn't ever one there, but it does seem strange," continued Watson.

Carmichael looked carefully at the first page.

"No, there has been one here," he replied. "You can see clearly in the way that rectangle hasn't aged as much in the top right-hand corner."

Carmichael showed Watson the page again.

"I think the photo has been removed," Carmichael said. "But why would Mrs Rumburgh do that?"

"I don't know," replied Watson. "Maybe she didn't. Maybe it's just fallen off somewhere, either in the cabinet or we've dropped it when we dashed out."

Carmichael nodded but looked unconvinced. "Maybe," he replied.

Chapter 65

Rachel was a touch surprised when she realised she'd arrived at Southport Hospital A & E department before Cooper and the ambulance carrying Tim Horton.

After having made sure they'd not already been admitted to one of the wards, Rachel bought herself a cold can of diet Pepsi from the vending machine and, finding a vacant chair in the waiting room, took out her mobile to check her messages.

She smiled broadly as she saw the latest text from her boyfriend, Matt, who'd been away all week in Leicester on some forensic course at the university.

Rachel was happy that he appeared to be having a good time, but even more pleased on his insistence that he was missing her badly.

She took a small sip of the Pepsi before starting to compose her reply to Matt, her fingers working at lightning speed.

She'd just pressed send, when the doors flew open and in came the ambulance driver and a paramedic pushing Horton, who was laid motionless on a trolley.

Although Rachel couldn't see his face, she knew it was Horton as just two paces behind them was Cooper, his face whitish, and clearly out of breath.

"What happened?" Rachel enquired.

"He was driving way too fast down the lanes up near

Hasselbury," replied Cooper, "hit a white van doing around fifty. To be honest, he's lucky to be alive."

* * *

Sonja Hanif looked as though she hadn't slept since receiving the news about her husband. She cut a forlorn figure as she sat alone in the centre of the sofa, her head bowed slightly, her thoughts clearly miles away.

"I'm sorry to trouble you again, Mrs Hanif," said Carmichael, a wealth of sympathy in his voice, "but we were wondering if Sajid ever talked to you about something that happened when he was a schoolboy."

Sonja lifted her head slightly and stared directly at Carmichael, her dark hazel eyes gazing out from an otherwise soulless face.

"Do you mean his friend drowning?" replied Sonja.

"Yes," replied Carmichael. "Billy Taylor."

Sonja's head dropped a few degrees and her gaze once again moved south to somewhere close to Carmichael's shoes.

"Sajid rarely spoke about what happened," Sonja said, "but it has always troubled him. And, lately, he was having bad nightmares about what he saw that day. He'd wake up suddenly, sweating and trembling. I told him to get some help about the bad dreams, but Sajid never did."

"What did he tell you about that day?" Carmichael asked.

Sonja shrugged her shoulders. "That they were being chased, that they split up. That he hid in the long grass and that he'd heard a loud splash, and his friend crying out for help, but that he was too scared to come out from where he was hiding until it was too late."

"But it was an accident?" Watson enquired.

"Yes," replied Sonja. "Sajid said that Billy must have just slipped, as the splash he heard happened before the boys that were chasing them arrived. But he has always felt guilty about it."

"Why?" Carmichael enquired.

"Because he was too scared to help when his friend needed him," replied Sonja. "But mainly I think, because he didn't tell the police about everything that happened that afternoon."

"What didn't he tell them?" Carmichael asked.

Sonja's dark piercing eyes again made contact with Carmichael's.

"That they were being chased by those monsters, who'd made their lives a misery," replied Sonja. "He hated himself for agreeing to stay silent."

Carmichael paused for a few seconds.

"So, why didn't he tell the police everything?" he enquired.

"Because he was told not to by his stupid, controlling parents," replied Sonja, her voice trembling with anger as she spoke. "You'll have to ask that mother of his why, as only she can say what was in her head that day, and what possessed her to make her boy carry so much guilt and hurt for so long."

As she spoke Sonja's eyes filled with tears which she allowed to cascade down her cheeks, making no attempt to stem the flow.

* * *

Stable but still unconscious, Tim Horton was admitted to Knowles ward an hour after arriving at the hospital, where he was given his own private room.

"What we do know is that he's fractured his right arm and right leg quite badly," the young junior doctor informed Cooper and Rachel Dalton after the hospital staff had finished their exhaustive examinations. "He's also broken a few ribs. What we can't be sure of is the extent of damage there is to his brain. The results of his MRI scan are being

268

analysed by the senior consultant now. He'll decide whether we need to operate."

"Do you think it's serious?" Cooper enquired.

The doctor shrugged his shoulders.

"The brain is badly swollen, but that may not mean that we need to operate," replied the doctor. "I'd not want to speculate as I'm not qualified to answer that question. It's something the senior consultant will need to determine. The good news is that he appears stable so hopefully for Mr Horton the prognosis will be positive."

The doctor then departed leaving Cooper and Rachel alone with Tim Horton.

"What now?" Rachel enquired.

"I guess one of us stays here while the other heads back to the station to try and get in touch with Mrs Horton."

Rachel nodded. "Do you want me to do that?"

Cooper smiled. "Yes please, Rachel," he replied. "And while I'm here I'll update Carmichael."

* * *

Carmichael and Watson had left Sonja Hanif's house and were already sitting in Sajid Hanif's mother's lounge when the call came through from Cooper.

"I'm sorry," remarked Carmichael who, seeing who was calling, quickly pressed the receive button and put the mobile to his ear.

"Is it important, Paul?" he said abruptly, followed swiftly by, "I'll call you in about twenty minutes," which indicated to the three other people in the room that the reply he'd received had been, "No."

"Apologies again," remarked Carmichael, with a faint smile as he placed the mobile back in his jacket pocket. "As I was saying, we'd like to find out from you why Sajid didn't

269

tell the police the full story about what happened to Billy Taylor."

"You don't have to answer if you don't want to, Mum," remarked Nora, her tone as abrupt and aggressive as it had been when Watson first visited the house.

Mrs Hanif put her hand on her daughter's leg, as if to indicate that she didn't want her to continue speaking.

"It's about time we told the full story," she remarked. "There's nothing to be gained now by hiding what really happened that afternoon."

Chapter 66

Rachel Dalton was just about to leave the hospital when she spotted a young woman who looked familiar.

Aged in her early thirties, the slim, attractive woman, with long hair tied back in a ponytail, rushed through the doors, forcing Rachel to step back.

Rachel remained motionless for the next few seconds as she watched the woman rush down the corridor, struggling to remember where she'd seen her before.

Once the woman had disappeared and with no luck in recalling who she was or where she'd seen her, Rachel turned, made her exit from the hospital and headed towards her parked car.

* * *

Carmichael and Watson spent no more than fifteen minutes with Sajid Hanif's mother, which was all that was required for the pair to learn exactly what had happened on the day Billy Taylor had drowned.

"So, what did you make of her story?" Watson enquired, as the two men sat together in Carmichael's stationary car outside Mrs Hanif's house.

Carmichael shrugged his shoulders.

"I believe what she told us is true," he replied. "And I

suppose part of me can empathise with their reasoning for staying silent, but they certainly made the wrong choice all those years ago; and you could see she realises that now, too."

Watson nodded. "So, do you think Horton and Attwood are in this together or do you think it's just one of them acting alone?"

Carmichael glanced across at his colleague.

"I'm not sure what we should be thinking," he replied. "But I don't think what we've just learned necessarily implicates either of them."

Watson's brow furrowed as he listened to his boss. He didn't agree but elected not to argue.

* * *

Sitting outside Horton's room, Cooper noticed the slim young woman, who had earlier caught Rachel's attention, walking briskly down the long corridor about thirty yards away. The anxious expression on her pale face immediately suggested to him that here was a distraught friend or relative who had come to visit someone. She carried no flowers, magazines, books or chocolates, so Cooper assumed her visit was, most likely, speedily arranged; an assumption supported by the fact that she didn't appear to know the precise location of the person she was visiting, looking frantically from side to side as she went along.

She stopped about fifteen yards away from Cooper and spoke to one of the nurses, who turned and pointed, firstly at Horton's room then at Cooper.

Assuming the woman was Horton's first visitor, Cooper stood up and walked slowly towards her.

A look of fear came across the woman's face as she saw Cooper approaching, an expression which remained as Cooper got closer.

Cooper was no more than five or six yards away when, suddenly, the woman turned and hightailed it down the corridor, at a pace so fast Cooper didn't even consider pursuing. The woman was clearly in great shape and he knew without trying that she would easily outrun him. He did, however, continue down the corridor to where the nurse was standing.

"I think I scared her off!" Cooper remarked, as he arrived beside the nurse. "Did she say who she was and what she wanted?"

The nurse smiled, "You certainly did. She was asking where Mr Horton's room was, and it was when I mentioned to her that you were the police that she took off."

"Did she say who she was?" Cooper enquired again.

The nurse shook her head. "She didn't say, but she didn't have to. She's Miss Templeton, one of the PE teachers at the academy. My daughters both go there."

"Really," replied Cooper, who continued to look down the corridor, even though Miss Templeton had long since disappeared.

Chapter 67

It was 7:15pm, and with his three trusted officers sitting opposite him in their office at Kirkwood police station, Carmichael started the debrief.

"I know it's been another long day," he announced, "but it's important everyone's up to speed before we go home. The good news is, I think we're starting to make some sense of this case; the bad news, however, is that if you had any plans for the weekend, they've all been cancelled. I need all four of us totally focused on getting these murders solved and apprehending whoever it is that's behind them."

As he spoke, Carmichael's eye line moved between his three officers, none of whom looked particularly pleased with the news that another of their weekends was to be taken from them, but none of them seemed surprised either, or dared to complain.

"What's the position on Horton?" Carmichael asked Cooper.

"He's stable, but still unconscious. So, it's still looking quite serious," Cooper replied. "I've made sure there's a uniformed officer outside his room twenty-four-seven, to be on hand if he does come around, but the doctors aren't sure what state he'll be in, even if he does. He's in a bad way."

"Do you think he's connected with the murders, sir?" Rachel enquired of their boss.

Carmichael shrugged his shoulders. "I've no idea," he replied.

"He must be," interjected Watson. "I can't think why he'd drive so recklessly down those narrow lanes unless he was trying to shake off his tail. He's got to be involved. Maybe he's not our killer, but if not, he's got to be hiding Attwood somewhere."

Despite Watson's view not being a million miles away from his own, Carmichael didn't want the team to get too fixated on just one scenario.

"You may be right, Marc," he said calmly, "but we're a fair way off being able to substantiate either of those theories."

"And what about Sonja's and Mrs Hanif Senior's confessions to us earlier today?" remarked Watson. "Surely that points the finger firmly at either Sean Attwood or Tim Horton."

On hearing Watson's assertion, Cooper and Dalton both turned to face Carmichael, each one eager to hear what it was that Sonja and Sajid Hanif's mother had told them.

Carmichael folded his arms.

"What they told us was very interesting and could well be significant," he conceded, "but in no way does it prove that either Sean Attwood or Tim Horton is our murderer."

"What did they tell you?" Rachel asked, her face clearly showing her appetite to learn what was said.

Carmichael looked back at his young colleague, his eyes fixed deeply into hers.

"They both told us basically the same story, that although Sajid had told the truth about most of what happened that afternoon, he'd not been totally honest and held back important information."

"So, what had he withheld from the police?" enquired the eager DC.

"According to them," continued Carmichael, "and I do believe what they told us is true, Horton, Attwood and, to a lesser extent, Brookwell had all been, in Mrs Hanif Seniors words, harassing young Sajid for some time. He was the only Asian boy at school, and because of that and with him being younger, quiet and quite shy, these older boys had been making his life a misery for months."

"Basically, they were bullies," remarked Watson, as if he needed to be more direct in describing what had gone on.

Carmichael nodded before continuing. "According to Sajid's mother, they'd also either turned the other children at school against him or made it clear to them that by associating with him they'd get similar treatment. They'd been so successful that poor Sajid had only a handful of friends and was terrified of going to school."

"Didn't his parents talk to the teachers about this?" Rachel enquired.

Carmichael nodded. "Mrs Hanif said they did, but they didn't get much support. They were just told by the head at the time that he'd keep an eye out for anything amiss. However, neither Mr nor Mrs Hanif felt that they did much to stop the victimisation Sajid was suffering."

"That's awful," remarked Rachel.

"You're right, Rachel," interjected Cooper, "but sadly, twenty or thirty years ago, many teachers weren't that clued up on the amount of bullying that went on in schools and how crippling such behaviour can be for a child."

His three colleagues all took a sideways glace in Cooper's direction, all thinking the same thing; namely that by the way he was talking, Cooper may well have, in his childhood, had first-hand experience of the sort of treatment Sajid Hanif had been receiving.

"Well, that wouldn't happen today," announced Rachel. "Schools are much more aware and take bullying far more seriously."

Carmichael nodded. "They certainly do at the academy," he remarked, "neither poor Mrs Rumburgh nor, from what I understand, Mr Wisset tolerate that sort of behaviour. Thank goodness."

"So, what exactly happened that afternoon?" Rachel enquired.

Carmichael unfolded his arms.

"According to Mrs Hanif, Sajid had been getting a fair amount of abuse that day at school at the hands of Attwood and Horton in particular. When it got to the end of the lunch break there was a lot of pushing and shoving going on, and Horton and Attwood managed to get Sajid on the ground where they were kicking him. It was then that Billy Taylor stepped in. Although he was the same age as Sajid, he was a bigger boy, played rugby and was much more robust. According to Mrs Hanif, he punched Attwood to the ground and the pair walked off…"

"But threatened to sort them out after school," interrupted Watson.

"Yes," continued Carmichael, "which Billy and Sajid believed they fully meant to do. So, when the bell went at three thirty Sajid and Billy made a hasty exit and ran down the footpath towards the canal; a long way home but a route they thought would give them the best chance of not being apprehended by pursuing thugs."

"But I guess they were wrong," remarked Rachel.

Carmichael nodded.

"They were, Rachel," he said. "Horton, Attwood and Brookwell chased after them and, according to Mrs Hanif, they were about twenty yards away from catching them when the boys split up; Sajid ran into some long grass where he lay low, while Billy continued to run on to the canal."

"So, did Attwood, Horton and Brookwell push Billy Taylor into the canal?" Rachel enquired.

277

"No," interjected Watson. "It does appear to have been an accident, but from what Sajid told Mrs Hanif and her husband, their three pursuers did very little to help Billy out of the canal."

"Certainly, that's true, initially," continued Carmichael. "But when Sajid heard the commotion of Billy thrashing about in the water and came out of his hiding place, it does sound like at least one of the older boys realised something needed to be done. According to Mrs Hanif, it was Brookwell and Sajid that went into the water to get Billy out."

"And what did the other two do?" Cooper asked.

Carmichael shook his head. "Nothing, by all accounts."

"And he was dead when they got him out then, presumably," remarked Rachel.

Carmichael nodded. "They tried mouth-to-mouth, but yes, he died."

"So why on earth didn't Sajid tell the whole story at the time?" Rachel enquired with incredulity.

"At first because Horton and Attwood threatened him that he'd get the same if he did," replied Carmichael. "Then, when he did tell his parents, they foolishly told him to remain silent, too."

"Why on earth did they do that?" Rachel asked, her voice shrill with fury.

Carmichael gently shook his head. "Because they were scared about how the village would react to them if they informed on the boys to the police. You have to remember this was over twenty years ago, the Hanifs were the only Asian family in the village and were trying hard to establish their small general store. In their eyes, the last thing they needed was to antagonise the village by accusing three white boys, born and bred in the village, of causing another boy's death. So, Mr Hanif made his wife and son promise never to divulge what really happened, which they stuck to until today."

"So, everyone including the police thought it was just an accident," remarked Cooper.

Carmichael nodded. "Which it was, of course," he said, "but driven by the bullying of Sajid and his close friends by Attwood, Horton and Brookwell."

The room fell silent for a few seconds as they all quietly took in the details of what had really happened all those years ago and the potential significance of the decision the Hanifs had made back then.

Chapter 68

Penny Carmichael was having a trying evening.

When Natalie had got home from school her mood was subdued to say the least. The death of Mrs Rumburgh was weighing heavily on her mind

"I know I'm being selfish," she'd eventually said to her mother, "but who's going to stop Jade Attwood and those other girls now?"

Despite all her efforts to reassure her, Penny felt as though she was losing the battle. She would have greatly appreciated her husband being there to assist in persuading Natalie that the bullying she'd been subjected to was over, in spite of the awful news about Mrs Rumburgh's death. But he wasn't, and her daughter remained quiet and continued to look as if her world was still in turmoil.

* * *

"I may be being a little dim here," remarked Cooper, "but what bearing does the death of Billy Taylor, and the fact that Attwood, Horton and Brookwell were partly to blame, have on our murders? Surely, Brookwell being one of the victims suggests that Horton and Attwood are innocent rather than pointing to one of them being the murderer."

"Not if, for some reason, Brookwell had decided to tell

the whole story," remarked Carmichael. "If that was the case, then you could argue it would make Horton or Attwood want to silence him."

"And Mrs Rumburgh and Sajid Hanif?" enquired Cooper. "How would their deaths fit in?"

"I'm not sure," Carmichael replied.

"Maybe Sajid had met up with Brookwell and between them they were going to tell the whole story," suggested Rachel. "And maybe Mrs Rumburgh twigged who was behind this and was killed because she knew who the killer was."

"That's possible," replied Cooper, "but it's a massive assumption to make."

Rachel couldn't help but agree. Even as she was speaking, she was also starting to challenge the plausibility of what she was saying.

"The fact that she'd been looking at some of her old pupil files the last time she was in her office and coincidently the files she'd been looking at were for Tim Horton, Sajid Hanif, and James Hampton," added Watson as he placed the pile of files they'd taken from the office onto the desk in front of his colleagues, " has got to suggest she was looking into something from the past involving those boys."

"How do you know she was looking at these files?" Rachel enquired. "And what has James Hampton got to do with it? He wasn't at the canal when Billy Taylor died, was he?"

"Good questions, Rachel," replied Carmichael. "We're pretty sure that she, or someone in her office, was looking at those files as they'd been put back out of order. We know this as her pupil files are all meticulously stored in alphabetical order and those three were the only ones out of place. Also, there had been a fragment torn off the bottom of Tim Horton's file which I'd found earlier on her desk in the office. So, I think it's safe to say that someone had taken those three files out recently."

"But you've seven files here," observed Cooper, flicking through the files that Watson had placed in front of him. "S A Attwood, G P Brookwell, J S Hampton, S Hanif, J A Heaton, T Horton and W Taylor."

"The others we extracted as we felt they may have some relevance to the case," replied Watson.

"And do they?" asked Cooper.

"Well, apart from James Hampton's being without a photo attached, we've not found anything particularly interesting, to be honest," replied Carmichael.

"Who is J A Heaton?" Rachel enquired.

"It's Jenny Attwood," replied Watson, "her maiden name was Heaton, remember?"

Cooper and Dalton both looked quickly at the contents of the seven files.

"So, are we saying that Mrs Rumburgh was killed by one of these people?" Rachel asked.

"Not necessarily," replied Carmichael. "Other than Horton, Hanif and Hampton, we're not totally sure which files she took out, but I think it is possible that our killer is one of the people from these files."

"And if it's not," continued Rachel, "then the killer surely has to be someone who works at the school."

Carmichael nodded. "That's also possible," he replied.

"What we really need," remarked Rachel, "is a link between someone in the files and someone currently at the school."

"But we don't have one," replied Watson.

"Actually, that's not totally correct," interjected Cooper. "I was going to tell you later, but when I was outside Horton's room earlier today, he had a visitor. She did a runner when she knew I was a police officer, but the nurse on the ward said she knew her. Her name's Miss Templeton; she's a teacher at the academy and she seemed very concerned about Tim Horton's condition."

Rachel nodded vigorously. "I saw her, too," she remarked. "I couldn't place her at first, when I saw her at the hospital, but she was with Miss Turner in the staffroom when I went to talk with her about Geoffrey Brookwell."

Carmichael raised one eyebrow. "That may well be our link," he remarked. "I think one of us needs to have a talk with Miss Templeton in the morning, don't you?"

Chapter 69

It was 9:25pm by the time Carmichael arrived home.

With the briefing concluded and the team having left the station with clear instructions about their tasks for the next day, Carmichael was looking forward to his dinner and a couple of glasses of wine.

"How's your day been?" he asked Penny, as he joined her on the sofa in the lounge.

"So, so," she replied, which Carmichael took to really mean pretty awful.

He put his arm around his wife's shoulders. "How's the team?" he enquired.

"Robbie's fine, I think," replied Penny, "he's got another new girlfriend and they're out at the cinema. Jemma and Chris are at the Railway Tavern; they had their tea here, then went over to meet some of their friends."

"And Natalie?" Carmichael enquired.

"She's in her room," replied Penny. "She's very upset about Mrs Rumburgh and is anxious about being bullied again by those horrible girls now that Mrs Rumburgh's not about."

"Understandable, I guess, but she's nothing to worry about," Carmichael remarked. "Jade Attwood's suspended and even with Mrs Rumburgh not around, I can't see Mr Wisset being anything but robust regarding any form of intimidation. Besides, young Jade and her family have more on their minds, I suspect, than terrorising other people."

Penny turned her head to face her husband. "So, how's the case going?" she enquired.

Carmichael shrugged his shoulders. "It's very confusing, to be honest," he replied. "We've got three murders in under four days, certainly all connected. We believe the death of a young boy over twenty years ago is linked to them all as well. We've got two main suspects, Sean Attwood and Tim Horton, but Attwood has disappeared and Horton was involved in a car crash earlier. He's still out cold and may not recover."

Penny continued to look at her husband, but her lips remained tightly shut.

"Then there's the academy itself," continued Carmichael. "I'm starting to think that someone there could be involved."

"Why's that?" enquired Penny.

"I'm not sure exactly," he replied with a mixture of tiredness and exasperation. "I can't bring myself to believe it's a coincidence that all three of our murder victims and our two main suspects went to that school."

"I went there, too," pointed out Penny with a wry smile. "I hope I'm not a suspect."

Carmichael smiled and pulled his wife close to him. "Absolutely you are," he remarked, before planting a kiss on her lips.

"So, I guess you'll be working this weekend," Penny pronounced, in the vain hope he'd say he wasn't.

Carmichael nodded. "I'm afraid so," he replied. "The team have their tasks sorted for the morning and we've another debrief at five tomorrow evening."

"I bet they were chuffed," remarked Penny sarcastically.

Carmichael smiled. "That's what they get paid for," he replied.

"So, what have you assigned them to do tomorrow then?" Penny asked.

"I've asked Cooper to have a rummage through Horton's house and his office at the spa," replied Carmichael, "I want to find out whether there's anything there that can help us."

"Can you do that," enquired Penny, "as I assume you've not charged him with anything?"

Carmichael stood up and walked over to a previously opened bottle of his favourite red wine standing enticingly on the cabinet.

"We're simply looking for an address or phone number for his wife in Spain," he replied with a wry smile, before pouring himself a large glass of the deep red liquid. "That's enough reason."

Penny shook her head. "What about the others?" she enquired.

"I've asked Watson to work with Rachel to try and track down someone from the drowned boy's family to see if they know anything that might help us, but his prime task is to locate and interview a teacher at the school called Miss Templeton," replied Carmichael. "She went to the hospital in a distressed state to see Horton this evening but then did a runner when she saw Cooper outside his door."

"Oh, I know her," Penny remarked. "She takes Natalie for games. She's really nice. I think she once played hockey for England, or maybe it was just the county."

"Well, I think she may be playing with Tim Horton, too," replied Carmichael, facetiously.

"And what about Rachel?" Penny asked. "What task has she been given?"

"She's got three areas of focus tomorrow," replied Carmichael. "To work with Watson to find someone from Billy Taylor's family, to find James Hampton, who also went to the academy, is Mrs Rumburgh's nephew and the estranged son of Mavis Heaton and, her main priority, to find this young person."

As he spoke, Carmichael took out the photo of the woman who'd been captured on CCTV posting the Jiffy bags to Geoffrey Brookwell and Sajid Hanif.

Penny grabbed hold of the photo and looked closely at it.

"Well, you tell Rachel she's just got two tasks now," announced Penny, "because I know who she is."

Chapter 70

Saturday 4th July

Jackson's Farm was located at the far end of Wood Lane, over a mile away from the last other inhabited dwelling on that long, narrow cul-de-sac.

Other than old Ben Jackson and his son, Wayne, no one else ever really used the bumpy dirt track that led the last three quarters of a mile, the occasional rambler, who took the wrong turning, being the only exception. Even less frequented was the ramshackle barn old Ben's father had last used thirty years earlier.

Located just off the lane about three hundred yards from Jackson's Farm, down a heavily overgrown track and almost totally obscured by bushes and foliage-rich trees, the dilapidated wooden structure was hidden from view.

It was the sight of the disturbed look of the grass and brambles leading down to the barn that caused Wayne Jackson to check it out. Maybe there would be another romantic couple in there, he'd thought, a sight he'd come across on more than one occasion over the last few years.

Carefully he tiptoed down the track, trying hard to keep his movements quiet so as not to alert any unsuspecting occupants, particularly if they were midway through their amorous activities.

As he reached the ancient gnarled and rotted door, Wayne Jackson could see that, unlike any of the times he'd been there before, the rusting brown chain, with its lock that had long since seized up, had been cut and was lying abandoned on the floor.

No loving couple would have done that, he thought, his mind now starting to race as he tried to imagine who had entered the derelict barn. Suddenly he became more preoccupied with his own safety than the infantile thrill of a quick flash of pink flesh in the throes of lovemaking.

He gently pulled the door open a few inches and gingerly peered inside.

* * *

Penny had identified the young woman in the CCTV footage as being Tim Horton's daughter, Hayley, a school friend of their eldest daughter, Jemma. So, before turning in that night, Carmichael had called all three of his team to give them the news. Without exception they were all in agreement that their prime suspect now had to be the man lying unconscious in Southport Hospital.

Although the main assignments Carmichael had set the team hadn't changed as a result of this breakthrough, Cooper's job to find Mrs Horton and her daughter in Spain was now even more critical, a point that Carmichael had made crystal-clear to him. Cooper had been given strict instructions to get them both back to the UK as soon as they'd been located, but not to mention to them anything about the CCTV footage.

Buoyed by the positive identification provided by his wife, Carmichael was in a cheerful mood when he awoke that morning, a disposition that was shattered completely when he received the call informing him that another body had been found in Wood Lane.

By the time he arrived at the old dilapidated barn, Dr Stock and his army of SOCOs, clad in their white overalls, were already in situ; a team which included Matt Stock, the chief pathologist's nephew and the main person in Rachel Dalton's life for the past seven or eight months.

"This one's a really messy one, Carmichael," remarked Stock, who was at the entrance to the barn when Carmichael arrived. "According to the credit cards in his wallet, he's a man called Sean Attwood," announced the seasoned head of the forensic team.

Carmichael peered over at the body, some ten metres away. With his legs, arms and torso all looking unblemished by the violent event which appeared to have taken away his life, Sean Attwood was slumped against the barn wall.

"Do you think it was suicide?" he enquired of the pathologist.

"That would be my guess," replied Stock, "and there was this note in his left hand, which would support that theory."

As he spoke, Stock handed Carmichael a clear plastic bag through which he could see the blood-spattered scrap of notepaper with just one word on it, handwritten in blue ink:

SORRY

Carmichael handed the note back to the pathologist and, with a degree of trepidation about what he was going to have to stomach, started walking gingerly towards where the body lay.

* * *

Having recalled that Mr Wisset had told him he'd be in his office on Saturday morning when they'd last met, Carmichael had suggested to Watson that he either call the headmaster at school or pop over in person, in order to get Miss Templeton's address and contact details.

With the academy being no more than five minutes away from his house by car, Watson had decided on the latter.

It being Saturday, the school seemed noiseless and as he wandered down the corridor, Watson thought it quite eerie. There were children around, mostly boys in their cricket whites, presumably about to start a game; however, in comparison to a weekday, the place seemed unnaturally silent.

Mr Wisset was where Carmichael said he'd find him, in his office.

After knocking loudly and being commanded to enter by the booming voice from within, Watson went inside.

Wisset seemed surprised when he saw it was Watson but quickly regathered his composure.

"Good morning, Sergeant," he remarked. "How can I help you?"

Watson smiled and took a few paces forward, so he was within a metre of the headmaster's desk.

"I'd like to ask you a few questions about one of your members of staff," he replied.

"Oh," remarked Wisset, whose facial expression suggested he may be reluctant to impart much in the way of information unless he was given a reason for doing so. "Which member of my staff are you talking about?"

"Miss Templeton," replied Watson. "Your PE mistress."

"Lauren," responded Wisset, with incredulity in his voice. "What do you want to know about her for?"

"Just background information to our investigations," replied Watson, with deliberate evasiveness.

"Surely you don't think she's involved in your murders," remarked Wisset.

291

Watson smiled. "We'd just like to ask her a few questions, that's all. Are you able to give me her address and telephone number, so I can make contact with her?"

Wisset, his face still suggesting he was bewildered by the police being interested in his PE mistress, slowly leaned back in his chair and ran his hands through his hair.

"If you want to speak with Lauren, you'll find her on the playing field behind the school," he announced. "Her sixth form girls are playing tennis against St Mary's School from Blackpool this morning."

Watson nodded. "That's excellent. I'll go and find her."

Watson smiled before turning to walk away. However, as he reached the door he turned back.

"Is Miss Templeton in a relationship to your knowledge?" he enquired.

Mr Wisset shrugged his shoulders and gently shook his head.

"I've no idea," he replied. "She's not married, but she may well have a boyfriend. Why do you ask?"

"It's just something we need clarifying," remarked Watson cagily.

Mr Wisset suddenly looked a little unnerved by Watson's reply.

"Are you talking about Tim Horton by any chance?" he enquired.

Watson's eyebrows raised a few millimetres.

"Why did you mention him?" Watson asked.

"Well, she did have a brief fling with him, but I think that's now over," replied Mr Wisset.

"And how do you know that?" Watson enquired.

"Because Mrs Horton came here to confront poor Lauren about it," replied Mr Wisset. "Mrs Rumburgh got involved, but my understanding was that the affair was then ended by Miss Templeton."

"And when exactly was that?" Watson enquired.

Mr Wisset took a few seconds before he answered. "About three months ago," he replied.

Watson nodded. "Thank you, Mr Wisset," he remarked before turning and heading out of the office.

Still looking perplexed, Mr Wisset waited until Watson had closed the door behind him before he picked up his mobile and started to text.

Lauren, a policeman has just left my office and is on his way to talk to you. I thought you'd stopped seeing Horton. What's going on? Nigel

Chapter 71

Carmichael's qualms about viewing the body and the possible effect it would have on him were well founded. It was certainly a grisly sight. With little left of Sean Attwood's head, which was now largely splattered all up the barn wall behind the body, it was as bad a scene as Carmichael had witnessed in years.

"How long has he been dead?" Carmichael enquired, diverting his eyes away from the corpse to look Stock full in the face.

Stock took a sharp intake of breath. "I'd say between twelve and twenty-four hours," he replied. "But I'll need to get him back to the lab before I can be certain."

As Stock was speaking, Carmichael's attention was drawn to the shotgun by the side of the dead man. He recognised it immediately. It was the one in Mrs Rumburgh's photograph.

"Be careful with the gun," Carmichael ordered. "Check it thoroughly for prints. And, of course, we need to see if any of the fibres you found under Sajid Hanif's fingernails are a match with the dead man's clothes."

The sides of Dr Stock's mouth turned downwards and the sound of him taking in breath was clearly audible.

"My team are always thorough," he snapped back at Carmichael, "and this incident will be no exception."

With a look of disdain, Stock left Carmichael's side and returned to Sean Attwood's lifeless torso.

Unmoved by Stock's petulant outburst, Carmichael turned to survey the rest of the crime scene inside the barn.

Apart from Attwood's pickup, which had been driven into the barn and lay silent with its driver's door still open, little else appeared to be there which would help him understand the violent act that had recently happened.

* * *

When Cooper arrived at Horton's Health Spa, none of the staff had any idea he'd been involved in a car accident and was critically ill in hospital. However, within five minutes of him telling Lynn, Horton's ultra-efficient PA, word had spread throughout the building like wildfire.

He'd spent less than ten minutes alone in Horton's office when a sheepish-looking Lynn knocked gently on the door, then entered.

"Sorry to disturb you," she said apprehensively, "but there's something I feel I need to tell you."

Cooper smiled. "Oh yes," he replied, "and what is that?"

"Well, it might not be anything," Lynn said, "but yesterday there was a very aggressive lady here who insisted she saw Mr Horton."

"Who was that?" Cooper enquired.

"She said her name was Jenny Attwood," replied Lynn. "And the reason I brought it up is because she maintained Mr Horton is her daughter's father."

The look of amazement on Cooper's face was so apparent to Lynn that she felt compelled to elaborate.

"I'm not sure how true that is, as Mr Horton's married and has a daughter," commented the PA. "He was adamant that the woman was lying, and she later did say that she meant

295

Godfather, but it did seem to upset him. I'm thinking maybe he was driving fast last night because he was angry with that woman."

Cooper nodded. "Maybe," he replied. "Did you hear what they talked about?"

Lynn shook her head. "No," she replied, "after she went in, I left them. And when she left, Mr Horton remained in his office for a while then went off; I presumed to go home."

"By the way you're talking I'm starting to assume there's something else on your mind," remarked Cooper.

"Well," replied Lynn, "you said the accident was on the Hasselbury Road. From here, that's in the opposite direction to where Mr Horton lives."

* * *

Lauren Templeton was tall, tanned and athletic-looking, three traits which appealed greatly to Watson.

When Watson located her, she was across the playing field and appeared to be talking with a youngish man, who Watson thought looked like the school caretaker or maybe someone who tended the sports pitches.

"I understand you want to talk to me," she said, after walking halfway across the playing field to meet the person she'd immediately identified as the policeman Wisset had texted her about.

"Word travels fast around here," remarked Watson, trying his best to make light of the situation and hopefully put the sombre-looking teacher at ease.

"Mr Wisset's very protective of his team," she replied in a tone that suggested she actually resented rather than approved of this. "He texted me just now saying you were on your way."

"I want to talk with you about Tim Horton," Watson said, having no desire to try and avoid why he was there. "Why did you go to see him at the hospital last night and why did you do a runner when you saw my colleague outside the door?"

"Well, you're the detective," Miss Templeton replied rather caustically, her arms folded tightly across her chest. "I'm sure you can work that out."

* * *

Back at Kirkwood police station, Rachel Dalton had spent the morning at her desk, her eyes rarely straying from her computer screen as she attempted to discover as much as she could about the whereabouts of any living relatives of Billy Taylor and glean as much information as she could on James Hampton, Mrs Rumburgh's nephew and the estranged first child of Mavis Heaton.

So far, she'd made no progress at all with Billy Taylor's relatives; it was as if they'd just disappeared. But, with the aid of social media, she'd found a lot of information on James Hampton, not that she could see it helping their team solve any of the recent murders. However, encouraged and intrigued by what she'd uncovered, Rachel was determined to try and amass as much as she could on James Hampton before the debrief at five that evening.

Chapter 72

Under normal circumstances Carmichael would have ensured that at least one of his close team was with him when he went to break the bad news to Jenny Attwood. However, he needed Watson, Cooper and Rachel to stay focused on their tasks. It may well prove to be a suicide and the note saying sorry may well have been Sean Attwood admitting that he'd committed all three murders, but Carmichael wasn't going to jump to any conclusions just yet. With plenty of doubt still in his mind, Carmichael wanted his team to continue to pursue their various lines of investigation as instructed.

Nevertheless, Carmichael wasn't about to break police protocol and deliver the tragic news about her husband's death to Jenny Attwood alone, so he'd swung by the station and picked up WPC Twamley before heading over to her house.

As soon as his car came to rest outside the Attwood residence, Carmichael's mobile started to buzz, and Cooper's name appeared on the screen.

"Hi Paul," Carmichael remarked. "How are you getting along?"

"I've located Horton's wife," replied Cooper. "I've asked her to contact either me or Rachel once she's sorted out her flight back from Marbella."

"I take it she's bringing their daughter back, too?" enquired Carmichael.

"Absolutely," Cooper reassured him.

"We've got another body," Carmichael announced. "It's Sean Attwood."

Carmichael could hear his colleague take a deep breath down the other end of the phone line.

"He was found this morning in a disused barn at the end of Wood Lane," continued Carmichael.

"How did he die?" Cooper asked.

"It looks like suicide, but until Stock confirms this, we need to keep an open mind on how he died," Carmichael replied. "I'm outside Jenny Attwood's house now with WPC Twamley. We're just about to go inside to break the bad news to her."

"Well, you might want to know something before you go in," Cooper said. "Remember I mentioned that PC Dyer and I saw Jenny Attwood leaving Horton's Health Spa yesterday when we were on surveillance? Well, according to Horton's PA, Jenny was very upset and demanded to see him even though he'd instructed the staff that he didn't want to be disturbed."

"Did the PA say why was she there?" Carmichael enquired.

"No," replied Cooper, "unfortunately she didn't hear their conversation, but she did say that Jenny Attwood had almost barged her way in, saying that Horton would see her as he was the father of her daughter."

"Jade Attwood is Horton's daughter!" exclaimed Carmichael. "Is she sure?"

"The PA maintained that Horton vehemently denied this and Jenny later said to her that she meant Godfather," replied Cooper. "But that's apparently what Jenny Attwood initially said."

Carmichael took a few seconds to digest what he'd just heard.

"Well, I'll need to ask her about that," he remarked, before saying, "Anything else, I should know?"

"No, that's it," Cooper replied.

"OK," continued Carmichael. "I suggest you get back to Kirkwood and see how Rachel's getting on. She may need some help tracking down Billy Taylor's family and finding James Hampton."

"Will do," replied Cooper.

"And let her and Marc know about Sean Attwood being found, too," added Carmichael.

As usual, he didn't wait for Cooper's response, ending the call in his customary abrupt manner.

"Deep breaths, WPC Twamley," Carmichael remarked before clambering out of the car.

* * *

It had taken Watson only a few minutes to get beyond the frosty façade initially put up by Lauren Templeton when they met. Once he'd managed to get her away from the hubbub of the sports field and they sat down together on the wooden bench outside the school's sports pavilion, the young teacher had become much less hostile.

"Will he recover?" she enquired, her watery eyes looking into Watson's with a longing to be told good news.

"He's stable," replied Watson reassuringly, "so hopefully he'll pull through."

Miss Templeton appeared to be heartened by Watson's brief synopsis of Horton's condition, allowing herself a tiny smile, before asking, "Does she know?"

"Mrs Horton?" remarked Watson to make sure the "she" that had been mentioned was Horton's wife. "My colleagues are trying to locate her as we speak."

Miss Templeton sighed and shook her head gently from side to side then quickly got to her feet.

"If he makes it, he's going to have to choose," she

announced. "I'm not going to allow this to carry on any longer. It's either her or me."

"So, how long has this been going on?" asked Watson, who remained seated on the bench.

"Too bloody long," replied Miss Templeton, who appeared to have regained her protective hard exterior.

As she spoke, her mobile indicated that she'd received a text.

After looking at the message, Miss Templeton shook her head and thrust the mobile into her tracksuit pocket.

"Mr Wisset again?" Watson enquired.

"Yes," replied the young teacher with a sigh. "He wants to talk to me before I leave today. Typical of him, he takes his pastoral duties way beyond reasonable limits. He thinks he's everyone's dad. God knows where he gets the energy."

Watson smiled. He could see she was clearly stressed out, anxious and worried about her lover. "Will you be going over to see Mr Horton?" he enquired. "If you want to see him before his wife arrives from Spain, you may want to go after you've finished here. I expect she'll get back later this evening."

Miss Templeton clearly appreciated Watson's kindness, which she acknowledged with a small smile.

"I'll go straight after the tennis here has finished," she replied. "Well, just as soon as I've finished seeing his nibs."

Then, without saying another word, the tall PE teacher strolled away, back towards the din of her students on the tennis courts.

She was only a few metres away when something suddenly occurred to Watson.

"Miss Templeton," he shouted. "I was wondering how you knew Mr Horton was in hospital?"

The teacher stopped and turned around.

"My neighbour knocked at my door to tell me about the crash," she replied. "She was driving home and recognised

301

the car. By the time I got there the ambulance had taken Tim away, but the policeman on duty told me where they'd taken him."

Watson smiled. "Thanks for clearing that up," he replied.

Chapter 73

No matter how many times he'd done it before, and despite all the advice he'd been given by colleagues and learnt on courses he'd attended, delivering that bombshell to relatives never got easier for Carmichael. It wasn't so much announcing the news itself that Carmichael dreaded, it was the sight of optimism being drained from the eyes of those who, only a split second earlier, had been clinging to a fragment of hope that everything would work out well and their fears and constant nightmares had been just a cruel, heavy load manufactured within their tired, confused minds.

For Jenny, Jade and Mavis, the news about Sean came as a mighty body blow, almost physical in the pained symptoms they all displayed as they hugged each other tightly and wailed uncontrollably.

"Shall I make us all a cup of tea?" asked WPC Twamley, who, like Carmichael, felt awkward, powerless and unable to think of anything more she could say or do to lighten the pain felt by the three women.

Jenny Attwood released her grip slightly from her daughter and mother, turned her head in Twamley's direction and nodded.

"Yes, please," she replied. "Two sugars for all three of us."

Relieved that she was able to provide at least a little

comfort, WPC Twamley smiled back at Jenny and headed for the kitchen, leaving Carmichael alone with the grieving ladies.

* * *

At first Rachel didn't notice Cooper when he entered the office, she was too transfixed by the subject matter on her computer screen.

It was only when the shadow of her colleague's imposing frame encroached on the outer limits of her vision that Rachel's eye line moved away from the Facebook page she'd been studying.

"Any joy?" Cooper enquired.

Rachel beamed. "With Billy Taylor's family, none whatsoever," she replied, "but I've found a lot out about James Hampton, and we can definitely rule him out as having anything to do with any of the three deaths."

"Really, tell me more," remarked Cooper who, interest now roused, walked towards Rachel. "And it's now four deaths," he added as he arrived at Rachel's desk."

Rachel looked up at Cooper. "Who now?" she enquired.

* * *

After the initial shock, but with tears still flowing freely, the three generations of Sean Attwood's grieving family sat in a line on their large sofa, facing Carmichael. Each had a steaming mug of tea in front of them, provided by WPC Twamley.

"I don't understand why he'd take his own life," Jenny remarked. "He wasn't that sort of man. He was a chancer, we all know that," she added, "but he loved life."

As soon as she'd finished speaking, Jade put her hands to her face and burst once more into uncontrollable wailing, before rising to her feet and making for the door.

"I'll go," remarked Mavis Heaton to her daughter, before springing to her feet and following the teenager out of the room.

Carmichael, Twamley and Jenny Attwood watched in silence and didn't speak until granddaughter and grandmother had left the room and the door was shut behind them.

"And all that was on the note was 'Sorry'?" remarked Jenny.

Carmichael nodded. "Yes," he said. "Do you know what he was referring to?'

"No idea," she replied, without hesitation.

Carmichael took a deep breath.

"I understand you went to see Tim Horton yesterday," he remarked. "Why was that?"

Jenny peered suspiciously back at Carmichael.

"I thought he might know where Sean was," she replied. "Thick as thieves, those two, so I thought if anyone would know it would be him."

"And could he help you?" Carmichael asked.

Jenny shook her head. "He reckoned he didn't know," she replied. "At the time I didn't believe him, but it looks like, for once, he was telling the truth."

"I also understand you told his PA that he's Jade's father," Carmichael added. "Is that true?"

"Yes," replied Jenny. "Well, it's true I said that yesterday, but it's not true. Sean's Jade's dad."

"So why say that Horton's the father?" enquired Carmichael.

Jenny shrugged her shoulders. "I knew he'd see me if I said that," she replied. "He'd helped me all those years ago when Brookie believed that he was Jade's father, but had hated having to keep it from Sean," she continued. "So, I knew he'd get annoyed with me dragging it up again."

"So, he knew about Geoffrey Brookwell thinking he was Jade's father?" Carmichael remarked.

"Yes," replied Jenny. "He caught us in the act, so to speak, so he knew there was a possibility that Brookie was the father. And he'd paid for the DNA tests we did, all those years ago, to prove to Brookie that he wasn't the dad. Back then you could only do those sorts of tests privately, so I was thankful to Tim that he agreed to sort it out."

Carmichael nodded. "Very generous of him," he remarked, "and the tests showed clearly that Sean is Jade's father?"

"Yes," replied Jenny.

Before Carmichael had a chance to ask any more questions, the door opened, and Mavis Heaton reappeared.

"I think you'd better go to Jade," she said to her daughter. "She's very upset."

Carmichael and WPC Twamley watched on as the two women changed places, Mavis Heaton now taking her position in the centre of the sofa in front of them, and Jenny Attwood making a quick exit from the room.

Carmichael allowed the old woman to take a sip of tea from her mug before saying a word.

"With Sean now gone, and it being in Jenny and Jade's interest to get to the bottom of his death, I think it's about time you stopped lying to me, don't you, Mavis?" Carmichael said, his voice clear and calm.

Mavis Heaton took a second sip of her tea.

"He made me keep quiet," Mavis said, her voice suggesting that she hadn't been given a choice.

"Quiet about what?" Carmichael enquired.

"About that car," continued Mavis. "And about seeing Brookie on Tuesday when he parked the damn thing near my house and went down the footpath."

"So, you saw him park," Carmichael remarked. "What time was that?"

"It would have been shortly after ten," replied Mavis. "I

306

recognised the car first as being Sean's; that flash thing he uses to impress people."

"And what did you do?" Carmichael enquired.

"I expected it to be Sean when it pulled up, but then I saw it wasn't," replied Mavis. "It didn't take long to recognise Brookie though. I'd not seen him in years, but he hadn't changed that much, and I realised it was him even before he'd reached the stile."

"Then what did you do?" Carmichael asked.

"I called Sean and asked him what was going on," replied the old woman. "He told me to mind my own business, and not to say anything to anyone about what I'd seen, even Jenny. He said there was a lot of money coming his way because of Brookie, and I needed to keep my nose out."

"So, you did just that," remarked Carmichael, "even though it meant lying to the police."

Mavis looked a little downcast at Carmichael's comments, but not enough to offer an apology.

"And did you see Brookie come back down the footpath and drive away?" Carmichael enquired.

Mavis nodded. "Yes, about an hour or so later," she replied.

Carmichael shook his head gently. "And what explanation did Sean give you about all this after I'd talked with you both on Wednesday?" he asked.

Mavis shook her head.

"He didn't say anything," she replied. "He just kept telling me to keep my nose out of it."

"What about the call you received from Mrs Rumburgh on Thursday evening?" he asked. "What did she say?"

"I told your sergeant everything about that call when he interviewed me yesterday," replied Mavis.

"As I remember," remarked Carmichael, "you told Sergeant Cooper that Mrs Rumburgh asked you where Sean was and then asked if you had any idea where Billy Taylor's family could be contacted?"

"That's correct," replied Mavis.

"What about James?" Carmichael enquired. "Did Mrs Rumburgh mention your son?"

Mavis screwed up her face as if the question was ridiculous.

"We never talked about James," she replied indignantly, "not then, not ever. I haven't seen my so-called son in over twenty years. I probably wouldn't recognise him now if I fell over him."

Carmichael got to his feet.

"In the light of what you've just told me, WPC Twamley will need to take a new full statement from you, Mrs Heaton," Carmichael announced, "but I'll not take up any more of your time. Once again, my deepest condolences to you all on your loss."

Carmichael glanced across at WPC Twamley who returned a gentle nod, to acknowledge she understood the instruction. Carmichael then walked over to the door, leaving WPC Twamley to wonder how on earth she'd be getting back to the police station once he'd departed.

Chapter 74

With several hours to go before the planned debrief with his team at Kirkwood, and keen to see how Stock and the team were progressing, Carmichael decided to return to the barn in Wood Lane.

Unsurprisingly, the scene was still a hive of activity when he arrived.

"How's it going?" he asked as soon as he saw the unmistakeable figure of Stock, bent over in his white overalls.

"We found the original plates from the Bentley behind an old wooden box in the corner," Stock replied, "along with the tools required to remove them; and I have to tell you, this was no suicide."

"Really," replied Carmichael. "How can you be sure it wasn't suicide?"

"Because he'd been tied up," announced Stock. "There are lesions to the skin on both of his upper arms, which suggests he was bound quite tightly. My supposition is that this was done behind his back like so."

As he spoke, Stock put his own arms behind his back, an action which instinctively made him lean forward.

"There's no way he'd be able to pull the trigger on the gun and cause the sort of injuries we can see here," continued Stock. "In my view, he was bound, sat down where we found him, shot at very close range by someone else, then the binding was removed."

Carmichael nodded gently. "And you're confident this is also the scene of the changeover of the number plates of Attwood's Bentley?" remarked Carmichael.

An audible sniff emanated from Stock as he took in a large breath of air up his nose.

"I can't be sure of that," he replied, "but as I said before, the tools to make the switch are over there with the plates, as are the remnants of the fixings that had held the original plates to the car; however, that doesn't mean the switch was done here."

"Great work, Stock," Carmichael remarked.

* * *

At Kirkwood station, Cooper and Dalton had been joined by Watson, all feeling positive, having made good progress with the tasks Carmichael had set them.

"Why don't we update the whiteboard?" suggested Watson. "It'll save us loads of time when Carmichael gets back and, with a bit of luck, we'll be able to get away before it gets too late."

"Good idea," remarked Cooper, "but you'd better do the writing, Rachel," he added. "My writing's not that legible and Marc's spelling is appalling."

Rachel Dalton smiled and walked over to the whiteboard.

* * *

With Carmichael still not back at Kirkwood, Cooper had just finished telling Rachel what she needed to write down to cover the results of his efforts so far that day, when the call came into the station to say that Tim Horton was regaining consciousness.

"Why don't you two stay here and finish that off?" Cooper suggested. "I'll get over to the hospital now. I'll call the boss on the way."

Watson and Dalton didn't protest at the suggestion, pausing briefly from their whiteboard updates until Cooper had disappeared out of the office.

* * *

Carmichael was heading towards Kirkwood police station when he received the call from Cooper, but keen to talk with Horton again about the deaths of Geoffrey Brookwell, Sajid Hanif, Mrs Rumburgh and Sean Attwood, he immediately changed direction and headed west towards Southport Hospital.

Although his mind wasn't totally clear on all the details of the case, he was now sure that at its heart was the man currently coming round in that hospital bed.

Chapter 75

With Cooper's input already added and having now been made aware that Sean Attwood had been found dead in the barn down Wood Lane, Watson and Rachel Dalton continued their update of the three lists on the office whiteboard.

By the time Carmichael arrived at Southport Royal Hospital, the updated lists were complete.

Standing back with his arms folded tightly to his chest, a pose more usually synonymous with Carmichael himself, Watson looked at the expanded list of bullet points that he and Rachel had just updated.

"Do you think that's everything?" he said.

"I think so," responded Rachel. "All we need now is the boss's input, when he gets here."

* * *

Once the tennis matches were completed and her girls had melted away from the school, Miss Templeton quickly made her exit. She'd decided to ignore Mr Wisset's text request to talk with her before she left. With Tim Horton being in hospital, her only thought was to get to see him before his wife arrived.

Out the corner of his eye, as he gazed out of his office window, the school's headmaster noticed her bright-yellow car disappear out of the gate. In frustration he reached for his mobile phone and started to type in a text message. Neither he nor Lauren Templeton saw Harry Bridge, the school's young caretaker, who was watching, too, from beside the bike sheds. Once Miss Templeton was out of sight, he also took out his mobile and started to text.

* * *

Cooper was already at the door of Horton's private room when Carmichael arrived.

"Has he said anything yet?" Carmichael enquired, his voice excited and impatient.

Cooper shook his head.

"They won't let me in," he replied. "The doctor said that until she's been given the go-ahead from the senior neurosurgeon, nobody other than family is allowed to talk with him."

"She did, did she?" replied Carmichael. "We'll see about that."

Carmichael disappeared into Horton's room, but only for a few seconds. Looking angry and somewhat shocked, Carmichael reappeared in the corridor followed closely by a tall, thickset woman doctor in her late forties who, in no uncertain terms, made it clear to Carmichael that she'd been given strict instructions. Her patient, as she called him, was not to be put under any stress whatsoever until he had been given a thorough examination.

"And when will that be?" Carmichael enquired, his voice hushed but showing his frustration.

The doctor shrugged her shoulders. "Dr McDonald is on his way here from his weekend holiday home," she replied. "He's expected at about seven this evening."

"Where the hell's his weekend holiday home?" snapped Carmichael.

"Somewhere in Wales," replied the doctor, who seemed to be getting a modicum of pleasure from seeing Carmichael's mounting frustration.

Carmichael turned to face Cooper.

"I'm going back to Kirkwood, but you stay here with him, Paul," he instructed. "And get a couple of uniformed guys here to help you. Place one outside the window. I don't want a potential murderer getting away, just because some senior quack can't get here quickly."

Unmoved by Carmichael's offensive language, the doctor smiled at the two officers and went back into Horton's room.

* * *

Although it took almost twenty minutes to get from the hospital to Kirkwood police station, Carmichael's mood was no better when he marched irritably into the office.

"Any joy with Horton?" Rachel enquired, as Carmichael approached her desk.

"No," snapped back Carmichael, "and we won't until some bloody specialist agrees to allow us to interview him. Cooper's still there, but it might be another five or six hours until he gives us his blessing."

"Right," replied Rachel. "Well, do you want to go through the lists again with Marc and me? We've updated them as best we can."

Carmichael looked over at the whiteboard. He seemed suitably impressed by their initiative.

"Yes, let's do that," he remarked. "But first I've got three or four things I'd like to add."

Once Rachel had written up Carmichael's new points she pressed "Print" on the side of the board, which immediately spewed out four A4 sheets of paper.

"A nice round fifty," Carmichael remarked, referring to the total number of items on the three lists.

Knowns:

- On Tuesday 30th June 10:30am, Geoffrey Brookwell went into Moulton Bank C of E church, with his hands covered in blood and confessed to a murder. He then disappeared.
- We know the blood in question was pig blood. Type O.
- Brookwell's body was found on Wednesday 1st July, in the boot of the car he'd been using which belonged to an old school friend, Sean Attwood. Car had false plates.
- SOCO indicate that Brookwell died between twelve noon and 2pm on Tuesday, his throat having been cut by his killer.
- Attwood and Brookwell made the handover of the car at the multi-storey on Saturday 27th June, which was done without them being together. The car, when it was driven away, still had its genuine plates on it.
- Brookwell received a Jiffy bag, postmarked on Wednesday 24th June in Kirkwood, which we found in his apartment in Knott End. No contents found yet.
- There were images of a girl confirmed as Jade Attwood in Brookwell's possession.
- The second dead man is Sajid Hanif, he also received a package recently. This was delivered to his work on 1st July, something the receptionist has confirmed. In that letter he is offered a job, given a thousand pounds and asked to book room seven at the Lindley Hotel for a meeting the following day (2nd July)
- According to his wife, Sajid received a call a week before from a man purporting to be Philip Dobson, basically offering him a job, which Dobson completely denies making.

- Sajid Hanif arrives at the Lindley Hotel at 9:15am and checks into room seven, an outside room facing the car park.
- Sajid is murdered between 9:15am and 11:30am when the young housekeeper finds his body.
- A pickup truck identified by one of the receptionists as belonging to Sean Attwood was seen leaving the Lindley car park at approximately 10am. This is the last known sighting of Sean Attwood before he dies.
- The same pay-as-you-go burner appears to have been used to contact Attwood, Hanif and Brookwell.
- A young woman has been identified on CCTV footage posting Jiffy bags at the same postbox at around 5pm on the two days we believe the parcels were posted to Brookwell and Hanif. We now know this woman to be Tim Horton's daughter, Hayley.
- Mrs Rumburgh died of carbon monoxide poisoning between 7pm and 9pm on Thursday 2nd July. Murder was staged to look like suicide.
- Mrs Rumburgh's guns were taken from her house, one later being used to kill Sean Attwood.
- Mrs Rumburgh called Mavis Heaton on the evening she died.
- According to Mavis Heaton she mentioned Billy Taylor and was keen to locate Sean Attwood.
- Sean Attwood, Geoffrey Brookwell and Tim Horton were all friends at school. Horton and Attwood remained close friends.
- Geoffrey Brookwell believed Jade Attwood was his daughter, Jenny Attwood denies this. However, the father of Jade is still unclear – it could even be Horton.
- According to Mr Wisset, Mrs Rumburgh wanted to see him about something urgent. They'd arranged to meet on Friday 3rd July.

- Mavis Heaton and Mrs Rumburgh were related by marriage.
- Mavis Heaton had been the long-term partner of Sean Attwood's father, and brought Sean up as her own son.
- Someone, assumed to be Mrs Rumburgh, had been looking at some old student files on the afternoon/ evening before she died (Tim Horton, Sajid Hanif and James Hampton's files all appear to have been taken out – possibly others too).
- Billy Taylor's drowning was witnessed by Horton, Attwood and Brookwell who had all been chasing him and Sajid Hanif. Sajid Hanif also saw Billy drown.
- None of the boys or Hanif's family offered up this information to the police at the time.
- James Hampton was Mavis Heaton's estranged son and Mrs Rumburgh's nephew.
- James trained as a teacher, emigrated to Australia but died in a car accident fifteen years ago.
- Billy Taylor was an only child and his mother, his only surviving relative, is now in a home suffering from dementia.
- Mavis Heaton lied when she said she'd not seen Geoffrey Brookwell on the day he went to the church. She now admits that she saw him arrive and leave.
- Sean Attwood was shot in the barn in Wood Lane. When found earlier today he had been dead for at least twelve hours, possibly since as long ago as Thursday evening.
- Attwood's death was staged to look like suicide.
- There is evidence to suggest that the false number plates were attached to the Bentley in the barn where Sean Attwood's body was found.
- Tim Horton has been having a relationship with a PE teacher from the academy called Lauren Templeton. This

was known by his wife, Mrs Rumburgh and Mr Wisset.

- The killer can afford to lavish multiple thousands of pounds to lure Brookwell and Hanif to their deaths.

Assumptions:

- There is a single killer.
- The four murders are linked – not random acts.
- Hayley Horton will know the killer.
- Mrs Rumburgh was killed because of something she knew or had worked out.
- The false number plate (WTR 1P) should be read as WT RIP (or Billy Taylor rest in peace).
- One of Mrs Rumburgh's stolen guns is still unaccounted for.

Questions:

- Who killed Brookwell, Hanif, Attwood and Mrs Rumburgh?
- Why has the killer spent time and money making Brookwell and Hanif believe they have new jobs before killing them?
- Who changed the plates on the Bentley – and why?
- If it was Mrs Rumburgh who took out the files, why would she want to look at those old student files shortly before she was killed?
- What did Mrs Rumburgh want to talk to Sean about?
- What did Mrs Rumburgh want to talk to Mr Wisset about?
- What has Billy Taylor's death got to do with the killings?
- What does Tim Horton know about the murders?
- Does the number plate, the pig blood on Brookwell's hands and the removal of Sajid's tongue have any relevance to the killer's motive?

* * *

The arrival of two plain-clothed PCs outside Tim Horton's room coincided exactly with the appearance of Lauren Templeton, who, this time, didn't scarper when she saw Cooper, but walked slowly in his direction, shoulders hunched and her worried eyes staring at the floor rather than the officers outside Horton's door.

Cooper, seeing her coming, quickly gave the two PCs their instructions, before standing and taking a few steps towards the nervous-looking woman.

Chapter 76

Carmichael looked up from his printed copy of their lists, his piercing blue eyes staring directly at Watson and Dalton.

"Fill me on these latest findings?" he said, his question suitably vague to allow either officer to feel free to answer.

It was Rachel who responded first.

"I managed to discover quite a lot about James Hampton," she replied. "I found out nothing for the period between Billy Taylor's death and James Hampton going to college, but I managed to find out that he went to a college in Cheshire to train as a teacher, qualified, and then emigrated to Australia."

"You have down here that he died," remarked Carmichael, pointing at the comment Rachel had written on the whiteboard.

"Yes," she replied. "There was a post on one of his college friend's Facebook page saying he'd died in a car crash. It was posted five years ago, one of those morbid 'ten years ago today' messages and a picture of him with other students at the college."

"So, he's not our killer," Watson interjected.

Rachel nodded. "No, we can scrub him out."

"Well, that narrows down our list of potential suspects," added Carmichael. "Although, to be honest, he wasn't very high on the list in the first place."

"Don't you think it's strange that his mother never mentioned the fact that her son was dead?" remarked Rachel.

Carmichael nodded. "That's true," he concurred, his words delivered slowly. "Mavis hasn't mentioned that."

"Maybe she doesn't know," Watson added. "If they were estranged, why would she know?"

"I can't see that," remarked Rachel. "Surely the Australian police would have contacted his next of kin when he died."

"Maybe they told his father," replied Watson, "but he wasn't in touch with Mavis, so maybe she just wasn't told."

Carmichael nodded gently.

"That whole situation is peculiar," Carmichael remarked. "The intertwined relationships between Mavis Heaton, her estranged son, Mrs Rumburgh, Sean Attwood and her daughter are totally bizarre. However, whatever happened back then, you're right, Rachel, we know for certain James Hampton isn't our killer."

* * *

Lauren Templeton gave Cooper a half-hearted smile.

"How is he?" she enquired.

Cooper returned the smile. "I'm Sergeant Cooper," he remarked. "I take it you're Miss Templeton."

"Yes," she replied.

Cooper smiled again. "Well, the good news is that he's conscious," he remarked. "But at the moment, until he's been seen by the neurosurgeon who's travelling back from Wales, it's family only allowed to see him."

"Then that excludes me," she replied.

* * *

"Let's step back and look at this from a broader perspective," suggested Carmichael. "What do we know about our killer?"

Rachel and Watson exchanged a quick glance at each other.

"Well, he must have known all four of his victims," suggested Rachel. "That suggests some connection back to when Billy Taylor was killed."

Carmichael nodded. "I agree. That's a reasonable assumption in my view," he remarked. "But do you think we're looking for a man?"

Rachel considered the question. "I guess it could be a woman," she replied.

"I'd say it's got to be a local," interjected Watson. "To know about the Lindley having outside rooms and especially to know about that old barn hidden away down Wood Lane tells me they are from around here."

"I'd agree with that," remarked Rachel enthusiastically. "There are probably people who've lived here for years that don't know about that barn, so it has to be someone from the area."

Carmichael nodded. "Anything else?" he enquired.

"They're connected with the school," Watson announced.

"Why do you say that?" Carmichael asked.

"Because, I think it's clear that the killer put back those files in Mrs Rumburgh's office," Watson replied.

Carmichael didn't look so certain.

"We don't know that for sure," he remarked. "It may well have been Mrs Rumburgh who did that."

Watson shook his head. "No, she was too fastidious," he remarked. "She'd have put them back neatly. I reckon someone snatched them from her hand then put them back. That would explain the small piece of one of the folders being torn."

"What about Billy Taylor's relatives?" Carmichael asked. "You say his only living relative is his mother and she's got dementia."

Watson shrugged his shoulders.

"I spoke with the care home and they say that she's quite bad," he replied. "Also, it's in Hampshire, so a fair way to travel to talk with her even if she wasn't away with the fairies."

Although she didn't say anything, Carmichael could see from the expression on her face that Rachel wasn't impressed with Watson's choice of words, but he decided to move the conversation on.

"Tell me about Miss Templeton?" he asked. "What sort of person is she and more importantly, tell me about her relationship with Horton?"

"She's a nice woman," replied Watson. "Clearly very worried about Horton and from what she told me, she's been in a relationship with him for some time. The affair, if that's what you want to call it, wasn't initially common knowledge from what I gather, but Mrs Rumburgh and Mr Wisset got to know about it and it was also known to Mrs Horton, but I think all three had thought it was over."

"Which it wasn't," added Carmichael.

"No," replied Watson. "It was Miss Templeton's house in Hasselbury that Horton was going to when he had the accident."

Carmichael nodded.

"What else did she tell you?" he enquired.

Watson shook his head.

"Nothing else really," he replied. "As I say, it's clear she cares deeply for him. She even said that when he recovers he'd have to make a choice between her and his wife."

Carmichael nodded again.

"It may be a choice of who visits him in prison," he remarked caustically. "Because, let's face it, he's certainly our top suspect at the moment. In fact, I'd go so far as to say he's our only real suspect."

* * *

Cooper and Lauren Templeton sat together outside Tim Horton's room, largely in silence but occasionally exchanging the odd few words.

It was clear to Cooper that she was relieved her lover was now conscious, but Cooper could sense that she was still very concerned.

"So, what are you going to do when Mrs Horton and their daughter arrives?" Cooper enquired.

Miss Templeton shrugged her shoulders.

"I guess that depends on how they react to me," she replied. "I'm not too concerned about his wife, as their relationship has been on the rocks for years, well before I came on the scene. It's Hayley I'm most worried about. I'd hate to fall out with her."

"You know his daughter?" Cooper enquired.

"Yes, of course," replied Miss Templeton, her face a picture of incredulity.

As she spoke, her mobile indicated that another text message had arrived. Although he'd not been counting, Cooper figured that it must be at least the fifth text she'd received since she sat down next to him.

As with all the others, Miss Templeton turned the mobile so Cooper couldn't see it.

Chapter 77

Nigel Wisset had arrived back home at about 2pm, after spending the morning in his office at the academy.

He had no thought of having lunch or even making himself a cup of coffee. His mind was too preoccupied with the events unfolding around him to think about anything as mundane as nourishment.

From his text conversation with Lauren Templeton before he'd left the academy and the text messages they'd shared since her arrival at the hospital, he knew that the relationship he and Mrs Rumburgh had thought was over was still going on, a fact that concerned him greatly. He also knew that Tim Horton was now conscious, but still in the hospital.

It was as he sat alone that he heard his phone ringing in the hallway. He allowed it to ring several times before he picked it up.

"Hello," he said, before listening intently to a voice he recognised immediately and the instructions he was being given.

There was no polite goodbye when the caller stopped talking, just an abrupt end to their conversation and then the familiar tone to indicate the other person had left the call.

Wisset sat back down at the kitchen table to consider what he should do.

***

Cooper decided to take a chance and leave Lauren Templeton outside Horton's room with one of the uniformed officers that he'd seconded to keep vigil.

He rushed down the corridor until he reached a point where the signal was strong enough to make a call, which Carmichael answered almost immediately.

"Hayley Horton works at the school," Cooper shouted down the phone. "She works in the office."

Carmichael didn't need to have the significance of this explained to him.

"Are you sure?" he replied.

"Yes," remarked Cooper. "Lauren Templeton's just told me. She's also just told me that Hayley is dating the caretaker there, a guy called Harry Bridge."

Carmichael thought for a moment.

"Where's Miss Templeton now?" he enquired.

"She's outside Horton's room with one of the uniformed guys," Cooper replied.

"Well get back to her," Carmichael ordered. "Don't let her out of your sight."

"Will do, sir," replied Cooper, just before the line at the other end went dead.

***

While Carmichael was talking, Rachel received a text message from Mrs Horton.

"They've got a flight that gets into Manchester airport at nine thirty this evening," she informed Carmichael and Watson.

Carmichael looked at his watch, it was still only 3pm.

"I'd like you there to meet them off the plane," he told Rachel. "But there's been a new development."

***

Nigel Wisset was torn between two choices. Should he follow the instructions he'd just received over the phone, or should he head to the hospital where Lauren Templeton was patiently waiting to see Tim Horton?

He spent a few minutes deciding what move he should take, before leaping up from the kitchen table and heading towards the hallway.

Chapter 78

"What's happening, sir?" Watson enquired as he, Carmichael and Rachel sped along the narrow country roads, Carmichael's foot heavy on the accelerator.

"I may have spoken a bit too soon when I said Tim Horton was our only real suspect," Carmichael replied. "According to Cooper, Hayley Horton works at the academy, as does her boyfriend, the caretaker, Harry Bridge."

"I think I may have seen him earlier when I was on the playing field looking for Miss Templeton," Watson remarked. "He looked a young guy to be a caretaker. He could have only been in his late twenties."

"That would make sense if he's dating Hayley," remarked Rachel. "She only looks like she's a late teen or early twenty-something."

"But what bearing does Hayley and her boyfriend working at the academy have on the case?" enquired Watson.

Carmichael looked sideways at his colleague, his face indicating he was amazed that Watson didn't get it.

"It means that the Jiffy bags Hayley has been posting may well have been in the school post, not given to her by her dad," remarked Carmichael.

"If that's the case it could be anyone working at the school that's our killer," Rachel said.

"Yes," replied Carmichael, "but I'm guessing it's most likely someone in particular."

* * *

Mavis Heaton took no more than two seconds to open her front door after the doorbell had sounded.

The stern expression on her face quickly turned to one of fear as, without a word exchanged between the pair, she allowed the visitor to come inside.

* * *

Carmichael's car screeched into the academy car park and the three officers got out of the car at a pace reserved only for emergencies.

Being Saturday afternoon, the car park was empty and, although they tried them one by one, all the doors to the school were closed and locked tight.

"Bugger!" exclaimed Carmichael.

Looking anxious and frustrated, Carmichael noticed the large board positioned next to the main entrance.

"There must be a telephone number on that," he remarked, a comment that sent Rachel to have a look.

"There's a caretaker's number," she replied.

"Call it and see if he has Wisset's address," Carmichael ordered.

As Rachel was tapping the number into her mobile and then putting the device to her ear, Watson, arms folded, turned to face his boss.

"Do you really think Wisset's our killer?" he enquired, his question said with great incredulity.

"I do," replied Carmichael firmly. "Well, sort of," he quickly added.

Watson didn't look convinced one bit.

"But Wisset's not a local man," Watson remarked. "Surely, if the caretaker is Hayley's boyfriend then he's more likely

329

to be our man than Wisset? Wisset's unlikely to have known about the Lindley having outside rooms and would certainly not have known about that barn down Wood Lane. And why would Wisset want to harm Geoffrey Brookwell, Sean Attwood or Sajid Hanif? He may have known Brookwell through him coming to the school to help out, and Attwood through Jade, but he wouldn't have known Sajid Hanif. He's no children here."

Carmichael listened intently to what his sergeant was saying.

"All really good questions, Marc," he reluctantly replied, "but it's his age that's the key. If the caretaker is in his twenties, he's far too young."

"I've got Wisset's address," Rachel shouted. "It's only ten minutes away."

"I think it's still more likely to be the caretaker or Tim Horton," remarked Watson, as the three officers clambered back into Carmichael's black BMW.

"Maybe you're right, Marc" replied Carmichael, "but for now, we're focusing on Wisset."

Chapter 79

As his car flew down the road on the short journey from the academy to Nigel Wisset's address, Carmichael's mobile rang. It was Stock.

"I'm impressed you're working today, Stock," remarked Carmichael.

"I'm not," replied Stock, who was on the fifteenth tee of his local golf course. "I just thought I'd let you know, the lab just called me to say we have some good prints on the shotgun that don't belong to the dead man or to Mrs Rumburgh. They also inform me that the fibres under Sajid Hanif's fingernails don't match the clothes that Sean Attwood was wearing when he died."

"That's great news," replied Carmichael, with a wry smile.

* * *

The door of Mavis Heaton's cottage slammed shut, leaving the old lady tightly bound to the wooden chair which had been rested on its side on the kitchen floor, her face and exposed nostrils a matter of inches from the punctured gas pipe that fed her combi boiler. The flannel that had been rammed into her mouth and then tightly bound with several rounds of wide brown tape, prevented any chance of the old lady calling out for help.

Also, with the landline telephone wire cut and Mavis's mobile smashed into several pieces on the floor in front of her, even if she could wriggle free, her ability to summon help would be greatly limited.

As she lay there breathing a mixture of oxygen and the gas that was slowly hissing its escape from the pipe, Mavis noticed an object standing proud from the floor under her cooker. It wasn't clear what it was, as the thing was now covered in a green furry layer. Mavis's eyes remained focused on that unwanted item for no more than thirty seconds before her breathing became shallow and she drifted into unconsciousness.

* * *

As he'd feared, when Carmichael arrived at Wisset's neat semi-detached house, it looked unoccupied.

With all its windows shut tight and no car on the drive, Carmichael knew the chances of anyone answering were small.

After five minutes of banging on the front door, peering through the downstairs windows and going around the back, the three officers got together at the front of the house.

"What now?" asked Watson.

Before Carmichael had a chance to answer, the next-door neighbour, a thin tall man in his late fifties, appeared over the hedge.

"Looking for Nigel?" he enquired.

"We're from Mid-Lancashire police," remarked Rachel, who was the nearest to the hedge that separated the two houses. "Have you seen Mr Wisset today?"

The neighbour at first looked suspicious, but on sight of Rachel's warrant card became instantly accommodating.

"He drove off about thirty or forty minutes ago," he replied.

"Which way did he go?" Carmichael enquired.

The neighbour pointed down the road where they'd just come from.

"Towards Moulton Bank," he replied. "Knowing Nigel, he'll be at the school. He's always there."

Rachel thanked the neighbour for his help and turned to face Carmichael and Watson.

"Wherever he's gone," remarked Carmichael, "it's certainly not back to the school."

* * *

Another text message arrived on Lauren Templeton's mobile.

With a look of frustration on her face, she stood up.

"When's this specialist going to arrive?" she snapped at the officious-looking nurse behind the desk.

The nurse looked back at her and shrugged her shoulders.

"Your guess is as good as mine," she replied vaguely, "but I'd say we've got an hour or two more to wait."

The teacher exhaled noisily as if to demonstrate her unhappiness.

"Look, I've got to be somewhere," she remarked to Cooper. "I'll be back in about an hour."

Without waiting for an answer, Lauren Templeton headed off down the corridor.

Remembering his last instruction from Carmichael, Cooper stood up too.

"You stay here and make sure nobody goes in or out other than the medical staff," he said to PC Hill, the uniformed officer by his side.

Cooper then followed the PE teacher, but at a reasonable distance so she wouldn't know he was tailing her.

PC Hill sat back in his chair and folded his arms.

"Let's get back to the station," Carmichael remarked despondently. "We can decide what we do when we're back there."

He flung his keys in Rachel Dalton's direction.

"Can you drive, Rachel?" he said. "It will give me some time to think."

Rachel caught the keys and smiled. "No problem, sir," she replied, before releasing the locks and clambering into the driver's seat.

Chapter 80

From behind the wheel of his car, Nigel Wisset watched as first Lauren Templeton then Sergeant Cooper emerged from the hospital and separately made their way to their cars. Having never met Cooper, he didn't recognise him as a police officer and didn't spot the fact that Cooper was attempting to follow the PE teacher.

He waited until Miss Templeton's car was safely out of the car park before moving from his vantage point. Wisset knew it would take her at least twenty minutes to arrive at the academy and probably ten more minutes before she realised he wasn't going to be there after all. So, he had the best part of an hour to complete what he wanted to do.

With the nonchalance of a professional assassin, he climbed out of the driver's door, removed the holdall which contained the second shotgun and the box of cartridges he'd taken from Mrs Rumburgh's house.

As he walked towards the hospital entrance, Wisset noticed the frustrated figure of Cooper climb out of his car and open the bonnet, but it meant nothing to him.

* * *

"Do you still think it's Wisset?" Watson remarked.

Carmichael turned sideways in his seat to face his sergeant, who was sitting in the back of the car.

"I'm not certain, for some of the reasons you articulated so clearly earlier, Marc," he replied, "but I think you were right when you said that it was the killer who put back the files so haphazardly in Mrs Rumburgh's office. Of course, that could have been anyone, Miss Templeton, Hayley Horton or even the caretaker. But they're all too young. And if it wasn't Wisset, I'd imagine he'd have seen whoever it was enter her room and would have told us."

"I guess that does make sense," Rachel added.

"If he was a local man I'd agree," Watson added. "But he's not. He's from…"

"Ramsbottom," confirmed Carmichael.

"So, he wasn't around when Billy Taylor drowned and there's very little chance he'd have known about that barn in Wood Lane," continued Watson. "I still think it will be Horton and maybe his daughter, or Lauren Templeton, or the caretaker, who are behind these deaths."

"You're right, Marc," he conceded, "we can't ignore the others but I think our killer is Wisset."

Carmichael turned back around and looked straight ahead through the car window, just as his mobile started to ring.

"It's Cooper," he remarked.

* * *

Nigel Wisset smiled at the receptionist behind the desk.

"Good afternoon," he said. "I've come to visit Tim Horton. Can you tell me what ward he's on please?"

* * *

"I'm sorry, sir," were the first three words Cooper said to his boss once the call had been answered. "Lauren Templeton left the hospital and although I tried to follow her, my damn car wouldn't start, so I've lost her."

"Where are you now?" Carmichael enquired.

"I'm in the hospital car park," replied Cooper.

"OK," continued Carmichael. "What about the consultant? Has he materialised yet?"

"No," replied Cooper. "The nurse reckons he may be an hour or two more."

"You go back into the hospital, Paul," instructed Carmichael. "One of us will join you shortly."

"Will do," replied Cooper, who ended the call and locked the door of his ancient Volvo.

* * *

Still reeling from the news about her father's death, Jade Attwood decided to walk to her nan's cottage. Despite being less than three miles away it was almost all uphill, so a feat which normally took her the best part of an hour. Not that she minded. She needed to get out of the house and get her head straight, free from her poor mother's sobbing and from a home that had suddenly felt so cramped and claustrophobic.

It wasn't that she was close to her nan, but at least at her cottage there was potentially some respite from the tears and the morose atmosphere that had gripped her own house.

She opened the creaky wooden gate and walked slowly up to the house and around to the green back door, which her nan only ever locked at night or when she was going out.

Jade didn't knock, she never did, she just barged into the kitchen.

It was the smell of gas that hit her first, followed a few seconds later by the sight of the diminutive figure of her nan, bound and gagged, and unconscious on the floor.

337

She rushed over to her and, as quickly as she could, removed the tape and flannel so she could breathe properly again. Although she was unconscious, her chest was moving, indicating that the old lady had not died.

Happy with that discovery, Jade rushed to the kitchen door and flung it open. Then she opened as many windows as she could before returning to her nan's side.

She pulled out her mobile and dialled 999, switched the mobile to speaker phone and then laid it on the floor beside them.

As the mobile rang, Jade started to untie the knots that had bound her nan to the chair.

* * *

After ending the call with Cooper, the three officers had continued their journey to Kirkwood police station without further comment.

As they were pulling into the car park Carmichael broke the silence.

"OK, guys, this is what I need you to do," he announced.

Chapter 81

"Any developments?" Cooper asked as he arrived back outside Tim Horton's room.

PC Hill shook his head.

"The nurse went in for a few minutes, then, after she came out, the porter arrived with his trolley to take away the old linen."

Cooper let out a huge sigh and sat down next to his uniformed colleague.

* * *

With her new instructions, Rachel started to scour social media to try and find anything she could relating to Nigel Wisset. And, although he didn't appear to be on Facebook, she found mentions of him on other teachers' social media sites. As the trail developed it became clear to her that Nigel had experienced a meteoritic rise in his career from when he left college, just fifteen years earlier.

"You were right, boss," she muttered to herself, scribbling down the details that emerged as she delved deeper into the past of the young headmaster of the academy.

* * *

When Carmichael arrived at the academy, he expected to see just one car in the car park but, although that was what confronted him, the car he saw wasn't Nigel Wisset's. Instead it appeared to belong to a tall woman in her early thirties, who was standing next to it, her eyes transfixed on her mobile phone.

"I take it you're Lauren Templeton," he remarked, much to the young woman's amazement.

Lauren Templeton looked suspicious of the man now walking towards her, despite his friendly smile.

"Who's asking?" she replied guardedly.

"Inspector Carmichael," he replied, while at the same time flashing her his warrant card. "Why did you leave the hospital so suddenly and what are you doing here?"

* * *

"Actually, he's been in there for ages," remarked PC Hill as they sat quietly outside Tim Horton's room.

"Who?" enquired Cooper, with a quizzical look on his face.

"The porter," replied the PC.

Cooper turned to face his colleague with a stunned expression on his face.

"Are you saying the porter never came out?" he said.

"Well, no," replied PC Hill.

"Bloody hell, man," shouted Cooper, while at the same time leaping to his feet and heading for Horton's door.

Within seconds, the two officers were in the room and, within seconds of them entering, they saw the man in the armchair next to a terrified Tim Horton, his shotgun barrel resting under the motionless patient's chin.

"Come in, gentlemen," said Wisset, his voice calm but authoritative. "Shut the door behind you and then walk over to the other side of the bed, where I can see you both. But move slowly, please. And keep your hands high above your heads. Otherwise I may accidentally blow Tim's head off."

* * *

Rachel was just about to call Carmichael, when the duty sergeant entered the room.

"Where's Carmichael?" he enquired.

"He's gone back to Moulton Bank, to the academy," she replied.

"Well, in that case you might want to know there's been another incident close to the scene where that man with blood on his hands was on Tuesday," he continued. "An ambulance has been called to attend to some old dear called Mavis Heaton, who lives in the cottage at the end of the footpath. It appears she's been bound and gagged and left for dead in a gas-filled room."

"What!" exclaimed Rachel. "Is she OK?"

"She's apparently still alive and on her way to the hospital," continued the sergeant, "but other than that, I've not much else to report."

Rachel sprang to her feet and grabbed her jacket.

"OK," she said, "I'll get up there. I'll call Carmichael on my way and let him know what's going on."

* * *

Having learnt from Lauren Templeton that she'd been summoned to school by Nigel Wisset, who had then failed to turn up, Carmichael knew the most likely place he'd be heading would be the hospital.

He was about halfway there when he took the call from Rachel telling him about Mavis Heaton and what she'd discovered online about Wisset.

341

"I'm not sure if Watson will be at the hospital yet," Carmichael said, "but call him and bring him up to speed. I'll call Cooper and do the same."

As usual, Carmichael didn't hang around once he'd given his latest instruction and abruptly ended the call.

Chapter 82

"Let's all just calm down," suggested Cooper, his voice as controlled and unthreatening as he could manage. "We don't want anyone to get hurt."

Nigel Wisset looked back at Cooper. "I am calm," he replied, "but you of all people should know that justice must be done."

Ramming the end of the barrel harder under Tim Horton's chin, the headmaster smiled. "Bullies need to be punished, don't they, Tim?"

Tim Horton remained silent, with no colour left in his face and numerous beads of sweat trickling down his head, some rolling onto the shotgun and the top of his hospital gown.

* * *

Watson was already inside the hospital when he took Rachel's call.

"I'm almost at Horton's room now," he remarked while making his way briskly down the corridor.

Rachel updated her colleague who listened intently as he walked. Suddenly he stopped in his tracks.

"So, he went to the same college as James Hampton, at the same time," he remarked. "That does put another dimension on all this."

"Best buddies, it would seem," Rachel remarked. "Carmichael's now totally convinced he's our man. He also lured Lauren Templeton away from the hospital earlier, so we think he may be trying to get to Tim Horton now."

Watson started to walk again, even more quickly than before.

"OK, Rachel," he replied, "let me know how you get on at Mavis Heaton's house, but from what you've just told me, it sounds like she was yet another target of Wisset's."

Watson arrived at the corridor where Tim Horton's room was located.

"There's nobody outside his room," he remarked, the concern clear in his voice.

"Be careful, Marc," Rachel heard herself saying, the last thing she said before she heard the gunshot and the line went dead.

* * *

"Pick up, pick up," Carmichael muttered as Cooper's mobile rang and rang again. He felt an uneasy feeling in his stomach, as if there was something churning around inside him.

He put on his blues and pushed his foot hard on the accelerator.

* * *

Watson had just reached Tim Horton's door when the second gunshot rang out from within. He burst through the door, his senses shocked by the sight and smell that hit him.

With blood everywhere and Cooper clutching at his badly injured leg, Watson's focus shifted to Nigel Wisset, who, still seated, was trying to reload the shotgun.

Within a flash he was on him, knocking the killer to the floor, pushing the gun out of his hands and away under the bed.

His whole being now filled with anger, Watson punched his prisoner with all his might, over and over again until he knew Wisset was incapable. Then he turned his thoughts to the other three occupants of the room.

Chapter 83

As his car neared the hospital gates, Carmichael's heart was pumping, and he could feel the adrenalin surging around his body.

Despite several attempts, he'd not managed to raise Cooper on his mobile and Carmichael instinctively knew something wasn't right.

His fears were only reinforced when, as he pulled into the hospital car park, he could see two police cars in front of the main entrance, empty of any occupants but their lights still flashing. Carmichael abandoned his car next to them, leapt out and rushed headlong into the hospital.

As he neared the corridor where Horton's room was located, he noticed numerous medical staff members rushing ahead of him, their sense of urgency merely confirmation that something was wrong.

As he reached the door, Nigel Wisset emerged, his hands cuffed behind his back and his head bent forward, flanked on either side by two uniformed officers who manhandled him roughly in Carmichael's direction.

"What's happened?" Carmichael shouted.

"Sergeant Cooper and PC Hill have been shot, sir," replied one of the officers, who had instantly recognised Carmichael. "PC Hill's not so bad."

"And Cooper?" enquired Carmichael worriedly.

"They're working on him now, sir," the PC replied, "but it doesn't look good."

For a split second Carmichael glared at Wisset, whose bruised and bloodied face showed no sign of emotion.

"Get him back to Kirkwood Station," he ordered them. "I'll talk with him later."

The uniformed officers nodded, before dragging him down the corridor.

Carmichael briefly stopped and watched as Wisset and his two captors walked away. His thoughts then returned to Cooper and he hurried inside the small private room.

The first thing that struck Carmichael as he entered the room was the sheer number of medical staff in there, all furiously attending to their patients. There was Horton, who was still in bed with what looked like a serious injury to his head, and PC Hill, who was conscious and sitting down on a chair to his left, the right side of his uniform shredded, blood pouring from his right ear and with clear injuries to his right arm and right leg.

Then there was Cooper. He couldn't see him at first, but quickly realised that he was the motionless figure laid on the floor in front of him, surrounded by a nurse and three medics frantically working on his limp, motionless body.

He then noticed the gun on the floor, broken open ready to receive more ammunition, and he became aware of the smell of gunpowder and the amount of blood, splattered on the walls and ceiling and lying in pools across the white lino floor.

Before he could say anything, one of the doctors attending to Cooper looked up, his worried face indicating all was not well.

"We need to get this man to theatre right now," he bellowed.

Seeing Carmichael and Watson standing helplessly, he

347

continued, "I'm not sure who you two are, but I want anyone not attending to the patients out of here."

Without a word, Carmichael and Watson did precisely as they were told, and quickly exited the room.

* * *

To Rachel's delight, the first person she saw when she arrived at Mavis Heaton's cottage was Matthew Stock. Dressed from head to toe in his white overalls, her boyfriend smiled at her as she approached.

"It's all go, today," he said.

"What do you mean?" Rachel enquired.

"Well, we've this crime scene to investigate and the old man and most of the others are now on their way to Southport Hospital. There's apparently been a major incident there, too."

Rachel's heart stopped as she heard the news.

"Did you hear what happened?" she enquired.

Her boyfriend shrugged his shoulders.

"He didn't tell me much," Matthew conceded, referring to Dr Stock, his uncle. "One minute there were six of us here, him moaning about being dragged away from the golf club, then he gets a call and now it's just me and Tony. I can only think what's happened there is considered more serious than what happened here."

Now very worried, Rachel grabbed her mobile from her pocket and started to call Watson.

* * *

"It's Rachel," Watson remarked seeing her name flash up on the screen on his mobile.

"Tell her you're with me and you'll call her back," replied

Carmichael angrily. "I want you to fully update me on what happened in there."

Without any argument, Watson did as he was told, cutting Rachel short with just five words, "I'll call you back later."

"So, what happened?" Carmichael enquired, as soon as Watson had ended the brief conversation.

Watson, his face pale and his hands shaking, shrugged his shoulders. "There were two shots as I got to Horton's room," he replied, "the last one just as I reached the door. I went into the room straight away and saw Paul on the floor. Horton was lying still on the bed, both had clearly been hit, and PC Hill was holding his arm. Wisset was sitting on the chair next to the bed. The shotgun he was holding was broken open and he was loading more cartridges into the barrels."

With Carmichael listening intently, Watson continued.

"I needed to stop him before he could fire more shots, so I rushed him. There was a struggle, but I managed to get the gun away from him and restrain him and get the cuffs on."

As Watson was speaking, Carmichael noticed that his colleague had a bruise on his cheek and the skin on the knuckles of both of his hands was cut and had been bleeding.

"Are you OK, Marc?" Carmichael enquired.

"A bit shaken up to be honest," Watson replied, "but I'm fine."

Carmichael gently put his arm on his colleague's shoulder. "Get yourself a coffee, then go back to the station," he said. "Charge Wisset with attempted murder and get him a brief. I'll hang around here for a while but will join you later and we'll both interview him."

Watson nodded. "Will do, sir," he replied sombrely. "I'll see you later."

As Watson ambled slowly down the corridor, Carmichael's thoughts turned to his other sergeant, fighting for his life in the room just yards away from where he was standing.

Chapter 84

Within two minutes of Watson leaving Carmichael, the medical staff had hurriedly taken Cooper away on a trolley, hooked up to breathing apparatus, a drip in one arm and a tripod on wheels supporting a bag of blood, which they'd also somehow attached to him. Propelled by three medics with a further two nurses in attendance, Cooper's trolley had disappeared down the corridor.

After all the commotion, suddenly he was alone.

Carmichael sat, helpless, on one of the plastic chairs outside Tim Horton's room. As he contemplated all that had just happened, a nurse in a dark-blue uniform appeared.

"How is everyone?" Carmichael enquired.

The nurse smiled. "The two in here are all fine," she replied. "To add to his existing injuries, Mr Horton's got a bad graze to the side of his head, but he doesn't appear to have been badly hurt from the gunshot. The other officer has some wounds to his arm and leg, but he's going to be fine."

"And what about Sergeant Cooper?" Carmichael asked.

"Is he the officer they've taken to theatre?" the nurse enquired.

Carmichael nodded. "Yes," he replied.

The nurse shrugged her shoulders. "I couldn't say about him, I'm afraid, but I can tell you they'll be doing everything to save him."

The words "save him" sent shivers down Carmichael's spine, as they served only to confirm that Cooper's fate was worryingly precarious.

Suddenly two thoughts came into Carmichael's head: he needed to let Hewitt know what was going on and secondly, and more importantly, he needed to inform Cooper's wife, Julia.

* * *

The next three hours passed painfully slowly for Carmichael as he waited in the corridor for news about his trusty colleague.

Although he'd hardly moved in that time, he'd not wasted a second.

His first task had been to call Julia Cooper and advise her of the grave situation her husband was in and that a police car would be with her to bring her to the hospital. He'd then updated Chief Inspector Hewitt, who, realising the gravity of the situation, had cancelled all his appointments for the afternoon and joined Carmichael.

Then he'd had brief conversations with PC Hill and Tim Horton, both of whom were able to add a little more to what Watson had told him about what had happened in the room.

From his conversations with them he now knew that Horton had tried to grab the gun, which prompted the first shot and his injuries, with Cooper and PC Hill being the recipients of the second shot as they tried to rush Wisset.

"He had the look of a madman," PC Hill had remarked. "I have no doubt at all that he intended to kill all three of us."

With Stock and his team taking photos and gathering evidence at the scene, Carmichael had then spoken to Rachel Dalton to get an update on her activities since he'd last seen her, to apprise her on events at the hospital and give her more instructions.

There were two tasks for her: to make sure that Tim Horton's wife and daughter were picked up from the airport, and then to come to the hospital and talk with Mavis Heaton about her ordeal, assuming the old woman had regained consciousness.

As for Watson, Carmichael checked to make sure he'd charged Wisset, and given him access to a solicitor. He also suggested that Watson call Lauren Templeton to let her know what had happened.

* * *

It was just before five o'clock when they received the initial update.

A surgeon, still wearing his greeny-blue gown and matching Croc shoes, joined Carmichael, Julia Cooper and Hewitt, who by then had been moved to a small private anteroom close to the theatre.

From his neutral facial expression, it was impossible for the two senior officers to gauge what he was about to say. They waited anxiously, longing for some positive news.

The surgeon smiled at Julia. "The good news is that your husband is out of danger; he's lost a lot of blood and may need to have more surgery in the days and weeks ahead, but he's currently stable. When he comes out of recovery and he's in the ward, you can see him."

The relief of the news caused Julia to immediately burst into tears, which in turn prompted Hewitt to place a comforting arm around her shoulders, a gesture Julia clearly needed as she wrapped her arm around the chief inspector and started to sob uncontrollably into his neatly pressed jacket.

"Why don't you get yourself back to the station, Steve?" Hewitt remarked. "I'll remain here while you get on with matters there."

Carmichael wanted to embrace Julia too, but for some reason he couldn't and although he tried, he couldn't think of any suitable words for her either.

"Will do, sir," he replied, before rising from his chair, placing a hand on Julia's shoulder for a few seconds and then quietly departing from the room.

* * *

Once he'd walked a matter of twenty paces, Carmichael was in the main corridor of the hospital, and it was as if nothing had changed. Staff, patients and the general public were going about their business as usual, some walking with purpose, others trying to get their bearings. Carmichael couldn't help thinking how bizarre that seemed, when no more than a matter of yards away, there were people fighting for their very survival.

As he exited the hospital, he noticed his car was still where he'd abandoned it earlier, only this time it wasn't flanked by marked police vehicles.

Under normal circumstances, the sight of a parking ticket stuck to his windscreen with yellow and black tape would have made his blood boil, however, on this occasion, it merely made him smile.

Carmichael gently peeled the notice off his window and without even bothering to look at it, opened his car door and threw it onto the passenger seat.

On such a day as today, the financial penalty of receiving a parking ticket was insignificant to the weary, but relieved, inspector.

Chapter 85

Carmichael sat across the table from Nigel Wisset, Watson to his right and to Wisset's left his brief, Mr Frazer.

With PC Newman standing by the door and the recorder running, Watson stated the date, time and place of the interview and the names of the five individuals in the room.

Although he was seething inside, Carmichael knew he had to stay calm and professional and be ultra-vigilant in observing the correct procedures. There was no way he was going to give Wisset or his legal counsel any opportunity to question how the interview was being conducted and hamper the prospect of Wisset receiving the long custodial sentence he deserved.

"Mr Wisset," he began. "Do you admit going to Southport Royal Hospital this afternoon with the sole purpose of killing Tim Horton?"

Nigel Wisset sat back in his chair and coldly and calmly looked directly into Carmichael's eyes.

"You must be mistaken," he replied. "You've got the wrong man."

Undaunted, Carmichael continued.

"What about the murders of Geoffrey Brookwell, Sajid Hanif, Brenda Rumburgh and Sean Attwood?" he continued. "And the attempted murders of Mavis Heaton, PC Hill and Sergeant Cooper. What have you got to say about all of those charges?"

"Why on earth would I want to kill or harm any of them?" Wisset replied. "What motive would I have? Since coming to the school I've never even met Sean Attwood or Sajid Hanif. I know Attwood's daughter, of course, that young delinquent. But I can't say I've ever met her father."

Carmichael paused for a few seconds before continuing.

"You're very hot on behaviour, aren't you?" he remarked. "Bullying is met with zero tolerance in your book, isn't it, Mr Wisset?"

"Absolutely," Wisset replied. "You, as much as anyone, should know how devastating it is to be bullied," Wisset replied. "Just consider what your own daughter has just gone through and what effect it's already had on her life."

"This interview's not about my family, Mr Wisset," Carmichael remarked, still calm, but his words pointed as if to let him know he wasn't about to tolerate any nonsense. "This interview is to try and get the facts from you about these murders and attempted murders. Your opportunity to explain why you did what you did."

Nigel Wisset shook his head gently.

"What evidence do you have to support this ludicrous claim?" he enquired.

Carmichael stared directly into Wisset's eyes.

"For a start we have found fibres under Sajid Hanif's fingernails," he replied calmly. "I'm confident when our SOCO team looks through your drawers and wardrobe and ferrets about in your linen basket, we'll find a garment that matches those fibres."

Wisset simply shrugged his shoulders.

"You have no idea at all, do you?" he remarked, a smirk of arrogant pleasure on his face. "And I'm certainly not going to make your life easier, Inspector. Search away."

Carmichael maintained his piercing stare.

"I think you've a lot of work to do yet, before you get the

right person for these incidents," continued Wisset. "You've charged the wrong man."

Carmichael sat back in his chair and considered his options.

"Let's leave it at that for now, Mr Wisset," he remarked. "We'll talk again in a few hours. Hopefully, it will give you some time to think more clearly."

Without bothering to say anything more, Carmichael rose from his chair and headed for the door.

"There is one thing," announced Wisset's brief. "My client would like to raise a complaint about the excessive force used upon him by this officer, earlier today." As he spoke, he pointed a finger at Watson.

Carmichael half turned and glared back at the brief.

"By all means," he replied. "You're free to register your complaint as you see fit. I'm sure the duty sergeant will take the details, but I don't think anyone in their right mind would uphold such a claim, when only seconds earlier, your client had discharged two rounds at almost point-blank range, with the intent to kill or injure three people. With him trying to reload the gun, I'd say Sergeant Watson deserves a commendation for his actions, and there's not a court in the land that would uphold any crazy claim you have regarding the use of excessive force; but, by all means, complain if you wish."

Carmichael didn't wait for any reply, he simply turned back around and exited the interview room.

* * *

It took Rachel almost five minutes to find Spencer Ward, where Mavis Heaton had been admitted.

When she eventually managed to locate the old lady, she found her semi-conscious, but with tubes and wires attached all over her.

Sitting silently on either side of her bed were Jenny and Jade Attwood, neither of whom said anything when Rachel entered the room.

"How is she?" Rachel enquired.

Jenny Attwood looked up at the young DC and shrugged her shoulders.

"The good news is that she's alive," she remarked, "but so far it's not clear how much damage her brain has sustained. The doctors say it may be some time before they can fully assess what state she's in."

Rachel smiled sympathetically. "Has she said anything about what happened or who did this to her?" she enquired.

"She hasn't spoken yet," remarked Jade Attwood, "but when I asked her she made a sign that she wanted a pencil and paper. When I gave her it, she wrote this."

Jade picked up a scrap of paper from the bedside cabinet and passed it to Rachel.

Rachel took the paper from Mavis's granddaughter and read the three spider-like words that Mavis had written.

"That can't be right," she remarked, her face showing her bemusement.

"That's what we said, too," said Jenny. "It just shows how confused she is."

* * *

"So, what do you make of all that, sir?" Watson enquired as he and Carmichael walked slowly down the corridor.

"He's playing games," replied Carmichael with a smile. "Hopefully, after he's had an hour talking to his brief, he'll be more rational."

"He showed no signs at all of any remorse," continued Watson, "kept saying we had the wrong man. It was almost as if he, smugly, knew something we didn't."

Carmichael stopped walking and smiled.

"He did, didn't he?" Carmichael remarked.

"What is it, sir?" Watson enquired.

"Have you not been wondering how Wisset knew about that barn and why he'd want to kill people he'd hardly met?" Carmichael remarked.

Watson nodded. "Of course," he replied. "His lack of local knowledge and the fact he wasn't around when Billy Taylor died were always the main reasons why he wasn't one of our main suspects."

"Well, I have a theory which answers both of those questions," remarked Carmichael. "I need you to do a bit of digging for me before I'm certain and we talk with Wisset again, but I think I know what's going on here."

Watson listened intently but said nothing.

"Go back over Rachel's work on Wisset's past, right back to his time at the college in Alsager," continued Carmichael. "Then check to see if Nigel Wisset has a police record. Go back as far as you can on that."

"Will do," replied Watson. "Is there anything in particular you want me to look out for in his past?"

Carmichael shook his head. "No, just find out as much as you can about Wisset and, while you're at it, his pal, James Hampton. I'd like to know more about them both and just how close their friendship was when they were at college."

"Will do, sir," replied Watson. "What are you going to be doing?"

Carmichael looked at his watch and smiled. "I'm going to call Rachel," he replied. "I need her to do something for me, too."

Chapter 86

With Mavis Heaton being unable to talk and drifting in and out of consciousness, Rachel Dalton had decided to go down three floors to where Cooper was being cared for.

When she entered the small anteroom where Julia Cooper and Chief Inspector Hewitt were waiting, she could feel the anxiety in the air.

"Any progress updates?" Rachel enquired in a whisper.

Julie Cooper looked over at Rachel, her eyes red and the skin below puffy and swollen.

"Not much," she replied. "He's alive and stable, but they say he may never walk again and could even need to have his leg amputated."

As she spoke her voice started to tremble and she broke down into floods of tears.

Rachel walked briskly over to Julia and embraced her tightly.

"We all have to be positive," she heard herself saying. "Paul's a strong man, a fighter. He'll not give up."

Still wrapped in her arms, Rachel could feel Julia Cooper nodding.

"Yes, he is," she replied. "But I'm so very scared."

At that moment Rachel's mobile started to ring. Her immediate thought was to leave it, but Julia Cooper, on hearing the call coming through, pulled herself away from Rachel's comforting hug.

"If I'm not mistaken, that will be Carmichael," she remarked. "He's got a knack for calling at the wrong moment."

Rachel smiled. "He certainly does," she replied, as she removed the phone from her pocket. "And you're right, it's the boss."

Even the normally undemonstrative Chief Inspector Hewitt couldn't help sharing a smile with the two ladies in the room as Rachel put her mobile to her ear and said, "Hello, sir."

* * *

With Watson and Rachel Dalton both in receipt of their instructions and having been told by Rachel whom Mavis was claiming to be her assailant, Carmichael went back to the office and started to jot down notes on the whiteboard against the various questions and unknowns.

He was now sure of his theory and was convinced that, between them, Rachel Dalton and Watson, with a little help from Stock, would provide all the evidence he needed to support it.

It took a little longer than he'd hoped, but within ninety minutes he'd spoken to both officers again and was now ready to re-interview the headmaster of his daughter's school.

* * *

"Well, have you had an opportunity to rethink what you'd like to say to us?" Carmichael asked, confidence oozing from him as he spoke.

Nigel Wisset sat upright with his arms folded but didn't reply.

"My client has decided he does not want to answer any more questions," replied Frazer, Wisset's brief.

360

Carmichael smiled and nodded sagely.

"Well, first of all, I'd like to say on behalf of the Mid-Lancashire police department, it appears that we've charged the wrong man for the murders of Geoffrey Brookwell, Sajid Hanif, Mrs Rumburgh and Sean Attwood. We've also charged the wrong man for the attempted murder of Mavis Heaton, Tim Horton, Sergeant Cooper and PC Hill."

After ending his surprise confession, Carmichael looked firstly directly into the eyes of Wisset, then his solicitor, with no trace of any emotion on his face. Watson, on other hand, couldn't disguise his small smirk of triumph, a look which clearly unnerved the silent headmaster.

Chapter 87

"So, my client is free to go?" Frazer enquired.

"Good gracious, no," replied Carmichael. "The person sitting next to you won't be going anywhere for a long time, other than prison. However, we do need to re-caution him, which my sergeant will do now."

"Is this some sort of game you're playing, Inspector?" remarked Frazer, who was clearly annoyed by the strange, sudden turn of events that was unfolding in front of him.

Carmichael smiled then turned his attention to Nigel Wisset, who no longer looked anywhere near as smug as he had in their earlier interview, or even a few moments ago, for that matter.

"Shall I tell him or will you?" he remarked.

Wisset remained silent but fidgeted anxiously in his seat.

"Mr Frazer," continued Carmichael, "what your client has been hiding from everyone, including you, is that his name is not Nigel Wisset. The man sitting next to you is, in fact, James Hampton."

Frazer's eyes almost popped out of his head and he turned to face his client.

Carmichael smiled, his voice sounding victorious, as he had no doubt that he was right. "Isn't that right, James?" he remarked.

"James Hampton's dead," replied the man sitting

opposite him. "He died in a car crash in Australia fifteen years ago."

Carmichael shook his head gently.

"No, James," he replied. "It was Nigel Wisset that died in that car crash."

"Prove it," the suspect remarked.

Carmichael smiled again.

"Can you remember that DNA sample you gave earlier, when you were charged?" continued Carmichael.

"What of it?" the man across the table replied.

"Well, we're currently comparing it to a DNA sample from Mavis Heaton, James Hampton's mother. And we expect our forensic team will shortly verify that the two samples could only have come from a parent and child. Now, unless you're going to tell me that Mavis Heaton is both James Hampton's and Nigel Wisset's mother, then the only conclusion we will be able to draw from that match is that you are not Nigel Wisset, you're Mavis Heaton's son, James Hampton."

James Hampton paused for a few seconds before unfolding his arms and clapping his hands, slowly but loudly.

"Congratulations, Inspector," he remarked. "Credit where it's due, you're right. Apart from Aunt Brenda, you're the only person who twigged that. Not Brookwell, not Sajid, not Attwood, not even Horton earlier today, and until a few hours before that, not even my precious loving mother knew I was James Hampton."

"Which is why you had to kill her," remarked Carmichael, "just like you had to kill your poor Aunt Brenda."

Hampton shrugged his shoulders.

"Very unfortunate, but I think they call it collateral damage," he replied coolly.

"So, do I take it the intention was only to kill Brookwell, Attwood, Hanif and Horton?" suggested Carmichael.

363

"Yes," replied Hampton, "the three bullies and the cowardly excuse of a friend. I wanted those three to be finally punished for all they put us through, and Sajid for not having the balls to tell the truth about what happened that day, when those three monsters drove Billy into the canal and to his death."

"Did you plan all this when you were at college with the real Nigel Wisset?" interjected Watson.

The man they now knew as James Hampton shook his head vigorously.

"No," he replied. "The plan was for us only to switch identities for a few years while Nigel was in Australia. Once he returned, we'd revert back."

"But why the need to do that?" enquired the brief, who was still looking somewhat confused and keen to learn more about what was unfolding around him.

"Oh, that's easy, Mr Frazer," replied Carmichael. "The real Nigel Wisset could not go to Australia as he had a criminal conviction for possession of drugs, some minor misdemeanour he'd picked up in his first year at college. We discovered that earlier. Isn't that right, James?"

James Hampton nodded. "Yes, he was desperate to work in Australia for a few years; he'd been there as a child and had fallen in love with the place. So, we decided to do the switch."

"But what about your friends and family?" enquired Watson. "How did you manage to hoodwink them?"

"Neither of us were close to our parents; estranged, you'd call it," replied Hampton. "We were also both only children, well I have a half-sister, but we have never had anything to do with each other, so it was easy. I'd never been abroad, so when Nigel needed to get a passport in my name it was a doddle. He just applied, sent his photo, with a forged verification in Aunt Brenda's name and we were away. It was also then I grew this beard. It's amazing what a beard does to alter your appearance, and it's fooled everyone since I've been here."

"Apart from Mrs Rumburgh," remarked Carmichael. "You said she spotted you straight away."

Hampton smiled. "She recognised me immediately," he replied. "As soon as I arrived at the interview."

"Did she not ask why you'd assumed a new identity?" Carmichael enquired.

Hampton nodded. "She did. I told her it was so I could have a fresh start back here and that I didn't want my mother or my half-sister to know I was back."

"And she believed that?" questioned Carmichael.

"I was always her favourite nephew," he replied. "She'd have believed I was Santa Claus if I told her."

Carmichael nodded.

"I can see what Nigel got out of the switch, but what about you?" he continued. "If the plan wasn't to use your new identity to help you commit these murders then what did you get from the exchange?"

James Hampton smiled.

"Nigel was far cleverer than me and had gained a first," he replied.

"I'd only got a two-two, so it helped me get a good job straight from college. The plan was that I could then use the work experience in Australia, when I became James Hampton again, to help me get other jobs. So, the only issue I had in all of this was that I could never travel abroad, as I did not look like my passport photo of Nigel. But I've never wanted to travel so that was no hardship."

"And then he died," remarked Carmichael.

"That was a shock," admitted Hampton, who looked genuinely sad as he spoke. "He was my only true friend, so that hit me hard. And, of course, it meant that I had to remain as Nigel Wisset forever, which I didn't mind as, if I'm honest, I liked being him more than being James."

* * *

After hours in surgery and an hour in recovery, Cooper was finally admitted to a private room where Julia and his other visitors were able to see him.

Hewitt and Rachel Dalton remained outside for a further twenty minutes, giving Julia time to be alone with her husband.

When they were finally allowed in, it was Chief Inspector Hewitt who spoke first.

"How are you feeling, Paul?" he enquired.

Hewitt had been the senior officer at Kirkwood for over twenty years, and in all that time Cooper couldn't ever remember him calling him Paul; he was even surprised he knew his first name.

"A bit dazed still, if I'm honest," he replied, "but not too bad, considering."

"You were incredibly brave in there today," continued Hewitt. "As a result of your actions, Tim Horton's life has been saved and who knows how many more people that maniac would have killed if you'd not intervened."

"Thank you, sir," Cooper replied. "It all happened so quickly, I really didn't have time to think about what I was doing or the implications. It just seemed the correct thing to do."

Rachel moved closer to the bed and placed her hand on her colleague's arm.

"You scared the hell out of us all," she remarked. "You even had Marc Watson worried about you."

Cooper smiled. "I expect he'll get over it pretty quickly," he replied.

Chapter 88

Carmichael looked up at the clock in the interview room. It read fifteen minutes to eight.

"Tell me, when did you decide to find and kill Geoffrey Brookwell, Sean Attwood, Sajid Hanif and Tim Horton?" he asked. "Was it before you saw the headmaster post advertised at the academy or after you'd arrived?"

Hampton smiled. "To be honest, that only came into my thinking after I'd met Brookwell," he replied, "and I'd seen how he'd managed to just get on with his life and forget the part he'd played in Billy's death. He even managed to get a job at the academy helping students. I ask you, a bully responsible for the death of a child, actually allowed to work with other kids, in the very school where he committed that crime. It's disgusting."

"What about the other three?" Carmichael enquired. "When did you decide to kill them, too?"

"You don't have to answer any of these questions," Frazer remarked.

Hampton just ignored him.

"Once I'd met Brookwell, the man, I decided to track the other three down," he replied. "It wasn't that hard as they'd not ventured too far away. They'd all done well for themselves, too. Horton was a successful business entrepreneur, Attwood seemed to be doing fine as a general builder and Sajid Hanif was an optician. Quite honestly, when I thought of the part they all played in poor Billy's death, it made my blood boil to see that they hadn't had any punishment for their actions, or in Sajid's case, his inaction."

"So, you decided to act as judge and jury and kill them," remarked Carmichael.

"Exactly," replied Hampton. "And it was a doddle. There were two common denominators they all shared: greed and ambition. I just appealed to those base instincts and regarding Brookwell, Hanif and Attwood, as they say, it was a walk in the park."

Not a hint of remorse could be seen on Hampton's face as he recounted the story of why he decided to kill. In fact, Carmichael had no doubt that the man sitting opposite him still believed what he'd done was no more than mete out fair justice.

* * *

Chief Inspector Hewitt and DC Dalton remained with the Coopers for only a few minutes before leaving Paul and his very relieved wife alone.

"Get plenty of rest," was Hewitt's last instruction before he left the room. "Carmichael will have to cope while you're out of action, so don't get any hare-brained ideas about coming back to work before you're ready."

Cooper smiled. "I suspect I won't be allowed to," he replied, his eyes moving sideways in his wife's direction.

"I'll pop in and see you tomorrow, if that's OK," Rachel remarked.

"That's fine by me," replied Cooper. "I've no plans to be going anywhere."

Rachel smiled at her colleague then, after giving Julia a massive hug, followed Hewitt out of the room.

As soon as the two officers were outside, Hewitt puffed out his cheeks. "Cooper has been very lucky," he remarked. "That could have all ended much more seriously."

Rachel nodded. "I know," she replied. "I reckon he'll be months in recovery before he can come back to work."

Hewitt turned to face the young officer. "It could be years, Detective Constable," he said. "That is if he ever does come back. Even if he makes a full physical recovery, psychologically this may take many years for him to come to terms with. I'd not build your hopes up too high."

Without bothering to wait for Rachel to say anything more, Hewitt straightened his cap and started to march down the corridor, leaving Rachel alone and somewhat stunned by what he'd told her.

Chapter 89

Had James Hampton or his brief pushed hard for an adjournment until the following day, Carmichael would have felt unable to refuse; however, Hampton seemed happy to tell his interrogators everything and as Carmichael wanted to get as much as he could on the tape, he was more than delighted to carry on all night if necessary.

"So, slowly talk me through each murder," he said. "In your words just explain how you went about planning and accomplishing them."

Carmichael selected his words carefully. In choosing the terms "planning" and "accomplishing" he wanted to appeal to Hampton's warped sense of achievement at his heinous crimes. He wasn't mistaken.

Hampton smiled, nodded gently then leaned forward.

"Being a struggling actor, I knew the one thing that Brookwell would be dreaming about was a big break," replied Hampton. "So, that's what I gave him."

A cruel smile came over Hampton's face as he thought back to what he'd done with Brookwell.

"A simple phone call, then a parcel with more detailed instructions, some cash and the carrot of a lucrative high-profile role was far too much for him," continued Hampton. "I knew it would be. I even got the fool to attach false plates to the car and smother his hands in pig blood. He hadn't an inkling about the significance of the number plate or what he was doing covering his hands in blood. He just thought, as I told him, that he was doing a role play with another actor playing a vicar to secure the part. The imbecile believed me when I said that there were cameras hidden about the church to capture his acting skills. What an idiot."

"Where did you get that blood?" Watson asked.

Hampton smiled. "The school has an arrangement with a local abattoir, which gives us blood at times for the biology department," replied Hampton. "I simply took a small bag from the refrigerator in the lab and enclosed it in the package I sent Brookwell."

Watson looked over in Carmichael's direction with a look that said, *I told you so.*

Carmichael remained totally impassive to both Hampton and his sergeant's glance.

"The 'Billy Taylor rest in peace' was a clever touch," Carmichael remarked, again trying hard to pander to Hampton's belief in his own intellect.

"You got that, did you?" replied Hampton, a small self-righteous smile appearing on his face. "Then at least it wasn't a total waste of time. I had to spell it out to Brookwell when we met in Wood Lane and to Attwood later, when I showed it to him in the barn."

"So, you met Brookwell down Wood Lane, did you?" continued Carmichael. "Was that in his instructions?"

"Absolutely," replied Hampton. "The idiot was supposed to go much further down the lane. I wanted to lure him into the old barn, but he parked up far too early."

"So, you planned to kill him in the old barn?" Carmichael confirmed.

Hampton nodded. "He couldn't even get that instruction right."

As he spoke, it was clear that Hampton was still annoyed

that Brookwell hadn't carried out his instructions to the letter.

"So, what happened when you met Brookwell down Wood Lane?" Carmichael asked.

"He'd parked about half a mile short of where he should have been," replied Hampton. "And when he saw me walk over to him, he was perplexed. Then when I told him there was no role and that I had called him and sent him the package, he went berserk."

As he recounted the details of their meeting, Hampton maintained an expression of calmness.

"I soon put an end to that," he continued. "Even then he never twigged who I was. He just kept asking why."

"And was there a struggle?" Carmichael enquired.

Hampton frowned. "No," he replied nonchalantly. "After shouting at the top of his voice for a few seconds, he then turned to walk back to the car. It was then I did it."

"Did what?" Carmichael enquired.

"Slit his throat," replied Hampton. "And as I watched him die, choking and coughing as he drowned in his own blood, I told him who I really was and why he was being punished. He could no longer reply of course, but I wanted to make sure he knew why he had to die, before he took his last breath."

It wasn't the first time in his career that Carmichael had been face to face with a man so void of morality, but even so, he found it almost impossible to listen to Hampton without feeling both anger and nausea welling up inside him.

"Why don't we take a short break there," Carmichael remarked, a suggestion that Watson and Hampton's brief both appeared to welcome.

* * *

Whether it was the relief of knowing he was going to pull through or the enormity of the uphill journey that Cooper would now be facing, she wasn't sure; however, as Rachel made her way down the M6 motorway towards Manchester Airport, tears streamed almost endlessly down her cheeks and she found herself having to deliberately control her breathing.

Although she was thankful that her colleague was alive, she realised that life for Cooper and his wife would never be the same, and that his absence, maybe on a permanent basis, would mean the small team she loved being a part of, would never be the same either.

* * *

Carmichael and Watson sat together in the canteen, plastic cups of coffee from the vending machine in front of them.

"What do you make of him?" Watson asked.

"Frighteningly calm about everything he's done," replied Carmichael. "There's not a shred of guilt or remorse; in fact he's actually enjoying telling us about what he's done."

Watson nodded. "I know," he replied. "It's chilling."

Carmichael took a small sip of coffee.

"But whilst he's happy to tell us everything, we need to plough on," he remarked. "I don't know about you, but I just needed a quick break."

Watson nodded again. "Me too," he replied.

"Well, we've had that now, so let's get back in there and get everything down on tape before he clams up."

Watson took a hasty last sip of coffee.

"I agree," he replied.

Chapter 90

Carmichael and Watson were just about to restart their interview with James Hampton, when Hewitt arrived back at Kirkwood station. Keen to hear what was being said, he quietly slipped into the small anteroom to watch and listen to proceedings, unnoticed, through the two-way mirror.

"So, James," Carmichael began, "you've explained why and how you killed Geoffrey Brookwell, now tell us about Sajid Hanif."

To Carmichael's relief, the short break had made no change whatsoever to Hampton's eagerness to talk openly. As Hewitt looked on, the man under caution continued to provide a full and detailed account of his actions, requiring only the slightest of prompts along the way from his questioners.

For two hours, Hampton told them everything: that Sajid Hanif had to die to be punished for not telling the whole story about Billy Taylor's death; that he'd removed Sajid's tongue as a punishment for him failing to use it when it was needed; that he'd chosen room seven at the Lindley as he'd stayed there for three weeks when he first got the job at the academy and he knew that the CCTV cameras did not extend to that room. He outlined how he'd arrived and departed on foot using the footpath that ran from the road to the outside rooms, how he'd made sure Sajid Hanif knew why he was being killed before he died. He explained how he'd lured Attwood to room seven,

374

through a call he'd made to him on his burner phone, pretending to be a potential customer wanting to show him some plans he had for a new house he wanted building in the village.

"Why did you do that?" Carmichael had asked.

"I hadn't made up my mind whether to kill Attwood or just frame him for the other murders," Hampton had calmly replied. "It was my plan B, a backup in case I changed my mind about killing him."

"But you didn't change your mind," Carmichael had said.

"No," Hampton had replied, coolly. "On balance, I decided I couldn't let him off with just a prison sentence. And there was always a chance a jury would have found him not guilty. I couldn't have that."

"Especially as Mavis brought him up as her own when she had abandoned you," Carmichael remarked cruelly.

Hampton glared back at Carmichael but said nothing.

Only when he talked about Mrs Rumburgh's death did Hampton show any signs of regret. But as he told Carmichael and Watson, "She knew something was up after you visited her. She got out some of the old files on us all and then asked me if I'd come in."

"Did she know it was you?" Carmichael had asked.

Hampton had paused for a few seconds before shaking his head and answering. "She wasn't sure, but I could tell she was starting to twig it was me. She had my folder out from when I was a pupil, along with Billy's and those of Sajid Hanif, Brookwell, Attwood and Horton."

"What happened?" Carmichael had asked.

"I snatched them from her and told her to get home and that I'd talk with her later," Hampton had replied.

"That's when you went round and killed her," Carmichael had said. "Then tried to make it look like suicide."

Hampton nodded. "I'd not had time to plan her demise," he'd remarked as if to excuse the way he'd despatched his

375

aunty. "But I did get her guns. I thought they'd come in handy."

When asked why he'd almost immediately told Carmichael that Mrs Rumburgh wouldn't have tried to kill herself, Hampton again smiled, an arrogant smile, from someone pleased with his own ingenuity.

"When I got home and had had a chance to think more clearly, I thought you may not buy it was suicide," he'd replied. "To try and stop you placing suspicion on someone from the academy, I thought I'd pre-empt you and hopefully throw any suspicion you may have away from me. And I succeeded, didn't I?"

Carmichael had just nodded gently, happy to allow Hampton to keep believing he'd been successful, although inwardly what he really wanted to tell him was far less flattering.

Moving on, Hampton talked in great detail about how he'd lured Attwood to the old barn down Wood Lane, killed him and left the number plates and suicide note.

"Did you think we'd believe he was the murderer?" Carmichael had asked.

Hampton had just smiled. "I wasn't sure, to be frank," he'd replied. "I hoped so, but I just wanted to buy myself time to kill Horton. Which it did. And had that old woman who gave birth to me not interrupted me, I reckon I'd have killed him too. I had to see to her first, as she'd realised it was me. If it wasn't for that delay, I'd have finished off Horton at the hospital."

"And my sergeant, too," Carmichael had said.

"Collateral damage," Hampton had remarked for the second time, a phrase that irritated Carmichael, who just about managed to keep his feelings in check.

With the time now close to 10:30pm and with a substantial confession safely recorded, Carmichael decided to end the interview.

"Take him to the cells," he'd instructed PC Newman. "We'll talk with him again tomorrow."

Chapter 91

As soon as Watson and Carmichael left the interview room, they were joined by Chief Inspector Hewitt.

"Good work, Carmichael," he remarked. "That confession you've taken should put him away for the rest of his life."

Carmichael nodded.

"When did you discover he was really James Hampton?" Hewitt enquired.

"As soon as we were aware of James Hampton being a pupil at the school I'd wondered if he could have come back," replied Carmichael. "He'd have the local knowledge and would have known all the people killed. However, when we learnt Hampton had died, he dropped out of the frame and with Wisset being from Ramsbottom, we assumed he wouldn't have the local knowledge to be a really serious suspect."

"So, what changed?" Hewitt asked.

"It was when Wisset was so insistent that we'd got the wrong man," replied Carmichael. "The way he looked at me when he was protesting his innocence was not the look of a man who genuinely thought he'd been wrongly charged, it was the look of a man who was smug, believing he was smarter than us. I then got to thinking of what Rachel had told us about Hampton going to college in Cheshire and I remembered seeing Wisset's degree certificate from Alsager on his office wall. It was then that it suddenly occurred to me that maybe the man we believed to be Wisset was actually Hampton. When that thought came into my head it suddenly explained everything. An explanation that was substantiated by the note Mavis penned from the hospital saying her attacker was James Hampton."

"You seem to have all the answers already, Carmichael," announced Hewitt.

"Not quite," replied Carmichael. "But what we don't know, we'll get out of Hampton when we talk with him again tomorrow, I'm sure."

After a brief pause, Carmichael looked directly at Hewitt. "How's Cooper?" he enquired.

"He's doing reasonably well, considering," Hewitt replied. "He's out of danger and they feel that there's a very good chance they'll save his leg."

"That's brilliant news," interrupted Watson.

"However," continued Hewitt, "he'll be out of action for months, maybe years, and we have to accept that he may actually never return to active duty."

Carmichael nodded. "I'll pop in and see him on my way home."

"I'd leave it for today," suggested Hewitt. "He's very tired and he's with his wife. I think tomorrow may be wiser."

Carmichael nodded. "You're right," he conceded.

"I'll go and make sure Hampton is properly processed," Watson remarked.

"Yes," replied Carmichael wearily. "Then get yourself off home, too."

Watson nodded. "Thanks, sir," he said. "What time are you planning on interviewing Hampton tomorrow?"

Carmichael considered the question.

"Let's shoot for eleven thirty in the morning," he replied. "Give us all some time to get some rest. Today's been a one hell of a day."

Watson smiled. "You can say that again," he replied, before heading away towards the custody suite.

"You've got a great team, Carmichael," remarked Hewitt as the pair watched Watson disappear down the corridor.

"I think so," Carmichael replied.

Thinking their conversation was at an end, Carmichael started to walk away towards his office. He was quickly brought to a halt when he heard Hewitt's voice once more.

"I guess now that Cooper's going to be out of action for a considerable period, bringing back Lucy Clark is a no-brainer. Don't you agree?"

Carmichael's throat suddenly felt dry and he could feel the small hairs on the back of his neck starting to rise.

"Don't you think that's a bit hasty?" he replied, turning as he spoke to face his boss. "We've no idea when Cooper will be back."

"Not at all," replied Hewitt. "We'd have to tell her that she's here purely on a temporary basis until Cooper returns, but it makes perfect sense. She knows us, we know her and she's clearly a great officer. I don't see any problem."

"Maybe," Carmichael remarked, "but I always feel that once an officer moves on, then it's best that they don't come back. I think she may find it hard to adjust back into our way of doing things."

"If I didn't know better, I'd say there was an issue between you and her, Inspector," remarked Hewitt. "I hope you don't harbour any of those old-fashioned misogynistic views."

Carmichael shook his head. "It's nothing to do with her gender," he assured Hewitt, "I just want to make sure whoever joins us fits in with the team in general."

Carmichael could see that his feeble protestations weren't having any impact on Hewitt, who just looked bemused at what he was hearing.

"Trust me, Steve," he replied. "If it doesn't work out, I'll be the first to send her packing; however, I've made up my mind and I'll be informing the powers that be that we have a position for her, albeit a temporary one, until we know more about Sergeant Cooper's situation."

Carmichael could think of nothing more he could say to stop what now appeared to be an inevitable disaster from happening.

He shrugged his shoulders and with a sick feeling in the pit of his stomach, turned away and headed towards his office.

* * *

Having collected Mrs Horton and her daughter Hayley from Manchester Airport and taken them both to Southport Hospital, it was close to midnight when Rachel arrived back at her flat, tired and still overcome by the events of the day.

She was delighted to be met at her door by Matt Stock who gave her a warm, engulfing hug.

"Are you OK?" he asked her.

Rachel shook her head and dissolved into floods of tears.

"No," she replied, "I'm not. I don't think anything will ever be the same again."

At about the same time, unbeknown to her, her boss was also arriving home. Like Rachel, he was exhausted and, although for altogether different reasons, he, too, now believed that life moving forward was not going to be easy.

What he hadn't expected, when he pulled up in the drive, was his soulmate, Penny, to be at the door to greet him.

With concern clearly etched on her face, she smiled. A smile that was as loving and caring as it always was.

Although Carmichael was able to return a smile back at her, inside he felt wretched and he was truly terrified about what may lie ahead with Lucy Clark returning to his team.

Chapter 92

Sunday 5th July

Carmichael hadn't managed to get to sleep until around 2am. After spending over an hour giving Penny the details of the case, and answering the many, many questions she had, he'd retired to his attic study where he'd drunk several glasses of malt whisky before finally to going to bed.

When he awoke, it was already 8:45am.

"I guess we're giving church a miss this morning," Penny remarked with cheery optimism as she rested a mug of coffee on the bedside cabinet next to her husband.

Carmichael sat up and looked at the time on the alarm clock next to him.

"Bugger!" he remarked. Then, "No, I think we can still make it. I'll just grab a quick shower and we can get off."

"OK, dear," replied Penny, who secretly thought she'd escaped the weekly family pilgrimage that she and their children disliked so much. "It will just be me, you and Natalie if she's up, as the other two have gone out already."

Carmichael leapt from his bed and headed off to the bathroom, leaving his wife alone, her comment unanswered.

An hour later, Carmichael, his wife and their youngest arrived at their parish church, perched halfway up Ambient Hill, the biggest hill for miles around.

Unusually, the church was almost full, which Carmichael guessed was due to people wanting to see if they could gather the latest information on the murders that had taken place that week. In the small community of Moulton Bank, the two pubs, the hairdresser's and the two churches were the places to go if you wanted to get the latest gossip.

As the congregation arrived, Natalie nudged her mother.

"There's Jade Attwood and her mum," she remarked, her head gesticulating in the direction of the two figures who were across the aisle a matter of three or four pews in front of them.

"I'm surprised to see them both here," Penny whispered to her husband. "After all they've been through, I'd have thought they'd have wanted to stay at home."

Carmichael nodded. "Me too," he whispered back.

* * *

Concerned about Cooper and feeling she should also check on the progress of Mavis Heaton and Tim Horton, Rachel had dragged Matt Stock out of bed at 8:30am and the pair were already at Southport Hospital by 10am.

She was relieved when she learned that all three had experienced uneventful, comfortable nights and that they were all awake and able to receive visitors.

Rachel's top priority was to see Cooper, who had been propped up in bed and was quietly talking with Julia, who held on to his hand tightly.

"It's the young lovers," he remarked with a friendly smile. "What brings you to my neck of the woods?"

Rachel smiled first at Julia, then at her colleague. "Well, you know, we were just passing so we thought we'd drop in."

Cooper smiled back. "It's really lovely to see you both," he replied.

*** *** ***

Although Penny never liked going to church on Sunday, the one saving grace was that Reverend Barney Green was a young man who always tried his best to make the services interesting and as enjoyable as possible; his services were invariably short, too, never going over forty-five minutes.

At 10:45, when the congregation started to depart, Penny knew that she had the rest of the day to herself. Steve had already told her he'd be going into the station as soon as he'd dropped her and Natalie off, and with Natalie planning to go and see her horse, and her other two offspring already out and about, Penny was looking forward to a day at home by herself.

As the congregation filed out of the church, shaking Barney Green's hand, the Carmichaels found themselves only a few people ahead of Jenny and Jade Attwood.

This proximity did not go unnoticed by Penny, who immediately felt anxious about how Natalie would feel, her tormentor-in-chief being so close.

She needn't have worried, as no sooner had they shaken Barney Green's hand and walked a few paces away from the church, their daughter, without saying a word, turned back and strode confidently over to Jade and her mother.

"I was really sorry to hear about your dad, Jade," Penny heard her daughter say. "And I hope your nan feels better soon."

From a few paces away, Carmichael and his wife listened as the two young ladies spoke.

"Thank you," Jade replied. "It doesn't seem real somehow, and it's really kind of you to say so, especially after the way we all behaved towards you."

Natalie gave Jade a hug, not an all-embracing smothering hug that happens between family and friends, but a gentle hug, to reinforce her words.

"That was really generous of you, Natalie," her mum said as they reached Carmichael's car.

Natalie simply shrugged her shoulders and opened her door.

"I feel sorry for her," she replied. "She's obviously going to be grieving and must have issues anyway, from the way she's been treating me. I just wanted her to know that, although she's a horrible person, it doesn't mean that others don't realise she's having a rough time."

"There's a career for you in social work, I'd say," Penny remarked.

Natalie smiled. "No way," she replied. "There's no money in that and I'm going to be a millionaire before I'm thirty. You can't do that being a social worker."

Penny looked across at her husband, who smiled back at her and started the car engine.

Chapter 93

Having left Cooper and his wife, Rachel Dalton and Matt Stock went over to Knowles ward where Tim Horton had spent the night.

As they approached the door of his private room, a tall woman appeared, who rushed quickly past them, her eyes streaming with tears and her left hand trying hard to wipe them away. The two watched as the woman disappeared out of sight.

"That's Lauren Templeton," Rachel remarked. "She works at the school and is Tim Horton's love interest."

Matt laughed. "Love interest," he repeated. "That's a bit Mills and Boon isn't it?"

"Girlfriend then," replied Rachel, digging her elbow deep into Matt's ribs.

"Ouch," yelled Matt. "Well, whoever she is, she's not very happy," he replied, rubbing his side.

"No, she isn't," Rachel replied. "I wonder what's happened."

The two exchanged a quick glance before entering Tim Horton's room.

* * *

Having dropped off Penny and Natalie at home, Carmichael sped down the country lanes which lead to Kirkwood.

No matter how hard he tried, his thoughts were never far away from the impending arrival of Lucy Clark and how that would play out given the circumstances when they last met.

Without reaching any conclusion, Carmichael found himself entering the car park at Kirkwood police station and coming to rest in his usual parking space.

He looked at his watch and took some satisfaction in the fact that he'd arrived with thirteen minutes to spare before the allotted time he'd given Watson the day before.

Although there wasn't much more he needed to glean from James Hampton, he wanted to spend a further hour or two with him, making sure he had all the evidence he needed to secure a safe prosecution and hopefully, a hefty sentence for the cold-blooded killer.

With thoughts of Lucy Clark now banished from his head, Carmichael strode purposefully towards the rear entrance of the police station.

* * *

Tim Horton lay propped up in bed when Rachel and Matt Stock entered his room. His wife, daughter and a young man Rachel didn't recognise, stood by his bed.

"More police, I suppose," he remarked caustically.

"Tim," rebuked his wife, "This is the kind officer who brought Hayley and me over last night."

"Really," replied Horton, his tone suggesting he was still not keen to talk with her.

"Harry and I are just going to the canteen," remarked Hayley. "Do you want anything?"

Tim Horton shook his head. "No, I'm fine," he replied, his response still grumpy.

Hayley and Harry both quietly crept out of the room, leaving Horton, his wife, Matt Stock and Rachel.

"Is that Hayley's boyfriend?" Rachel enquired, her question aimed at Horton's wife.

"Not if I have anything to bloody do with it," snapped Horton. "She's too bloody good for a caretaker. I ask you, what sort of provider is he going to be for her?"

"Well, it's not up to you, Tim," replied Horton's wife. "I don't think it's a serious relationship, but if it does grow more permanent then it's her choice. He's a very nice boy, as it happens."

"Over my dead body," retorted Horton angrily.

"You're looking really well, considering," Rachel remarked, trying to change the subject.

"Considering I almost got my head blown off yesterday. Is that what you're saying?" replied Horton, grumpily. "If your colleagues had done a better job of guarding me, I wouldn't have had to experience any of this. The injuries from the car accident were bad enough."

Despite feeling great empathy with Mrs Horton, who seemed a really pleasant lady, Rachel wasn't about to be bullied by the rude man in the hospital bed, irrespective of his pain and injuries.

"My colleagues saved your life, Mr Horton," she responded angrily. "One of them is now very seriously injured and may never return to duty, and if it wasn't for Sergeant Watson, who risked his life to stop James Hampton, he'd have certainly reloaded the gun and killed you. And as for your other injuries, they were all self-inflicted, due to your reckless driving."

By his open mouth it was clear that Tim Horton hadn't expected a response like that from the slightly built young woman at the end of his bed.

"James Hampton?" remarked Horton. "What are you talking about? The man who tried to kill me was Wisset, that nutcase school headmaster where Hayley works."

Rachel shook her head. "No," she replied. "My boss spoke to me on the phone last night and the man who was trying to kill you was James Hampton, one of the guys that you, Geoffrey Brookwell and Sean Attwood used to bully at school."

Tim Horton, eyes and mouth wide open, was visibly shocked.

"Bugger me," he said.

"He nearly did," replied Rachel, brusquely. "If not for the bravery of my colleagues you'd be a goner, Mr Horton. Just like the other two who were in cahoots with you all those years ago."

Still angry with the ill-mannered, arrogant man in the hospital bed, Rachel did something that was totally out of character for her, but she just couldn't help herself.

"Tell me, Mr Horton, who was the distressed lady who came out of here just now?" she enquired, although she knew full well.

Tim Horton looked decidedly uncomfortable but said nothing.

"It was his latest fling," replied Horton's wife firmly. "He's prone to his little dalliances, aren't you, Tim? Well this latest one, Lauren Templeton, has just been given her marching orders by yours truly."

In truth, Rachel regretted asking the question as soon as it had left her mouth. She turned to face Mrs Horton and tried to produce a comforting smile.

"I'm glad your husband is on the mend, Mrs Horton," she remarked, "but, just so you know, I think my colleagues from traffic will be wanting to talk with him further about the road accident he was involved in."

Mrs Horton shook her head slowly from side to side. "Why on earth were you driving so recklessly?" she asked her husband.

"That's easy to answer," remarked Rachel. "He was trying to lose our officers who were tailing him."

"Your officers!" exclaimed Horton. "I thought they were…"

Realising he was about to dig himself into an even bigger hole, Horton stopped abruptly.

His wife folded her arms and stared sternly at Horton.

"You idiot," she remarked. "You thought I'd had you tailed, didn't you?"

Tim Horton said nothing, but his expression couldn't conceal his guilt.

"I don't have to get you followed," she continued. "I know when you're playing away. You've been doing it for so long that I can spot the signs immediately. Do you think I'm stupid?"

Tim Horton looked back at her but remained silent.

"Anyway, I doubt my colleagues in traffic will let this go without there being some further investigation," continued Rachel. "I suspect you may well be charged."

Mrs Horton, arms still firmly folded, turned her head to face Rachel. "I think he should count himself fortunate. If it hadn't been for you lot, he'd be dead. So, if he's only got me and a driving indiscretion to worry about, he's very lucky. I actually hope they take his licence away from him for a while. It might make him think a little more about his family, rather than that spa and all those female distractions he has to cope with."

Rachel smiled broadly but said nothing. Then with Matt Stock a few paces behind her, the pair left the room.

* * *

Watson was already in the incident room when Carmichael arrived.

"Morning, sir," he said cheerily. "Have you heard from the hospital about how Paul's doing?"

Carmichael shook his head. "No, have you?" he replied.

Watson smiled. "I called just now, and they say he's had a good night and is doing well."

Carmichael smiled. "Excellent," he replied. "What about PC Hill, Mavis Heaton and Tim Horton?"

Watson shook his head. "I know PC Hill was discharged last night, so he's obviously doing fine, and Rachel's planning to go in and see the others today, but I've not heard from her so far this morning."

Carmichael nodded sagely. "OK, it sounds positive, which is a relief. Now let's get Hampton out and see what he's going to tell us today."

* * *

"You were a bit heavy on him," remarked Matt Stock as he and Rachel Dalton walked towards Mavis Heaton's room.

Rachel was still angry. "Well, what a prat," she replied. "If it wasn't for Cooper, PC Hill and Watson, he'd be dead. It just annoyed me to hear him be so thankless. It makes my blood boil."

"I saw," Matt acknowledged with a smile.

As the pair arrived at Mavis Heaton's room, Matt decided to let his partner enter alone.

"I'll wait out here," he remarked.

Rachel smiled and kissed him on his cheek. "I doubt I'll need to give poor Mavis a hard time, but by all means you take a seat if you're not up to it."

Matt Stock hardly had time to get comfortable before Rachel reappeared out of Mavis Heaton's room.

"She's asleep," she replied. "The nurse in there says she's doing fine but needs rest."

390

Matt Stock smiled and put his arm around Rachel's waist.

"Can we get out of this place?" he said. "Hospitals give me the creeps."

Rachel turned her head to face her boyfriend, her brow furrowed in surprise.

"But you work in forensics," she exclaimed.

"That's different," he remarked. "The people I work on are dead and I'm just doing exploratory science. These places are full of sick people who are alive. I can't think of anything worse."

Rachel chuckled and shook her head. "I'm speechless," she replied. "Now come on, you wimp, let's go."

Chapter 94

Carmichael and Watson started their interview with James Hampton at precisely 11:40am with, once again, Hampton's solicitor, Mr Frazer, sitting to Hampton's left.

Watson attended to the preliminaries of starting the recording equipment and confirming the date, time and the details of those present in the room.

Carmichael already had more than enough on tape from the interviews the day before to convict James Hampton ten times over; however, there were still several loose ends that he felt needed to be clarified.

"Good morning, James," Carmichael stated. "I'd just like to ask you a few more questions if that's OK with you."

James Hampton sat upright, shrugged his shoulders, placed his arms on the desk but said nothing.

"Tell me about the calls and the packages with instructions?" said Carmichael. "How many calls did you make to the various people you killed and how many parcels of instructions did you send out?"

James Hampton scratched his head.

"I made just one call to Brookwell and just one to Sajid," he replied with a smile. "That's all I needed to make as they were so gullible. I made a couple to Attwood, one when I told him I was a potential customer, asking him to meet me at the Lindley on Thursday, then later that morning I called him again to say I was one of your lot, told him we thought he was in danger and that I needed to meet him down Wood Lane to take him somewhere safe."

"And they all bought what you told them each time?" Carmichael asked.

"Attwood was very suspicious when I called him the second time," Hampton conceded, "but he came around after a few minutes of reassuring. Accents are one of my party pieces. So why wouldn't Brookwell be taken in by a big TV producer with a posh voice?"

As he spoke James Hampton changed his voice to sound unerringly good as a well-spoken man from the home counties.

"Or like a man from the West Country for Hanif," continued Hampton, his voice now sounding like a country bumpkin.

"Or like a local man with brass to spend," added Hampton in a strong, confident, brash Lancashire accent.

"Very good," remarked Carmichael. "And you made these all on the same pay-as-you-go mobile?"

"That's correct," replied Hampton with a smile. "Untraceable."

"And the packages," continued Carmichael, "you say you just sent out two of them, is that correct?"

"Yes, one to Brookwell and one to Hanif," replied Hampton.

"You cut it fine with the one to Brookwell," remarked Carmichael, "he would have only received it on Thursday 25th June, and he had to pick up the car from the car park on Saturday 27th June. Did you not worry about him not sending over the thousand pounds you'd enclosed in time?"

Hampton shook his head. "No," he replied firmly. "Brookwell was so suckered in when I'd called him on the Tuesday that I knew the plan would work and that he'd send that envelope out as soon as the money arrived."

"And you put both Hanif and Brookwell's packages in the school out-tray to be mailed?" Carmichael added.

"Yes," Hampton replied. "They always make the last collection each evening, so I made sure the right postage was on them and just slipped them into the pile for young Hayley Horton to post. An ironic touch, I thought, given that her father was on my list to be dealt with."

"I see," remarked Carmichael.

"So, it was Brookwell who liaised with Attwood about the car hire?" Watson asked.

"Yes," replied Hampton, "he did all that, but was instructed not to reveal who he was."

Watson shook his head. "I can't believe how anyone could fall for such a scam," he remarked.

Hampton laughed. "Greed and stupidity," he replied. "The two keys to successful deception. Supported in these circumstances by my impeccable made-up characters. Actually, maybe it should have been me that embarked on the acting career. And, of course, enclosing the money in the packages to Brookwell and Hanif gave them the ultimate proof that the person they were dealing with was genuine."

"You did that deliberately to support the scam?" Carmichael enquired.

"Of course," replied Hampton. "Who in their right mind would send you money if they weren't genuine? As I said before, they were greedy and stupid."

As Carmichael listened, he couldn't help thinking that either Hampton had no comprehension of the seriousness of his crimes, or he was totally insane. He decided that probably both were true.

"Yesterday you mentioned luring Sean Attwood down Wood Lane, pretending to be a police officer," continued Carmichael. "When was that exactly?"

"It was around lunchtime on Thursday," replied Hampton. "I asked him to meet me near the old barn. I used to play there with Billy and a few others when we were kids. Once I got him there, I overpowered him and tied him up."

"And when did you actually kill him?" Carmichael asked.

"Friday," replied Hampton. "It was after I'd spoken to the teachers and governors about Aunty Brenda being murdered, but before I made the announcement to the school."

"So, you kept him there overnight?" Carmichael remarked.

"That's right," replied Hampton, "all neatly tied up and gagged."

"That didn't give you long," Watson remarked.

"What do you mean?" Hampton asked.

"To get from the school to the barn, kill him and then get back to make the announcement to the school about Mrs Rumburgh's death?" explained Watson.

Hampton smiled. "Long enough," he replied.

* * *

Rachel Dalton and Matt Stock were about to leave the hospital car park in Matt's shiny red Audi, when Rachel spotted Hayley Horton and Harry Bridge wandering out of the hospital entrance.

"Stop," shouted Rachel. "I want a quick chat with those two."

Matt Stock did as he was told, briefly remaining stationary as his girlfriend clambered out of the car. However, a sudden blast from the horn of the car behind forced him to push the gear lever into first and move on to look for a place to park until Rachel returned.

Chapter 95

Rachel quickly made her way over to meet Hayley Horton and Harry Bridge.

"Hi," she said as she reached them, her smile broad and friendly. "Can I talk with you both for a few seconds?"

Hayley returned a smile. "Yes, of course," she replied.

"It's great to see that your dad is on the mend," Rachel remarked.

"Oh yes," replied Hayley, "he's fine. Complaining and trying to boss everyone about as usual."

Rachel laughed. "I was just wondering if you could tell me about a few parcels you posted a week or so ago?"

Hayley frowned and shrugged her shoulders. "Apart from the school post, I don't recall posting any parcels recently," she replied.

"These would have been in with the school post," replied Rachel. "One was to a man called Geoffrey Brookwell at an address in Knott End. The other was to a man called Sajid Hanif who lives in Moulton Bank."

Hayley, her face blank, just shrugged her shoulders.

"I don't recall either of them," she replied. "What was in them?"

Rachel shook her head. "It's not important," she replied. "I just wondered if you remembered either of them."

"Sorry," replied Hayley. "I don't."

"So, is it true that Mr Wisset killed all those people?" Harry Bridge asked. "Including Mrs Rumburgh?"

Rachel shrugged her shoulders. "I can't tell you anything at the moment," she replied. "I'm afraid we're still conducting our enquiries. But we do think the man we have in custody is the killer."

"I've been watching Mr Wisset for a few weeks," remarked Harry Bridge. "He kept shooting off from school at funny times during the day, and he kept coming in late and was behaving really strangely. I wasn't sure what he was up to, but I could tell he was involved in something. To be honest I thought he was having some clandestine relationship, he was being so secretive."

"Like my dad and your chum Lauren Templeton," remarked Hayley.

Harry Bridge's face suddenly looked uncomfortable. "I honestly didn't know about that, Hayley," he replied. "I promise you, Lauren never told me."

From the glare that Hayley gave her boyfriend it was clear that she wasn't totally convinced.

* * *

"Is there anything else I can help you with?" Hampton asked, as if the information he'd been so readily giving Carmichael and Watson was of no great importance to him.

Although Carmichael could scarcely believe how relaxed and untroubled Hampton appeared, he welcomed his keenness to talk and was determined to glean as much as he could from the killer.

"Tell me about the number plates?" he enquired. "Who had them made and who switched the plates on the car?"

Hampton smiled. "That was a clever touch, don't you think?" he replied. "I bought them online and had them

397

delivered directly to Brookwell's house. They did them in twenty-four hours, so he received them the same day he received the package. It was all very simple."

"But wasn't there a risk that the package would have your details on the paperwork?" Watson asked.

Hampton shook his head. "I just stated on my order that it was for a friend as a present, so they sent it out without any mention of me. You know like you can do with flowers and chocolates that you order online."

"Very clever," remarked Carmichael.

"I thought so," replied Hampton, who was clearly enjoying the admiration he felt his revelations were receiving.

"And presumably Geoffrey Brookwell was told to switch the plates in the package you sent him?" Carmichael added.

"Correct," replied Hampton. "He thought that was for another outside scene we were going to re-enact down Wood Lane after he'd done the church improvisation."

"But we found the real plates and the old fixings at the barn," remarked Carmichael. "Was the change of plates not done there?"

Hampton shook his head. "No, I instructed him to leave the real plates and their fixings in the boot," he replied. "I took them when I put his body in the boot and left them in the barn later."

"When you tied up Attwood?" suggested Watson.

"That's right," replied Hampton.

* * *

"What now?" Matt Stock asked, as Rachel climbed back into his car.

"I need to get to the station in Kirkwood," replied Rachel. "I suspect Carmichael will be interviewing Hampton again, and I'd like to find out what he's telling the boss."

398

"OK, madam," remarked Matt, who started up the engine and headed out through the hospital gates.

* * *

"Is that everything?" Hampton asked.

"Just a few more questions," replied Carmichael.

Hampton sighed. "Just a few," he replied, as if his willingness to cooperate was shortly about to change.

"When we looked at your old school folder from Mrs Rumburgh's filing cabinet, there was no photo," remarked Carmichael. "I assume you took it."

Hampton laughed. "Yes," he replied. "I know this beard hides a multitude of sins and the photo in the file was of me when I was no older than sixteen; however, it was still me and I couldn't risk you seeing it and making the connection. So, I removed it when I put the files back on Wednesday evening."

"You mean Thursday," remarked Carmichael. "You had your heated discussion on Thursday evening in Mrs Rumburgh's office, just before you went to her house and killed her."

Hampton's expression showed quite clearly that he didn't like being corrected by Carmichael.

"I'm only going to answer a couple more questions," he announced.

Carmichael had no doubt that Hampton meant what he was saying. In his opinion Hampton was a control-freak, and in Carmichael's experience, people like that had a need to manage the agenda.

Carmichael, therefore, thought for a few seconds before deciding what were going to be his last few questions to James Hampton.

"You've mentioned that your desire to kill Geoffrey Brookwell, Sean Attwood and Tim Horton was driven by the fact that they were, in your eyes, to blame for Billy Taylor's death, but tell me where were you, on that day?"

Hampton nodded gently. "I was at home in bed," he replied. "My dad had kept me off that day as I'd got some bug and had a fever."

"I see," replied Carmichael. "So, when did Sajid Hanif tell you about what really happened? I assume it was Sajid who told you?"

Hampton's facial expression changed. It became more intense, almost angry.

"It was over a year afterwards," replied Hampton, "on the day that I left the school. My dad and I had to move away for his new job, so I had to change schools. The weasel only told me on that last day. What a coward. I couldn't believe he'd been so weak. But what could I do?"

"So, you weren't there for your friend when he died," remarked Carmichael, "and when you did know the truth, you did nothing either. Stayed silent just like Sajid Hanif."

Carmichael's remark appeared to touch a nerve with Hampton, as Carmichael had intended. He glared back at the inspector.

"That's your last question, Inspector," Hampton said, "I'm telling you no more."

Carmichael didn't mind in the slightest. He already had more than enough to put Hampton away for a long, long time.

Carmichael stood up.

"You seem very relaxed telling us about how you went about luring these people to their deaths and you've explained why you killed them," he said. "But surely, deep down, you must now realise that what you did was wrong. Is there no part of you that feels remorse for what you did to those poor people?"

Hampton folded his arms and sat back in his chair.

"Spoken by a man that quite clearly has never been bullied," he remarked. "You've just no idea how devastating being bullied is, at the time and for years after. They just got what they deserved."

Carmichael shook his head, then leaned over the desk so his face was no more than inches away from Hampton's.

"And so, will you," he remarked, his anger and disgust evident in his voice.

Chapter 96

"He's completely barking mad," proclaimed Watson, as he and Carmichael made their way from interview room one to their office.

"I think you're right, Marc," replied Carmichael. "Mind you, I suspect some would argue that anyone who kills is mad to some extent."

"I guess so," Watson concurred, "but Hampton is in a league all to himself."

Carmichael smiled. "Fortunately, that's for others to decide. Our job is just to bring the killers in and make sure we have enough evidence to charge and convict," he remarked. "And in the case of James Hampton, we've got all we need."

As the pair reached their office, they spied Rachel sitting alone at her desk.

"How's it going?" she enquired.

Watson smiled. "He's been singing like a bird," he replied. "The boss got everything out of him. Where, why and how, it's all nicely on tape."

Carmichael allowed himself a small smile of satisfaction, too. "The key thing is that we make sure we dot the i's and cross the t's, Marc," he remarked. "So, can you work on sorting all the paperwork out?"

Watson nodded and walked away towards his desk.

"How's everything at the hospital?" Carmichael enquired. "How's Paul?"

"He's doing really well," replied Rachel. "He was in good spirits."

"Excellent," replied Carmichael. "I'll drop in and see him on my way home. What about Mavis Heaton and Tim Horton?" Carmichael asked.

"Mavis was still asleep," replied Rachel, "so I didn't talk with her. But Horton was awake and very lucid. His wife and daughter were there, too, and Harry Bridge, Hayley's boyfriend."

"Did they tell you anything?" Carmichael asked.

Rachel shook her head.

"Hayley reckons she can't recall the two Jiffy bags she posted and Harry Bridge told me that Wisset, I mean Hampton, had been behaving very unusually in the last couple of weeks. Arriving late, popping out at strange times, that sort of thing. Harry thought he'd got some secret lover."

Carmichael laughed. "A reasonable assumption to make," he replied.

"I saw Miss Templeton, too," Rachel added. "She was very upset, and it turns out Mrs Horton sent her packing in no uncertain terms."

"I bet Horton won't be happy about that," piped up Watson from behind his screen. "She's a stunner."

Carmichael rolled his eyes which made Rachel smile.

"Get back to your paperwork, Marc," he said. "I have it on good authority that remarks like that are totally unacceptable in today's police force."

"Quite right too, Inspector," announced Hewitt, who suddenly appeared through the door.

Carmichael, who had his back to Hewitt as he arrived, rolled his eyes skyward once more, making Rachel's smile widen before quickly looking away, so the chief inspector couldn't see her.

Carmichael turned around to face his superior.

"Good afternoon, sir," he remarked as cheerily as he could.

"How did it go this morning, with Hampton?" Hewitt enquired.

"It went well," replied Carmichael, "we've all we need, and more, to charge him with the murders of Brookwell, Hanif, Mrs Rumburgh and Attwood; and the attempted murders of Mavis Heaton, Tim Horton, Sergeant Cooper and PC Hill."

"Well done, Inspector,' Hewitt continued.

"Well, it was a team effort," replied Carmichael.

"Oh, yes, of course," remarked Hewitt. "And talking of the team, I can confirm that Lucy Clark has agreed to return to stand in for Sergeant Cooper until he's ready to return to active duty."

"It will be Lucy Martin as from next Saturday," remarked Watson.

"Yes, you're quite right," confirmed Hewitt.

"What do you mean?" Carmichael asked.

"Lucy's getting married next Saturday to her politician boyfriend," Watson replied. "Sue and I both got our invites a few months ago. It's at some swanky place in Durham, where her folks live. Did you and Mrs Carmichael not get an invite?"

"Er, no," replied Carmichael, "but Lucy and I only worked together a short while before she moved on, so that's no great surprise."

"I got one," announced Hewitt. "Mrs Hewitt and I are very excited about going over to the North East. We honeymooned at a little cottage near Alnwick when we were married, so we're taking a few days off afterwards to reminisce."

"How lovely," remarked Carmichael.

"Anyway, she and the Labour MP for Ribble South

already have a place here, so she's starting in the first week of August, when they return from their honeymoon in Antigua," continued Hewitt. "I suspect you'll appreciate having another female on the team, DC Dalton?"

Rachel shrugged her shoulders. "I suppose I will, sir" she replied, although in truth she preferred having just males in their small team and the thought of a more senior woman officer coming in wasn't something that filled Rachel with too much joy.

Chapter 97

With the news of Lucy re-joining the team now public knowledge at the station, Carmichael couldn't wait to get out of the place and away.

Why on earth would she want to come back here? he kept asking himself on the drive over to Southport Hospital. *And what purpose would her being back working with me serve? Especially now she's to be married, too.*

He was thankful that at least he and Penny hadn't received an invite to the wedding as he would have felt awkward attending. But he also realised their omission may appear strange, and knowing Watson as he did, Carmichael was sure his nosey sergeant would be trying his best to find out why they weren't invited.

"Bugger it!" he exclaimed aloud, before opening his driver's window wide to allow the warm summer air to rush in.

* * *

Safe in the knowledge that Cooper was comfortable, Carmichael decided to pay a visit to Mavis Heaton first.

When he entered Mavis's small private room, he saw that Jenny Attwood was already at her mother's bedside.

As soon as Jenny saw Carmichael she leant over and kissed her mother on the cheek.

"I'm just going to get a sandwich and a coffee," she said. "I'll leave you alone with the inspector."

Carmichael smiled at Jenny and waited for her to collect her handbag from the floor and make her exit.

"How are you feeling, Mavis?" Carmichael enquired.

Mavis nodded, her face grey and sombre.

"I'm OK," she replied. "A bit shaken by my experience, but I'm fine."

"What exactly happened?" Carmichael enquired.

Mavis shook her head.

"What sort of mother am I if I can't identify my own son?" she remarked. "And what sort of mother have I been so that when I do, he just wants to kill me?"

Carmichael put his hand on her arm.

"I fear your son has many issues," he replied. "He needs specialist help."

Mavis shook her head.

"He may well do now," she replied. "But now's too late. What he really needed was his mother to be there when he was growing up, and of course he didn't have that."

Although Carmichael suspected that her words were very close to the nub of James Hampton's problems, he saw no value in telling her so.

"When we found out that James had died in Australia, we couldn't believe you hadn't been informed," Carmichael remarked.

"I can assure you I wasn't," replied Mavis. "His father would never have told me as our split was so acrimonious. I'm sure he would have told Brenda, but again it doesn't surprise me that she didn't tell me either. They all hated me."

Carmichael nodded gently.

"So, when did you realise that Nigel Wisset was really your son?" he asked.

"It was when you mentioned him yesterday," Mavis

407

replied. "It got me wondering why you brought him up. I also got to thinking why it was that Brenda Rumburgh called me that night wanting to locate Billy Taylor's relatives. It just all seemed to fall into place and before I knew it, I'd convinced myself that Nigel Wisset was in fact my son James."

"So, you called him?" Carmichael said, keen to get Mavis to tell him everything.

"I did," she replied, "and I knew, as soon as he heard what I was saying, that I was right."

"What did he say?" Carmichael asked.

"Not much," replied Mavis. "He didn't try to fob me off when I said I knew he was James, but he didn't confirm it either."

"Then he came over," Carmichael continued.

"Yes," replied Mavis. "I told him if he didn't come over, I'd tell the police, and he was there within twenty minutes, standing on my doorstep."

"What happened then?" Carmichael enquired.

"Without saying anything he came in," continued Mavis. "He asked me if I was alone. I said yes, then the next thing I remember was feeling a massive pain in my head, and then seeing Jade crouching next to me and realising I had been bound and gagged."

Carmichael smiled. "You've had a lucky escape," he remarked with a smile.

As he spoke, the door opened and in walked Jenny Attwood holding a plastic container with "Costa" emblazoned on the side.

"I'll leave you ladies alone," Carmichael said, before exchanging a smile with Jenny Attwood and heading for the door.

"What will happen to James?" Mavis asked.

"I'm not sure," replied Carmichael. "I suspect he'll be put away for life somewhere, but whether it's in a prison or in a psychiatric hospital, I just couldn't say."

The dazed, pale-faced old lady just nodded, but said nothing.

* * *

The walk between Mavis Heaton's room and the almost identically laid out room where Cooper was recovering took Carmichael a matter of minutes.

The first thing he saw when he entered Cooper's room was Julia Cooper fussing over her husband, who was propped up in bed looking remarkably well for someone who had been close to death a matter of twenty-four hours earlier.

"Hello, Paul," he said, a broad smile across his face. Then, "Hello, Julia," as he turned his head to make eye contact with Cooper's wife.

For the next forty minutes, Carmichael and Cooper talked about what had happened, the interviews Carmichael had conducted with James Hampton and what the Coopers' expectations were concerning his recovery.

Just as Carmichael stood up to leave, Cooper grabbed him by the arm.

"I just thought I should tell you, sir," he said, "even though I'm sure, in time, I'll be right as rain, I'm not sure I'll ever return to work. Julia and I have been talking and I'm almost fifty now, so maybe it's time for me to think about life outside Mid-Lancashire Police."

Carmichael smiled and nodded his head. "Whatever you both decide is all right by me," he replied. "My advice is not to think too much about that now. Just concentrate on getting better. Then, if you decide to call it a day, I'll support you all the way. But just get better first."

Cooper smiled and nodded. "I will," he replied. "I just wanted to let you know."

As Carmichael reached the door, he heard Cooper speak again.

"All this also means we'll miss Lucy Clark's wedding," he heard him mention to his wife. "That's a real shame, I was looking forward to seeing Lucy again."

Carmichael didn't bother turning around, he just quickly made his exit.

Chapter 98

It was five o'clock precisely when Carmichael finally arrived home.

When he opened the front door and walked into the hallway, he thought for a few seconds that the house was empty, but then he heard laughter coming from the back garden. He hadn't even reached the kitchen when he could smell coals burning, a sure sign that their barbecue was on.

"Is this a private party or can anyone join in?" he enquired as he emerged from the kitchen door.

"Steve," exclaimed Penny who was sitting on one of their loungers with a glass of wine in one hand.

Since their children had all reached, and in Jemma's case passed through, their teenage years, it was unusual for the whole Carmichael family to be at home together at the same time.

With the exception of Christmas, Carmichael could probably count on one hand, with a few fingers to spare, when such rare, joyful events now came to pass.

However, that afternoon was one such occasion, and with Jemma and Natalie sitting either side of their mother while Carmichael's son Robbie and Jemma's boyfriend Chris (aka 'Spot-On') were busily attending to sausages and pieces of chicken suspended over the hot coals, Carmichael became filled with a sense of contentment.

"You're back," Penny continued. "Just in time for dinner."

After pouring himself a large glass of pinotage and settling down on one of the vacant iron chairs under the large red garden parasol, Carmichael raised his glass.

"Cheers," he said before taking a long welcome gulp of his favourite red wine.

"How's Cooper?" Penny enquired.

"He's doing quite well, considering," Carmichael replied. "They're confident they can save his leg, which they did think might not be the case, but he will need more surgery and he faces a long road back."

"Julia must be distraught," Penny remarked.

"She was putting on a brave face this afternoon when I popped in to see him," he replied, "but I'm sure you're right. I'm thinking about talking to Hewitt about putting Cooper, Watson and PC Hill all forward for a bravery award," Carmichael added.

"I should think so, too," replied Penny.

Carmichael nodded and smiled. "I'm glad you agree."

"And what about you?" Penny asked. "How do you feel?"

Carmichael shrugged his shoulders.

"Well, we'll get a conviction for Hampton," he replied. "Cooper will live, and I've not been shot, so I guess I should be pleased, but this case has been a tough and nasty one in every sense, I have to admit."

Penny stood up, walked over to her husband and gave him a massive hug.

"Grub's up," announced Spot-On in his thick Cumbrian accent.

"Excellent," exclaimed Natalie, who was the first to rush over, plate in hand, to the barbecue.

"One good thing, though: I think she's fine now," Carmichael whispered in Penny's ear, his head nodding over in Natalie's direction.

"Yes, she's back to normal," replied Penny. "Thank God."

Having eaten, drunk and laughed for over an hour, Carmichael suddenly remembered something.

Leaping to his feet and then rushing into the house, Carmichael went to retrieve the folder he'd borrowed from Mrs Rumburgh's office.

With the other five people in the garden all still perplexed as to what had made him move so quickly, Carmichael reappeared clutching a green faded folder.

He sat down in his seat and opened it up on his lap.

"In the course of my enquiries," he said in as pompous a voice as he could muster, "certain information pertaining to one of you was brought to my attention."

The looks of puzzlement remained on the faces of the five people, who listened intently to what he was saying.

"I have in front of me," continued Carmichael, "a detailed report on a certain Penny Lathom, now Penny Carmichael."

As his audience realised what he was holding in his hand, four of them started to smile broadly, the fifth, her eyes and mouth wide open, made a lunge at her husband to snatch the file from his hand.

She wasn't quick enough, as before her hand was anywhere near the folder, Carmichael had moved it out of her reach.

"Is that mum's school file?" Natalie asked, her eyes shining with excitement.

"It is indeed," replied Carmichael, still maintaining his fake pompous voice.

Standing up and taking a few paces backwards, to avoid the file being successfully extracted out of his hands, Carmichael continued. "This is the school record of the said individual from the age of eleven until she was discharged from the said establishment at the age of eighteen."

"Discharged," remarked Penny loudly. "You make it

413

sound like I was in a young offenders' institute, not the most prestigious school in Mid-Lancashire."

Carmichael ignored her comments and started to read from the file.

"Well, it would appear that this young lady was a model student from the age of eleven until she was sixteen," he reported, "achieving good end-of-year grades, playing in the school netball team and, it says here, was a pleasant and friendly young lady."

Penny smiled, shrugged her shoulders and with the palms of her hands facing upwards nodded gently. "What did you expect," she remarked, "I was a good girl when I was at school."

"Well," continued Carmichael, "that's true up until an incident that appears to have taken place when you were about sixteen and went on a trip with the school to France. According to a report here by a teacher called Mrs Ambrose, on that trip there was a major blot on your goody-goody image."

It was clear by the horrified look on her face that Penny not only realised what her husband was referring to but also wasn't keen on the disclosure he was about to make being shared with their children.

"I think you should stop there," she said firmly to her husband.

Carmichael peered across at her and grinned.

"What happened in France?" Jemma enquired.

"Well, if this report from Mrs Ambrose is correct," continued Carmichael, with an air of pleasure in his voice, "this young lady who, to that point, had had a flawless record, appears to have been caught with a fellow pupil, a girl called Beverly Wright, with a quantity of alcohol and two local French boys in their room, at eleven thirty one evening."

"That was all Beverly Wright's fault," Penny pleaded. "I was already in bed when she came back to the room with those boys and the cider. I was totally innocent, and in any case, nothing happened, and the boys behaved like gentlemen."

Robbie Carmichael shook his head and tutted loudly. "Mother, how could you," he remarked in mock disgust. "What a dreadful example that is for young Natalie. What must she think?"

"She thinks that Mum is telling the truth and that it wasn't her fault," remarked Natalie, much to her mother's delight.

"You can just hand over that file, right now," Penny ordered, her hand thrust out in her husband's direction.

Carmichael did as he was instructed and passed over the file to Penny, the mischievous grin he'd been sporting for the last few minutes still etched on his face.

Penny grabbed the file and put it under her arm.

"I don't know," she said, "just one little blemish on an otherwise flawless record and you have to broadcast it, Inspector Carmichael. I only hope you've no sins in your past, because if you have and I find out, there will be hell to pay."

As his wife headed into the house with her school file under her arm, and his three children and Spot-On laughed and chatted between themselves about the revelation they'd just heard, Carmichael took a small sip of wine and stared aimlessly into the distance. His thoughts were no longer on Penny's school report, but on Lucy Clark re-joining his team and whether the sins from his past would soon come back to haunt him.

415